MERLIN'S MAGICAL MYSTERIES

COMPLETE TRILOGY EDITION

MOLLY FITZ

Editor: Jennifer Lopez, Mistress with the Red Pen
Cover: TM Franklin

PO Box 873543
Wasilla, AK 99687

MERLIN TAKES A FAMILIAR

My name is Gracie Springs, and I am not a witch... but I'm pretty sure my cat is. I first started to get suspicious when he jumped just a little too high while chasing after a robin in our front yard. I knew for sure when he opened up his mouth and addressed me by name!

The first thing he told me? That he doesn't like the name I gave him—even though "Fluffy" fits him like a warm sweater at Christmas. Now we've compromised on "Merlin the Magical Fluff," which according to him references his long and proud lineage just fine.

After that small matter was settled, he informed me that I must uphold his secret or risk spending the rest of my life in some magical prison. I agreed, not knowing it would turn into a full-time job of covering his tracks and fibbing our way out of some pretty tight spots.

When my boss at the local coffee shop turns up dead as a

dormouse, things go from challenging to practically impossible… especially since all my coworkers seem to think I'm to blame.

Here's hoping my witchy cat can charm our way out of this one, because right now it looks like I'm cursed if I do and charged with murder if I don't. Yikes!

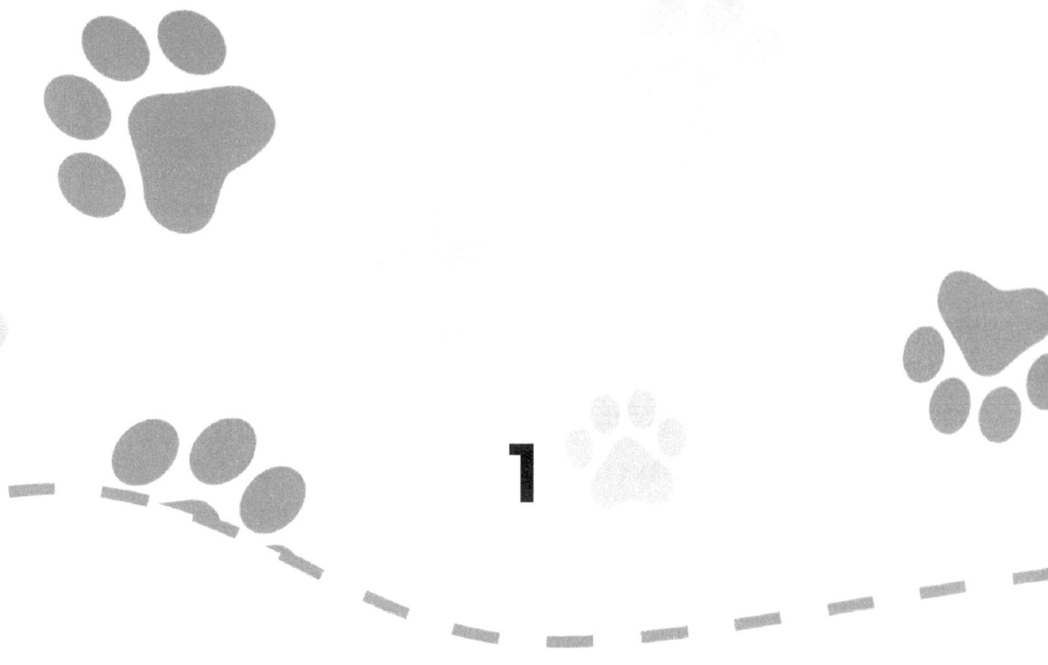

1

My name is Gracie Springs, and I've always been a pretty normal girl. I work as a barista while working toward my master's degree in Sociology. I've finished all my coursework but still haven't landed upon the perfect thesis topic. And I can't earn my degree until I do.

Oops.

Meanwhile I live in a small suburban town in Southern Georgia called Elderberry Heights. And the name fits it to a *T,* because most of my neighbors are somewhere north of seventy years old. I'm living in my grandma Grace's house, which she left behind when she chose to move south to a trendy retirement community in the Florida Keys.

She gave me the home where she raised my father and all my uncles, saying it was my early inheritance and that I'd always been her favorite, anyway—and not just because we shared a name.

She left all her furniture and decor, which means my house has at least three dozen hand-crocheted doilies and the living room is made up of brown floral couches and honey oak side tables. I don't have the heart—or the money—to change anything.

Grandma Grace also left me this ragamuffin cat that turned up at her doorstep only days before she'd been scheduled to move out and me to move in. The vet says he's a Maine Coon. I say he's much larger than any cat should ever be, especially considering all that stripey fur that poofs out from his body and makes him look like a literal fluff ball.

I guess that's why I named him Fluffy.

Keeping a cat I hadn't wanted was a small price to pay for being handed a free house, and over time Fluffy has started to grow on me. He's not exactly the cuddly type. In fact, every time, I've tried to pick him up, he's gone for blood. And succeeded in getting it twice.

I don't try to pick him up anymore, but if I sit really still and pretend I'm not interested, sometimes he'll help himself to my lap. Once he even purred.

Fluffy does love food and often takes a bite of whatever I'm having for dinner. He also enjoys running up and down the hallways in the middle of the night like a creature possessed.

I hadn't meant for him to be an outdoor cat, but he's such a good escape artist that eventually I just installed a pet door so I wouldn't have to worry about it, anymore.

That brings me to this morning...

I was running late for work, thanks to having a particularly difficult time following a new makeup tutorial from my favorite beauty Tuber. In the end, I scrubbed off the whole thing and went with a smoky eye and nude lip. That'd teach me to try something new so close to the start of my shift.

Especially since my mean old boss would take any excuse to dock my pay. He's still bitter that a popular franchised cafe moved in a couple streets away and cut his profits considerably. But he's also stubborn and not quite ready to admit defeat, which is why he's kept the whole staff on while slashing our hours and looking for any excuse to pay us less.

Great guy, that boss of mine.

I hadn't seen Fluffy since breakfast and wanted to make sure everything was okay with him before taking off for my shift.

"Fluffy! Fluffy! Here, kitty, kitty!" I called and clicked my tongue, but he didn't come running. He never comes running. It's always up to me to find him.

And so I looked under the bed, behind the couch, and out the front window.

Finally I spotted him with his butt in the air and face toward the ground in that classic pre-pounce pose. Across the way stood an unaware robin bathing in the stone birdbath Grandma left behind with whatever few drops hadn't yet been evaporated by the hot summer sun.

Wiggle, wiggle, went Fluffy's butt.

He leaped, but the robin saw him coming and flittered away.

Fluffy flittered after him.

Not just a normal cat leap, either. He looked like a tiny feline athlete about to slam dunk a basketball. Up and up he went after that frightened avian target. He must have gone at least six feet into the sky and was still climbing up, up, up.

That's when he turned his head my way and saw me watching. Those emerald eyes bored straight into mine, and for a moment he remained stuck mid-jump just hanging in the air.

Then he turned again, and the sudden movement broke the spell. Fluffy came crashing straight back to earth, then skittered out of sight, leaving me to wonder: *What in the heck just happened?*

* * *

I chalked the whole gravity-defying cat episode up to poor sleep and an overactive imagination, then hurried my way over to Harold's House of Coffee.

Despite ignoring both speed limits and stop signs, I wound up three minutes late for my shift. My boss, Harold himself, stood just inside the front door waiting for me.

He tapped his wrist even though he never wore a watch and shouted, "When will you learn? Three minutes means three dollars, and since this is your second offense this week, I'm doubling it."

I snorted and rushed past him to clock in.

"Gracie! Aren't you listening to me?" he demanded, trailing after me like a demented duckling.

"Yes, you're docking me six dollars for being three minutes late, even though we have no customers and you only pay us minimum wage. And even that's because you're legally obligated. Pretty soon I'm going to be paying you for the pleasure of standing around with nothing to do while our customers hang out at Mermaid's Brew down the street. Does that sound about right?"

Harold's face turned bright red. "The insolence!" he screamed. "If it didn't cost so much to train someone new, you'd be out of a job. In fact you're lucky that I—"

He took a step back, shook his head, and tried again. "Listen here, Gracie. You're lucky that—"

His words stopped coming as he gasped and crumpled to the floor. From hotheaded to out cold in mere seconds.

"Harold, Harold!" I cried and fell to my knees to check if he was breathing.

He wasn't.

I grabbed his wrist and tried to find a pulse.

I couldn't.

Ruh-oh.

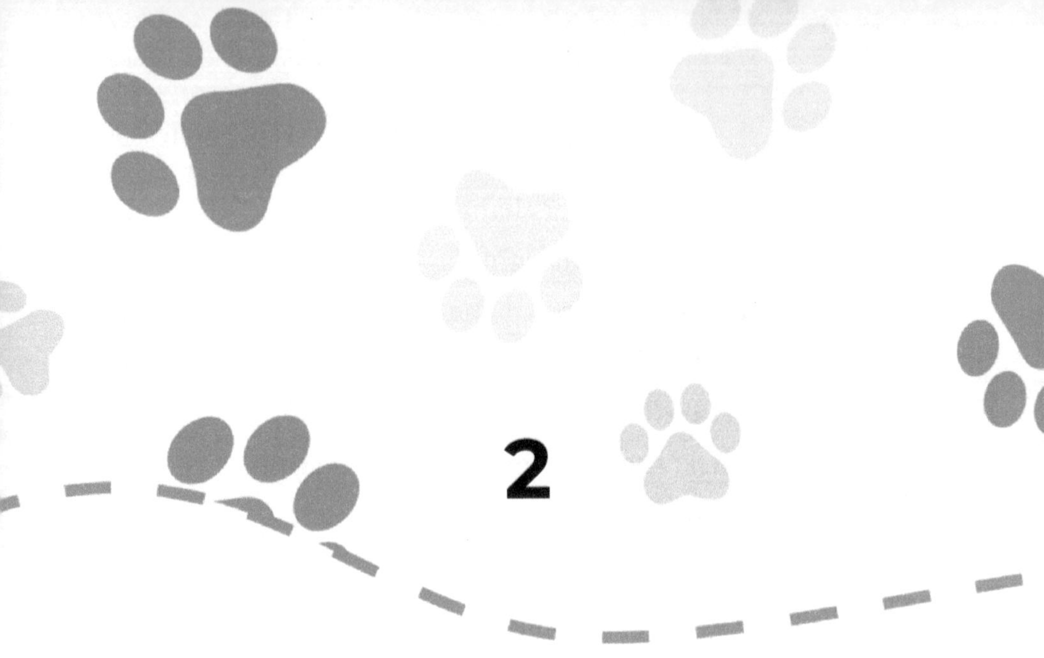

2

My boss had just dropped dead, right here in front of everyone—well, at least a couple coworkers and one customer who sat sipping a cold brew in the corner. Even though I couldn't find a pulse, I attempted chest compressions. But Harold was already gone.

"I'm calling an ambulance!" Kelley, our newest barista, shouted from behind the cash register.

Drake, our shift manager, tromped over to the door and flipped the open sign around, then drew the blinds.

"I'm sorry, Miss," I told our lone customer. "We're going to have to ask you to leave now. If you have your punch card handy, I can give you a couple extra points as an apology for the inconvenience."

Had Harold been alive, he would have fired me for that, given his propensity to nickel and dime both his staff and his customers for all they were worth. But I guess that didn't really matter now.

The woman took a long swig of her cold brew, her green eyes wide as she regarded me, then tossed the remainders in the trash can, gathered her belongings, and high-tailed it out of there. I couldn't say I blamed her.

Kelley rushed over to my side and glued herself there. "An ambulance is on the way."

"Won't do any good if the jerk is already dead," Drake said with a scowl.

"Don't talk like that," Kelley shrieked, clutching a hand to her chest. "A man just lost his life!"

"Probably a heart attack," I offered with a shrug. "It's sad, but it happens all the time. Harold wasn't exactly in the best of shape, besides."

"Yeah," Drake added with a sarcastic laugh as he crossed his arms and leaned back against the counter. "And considering his heart was at least three sizes too small, I'd say it had a pretty hard time keeping up."

I kept my lips pressed together in a tight line. Even though I agreed with Drake's assessment of the man, it was a terrible thing to witness his death. Add to that the uncertainty of my future employment, and today was just an all-around crummy day.

We had a few gawkers peek through the edge of the windows where the blinds were cut slightly too short and thus allowed a glance inside. One even knocked despite the CLOSED sign. Drake pounded on our side of the door and screamed threats at the would-be customers.

I decided to focus on my work even though there was no one to make coffee for. I cleaned down all the tables and counters, praying help would arrive soon. There was something so creepy about being locked in with a dead body.

I think Drake felt it, too, because he continued to pace and prowl, all the while muttering something under his breath.

By the time the emergency workers arrived, Kelley had taken up a spot on one of the squishy club chairs, her knees drawn into her chest as she sobbed silently.

Since neither of my coffee colleagues were in shape to play host, I welcomed the paramedics and the policewoman inside, then relocked the door behind them.

"He's right over here," I announced, walking them toward the back area that housed Harold's small office and gave the rest of us a place to stash our coats and scan our timecards.

Poor Harold lay on his back with his head slouched against the wall and his neck bent uncomfortably. One hand set atop his chest and the other lay splayed out at his side. His face had already started losing its color, giving him that waxen appearance that no amount of postmortem makeup could hide.

The paramedics bent to examine Harold while the policewoman remained standing at my side. "Is there a place we could go to have a chat?" she asked, her face giving nothing away.

"Sure." I led her to the one booth we had in the back corner of the cafe, a relic from the shop's previous life as an old pancake place. "Would you like a coffee or something?"

She shook her head and pointed to her shirt pocket. "I'm Officer Dash. And you are?"

"I'm Gracie. Gracie Springs."

She took out a notebook, licked her finger, and flipped to a fresh page, then drew a small pen out of the binding and held it poised above the paper. "And you worked for the deceased?"

"Yes. For the past few months."

Officer Dash scribbled away with a frown.

"Why is this important?" I asked, tapping my fingers against the tabletop.

"Just getting the facts down now in case we need to revisit them later."

"But what do you mean?"

She raised an eyebrow at me. "Ever heard the phrase presumed innocent until proven guilty?"

I nodded.

"Well, in this case, our stiff is presumed murdered until proven dead by natural causes. We can't just assume there's no foul play involved here, because by the time we get the coroner's report, we'll have already lost the opportunity to investigate the crime scene."

My head spun. There was no way Harold had been murdered. And yet…

"Wait," I mumbled, a horrifying thought settling into my brain. "You don't think I had something to do with this. Do you?"

Officer Dash smirked. "From what the dispatcher told us, you were having a heated exchange with the deceased right before he keeled over."

"Yes, but you couldn't possibly—"

"And were these fights a regular thing?"

"Yes, but I didn't—"

"Well, Gracie Springs. You better hope that Harold died of a heart attack or an aneurysm or some other kind of commonplace medical tragedy. Otherwise you are definitely at the very top of my suspect list."

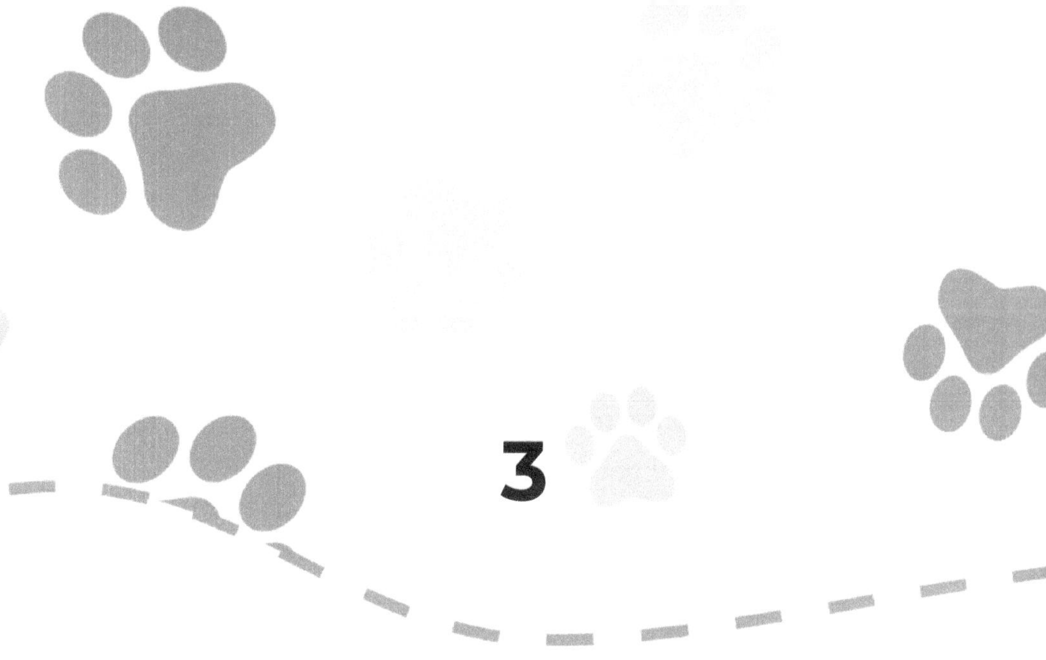

3

I returned home physically exhausted and emotionally wrung out. Everything happened so fast after Harold collapsed. The severity of Officer Dash's implication didn't fully sink in until I finally escaped the coffeehouse and began my quiet drive home. Now that I had a moment to think, a few very important questions crowded into my mind. Why was she so sure that he had been murdered? And even more puzzling, why did she believe I'd done it?

True, lots of people disliked Harold, but nobody had a reason to kill him—least of all me. I mean, why would I when I could have just quit my job and never seen him another day in my life?

The whole thing made me sick... and terrified. All I wanted to do was wake up from this horrible nightmare and go back to my normal, if a tad unexciting, life.

So I changed into my favorite matching flannel pajama set even though it was still the afternoon and the outside temperature was well over eighty degrees. Sometimes I missed my hometown in Northern Michigan where it was chilly more often than not, and my jammies—along with the added help of an overworked tabletop fan—helped allay the occasional bout of homesickness.

Right now, I wanted my mama. It didn't matter that I was an independent twenty-something. I'd been hurt, and I was scared. And just because I'd grown up didn't mean I couldn't turn to my mother in times of great need...

The fact that she didn't answer the phone when I called, however, meant precisely that. I hung up instead of leaving a voicemail, then fired off a quick text asking her to call me back whenever she got the chance.

Fluffy meowed and jumped up on the couch beside me. His whiskers twitched as he tried to discern whether I had anything worth eating. When he didn't find any food, he sunk his teeth into the edge of my sleeve and growled softly.

"Good idea," I said. "Today definitely calls for some ice cream."

I scooped up some of our favorite flavor—plain vanilla bean—into one of my lesser used breakfast bowls, grabbed a spoon and the remainder of the gallon, and settled myself back on the couch. The bowl was for Fluffy. I needed the entire container.

As we ate together, I began to share the events of my day with my feline companion. "That cop was so mean," I whined. "I mean, why would she just automatically assume I killed my boss? It was terrible. Just awful. To see the life leave his eyes. I don't think I'll ever forget it."

Fluffy sat up straight and cocked his head to the side. Sometimes, in moments like this, it felt like he could actually understand me.

"Mew?" my Maine Coon asked.

"Oh, yeah. I guess I should start at the beginning, huh? Well, my boss at the coffee shop, Harold. He died today."

"Harold is an awful name," Fluffy rasped.

"I know. I never thought anyone in the—" I stopped suddenly and closed my mouth up tight, then just stared at Fluffy for a long moment. Was I really so worked up that I was now hearing things?

I laughed at myself. "Silly me," I said with a deep breath out. "Thinking you're talking to me, Fluffy."

"My name's not Fluffy," the cat said, then hopped off the coffee table and onto the sofa beside me. "So don't call me that anymore."

"Wh-wh-what?" I sputtered, rubbing my eyes until I saw stars. "I'm seeing things. This isn't real."

Fluffy clucked his little sandpaper tongue. "You meant to say you're hearing things, and no, you're not. I'm talking to you, Gracie."

I jumped off the couch and spun wildly around the living room. "Come out, come out wherever you are!" I shouted with a mad laugh, not really sure who I was confronting here. "The joke's up. Haha, you actually had me convinced Fluffy was talking. Yup, I'm crazy! You win! Now come out and fess up!"

Fluffy let out an enormous yawn, then settled down with his paws tucked into himself. "You are most definitely acting crazy. Also I already told you my name's not Fluffy, so will you please stop calling me that?"

I gasped, then sunk to the floor before I could pass out and crash down onto it. “This is not real. This is not real,” I murmured, acting quite similarly to how Kelley had when she was balled up and rocking in that club chair back at the coffee shop.

“What’s not real?” Fluffy asked, jumping off the sofa and striding over to me.

“You can’t talk.”

“I can talk, but it seems you’re not very good at listening.”

“Are you going to hurt me?”

“Of course I’m not going to hurt you. I need you to feed me, don’t I? Silly human.”

“What do you want from me?”

“The aforementioned food and also for you to stop calling me Fluffy. I much prefer the name given to me by my ancestors, thank you.”

“Um... Okay. What should I call you?”

“The name’s Merlin, and I come from a long and noble lineage of wizards dating all the way back to King Arthur.”

“You’re magic?” I asked with a quick breath in.

“Duh,” my cat spat, and then I officially passed out.

4

Night had already fallen by the time I regained consciousness. I'd like to say that I experienced a few blissful moments of ignorance as to the day's events, but that's not what happened.

First one eye squinted open… and I remembered my boss had died right in front of me and that I was a suspect in his possible murder.

And when my other eye popped open… I remembered my cat could talk and also claimed to have descended from wizards.

Ugh. I just wanted to go back to sleep and wake up when this was all over. Was it too late to drop out of school and move far, far away from this place?

Well, I was awake now, and I had to do something. I had no idea what to do about my cat, and I felt uneasy being home alone with him here in my dark house, so I decided to drive to the coffeehouse and see if I could find something that would prove my innocence.

Thankfully, I had a key from the many times I'd been forced to work both opening and closing shifts. I parked at the other end of the strip mall out of some small sense of self-preservation, then crept toward Harold's House of Coffee and let myself in.

A shiver wracked through me as I used my cell phone's flashlight to guide my steps toward the tiny back office. I probably shouldn't have been there, but I definitely shouldn't have been blamed for a crime I didn't commit. Maybe Harold's paperwork would reveal a secret mistress or embittered rival. I thumbed through stack after stack of timesheets, noting that despite having less seniority Kelley earned more per hour than I did.

And that jerk Harold had told me minimum wage was the best he could do! I continued flipping through the records of money in and money out, finding no alarming departures from the standard totals week after week. I was just about to move my attention away from the desk and toward the filing cabinet when a *clack-clacking* sounded just outside the office door.

I froze in place and willed my galloping heartbeat to settle.

"Please be a rat. Please be a rat," I whispered to myself when I realized it would be impossible to hide from an intruder, then grabbed the biggest, most solid object I could find—a stapler—and crept out of the office.

"You're about as stealthy as a one-winged bird," a deep, vaguely familiar voice said from the shadows.

And then Fluffy—I mean, Merlin—stepped forward, his pale green eyes giving off an eerie otherworldly glow.

"What are you doing here?" I whisper-yelled.

"I know you left the house to get away from me," he said, his tail swaying in a large sweeping motion behind him.

"What?" I said. "That's—no. No, I didn't. Um, how did you get here?"

He sighed, letting out the unpleasant scent of stale milk, thanks to the ice cream we'd shared earlier. "I used magic, obviously."

"Oh, um. Why? I can handle things on my own here?" I wasn't sure why that came out as a question. I guess my nerves were still rattled by the fact my boss was dead and my cat could talk.

"Sure, you can." Merlin scoffed at my alleged independence, then shook his head and continued. "Look, I don't care why you killed this Harold guy. That's your business, not mine. But the thing is since you're my familiar now, I'm going to have to ask you to stop taking wild risks with your safety."

"Come again now? I'm your what?"

"My familiar. All good witches and wizards have them, and you're looking at one of the best."

"I don't want to be your—"

"Too late! Since I confided my secret in you, we are now bonded. No take-backsies." That irksome feline had the audacity to smile as he announced this.

I swooned and staggered backward. "I'm sorry. This is all a little much. Also I didn't kill Harold."

"Sure, you didn't."

"I didn't! That's why I'm here. I'm looking for proof that someone else did it. Although the best option is still that he died of natural causes."

"He didn't," my cat informed me matter-of-factly as he sniffed at the air. "I can sense the rage and ill feelings in this place. It's thick like a smog."

I raised an eyebrow. "Oh, then you know who did it, too?"

"Not a clue, but it's probably better you let the police handle this. You'll have enough to keep you busy now that you need to learn the ropes of being someone's familiar."

"I really don't have the energy for this," I pouted, then let out a long yawn.

Merlin touched my foot with his paw, and a little jolt of energy ran through me—a sudden pick-me-up that was even more powerful than a double shot of espresso.

I stopped to gape at my feline companion. "Whoa, you really are magic. Aren't you?"

"Yes, clearly." He rolled his eyes at me, a gesture I didn't even know a cat could make. "Oh, and also, you can't tell anyone."

"I won't," I promised as my hands shook with fear. "Who would I tell?"

"Not my problem," he informed me, turning to trot away. "But if you do tell, you'll be immediately transported to the dirtiest, seediest, awfullest magical prison that ever existed."

"Oh." My hands shook even harder now, and I dropped the

stapler. A loud clatter rang through the empty coffeehouse, and my heart practically stopped beating in my chest.

My cat returned with a sneer. “Stop futzing. You’re my representative now, and I don’t take kindly to being embarrassed.”

Ugh. What had my life become?

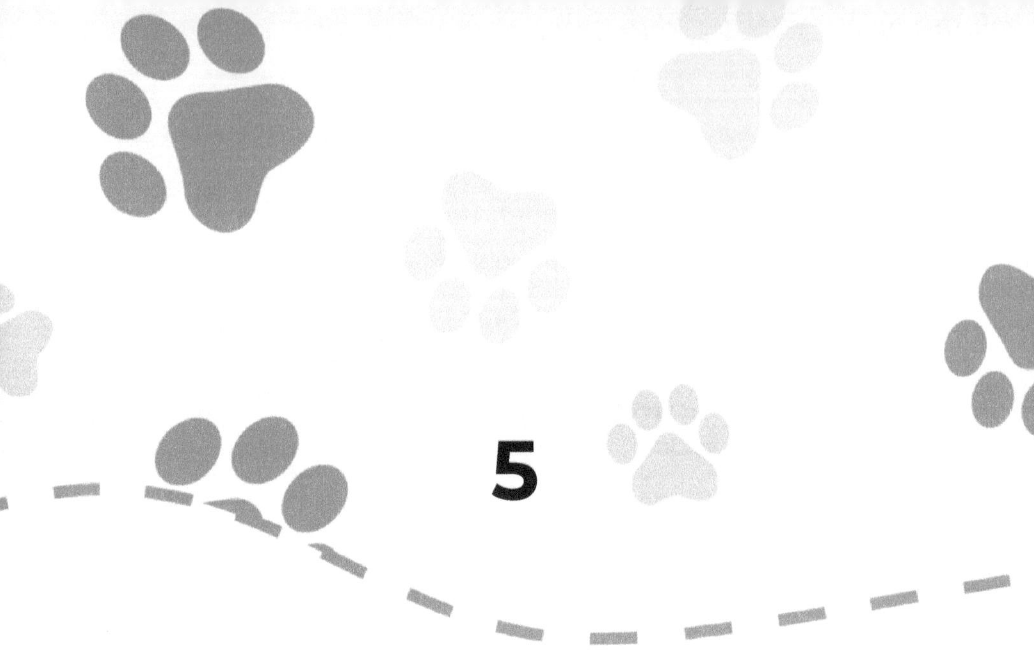

5

When we returned home, Merlin disappeared into the darkness, mumbling something about witchy business that needed seeing to and continuing my familiar education tomorrow.

I fell into bed in an exhausted heap and with a desperate prayer that tomorrow would be different.

I awoke the next morning to an insistent pounding on my front door. Upon squinting my eyes open, I realized that the sun already hung high in the sky. Normally my cat woke me in the pre-dawn hours to demand I refill his food bowl, but today he'd allowed me to sleep in. Why?

Knock, knock.

And who was that trying to break down my front door?

"I know you're in there," that unpleasant policewoman I'd met yesterday afternoon cried from the other side.

I groaned and pulled myself out of bed, quickly running my hands through my hair in a half-hearted attempt to tame it. When I flung the door open, Officer Dash snorted and pushed her way inside.

"Oh, please. Come right in," I muttered and closed the door behind her.

"Coffee?" I offered as I padded toward the kitchen and let out an enormous yawn so she could see firsthand how much she was inconveniencing me.

"Just waking up, I see," she noted with a disappointed shake of her head. "You sleep pretty easy for someone who just committed murder. Guess that makes you a psychopath."

I shook off her over-the-top insult and forced a smile. "Do you want the coffee or not?"

Officer Dash held up a hand. "None for me. Thanks."

I sighed and turned my back to her as I went about the business of rescuing my favorite mug from the dishwasher and sticking a pod in the Keurig so it could begin the brew cycle.

When I turned back around a couple minutes later with a full cup of coffee in my hands, I found she had made herself comfortable at my messy kitchen table.

I set my mug down and grabbed the scattered articles I'd printed for my thesis research, arranging them into a sloppy pile just out of the officer's reach.

She waited for me to sit and take a blessed sip before bombarding me with whatever news she'd come to share. "The M.E. has now confirmed that Mr. Harold Harris was murdered. We're still waiting on the full toxicology report to come back, of course, but you could save us all a lot of time if you just confess now."

I refused to be baited like this, no matter how insistently this detective clung to her false accusations. "I didn't kill my boss," I ground out from between clenched teeth.

"Uh-huh. That's what they all say."

"I don't know who 'they' are, but I'm telling you the truth about me."

Officer Dash widened her eyes and leaned toward me in what appeared to be an intimidation tactic. "If you didn't kill him, then who did? Huh?"

"I have no idea. I'd only just arrived when he keeled over, so anyone could have come and gone by then without me knowing. Besides, I don't even know what killed him, so I can't really speculate." Okay, that was probably a bit insensitive, but this whole thing was causing me way too much stress, way too early in the day. I just wanted Officer Dash to accept my innocence and leave me be.

She grew even more frustrated, a sheen of sweat rising to her brow. "Are you even paying attention? Toxicology means poison. We're just waiting on the particulars."

"Poison, huh? Well, Harold pretty much always had a coffee in hand. We often joked that he'd set up shop primarily to save on his habit." I studied my coffee suspiciously, then deciding it was okay took another long swig. Heavens knew I would need all the caffeine I could get to make it through this conversation.

Officer Dash pulled a small notepad out of her pocket and clicked her pen. "We? Who's we?"

Shoot.

"Oh, um. Just the others who work there. Drake and Kelley are the two who're usually around for my shifts, but there are others, too."

She studied me carefully. "So you believe one of your coworkers poisoned Mr. Harris?"

"I didn't say that. I honestly have no idea. I'm just as shocked by all this as you are."

"If the poison was delivered via his coffee, then you three baristas on shift had the greatest opportunity to pull off the crime," she pointed out with a shrug that came across as incredibly unnatural.

I shook my head. "I didn't say Kelley or Drake did it. Kelley was really, really upset."

"And Drake?"

Instead of answering, I took another long gulp of coffee. I didn't want to prove my innocence by throwing someone else under the bus, and there was no rule saying I needed to play Officer Dash's little game. When I lowered my cup, Officer Dash was still staring at me intently.

She stood and pushed her chair back in toward the table. "If I find out the poison was delivered via his coffee, you better believe I'll be right back here asking more questions."

"I didn't kill Harold, but I'll do what I can to help you find out who did," I called out half-heartedly.

She huffed. "They all say that, too," she said with a sarcastic smirk. "I'll tell your buddy Drake you said hi."

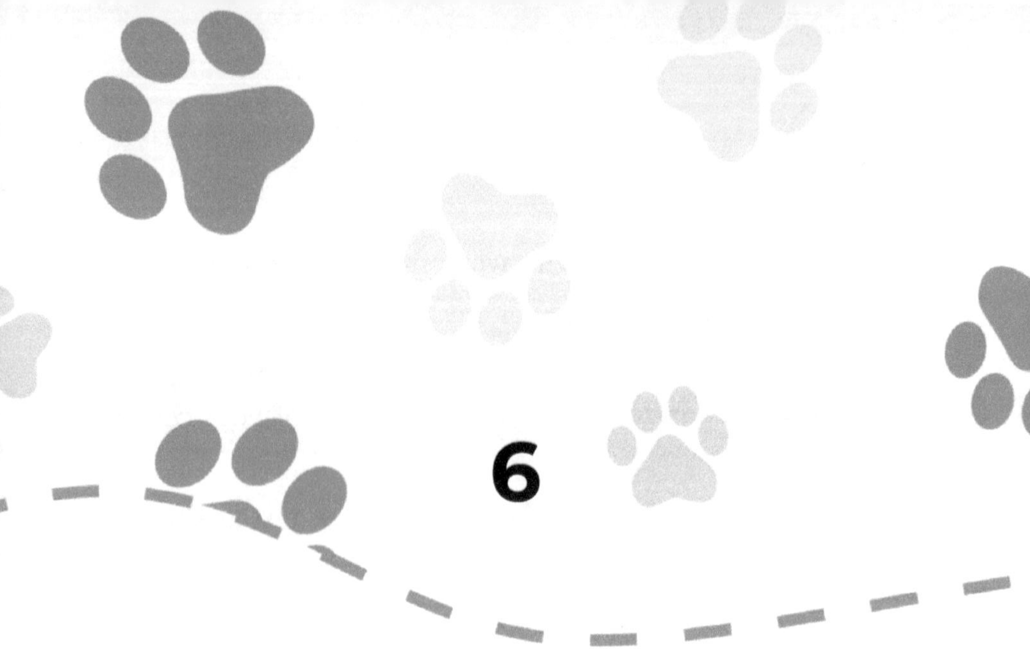

6

After Officer Dash saw herself out, I threw on a worn pair of jeans and a fresh t-shirt from my laundry basket, popped another pod into my coffee maker, and waited for it to brew. Before it even had a chance to finish, Merlin came racing in through the pet door, a cat possessed.

"Come, there's no time to waste!" he shouted, running laps around the kitchen with his tail flat.

"What's the matter?" I choked out. I may have started getting used to the idea that my cat could talk, but I was still having a hard time following his dramatics.

He stopped in place, fell over onto his side, and yowled. "Wrong! Now we're both dead."

"Dead? What?"

"A familiar should always be in tune with her witch. A quick response could very well be the difference between life and death, between freedom and capture," he lectured from his place on the floor.

I rubbed at my eyes. "You've gotta give me some time to catch up here. And to wake up a little."

Merlin hung his head and let out a dry laugh. "I chose poorly. Of course, I did."

"Insulting me isn't going to help me learn any faster," I pointed out as the last drips of coffee landed in my cup with a *plop* and a *plip*. "By the way, when do I get magic?"

Merlin's laugh came on loud and hysterical as he rolled from side to side on the linoleum kitchen floor. "Magic! You? Hoo, that's a good one. Thanks, I needed that laugh."

"It's not a joke. You forced me into whatever this is, the least you could do is make it worth my while."

"Oh, my dear sweet human..."

"Gracie," I reminded him. "I have a name, use it."

"Gracie," he spat out, then wrinkled his nose unkindly. "Would you be open to changing that?"

I scowled at Merlin as he dragged himself to his feet.

"Fine, Gracie, it is. And, no, you don't get magic. That's not a familiar's role."

He was proving to be even more tiresome than Officer Dash this morning. "Then what do you even need me for?"

"In addition to your previous duties of filling my food bowl and cleaning my kitty box, it is now up to you to be my face."

I stared at him deadpan.

"What part of that was a problem?" Merlin asked, tilting his head to the side.

I crossed my arms over my chest and sighed. "What do you mean by be *your face?* That makes zero sense. You already have a face."

"I can explain by sharing a story. Once there was this ugly guy with a long nose. He loved a gorgeous lady, but was worried she would reject him, so he struck a deal with a brainless pretty boy to—"

"Are you telling me the story of Cyrano de Bergerac right now?"

"Oh, good, so you know it."

"And in this scenario, I'm your..." I raised my fingers in air quotes. "Brainless pretty boy."

"Sure. I mean you're a little better than brainless and a little worse than pretty, but it averages out."

"Sorry, I can't deal with this right now." I grabbed my fresh cup of coffee and marched toward my room, ready to slam the door in his face.

Merlin trailed behind me, too fast for me to shut out without spilling my precious coffee along the way. "I'm sorry. I forget how sensitive you humans are about things like that. I chose you because I believe you have what it takes."

"To be the brainless face of your operations?" I asked with a growl.

But Merlin either didn't pick up on my ire or chose to ignore it. "Exactly. I'm so glad you understand now."

"I'm sorry, but I have bigger plans for my life than that."

Merlin's eyes glistened with mischief. "What plans? Tell me, and I can make them happen."

I stared at him quizzically, afraid to ask for more.

"You don't have magic, but I do. Remember? Being a familiar is an important job, but not a thankless one. Many of the famous folks in your human history were secretly familiars."

I crossed my arms and glared at him. "Really? Like who?"

"Well, consider my namesake," he said with a smile stretched wide between his whiskers.

I balked at this. "Merlin. The wizard?"

"Ha, he wishes! The Merlin you humans know about was actually the familiar for an extremely powerful cat witch. His name was also Merlin, which makes it a bit confusing. The human Merlin wished to achieve power and fame in exchange for aiding his cat. But he became greedy and self-important, which is why the real Merlin cursed him to age backward. Meanwhile, he found a much more suitable familiar in a new human called Arthur. He only wanted power and prestige in the human world, which was much easier for my great ancestor to cope with."

"So Merlin was a fraud and King Arthur was just somebody's familiar?" I summed up.

"There's no *just* about it. Familiars are incredibly important. We witches do what we have to in order to keep you happy."

I raised an eyebrow in question.

"So could I be the next Lady Gaga?"

"That would take some talent. You may not have been born that way, but I can sure make it happen." Merlin paused and flexed his paws. "Is that what you want?"

"No, it was just a hypothetical," I rushed to explain.

"Careful then, because wishes that size only come around once.

There's a lot of small stuff I can do on the regular, but truly life-changing alterations are a one-time deal."

"I'll keep that in mind," I promised, still not quite believing all this.

"As you should." Merlin appeared to be satisfied now. "Come. Let's begin."

7

"Where are we going?" I asked as I chased my cat through the house.

Instead of answering, though, he ran through the pet flap and outside.

Hurriedly, I pushed my feet into a pair of cheap flip-flops I kept by the door, then swung the door open in just enough time to see him jump into the birdbath and splash around. I knew Maine Coons liked water, but it was still strange to see him enjoying himself in this way. Back where I came from, cats were cats—they hated water and they definitely did not talk.

"I saw you the other day," I said as I approached cautiously. "Yesterday," I amended.

Wow, that felt like a week ago at least.

Merlin stopped splashing and glanced over his shoulder at me. "Yes. And what did you see?"

"You f-fl-flew," I sputtered, wrapping my arms around myself in a hug. "After a bird you wanted to eat."

Merlin sighed. "First thing's first, I did not want to eat him. That guy owed me money."

I blinked hard. "Money?"

"Yes, money." He smiled now. "Secondly, I wanted you to see me. It was a test."

"Test?" A chill ran through me, even though the Georgia morning was already bright and warm.

Merlin rolled his eyes. "Stop repeating everything I say as a question." He stared me down, waiting for whatever it was he needed from me.

I gulped and nodded, still stuck on the fact my cat used money and that a neighborhood bird owed him some.

"I had to see how you reacted to your first glimpse of magic. Some humans can't quite handle it."

"And I did? Handled it, I mean?"

My cat looked me up and down then smirked. "You're still standing. That's a good start."

"What could have happened?" I demanded, quite angry that he would knowingly put me in danger.

"You could have lost your mind," he said flatly. "Many do. That's why one must always exercise extreme caution when selecting and testing a familiar."

"So you mentally break people?" It took everything I had not to yell that. Still, we were outside in the middle of a neighborhood street. If someone happened by and saw me not only talking to—but arguing with—my cat, the crazy train would be at my door by noon, ready to lock me up and throw away the key.

My cat remained calm, casual, as if he were discussing meaningless trivia and not the very real facts of our lives. "Yes, not everyone can handle the existence of magic. A sad truth." Merlin straightened and puffed his fluffy chest out. "Anyway, glad you're still with me."

"Do I have a choice?"

He chuckled. "No."

"I didn't think so."

"Come closer," my cat urged, and I immediately did as told.

"What's this? What are were doing?" I asked, feeling awkward as we stood in the middle of my yard and continued to converse in broad daylight. Seriously, why couldn't we have done whatever this was inside?

"How to be a familiar, lesson one!" he declared with pride, then moved to the edge of the birdbath, balancing somewhat precariously. "Protect the cauldron at all costs."

"That's a birdbath," I pointed out.

He raised his arm high, then face-pawed. "It's a cauldron. The source of my power and my connection to the larger magical community. Without it, I am a witch at large. Not a proper witch at all."

I looked from the birdbath to him and back again.

Merlin sighed. "Lesson two, believe everything I say without question. For example, this is a cauldron. In the olden days, witches used giant black pots. But in the modern era, we use other commonplace items that are easy for a witch to access but go largely unnoticed by others. Observe."

He walked to the center of the small fountain and dipped his paw in. Instantly the thin layer of water began to glow a pale green, not unlike the color of Merlin's large eyes.

"Whoa," I said, the air whooshing right out of me in surprise.

Merlin tapped the water again, and it returned to its normal state. "This is why we cats choose to adopt humans. There is no guaranteed safe place on the streets. We need the guise of domesticity to protect our secrets. And also the shade of night. Naturally, we would prefer to keep away during the day, but it's easier to hide our true ways when most of you humans are tucked away in your beds."

I nodded along. Everything he was telling me made sense, now that I thought about it. Everything except...

"What do you need money for?" I asked, still stuck on his revelation about that poor robin who owed him money.

"You're still stuck on your own world. In mine, we... *MEOW!*"

"Huh?" I spun my head to see where he was looking and caught sight of a neighbor powerwalking by.

She smiled and waved a hello, and I could swear I recognized her from somewhere. I just didn't know where.

But then just as quickly as she'd approached, she passed out of view.

I turned back to my cat, whose tail flicked wildly as it hung down from the stone bath. "Watch out for that one," he growled.

"What? Why? She seemed friendly enough."

He sneered unkindly as he stared in the direction the woman had gone. "Remember lesson number two?"

"Trust everything you say?"

"Yes. That was Virginia. She's the familiar for a very troublesome witch who lives on the other side of town. Luna," he bit out.

"Did she come to spy on us?"

Merlin jumped down from the bath. "I wouldn't put it past her. Luckily, the cauldron is protected from other magical practitioners and their familiars. Come. Let's return inside where we cannot be watched by those who would do us harm."

Harm? It seemed I'd only survived the first of many trials when it came to joining my cat in his magical world, which left one question playing on loop in my mind: *WHY ME?*

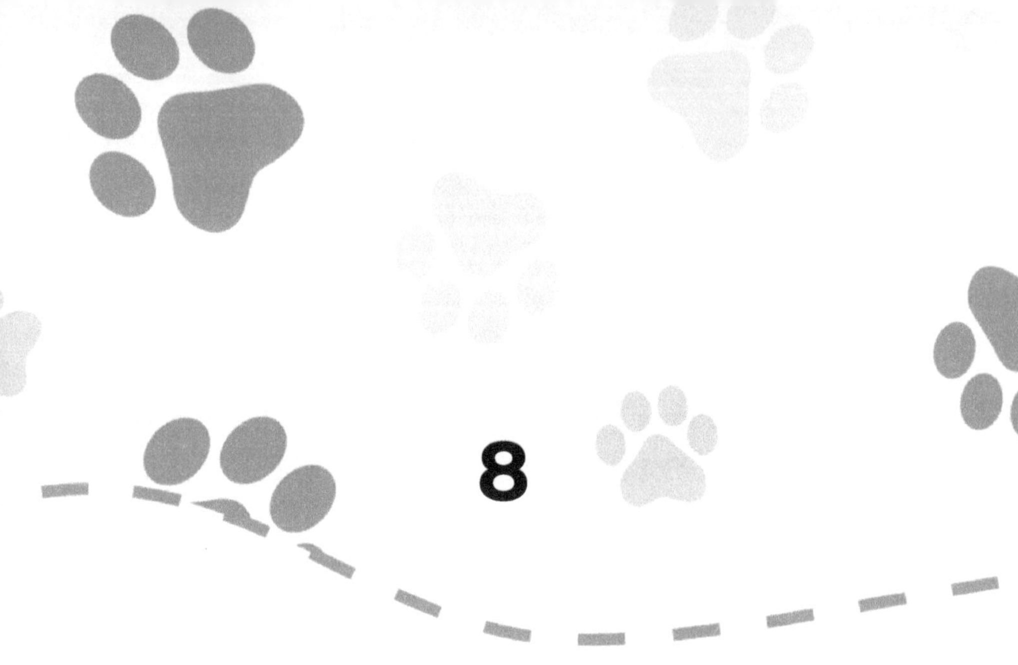

8

"We're going to Luna's," Merlin announced as soon as I'd shut the door firmly behind us. Of course, I didn't like this one bit.

"What? Why?" I moaned.

Unfortunately, Merlin remained steadfast in his demands. "If she's spying on us, that means she herself probably has something to hide."

"We're going to break and enter based on a probably? In case you haven't noticed, I'm already a suspect in a murder investigation!" I exploded, and I had to admit it felt good to yell after working so hard to keep it together outside.

"Lesson number two," he reminded me yet again, and I could already tell that this would be my least favorite of all the lessons, no matter what came next.

I huffed and crossed my arms. He couldn't make me do something I didn't want to do… Could he?

Merlin softened a bit. "Look, I know this is all new to you, but you have to trust me. I will protect you. And right now, protecting you means making sure Luna doesn't try something while I'm working to get my new familiar on board. We're both incredibly vulnerable right now, which means we must be vigilant."

He paused to suck in a deep breath here, then resumed in an even more somber tone. "You think human prison is scary? It doesn't hold a candle to the living horror that is a magical prison. If Luna exposes us, then we'll both go there with no hope of ever getting out. You get taken to human prison, I can break you out in a blink and help you create a new identity. Trust me, this Harold guy's murder is the least of our problems right now."

"Okay," I said, too tired to argue any longer and too afraid to learn any more about the possible repercussions of failing to do this familiar thing the right way.

He studied me with those curious green eyes of his and asked, "Okay what?"

"I trust you," I said, praying I wouldn't come to regret this assertion.

"Really? I expected you to put up more of a fight."

I shrugged. "What good would that do if we're just going to end up doing what you want, anyway?"

"I'm glad you agree." Merlin nodded, then blinked slowly two times.

I must have blinked, too, because one second we were standing at the edge of my kitchen, and the next I found myself under the shade of an unfamiliar magnolia tree by a small ranch-style home with a carefully tended garden.

I took a step back, pushing myself against the tree for support.

"What… What just happened?" I gasped.

Merlin stalked toward me and snickered. "Your first teleportation. So sweet."

"Teleportation?" I whisper-yelled, in case anyone was nearby and paying attention to us. "Next time give me a little notice, please."

"No," he said firmly. "It's much easier if you don't know it's coming."

I groaned and clutched at my head. Really that was just for show, though, because other than being shocked witless, I felt perfectly fine. "Where are we?"

"Luna's. Now c'mon." Merlin turned away from me and began trotting toward the back of the nearby house, his fluffy striped tail held high and proud.

"Wait. How are we going to get in?" I called after him.

But Merlin just ran faster, then jumped into a window box fitted with perky yellow daffodils.

I crept after him, one second moving through soft, spongy grass and the next stomping across a smooth hardwood floor. Great, now we were inside the house.

"Stop doing that," I hissed.

"Stop complaining," he hissed back, "and help me look."

"For what?" I said, taking in the homey decor.

Luna's owner—or familiar, I guess—certainly loved floral prints.

They covered everything. I was pretty sure I'd seen that exact couch pattern on a pregnant B-list celebrity once upon a time. In addition to the floral fabric, drapes, and decor, more than a dozen vases of fresh-cut flowers filled the modest home.

I couldn't help but sneeze in response.

"Luna's a garden witch," Merlin explained when he caught me staring.

"What kind of witch are you?" I asked, mouth agape. First I learn that witches are real, then I find out they come in multiple flavors.

"Sky," he informed me placidly.

But my head was positively spinning from all the new information flying at me in rapid succession. "Come again now?" I squeaked. This seemed like one thing I just couldn't let go without getting at least some kind of quick explanation.

"I'm pretty well-rounded, but my specialty pertains to things that come from the sky. You know, wind, water, ice. The occasional burst of electricity, if the mood is right."

Finally, part of this was beginning to make some sense. "Oh, so you're all elemental? Like Pokémon."

His expression instantly turned dour. "No, not like a children's video game."

"Yeah, actually, I think it is. Luna's a garden witch, so plants and earth, right? That would make her grass and ground type," I recited, glad the many hours I'd invested playing Pokémon Go were good for more than just getting my steps in. "And you're water, flying, and ice, so you're kind of an even match. I suggest you use your ice powers in battle."

"This is not a game, and there are no battles. Now stop yammering and help me search for anything suspicious."

"Like that?" I asked, pointing to an old leather journal that lay open on the coffee table.

"No," Merlin began, but then he turned to look where I was pointing, and his eyes lit with delight. "Actually, yes. Good job. Now grab the book, and let's get out of here before someone notices our intrusion."

Well, he certainly didn't have to tell me twice. I hustled for that journal as fast as my flip-flopped feet would carry me, more than ready to head home.

9

Merlin blinked once, and I braced myself for another unnerving journey by teleportation. Before he could blink a second time, however, a nearby flower vase shattered and the thorny stems flew to my cat, locking him in place.

"Well, well, well..." A husky female voice floated toward us from the doorway. I hadn't even heard anyone enter. How could we have been so careless?

I craned my neck, too afraid to move the rest of me, and spotted a lanky white cat with bright green eyes staring right back at me.

"Luna," Merlin growled. "What do you want?"

She stalked over to him and slowly circled her entrapped rival. "I think I should be the one asking questions here, since you're the one who broke into my house."

"I owe you nothing," Merlin spat and hissed.

While the two felines continued to argue, I carefully slipped the journal we'd found into the waistband of my pants.

"Why was your familiar at my house?" Merlin demanded. He looked so pathetic in that cage of flower petals and stems.

"Why is your familiar *in* my house? We can do this all day, Fluffy." She cackled at him, leaving no doubt who was the wicked witch in this scenario.

"His name's Merlin," I corrected angrily and grabbed for the white cat. Even though I didn't have magic, I did have almost one-hundred and fifty pounds on the skinny feline. Surely, I could overpower her.

But no. She escaped my reaching arms and turned back to hiss at me. "I'll only tell you this once, so make sure you're paying attention." Luna's back arched and her tail grew extra poofy. "If you ever break into my house again, I won't be so forgiving a second time."

I gulped hard, choosing not to point out that we teleported in, that there was no breaking at all.

Luna inched forward with claws extended. "What are you, stupid? Get out of here!"

I didn't need to be told twice. I picked up Merlin, thorny cage and all, and bolted through the front door. Outside now, I ran toward the street, which I could just barely see in the distance. Luna's large front yard sat at the intersection of two side streets. I tried to read the signs as I got closer but struggled to make out either very clearly.

Persimmon, I read just as my feet made contact with the pavement. Now that we'd stepped off Luna's property, the thorns and flowers that held Merlin fell away.

He jumped from my arms, shook off, blinked once, twice… And we were back home.

“All that for nothing,” he mewled, padding toward his water bowl then taking a few long laps to refresh himself.

“Not for nothing,” I revealed, tugging the filched journal from my waistband and bringing it into view.

“Gracie,” my cat exclaimed. “Good girl. Very good girl.”

I basked in his praise despite his dehumanizing tone. “I can see why you don’t much care for Luna,” I added softly. “Or the name Fluffy. I’m sorry.”

“She’d have killed me if you weren’t there,” he said with a casual shrug. “She’s been like that ever since I dumped her to take my place as a full witch.”

I threw my hands up and took a step back. “Whoa, whoa, whoa. Back up there.”

Merlin turned away but kept one eye trained on me from the side. “A cat doesn’t become a full witch until he takes a familiar.”

“Not that part. The dumping part?” I clarified, wondering why he hadn’t told me this bit of his history with Luna in advance of our trespassing—and me stealing the journal.

Merlin yawned and stretched his back legs lazily. “Oh, yeah. We used to date. Not a big deal.”

“Actually, it seems like a very big deal,” I corrected, hoping he would tell me more.

“It’s not my fault the rules state that no two witches may live under the same roof. It was fine when I was stray, but things change. There was no way I’d give up my awesome powers in favor of a fling.

Nope. Anyway… No need to dredge up the past when we have our futures to worry about. Now show me the book," Merlin commanded without a second thought about his past love affair.

I tromped over to the couch and set the journal in my lap so we could read through it together. "What is all this?" I asked, squinting at the strange series of symbols interspersed with sketches of various flora and fauna.

"It appears to be a grimoire. Not her primary one, mind you, but something new she's working on."

"A spell book? Do you have one of those, too?"

He nodded, continuing to study the page. "I have many, but I would never leave them in plain sight."

"Where are they?" I wondered aloud.

"That's privileged information, aka on a need-to-know basis. And you don't need to know right now."

"Ouch. Okay."

Merlin mumbled to himself as he flipped through the pages, completely unbothered by the fact that he'd hurt my feelings.

"So what are we looking at here?" I asked after a little while of watching, waiting, and understanding absolutely nothing.

"She's developing a new potion. A powerful one. But she doesn't seem to quite have it yet."

I stared at the book harder but still couldn't make heads or tails of it. "To do what?"

"I can't quite tell. This is all garden witch stuff. They're big on brews. Me? Not so much."

"Do you think it could be a poison?" I asked, thinking of poor

Harold. Yeah, he may have been stingy and mean, but he certainly didn't deserve to be murdered over it.

Merlin immediately picked up my suggestion and ran with it. "You think Luna could be behind Harold's death?"

I nodded. "Yeah. I mean, why not? We don't really have any other suspects that make sense."

Merlin slammed the journal closed. "A very interesting theory. She may have been trying to get to you, but nabbed Harold instead."

I gasped, unaware of just how much danger I'd been in this whole time, how much danger I was still in. "She would do that? Kill me?"

"Duh." Merlin yawned as if this very important conversation bored him. "Luna is very dangerous, and she has it out for me, which means now she has it out for you, too."

"Maybe you shouldn't have broken her heart then," I mumbled, adding to the long list of reasons why I was very upset with my cat that day.

If only I'd have adopted a dog instead...

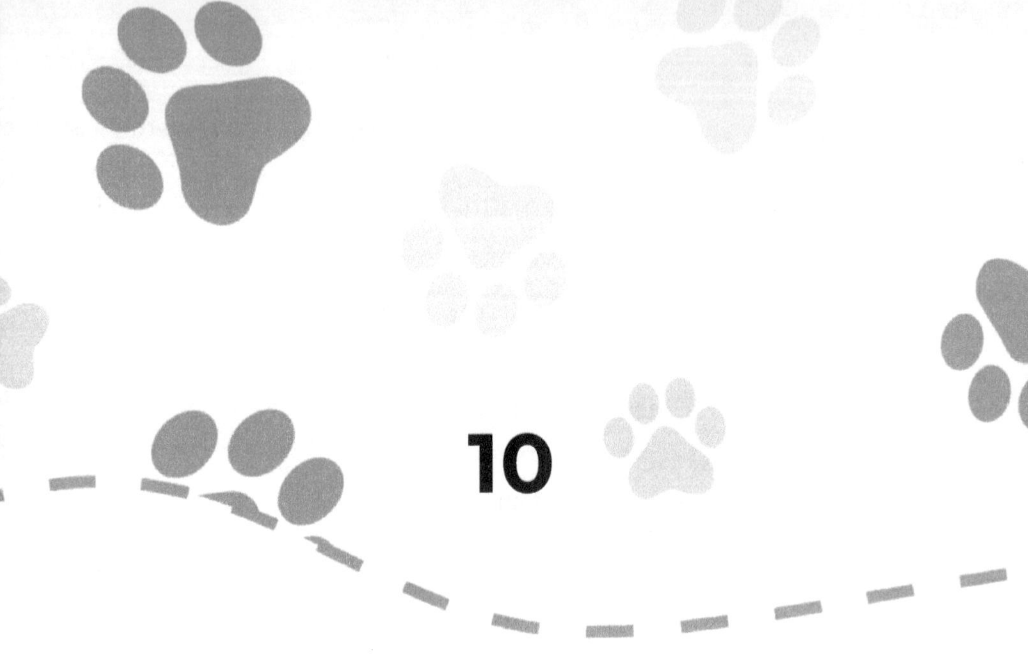

10

"I have to get to work," I said before shuffling my way toward the shower. We'd spent the better part of the last hour poring over that stolen grimoire and still had nothing to show for it. Well, except for my poor frazzled nerves.

"If Luna's so dangerous, perhaps you should return that journal," I shouted back toward Merlin before I closed the door and enjoyed some much-needed time to myself.

And he seemed to have taken my advice, because by the time I finished getting ready for my shift, neither he nor the journal were anywhere to be seen.

Honestly, I didn't know whether I was expected to show up for work that day, given the whole crime scene thing, but I decided it would be best to at least try to honor my responsibilities to the late Harold.

When I reached the coffeehouse, I found that it was still blocked off by police tape but that my coworker Kelley was moving about inside.

I let myself in, too.

Kelley glanced up suddenly from her place behind the glass pastry display case. “Oh, hi, Gracie,” she said with a frown.

“How are you holding up?” I asked gently, coming over to stand beside her.

She shrugged. “Honestly, I don’t know.”

I glanced down at her hands, but they were empty. In fact, Kelley appeared to be doing nothing more than standing there in a mournful trance.

She’d been upset while we were waiting for the police yesterday, but I’d assumed that was more of an in-the-moment reaction. If possible, she seemed even more torn up today.

And that made me feel guilty that I hadn’t spent any time mourning for Harold. Instead I was too focused on my worry that I might be pegged with his murder.

Even if Harold had been a bad boss, I still wanted to be a good person. Maybe if I helped Kelley now, it would make up for my earlier failures.

“Yeah, it’s hard,” I said, keeping my eyes downcast. “He may not have been the best boss, but he was still a person we knew.”

Kelley sobbed into her hands. “Not me. I hardly knew him. Not yet. I thought we’d have more time.”

I didn’t know Kelley all that well myself. I hadn’t realized she’d wanted more than a casual work acquaintanceship. Had she been crying out for a friend, and we'd all been too busy to catch on? If so, I felt horrible about it.

Kelley had only been working at our coffee shop for about a month. She was a sweet girl who'd recently graduated high school and moved to our area for a gap year. I always wondered why she'd chosen to move to rural Georgia rather than backpack through Europe, but who was I to judge? Maybe she'd inherited a house just like I did. I could have asked, though. I should have asked.

I placed a hesitant hand on her shoulder. "Trust me," I said with a small smile. "You aren't missing much."

She turned to me with red-rimmed eyes. "Aren't I, though? I've spent my whole life wondering about him, imagining how it would be when I finally got to meet him face to face, but now we'll never get the chance to form a real relationship."

The revelation slammed down on me like a falling stack of bricks. "Kelley, was Harold...?"

"My dad," she finished, reaching into her pocket and pulling out a crumpled tissue. "He dated my mom way back when. By the time she found out she was pregnant with me, they'd already broken up and he'd moved away."

I hugged her hard. "I'm so, so sorry."

She tried to smile, failed. "I guess I wasn't meant to have a dad. I also guess there's no reason for me to stick around here anymore. I never should have come. That police officer says my dad was murdered. What if it was my fault somehow?"

"Oh no, sweetie. It definitely wasn't your fault," I assured her, but Kelley was not easily assured.

"Think about it," she said, knitting her brows together in frustration. "I show up in town, and a month later he's dead. That can't be a coincidence."

"Of course it's a coincidence. A horrible one, but definitely not your fault. You aren't responsible for your parents' decisions, and you're definitely not responsible for Harold's death."

She blinked up at me. "Do you mean it?"

I bobbed my head vigorously. "Yes, absolutely."

Finally Kelley chanced a small smile. "Thanks."

"If you've got some time, I can tell you some stories about him."

Her smile grew wide and bright. "Really?"

"Yeah. It's not like we're open for business. Let's grab ourselves a snack and settle in for a chat."

"I'll make us a couple of pumpkin spice lattes," Kelley volunteered.

"And I'll get the snacks!" I headed to the walk-in cooler and grabbed some "fresh-made" banana bread to thaw. When I came back out, Kelley motioned for me to take a seat while she finished up with the drinks.

"You know," she told me when she came to join me in the lone booth. "My mom told me I was crazy for coming here. For trying to get to know him. I probably should have listened. At least then I'd still be able to imagine what he was like, what he might be doing. Rather than knowing for a fact he was dead."

And so began a very uncomfortable conversation, indeed.

Well, at least it was for me.

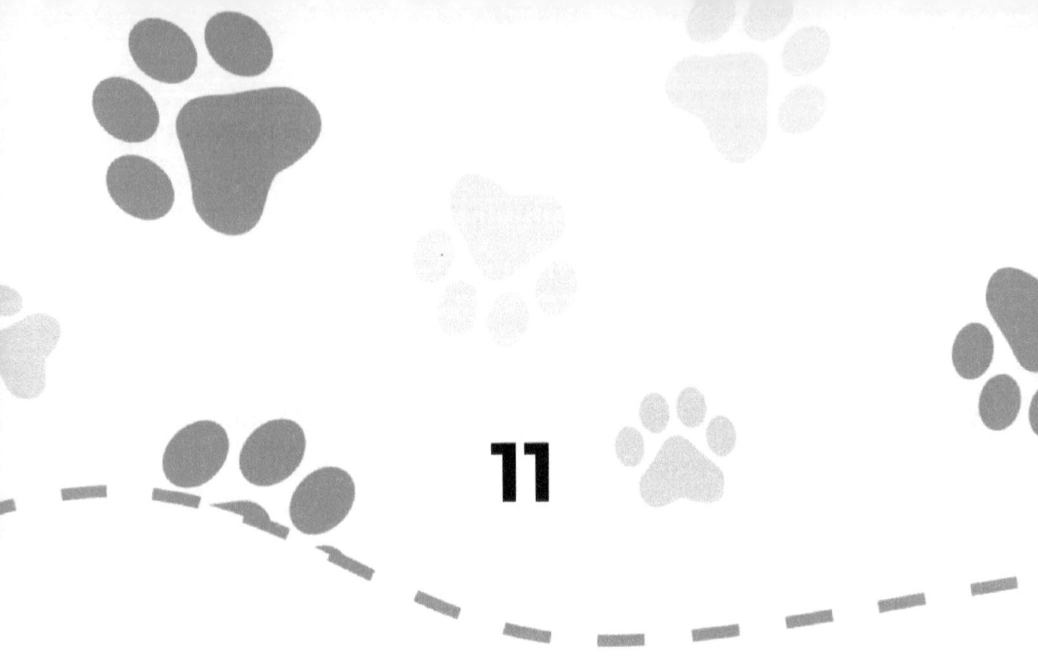

11

I pressed my lips in a firm line and nodded as Kelley shared a small glimpse into her family history. The whole purpose of this conversation was for me to help her get to know her late father better, but what if she actually knew more than she realized? What if Kelley had some special glimpse into Harold's life that helped pinpoint his killer?

She'd certainly been paying better attention to his comings and goings than I ever had.

But my young coworker was also already so distraught over his passing, it seemed wrong to push her for information when that could possibly make things worse for her.

And yet if someone didn't find out who actually killed Harold—and soon—I could end up taking the blame. Thinking of it in this way made my path obvious.

I cleared my throat and cast my eyes toward the table. "Did things end on bad terms with your mother and father?" I asked, seeing no other option but to nudge her gently and hope for the best.

Kelley sighed and reached for one of the pieces of banana nut bread, then realizing it was still ice cold, placed it back on the plate and wrapped both hands around her to-go cup. "Mom said if she never saw him again it would still be too soon," she murmured.

"That bad, huh?"

Kelley leaned back against the booth and let her head rest against the worn vinyl cushioning. "Yup."

"Did I ever tell you about the first time I met Harold?"

Kelley shook her head and her eyes widened. "No, but please do."

"Well, I was coming in for my interview. Late. And when I showed up, I found him sitting in the office going over his papers while belting out that one song from Phantom of the Opera."

Kelley sat up straight and actually let out a small chuckle. "No way!"

"Yes, way. And that's not all…"

I shared the few pleasant memories I had of my former boss, and Kelley proved to be a rapt audience. By the time we'd drained our lattes, I'd run out of stories to pass on. Also the banana bread had at long last thawed.

I lifted a piece and nodded to Kelley before taking a huge, delicious bite. Hey, even though it wasn't made fresh, it was still freaking delicious.

"So what do you think you'll do now?" I asked as Kelley picked all the walnuts from her bread and popped them into her mouth one by one.

"My mom's on her way to pick me up and drive me back home," she revealed with a grimace.

"Where's she driving from?" I asked conversationally, although it didn't escape my notice that Kelley seemed unhappy about her mother's impending visit.

"Ohio."

"No way." I reached across the table and lightly slapped her hand. "I'm from Michigan."

"Natural enemies," Kelley teased, referring to our home states' bitter rivalry. In reality, though, us both being from the Midwest meant we had more in common than not.

I wanted to know more about her mother, just in case she was a person of interest in this investigation. But I had to be careful about how hard I pressed. Hopefully the light playful moment would help me get further with my next line of questioning. Again, the next to last thing I wanted to do was kick Kelley when she was down. The very last thing I wanted to do was go to jail for a crime I had no hand in committing.

"Your mom must be happy that you're coming back home. Huh?" I ventured, licking my thumb and then pressing it into the crumbs that lay scattered on my plate.

"Yeah." Kelley said, finally taking a proper bite of her dessert. "Like I said, she never wanted me to come in the first place. She said the only good thing my dad had ever done in his whole life was to give her me." She smiled shyly.

"Why'd they break up? Did she ever say?"

"She didn't want to spoil my impression of him. Kind of ironic, huh? She said just to take her at her word and be careful."

That reminded me of rule number two of being Merlin's familiar: Do whatever he says without asking any questions.

"I know things didn't end well, but I think it's really good you got the chance to meet him," I offered with a small smile.

Kelley sniffed and shook her head. "I don't know."

"You'll get there," I said as if speaking from experience.

"You're probably right." She shrugged and leaned back in the booth, eyes closed. "It's just still all fresh and new, and I'm not sure I can handle my mom trash-talking him before he's even laid to rest."

"Yeah, that's hard." Suddenly I got an idea that could help both of us. "Tell you what, if she gives you any trouble, come see me. Tell her we already had plans before this all happened. I can serve as a buffer."

Kelley opened her eyes and stared at me in silent shock before saying, "Wow. Thank you, Gracie. You are being so nice."

"You deserve a friend right now, and I'm willing to bet you need one, too." I pushed my phone across the table toward her. "Here, enter your phone number, and I'll text you my address."

Kellie grabbed at it eagerly and began to type. As she did, a knock sounded on the door to the coffee shop.

I glanced over and immediately recognized the silhouette of the last person I wanted to see just then.

Officer Dash had come to pay us a visit.

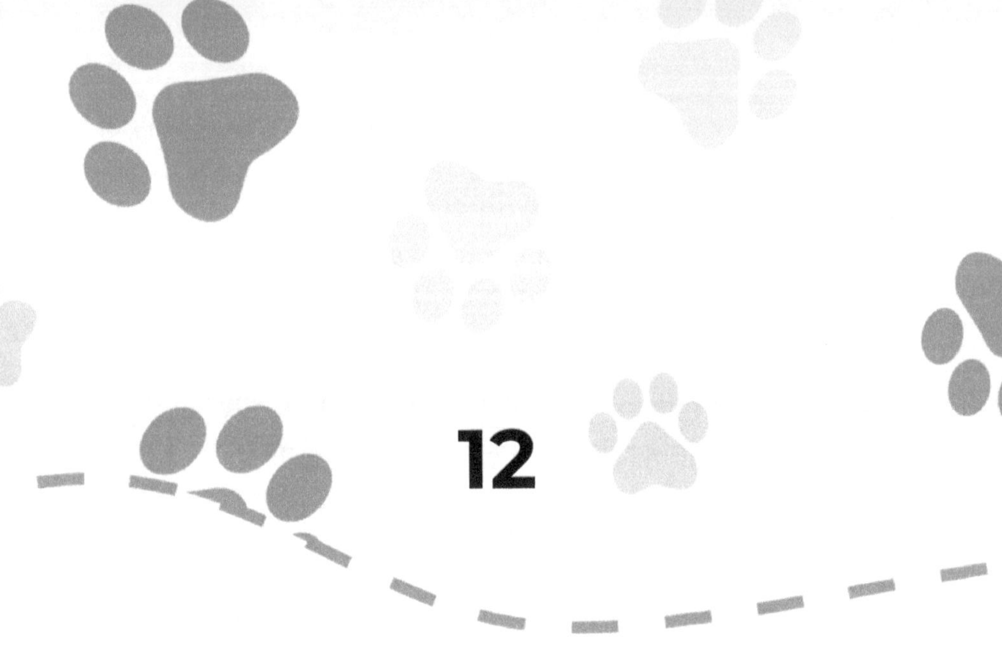

12

As soon as we heard the knocking, Kelley immediately jumped up to let the policewoman inside.

Officer Dash smirked when she saw me. “Figures you’d be here, exactly where you aren’t supposed to be.”

“We were scheduled to work today,” Kelley explained, jumping straight to my rescue. Now that I was getting to know her better, I really did like her.

“Well, sorry to say, this place of business is closed until further notice.” Dash didn’t look sorry, though. Not one bit.

“Do you have any idea when that might be?” I asked, gathering the two empty plates and taking them back to the small sink we used to keep things tidy.

Dash’s eyes followed me, tracing every movement. “Not until we conclude our investigation and Harris’s attorney settles his estate.”

“Do you happen to know who’s handling his will?” Kelley asked, tucking her hair behind each ear and glancing down. Well, at least I wasn't the only person intimidated by the brusque policewoman. Still, this was the last thing that poor Kelley needed right now.

"That's private family business," Officer Dash snapped, only glancing toward Kelly for a moment before staring me down again.

"I know," Kelley mumbled as she studied her shoes. "I'm his daughter."

"If you're meant to be included, his attorney will contact you," the officer explained with a hard gaze. "How come you didn't disclose your relationship with the deceased the first time we talked?"

Kelley shook her head. "I'm still coming to terms with all of this."

"They were estranged," I piped up. "Until very recently."

"Interesting." Officer Dash pulled out that little steno notebook of hers and jotted a few things down. "Do you mind accompanying me to the station for a few questions?"

Kelley's eyes widened in horror.

"Is that really necessary?" I argued, moving in front of Kelley protectively. "Can't you see how upset she already is?"

"Oh, did I hurt your little friend's feelings?" she asked with a cruel smile. "Silly me, I was just trying to bring a murderer to justice here!"

Officer Dash stomped her foot, and Kelley's trembling fingers reached for my arm.

I turned to face my frightened young colleague. "You didn't do anything wrong, which means you've got nothing to hide. Even this one is going to see that," I said, hooking a thumb back toward a very cranky Officer Dash.

"Stay?" Kelley begged.

"I really need to question each suspect separately," the policewoman informed us.

Kelley gasped. "Suspect?"

"Look, she's a little rough around the edges—okay, a lot. But she can't do a thing to you. You have my number now, call me anytime you need me. Any reason."

Kelley nodded, and I stepped aside.

"Ever ridden in the back of a cop car before?" Officer Dash asked with a bemused expression, sending Kelley shrinking back.

"Enough," I growled. As soon as this investigation was over, I would be filing a big fat complaint about Officer Dash's lack of professionalism. Anonymously, of course.

"You can talk here," I continued. "I'll leave to give you both some privacy."

I squeezed Kelley's hand and told her it would be okay, then saw myself out. Neither of them tried to stop me.

I waited in the parking lot for a few minutes just to make sure Officer Dash wasn't honestly planning on carting the poor aggrieved daughter to the station for an interrogation.

Once I was satisfied that she wasn't, I began the short drive home.

In my distracted state, I almost ran a red light and drove up over the curb more than once. Why did Officer Dash have to be so combative about the investigation? Moreover, why had she come into the coffeehouse that afternoon? Had she been looking for me?

I worried now that if they didn't find the real killer soon, Officer Dash might even stoop to fabricating evidence just so she could close the investigation and move on.

Scary.

Maybe I should file that complaint against her sooner than later…

One more chance, I decided as I pulled into my driveway. One more encounter. If Officer Dash didn't start behaving more professionally with her very next visit, I would be heading into the station to discuss matters with her boss.

That small thing decided, I pushed my car into park, took a deep breath, and headed inside to see what new trouble my cat had gotten us into during my brief absence.

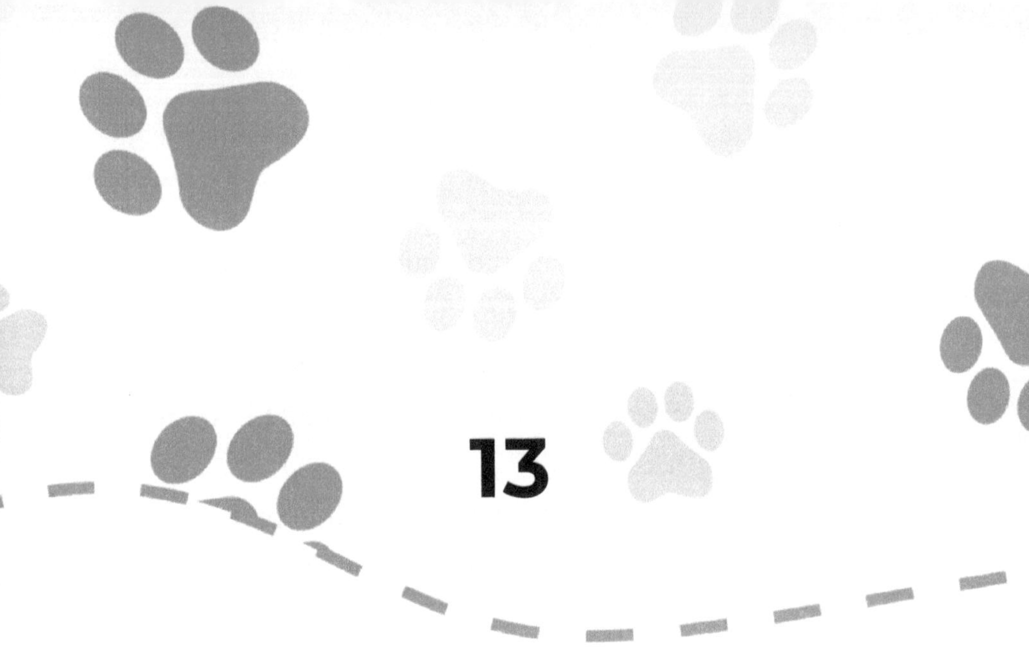

13

I crept into the house, not sure what I would find. Merlin had been alone for almost two hours, thanks to my strange shift at work. Funny, I'd never had to worry about what he did while I was away before. Now all I did was worry… about him, about Harold, about life on the whole.

Well, whatever he had gotten up to in my absence, it hadn't caused any obvious damage. In fact, the house was exactly as I'd left it. Even Luna's journal still lay open on the couch, exactly as it had been when we'd reviewed it together earlier. He must have taken it, and then brought it back. But why?

"Merlin?" I called as I moved toward the couch and peered down at the filched object. The two-page spread on display was filled with furious illegible scrawl, and I couldn't make any sense of it.

Yeesh. I'd hoped he would have returned his nemesis's journal when he was done with it, or at the very least hid it somewhere. It was like he was courting trouble here and doing it on purpose.

I took a quick picture of the journal's pages on my cell phone, then grabbed it up and headed out to return it myself.

Problem was, I didn't know exactly how to get to Luna's cottage, seeing as we'd teleported there and back, but I remembered seeing the crossroads at the edge of the property when we escaped. One of the roads was called Persimmon. I typed the street and city name into my phone's GPS and got directions to the general location. Thank goodness for modern technology.

Persimmon lay on the other side of town, but still it only took me ten minutes to find Luna's home and park outside. I tucked the journal into my purse and moved toward the door.

An older woman answered before I even had the chance to knock.

"Hello. Virginia?" I asked hopefully.

"Gracie," she answered with a sigh, then stepped back and allowed me to enter.

Good. This was good.

Now I just had to find a way to return the journal without her noticing I'd taken it in the first place.

So I put on my best, most cordial smile, and said, "I just wanted to stop by and introduce myself. I know our cats are fighting, but I see no reason why we can't get along."

Although she was much older than me, Virginia seemed to possess a grace and easiness within herself that I'd never known. Her blonde hair was an obvious dye job even though I couldn't see any dark roots peeking through, and her green eyes studied me with a quiet intelligence I found comforting.

"Would you like some sweet tea?" Virginia offered, gliding toward the kitchen.

"Please." I knew it would rude not to accept, but also kind of stupid to actually drink anything she gave me, given that I didn't know if we were on good terms. Still, I liked her, despite Merlin's warnings. There was something I instantly related to, although I couldn't say what. Maybe we familiars had more in common than just our job. I thought about all this as I stood waiting awkwardly near the door.

Virginia cracked a tray of ice cubes and dropped several into each of two glasses.

Focus. I needed to focus. Remember the purpose for this visit.

Hmmm. Could I just stick the journal on the entry table and call it good?

No, no. Too obvious.

"Come. Let's have a seat." Virginia guided me to the tacky floral couch I'd spotted on my first visit, and we both settled in with our sweet tea. She smiled warmly at me as if we were old friends and not new acquaintances.

I placed my purse on the floor by my feet. When she wasn't looking, I could take the journal out and kick it beneath the couch for them to find later. I just had to wait for my opportunity.

"You're still very new," Virginia pointed out. When I looked at her askance, she added, "To the familiar life."

I bobbed my head and pretended to take a sip from my glass.

Virginia's casual smile faded at once. Even the soothing green of her eyes appeared to sharpen in an instant. "Our witches' feuds are ours, too. We don't have any autonomy in their world. So if our cats are fighting, then we are, too."

I coughed and set my sweet tea on the coffee table. It seemed there was no need to keep up appearances if she was going to wear her hostility on her sleeve here.

"Are you sure?" I asked with a frown. "It just seems so silly. Shouldn't we witches and familiars stick together?"

"That's not our decision. Now that we've met, I hope you're satisfied. You may finish your tea and leave." Virginia drained hers in a single gulp, then wandered off down the hallway and let herself into a private room.

I had to act fast. Something told me if I wasn't gone by the time Virginia came back, I might not be able to get away. How quickly she had transformed. This frightened me. Would I one day become like her, too? Was this the life my witchy cat had cursed me to live in choosing me as his familiar?

Desperate to get out of there and fast, I knocked my purse onto its side with my heel, trying to make it look like an accident in case anyone was watching. Then I bent down and grabbed it, taking care to shove the journal as far back as I could.

Satisfied with my work, I took my still full beverage to the kitchen and dumped it down the sink drain, then let myself out into the yard and bolted for my waiting car.

So much for diplomacy.

Whatever our cats' problem with each other, the two felines would just have to find a way to work it out for themselves.

14

I thought about my strange encounter with Virginia the entire drive home. How she had transformed from pleasant to frightening in the quickest of moments. Merlin had said that familiars themselves don't possess magic, but Virginia's personality shift had felt wholly unnatural. Did Luna bespell her somehow?

And, more importantly, would Merlin do something similar to me?

I didn't like this one bit. Was it too late for me to tell him "thanks, but no thanks" and leave him to find someone better suited to lifelong magical servitude?

I had a feeling that no matter where I ran to, Merlin would find me and drag me back. And other than being a little rude, he hadn't done a single thing to hurt me. In fact, he'd promised to protect me, at least when it came to Harold's murder investigation.

Whatever the case, he and I clearly needed to have a long talk before he asked anything more of me. Lesson two said that I was supposed to trust him, but he needed to trust me, too. And he needed to offer some kind of guidebook into my new life if he expected me to assimilate.

Yes, we would have a nice long chat, provided I could find him. I took a deep breath and pushed open the door to my home, more than ready for a heart-to-heart.

But I didn't find Merlin waiting for me.

Instead, the house had been ransacked during my brief visit with Virginia. I'd only been gone half an hour, tops, but cushions had been torn off the couch, chairs overturned, the whole nine yards.

Thinking fast, I grabbed a broom from the front closet and proceeded deeper into my house with the end raised like a baseball bat.

"Who's there?" I called as my eyes darted all around. Who would burgle me in broad daylight? And why? I didn't have anything good.

Suddenly the broom flew from my hands and whipped back around to pin me against the wall.

"Where is it?" a lanky white cat demanded, tiptoeing toward me. *Luna.*

"Let me go," I cried, struggling against the broom, but Luna's magic proved stronger than my muscles.

"Not until you tell me where it is!" She stopped about a foot in front of me and unsheathed the claws on one paw. "Tell me right now!"

I could play dumb and pretend I didn't know what she was

talking about, but it seemed easier to give in to her demands. "The journal?" I asked.

Her glowing green eyes widened. "So you admit to the theft?"

"I admit I took it, but I also brought it right back. I'm sorry."

"You have no idea what you've done. What trouble you've caused."

"Again, I'm really sorry. Please let me go?" I begged meekly.

"No," she told me with a beastly growl. "You started this, and you'll be the one to finish it."

The broom dropped, and I lurched forward. No sooner had I been freed than one of my wooden dining chairs slammed into me from behind. I fell into a sitting position and then the broom pressed me against the chair, securing me in place.

"Please..." I cried actual tears now. "I never asked to become Merlin's familiar. I never asked for any of this."

"You're coming with me," Luna said, then blinked once, twice...

And we were back at her cottage. "Are you going to kill me now?"

"Where's the journal?" Luna hissed, ignoring my desperate question.

"Under the c-c-couch," I sputtered, seeing no point in lying now.

The thin cat ran beneath the couch, then came out with the notebook gripped between her jaws.

I remained stuck in the chair, only able to watch as she levitated the book to the coffee table and flipped through its pages.

Apparently having found what she was looking for, she smiled, blinked, and took us into her rear garden. Then she approached an old stone wall, dragging me along with her magic.

"What are you doing?" I ground out.

"That doesn't concern you." Luna hopped onto my lap and pawed at my pants, picking something up and dropping it into the well.

Then she ran back and chomped at my hair, ran back to the well, and spit inside.

"Is that your cauldron?" I guessed.

"Ah, so he has taught you something, at least. Not enough to keep you from playing right into my paw, though."

"What? I don't understand."

"Good, then your boss won't see it coming, either."

"What are you plotting?"

"Nothing that concerns you. I'm just setting things right," she said, walking through her garden and plucking various leaves and petals to drop into the well.

I watched her work for at least twenty minutes, but nothing I said could convince her to tell me anything more. Sometime later, a shimmering emerald puff rose from the well and Luna laughed girlishly rather than wickedly.

"Purrfect," she exclaimed. "Now return home and mix this in your master's water dish." She pushed an empty plastic bottle into the well with her paw. And when she brought it back up with her magic, it held a small amount of liquid. No more than half an inch deep.

"I won't do it," I said, struggling against the broom and chair once more.

Luna laughed again as the broom snapped away and the chair crumbled into a pile of sawdust. "Funny thing is, you don't have a choice. And you won't be able to warn him, either. It's brewed right into the spell."

"That's why you took my hair," I realized.

"Yes. And his. It's lucky for me he sheds so much and can't resist a warm lap, eh?"

"I don't know what you're planning, but you won't get away with it."

"I already have," Luna said with a smirk.

She blinked once, twice…

And I was back home with the water bottle clutched firmly in my hand. Before I could stop myself, I poured its contents into Merlin's bowl. As soon as I did, the plastic container dissolved into thin air and completely disappeared.

No, no, no! I strained for his dish, but something yanked me back. I couldn't stop whatever Luna had planned from happening, and I couldn't find Merlin anywhere to keep an eye on the situation.

What now?

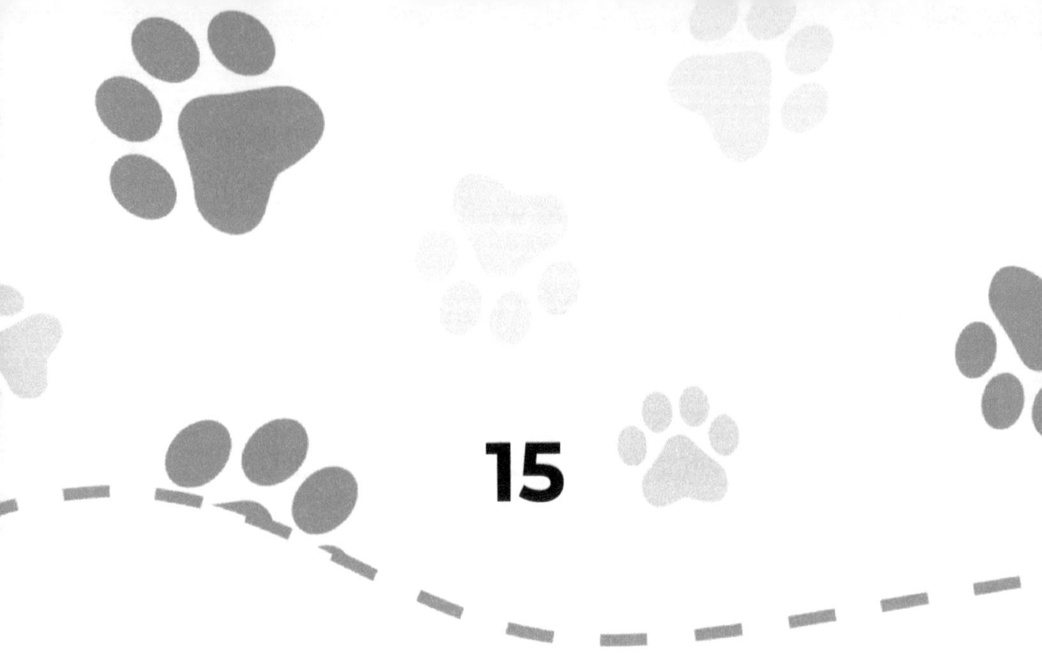

15

I must have fallen asleep at some point, because the next thing I knew the sun had crept between my bedroom blinds and was now beaming directly into my eyes.

Merlin jumped onto my chest and brushed his fluffy tail in my face. "You sleep a lot for a human. Are you sure you're not part cat?" he quipped. A wry smile stretched between his bright white whiskers.

And that was when everything came rushing back—Luna, the potion, my part in it all.

"Merlin!" I cried and hugged him hard against my chest. "You're okay!"

He struggled from my grip and then jumped out of reach, looking at me like I was crazy. "Of course I'm okay. Why wouldn't I be okay?" His fur twitched in odd spasms across his back, a sure sign I'd overstepped my bounds as a cat owner.

"Because I—" I began, but my words were abruptly cut off.

"Well, yester—" I tried again. "L—"

Each time I tried to speak, I found myself gagged mid-sentence.

"You're being weird," my cat said, his ears pressed back against his head.

And he was right; I was being weird. I also didn't know how to stop. Maybe if I tried talking about something else...

"Want breakfast?" I asked casually, and sure enough, that I could get out without being magically silenced. Whatever Luna had worked into her spell, it seemed impossible for me to get around it.

Perhaps if I had more knowledge or guidance, I'd be able to find a way... but only Merlin could give me answers, and I wasn't even able to ask him any of the right questions.

"Yes, I want breakfast. Do you even need to ask?" Merlin hopped off the bed and slipped through the doorway.

Worry gnawed at my brain as I followed.

In the kitchen, I found that his water dish had been licked dry. I wanted to ask how he was feeling after lapping up Luna's potion, but couldn't. So I simply shook my head and refilled his dish from the tap.

"Are you going into work today?" Merlin asked as I opened a can of wet food and plopped it in his bowl.

"Not today."

"Good. We can continue your training." His piece said, Merlin turned his attentions toward his breakfast.

Biding my time until Luna's spell activated proved to be complete agony. I was glad that everything appeared normal thus far today, but waiting for the other shoe to drop made it hard to focus on anything else.

"Aren't you going to make some coffee?" Merlin asked me some time later.

I glanced toward his bowl and saw he'd already polished off his breakfast. Wow, I must have been lost in space for the last few minutes.

"Yes, coffee," I said, not unlike a zombie as I made my way to the Keurig to brew some liquid energy.

"Lesson number three," Merlin announced from his spot on the linoleum kitchen floor. "In all things you do, you are a representative of me. If you do something good, I will receive the praise. If you do something bad, I will receive the punishment."

"Why are you telling me this?" I asked nervously.

He stared at me unblinking, unmoving even. "So you don't mess up."

I gulped hard. I'd already messed up and messed up big, but I also had no way of telling him that. Shoot.

"You are not magical," he continued, unaware of my raging internal conflict. "But you are a reservoir. Kind of like a living, breathing cauldron. Your presence amplifies my magic. The longer we spend in each other's company, the more of my magic will bind to you. You can't use it for yourself. Only contain it for my later use."

Now this was a big revelation, far too big for me to understand pre-coffee.

Merlin hopped up on the counter and studied my face. "In fact, it seems you've already collected some," he said.

"What?" I croaked, lifting my fingers to my face.

My cat smirked. "Your eyes."

"What about my eyes?"

"Stop panicking and go have a look."

I marched toward the bathroom and flicked on the light. Instead of my usual dark brown, my eyes now appeared a deep forest green.

"Green!" I shouted, unable to believe the image that floated right before me. "Why are my eyes green?"

"Well, that's easy," Merlin said, appearing in the hall outside the bathroom. "Eyes are the window to the soul. Green is the color of magic. Now you are magic, thus your soul is tinted green."

"You said I wasn't magical," I argued hopelessly. It was really hard to trust everything he said when so much of it seemed contradictory.

Merlin yawned and stretched out in a yoga-like pose. "You're not *magical.* You are magic. It's a subtle distinction, but you'll get it eventually," he assured me.

Either Merlin had faith in me or was too stubborn to admit he'd been wrong in choosing me as his familiar. And at that precise moment in time, I really didn't care to know which.

Ugh. Why was this my life?

16

I still hoped to speak with Merlin about Luna, but my magic bindings shut me down every single time I even thought about it too hard.

To avoid wasting time completely, I decided to ask him about something much safer—the open murder investigation.

"Merlin?" I asked as my second cuppa brewed. "Can you use your magic to find out who killed Harold?"

He thought about this for a moment as he shifted to follow the sunbeam that had slowly begun to migrate across the living room. "Possibly. But I would need to see his corpse to do so."

I shuddered. "Let's make breaking into the morgue our backup plan," I suggested, wrapping my arms around my torso to hug myself.

"Suit yourself," Merlin responded, then closed his eyes and purred. "If you do end up needing me, you know where to find me."

Yes, I did. For right now, at least. His constant coming and going hadn't bothered me much before. But now? Now every time we were apart presented another opportunity for one of us to be kidnapped.

Oh, if only I could warn him.

I knew he had just recently been made a full witch—something he said only happened when a cat officially took on a familiar. But still it seemed his casual attitude could be putting us both in danger. I, of course, was even newer to the whole magical powers thing, which meant he had no reason to listen to me if I asked for better protection.

And seeing as I couldn't come right out and explain why I needed that protection, we were both stuck.

I sighed and added some milk to my new cup of coffee and stirred while I mentally sorted through what I already knew about my late boss's death. It would be easier to focus on my magical problems if I got my more mundane ones out of the way.

Of course, I hadn't ever conversed with Harold outside of work, and it was perfectly probable that some scandal in his personal life had led to his forced demise. Given my butt was on the line here, though, it made sense to at least consider the clues I'd picked up.

First, there was the fact that his long-lost daughter Kelley had recently reappeared in his life. And that Kelley's mother had tried to prevent this reunion. Kelley was also present when Harold took his last breath, but she was too obviously distraught to even be considered a suspect.

Drake had been there, too. Come to think of it, I hadn't seen him since. Was it possible he hated our boss so much that he'd slipped him some poison?

I'd definitely have to look into that later.

The coffee house had been mostly empty besides the three of us and Harold. Only one customer had sat in the corner sipping her coffee, and she'd left as soon as we asked her to.

Hmmm.

Another thing to consider was that the poison could have been meant for me, and Harold was merely collateral damage. The more I thought about it, the more I feared this could be the case. I'd only just witnessed Merlin's magic for the first time before rushing into work. That had been a test, he'd told me, to see if I was ready to serve as his familiar. Then later that night he had revealed himself to me.

I already knew he had an enemy in Luna, and she lived very nearby. She was also crazy enough to kidnap me and brew some kind of voodoo potion, which she forced me to slip to my cat last night.

Was this because her first attempt to get at me had failed when Harold took the poison instead?

Officer Dash had hinted at a toxicology report but never shared the results. Had it been completed? Did we know for sure we were dealing with a poison—or could some kind of magic be at play?

So many questions, and literally no one to ask. Maybe if I was careful about how I spoke with Merlin, I could suss out some answers about Luna indirectly. I finished my coffee and lowered myself to sit beside him on the living room carpet.

"Do you have any idea who might have killed Harold?" I asked him softly.

Merlin kept his eyes closed, but his whiskers twitched, telling me he had heard my question but didn't much like it. "Do you want to break into the morgue?"

I shivered at the thought. "Can you go without me?" I asked, preferring that option much more. "Just teleport in, check things out, and come back."

"I could," he said, squinting one eye open to look at me. "Except I don't know which one is him."

Crud. I really didn't want to go sift through a bunch of cold corpses, but I also really didn't want to go to jail. Could I suck it up for the greater good?

"Got a picture?" Merlin asked, rolling onto his feet and standing on four shaky legs.

Ooh, a picture. Smart! Why hadn't I thought of that?

"Let me search the coffeehouse's Facebook page. I'm sure there's at least one useable shot there," I told him and then trotted off in search of my tablet.

Why hadn't we thought of this option sooner?

Well, better late than never, I supposed...

17

It didn't take long to find a clear photo of Harold on the company's Facebook page. Even though Harold's House of Coffee only had a handful of likes, its former owner wasted no opportunity to get in front of the camera and show everyone how important he fancied himself to be.

"I can work with this," Merlin informed me when I shared the image with him. "I can't teleport directly into the morgue, so this little fact-finding mission may take me a while."

"Why can't you?" I asked, uneasy at the thought of being away from him—and his magical protections—for an extended period.

"Same reason I took us outside of Luna's house, then flashed us in through the window. If you're going someplace you can't see and don't know well, you risk getting yourself stuck in a wall or in some other precarious situation," the novice feline witch explained.

"Oh," I said stupidly.

"Lesson number four. Magic is much harder to wield than it may look to outsiders," he announced and cracked his neck to either side.

"I'm beginning to see that."

A knock sounded on the front door, and I briefly glanced over to it. By the time I turned back to Merlin, he had already vanished.

I groaned and headed to find out what Officer Dash wanted. Because, yes, I already knew it would be her. She'd bothered me so much the past couple of days that I readily recognized the unique cadence of her knock.

Bang. Bang. Tap, tap, tap. BANG!

I flung the door open, reminding myself that if she didn't behave more professionally in this exchange, I'd be taking a trip to the station to issue a formal complaint. That at least brought me some satisfaction as I came face-to-face with my current least favorite person in all the world.

"The toxicology report came back," Officer Dash informed me as she hooked a finger into her belt loop.

I crossed my arms and remained planted in the doorway, not allowing her into my house. "And?"

Officer Dash hooked her other thumb in her belt loop and rocked back on her heels. "Gas Line Antifreeze. Not something most people need for a summer in Elderberry Heights. Say, you're from up north, right?"

"Michigan," I managed as my stomach roiled. "What's your point?"

"And is that your car in the driveway there?"

"Yeah." I definitely did not like where this was headed.

"Huh," the policewoman said simply.

"C'mon. You can't honestly think that this proves anything! Antifreeze is readily available. Even here in Southern Georgia, I'm sure."

Out came that stupid notebook of hers. "*Uh-huh. Uh-huh.* And how do you happen to know that?"

"I didn't kill Harold," I said between gritted teeth.

"Sure, you didn't." She smiled. "I'll be back with a search warrant. Oh, and I wouldn't leave town if I were you."

Fantastic.

I slammed the door shut as soon as Officer Dash sauntered away. She looked like the cat who was about to eat the canary, so happy with her upcoming kill she couldn't see anything else... Like the fact that I was not guilty!

My phone buzzed in my pocket, and I took it out to find a next text from Kelley.

I told my mom I'd be meeting you for lunch. She insisted on coming along.

Hmm. So Kelley's mom was now in town and causing problems for her.

Where? I texted back.

The BBQ Shack at 12.

I'll be there.

I still thought Officer Dash was grasping at straws, but if her antifreeze theory played out, then I knew at least one other potential suspect who'd come from colder climates.

And I was about to have lunch with her.

18

Despite my ardent hope, Merlin didn't return before I had to leave for my impromptu lunch date. I wished I could call him back now that Officer Dash had told me the exact cause of death, but unfortunately I had no way of getting in touch with him.

He'd find out soon enough, I supposed. And I could rest a little easier knowing that our dear Harold hadn't been killed by magical means.

I applied my normal going-out face of makeup. Then, hating what I saw, I washed my whole face clean. The striking blue eyeshadow I normally wore to complement my dark brown eyes appeared clownish when paired with my new forest green irises. I'd have to add a trip to the drugstore cosmetics aisle to find something more fitting to my lengthy to-do list... or I could just get used to going everywhere fresh-faced.

Haha, right. It's not like I had many wrinkles or pimples to cover up, but the simple act of applying my daily powders and glosses gave me a special kind of courage. Knowing I looked good helped me get through the day. I'd never been a great beauty, but I liked showing others that I cared about my appearance and thus myself. It was a routine my mom had taught me while I was quite young. I still fondly remembered those middle school mornings spent applying our foundation and blush side by side in the massive bathroom mirror.

I smiled as I thought of Mom all the way back home in Michigan. Once this investigation was officially closed, I'd have to give her a call to catch up. Unfortunately, if I called any sooner, she'd see right through any attempts I made to downplay my anxiety.

And so it would have to wait.

In all the talk about Harold and the non-talk about Luna, I hadn't managed to eat breakfast, so by the time I reached the restaurant my stomach had begun to sing a mournful tale of neglect, one growl and one grumble at a time.

The BBQ Shack was something of a local legend and often boasted a long wait for anyone to be seated. I hadn't yet been, but the moment I stepped inside and smelled the sweet, tangy scents of barbecue, saliva began to pool in my mouth.

Kelley was already seated at a table toward the front and motioned for me to join her. She stood when I arrived and motioned between me and her mother, a dour-looking woman who was so thin, her cheeks appeared sunken in. "Gracie, this is my mom. Mom, Gracie."

Kelley's mother remained seated but extended her hand for a limp shake. I couldn't tell whether I disliked her or whether I simply had a bad reaction to believing she didn't like me. Whatever the case, I immediately became very uncomfortable. The only saving grace was that the noisy revelry of the other diners was enough to drown out the sounds my singing stomach.

Nobody said anything until the waitress arrived to take my drink order. Kelley and her mom had already settled in with a couple Arnold Palmers, so I ordered the same.

When it became clear that Kelley still didn't know what to say and her mother had no desire to start a conversation herself, I folded my hands in front of me and did the deed myself. "So what do you think of Elderberry Heights, Mrs....?" *Shoot,* I didn't even know Kelley's last name.

"Carmine," my friend supplied with a tight grin.

"And it's Miss, thank you very much. I never married after a certain boyfriend turned me off of love and marriage forever." She sniffed and grabbed the small mesh container that housed packets of multi-colored sugars and artificial sweeteners.

"Mom," Kelley whined, kicking her heels back against her chair with a thump that resonated through the table. "You promised you wouldn't talk about Dad anymore.

"Well, it's not my fault, your friend brought him up. Also don't call him 'Dad.' that man was never a father to you."

"I didn't... I mean, I'm sorry if—"

"No, no. Don't apologize," Kelley said gently to me, then turned her head to glare at her mother. “Stop trash-talking him. I get that what happened between you wasn’t great, but the man is dead. Just let it go.”

Ms. Carmine snorted and dumped two packets of Splenda into her cold drink, taking care to stir them vigorously with her straw.

Seeing as things were already tense, I decided to prod a little. “What did happen between you?”

Kelley’s eyes widened and her lips puckered, but she made no move to argue. The look on her face said it all, though. I’d betrayed her in the worst possible way.

I hated that I’d hurt my new friend, but I could apologize for that later. She’d thank me once I helped to bring her father’s murderer to justice—even if that murderer ended up being her own mother.

“What happened between us?” Ms. Carmine repeated, her voice pitchy and agitated. “What happened between us?”

Kelley placed a hand on her mother’s shoulder and mouthed something I couldn’t decode. “Same old girl loves boy, boy cheats on girl, and they lived unhappily ever after story,” she told me, then raised an arm and shouted, “Waitress! I think we’re ready to order.”

“He didn’t just cheat on me,” Ms. Carmine bit out. “He did it with my roommate who also happened to be my very best friend. I had nowhere else to go, so I left town. I vowed if he ever turned up at my door again, I’d kill him with my bare hands.”

“Mom!” Kelley cried, jumping to her feet. “Enough!”

Ms. Carmine silently sipped at her tea. To her credit, she was in a much better mood for the remainder of our meal after she’d gotten whatever that was off her chest.

And the whole time we ate and made small talk, I kept on wondering: Had Kelley's mom just confessed to Harold's murder?

And if so, what should I do next?

19

When I returned home from my lunch outing, I found my cat waiting for me by the front door.

"Where were you?" he demanded with an angry flick of his tail.

"Something came up, and I had to help a friend," I explained as I crossed the room and flopped down on the couch.

"You smell like barbecue sauce," Merlin accused. His nose twitched unhappily.

"That help involved taking her out to lunch. But that's not what's important here." I leaned forward and steepled my fingers. "I think I know who killed Harold."

Merlin jumped up onto the sofa beside me and allowed me to run my fingers through his thick double coat. "So you've got it all figured out, do you? Enlighten me, then."

"It was Ms. Carmine. She's the mother of one of the other baristas, Kelley. And Harold was Kelley's father. There was no love lost between them, let me tell you. Add in the fact that Harold was poisoned with gas line antifreeze and that Officer Dash is convinced someone from out of state did the deed, and the fact she all but confessed over lunch, and there you have it."

"Interesting," Merlin said from his place beside me. "One hundred percent wrong, but interesting, nonetheless."

"Wrong?" My heart sank, and I pulled my hand away. "Why do you think that? I've already thought really long and hard about this, and Ms. Carmine definitely did it."

"I don't merely *think* you're wrong. I know it." He sat up and puffed his furry chest with pride. "I just paid a visit to our old friend Harold, and I can say with absolute certainty that he was poisoned by a magical potion. Not... what was it you said? Antifreeze?" He chuckled quietly and shook his head.

"But Officer Dash said—"

"Officer Dash lied," he said flatly.

No, this didn't make sense, and I'd tell him that if he would just let me finish a sentence. "Why would a police officer lie?"

Merlin hung his head, his ears thrust back in consternation. "That's a good question. You can't exactly ask her. She'll just lie again."

"I'm going to the station," I said, shifting back toward the door. "Something's not right here."

"I'm coming with you," he insisted.

"Are we going to teleport? Because the station is on a pretty busy street. Someone will see."

Merlin jumped off the couch and then turned to face me. "You drive. I'll meet you there. First I have some business with my cauldron."

"What are you going to do? Can't we just drive together? I'd feel safer if I had you with me." I was in a sad state considering I felt that I needed my cat's company in order to stay safe.

He didn't budge despite my pleas. "I'm a cat, Gracie. Cats don't do cars. Besides, I'll already be at the station and waiting by the time you get there. I just need a few minutes to mix a truth potion. Since I'm a sky witch, I can deliver it by air. All your officer... what was it? Nash?"

"Dash," I corrected. "She's the one with the bad attitude and permanent scowl, remember?"

He grimaced then, showing off one pearly white fang. "Dash, okay. But how could I remember when I have yet to meet her?"

"She's already been here two times in less than twenty-four hours. How is it you haven't been here for any of her little visits?"

"Dunno, but don't worry about it too much. My truth potion will be a gas rather than a liquid. I only need to breathe it out and she to breathe it in for her to fall under its spell. We'll know everything within a matter of minutes."

"Great, because I am already so sick of this investigation."

Merlin shook his head. "We still need to toughen you up. You'll deal with much worse than this serving your role as my familiar."

I rolled my eyes hard. "Oh, goody. I can hardly wait."

Merlin clearly didn't appreciate my attitude, but that didn't stop me from feeling exhausted, afraid, and in a foul mood.

"Stop with the sarcasm. It's not very becoming for a familiar," he hissed.

"I'm more than just a familiar. I'm a person, too," I reminded him, not exactly sure where this was coming from. I guess I just had things to say, questions that had gone unanswered for too long, even though it hadn't been long at all.

"Why did you choose me?" I blurted out.

Merlin turned to stare at me head on. He blinked slowly, then stopped. "I didn't choose you, Gracie. I chose your grandmother. Remember, I was already here when you showed up."

"So you wanted her but got me. Right, I'm just one big mistake," I pouted. His confession hurt far more than I'd have expected it to.

"An accident, yes. Mistake, no. I watched you for months before revealing myself. I had to make absolutely sure," he confessed softly. "I hadn't planned for it to be you, but I'm glad it is."

I chanced a smile. "Really?"

"Really. Now enough with the mushy stuff." He moved toward the door and stopped in front of the pet flap. "We need to focus on the task ahead. I want you to drive straight to the police station. No pit stops or detours. Straight there, and I'll be waiting with the truth potion ready to go. We'll go in together."

"Yes, boss," I said with a nod. Our short chat just now had given me a renewed sense of purpose. Merlin hadn't chosen me initially, but he chose me now.

As it turned out, that mattered a lot.

With his support and encouragement, I would be okay. And thanks to the plan he'd concocted, we could scrub my name from the suspect list within mere minutes.

I was going to be okay...

In part, because I didn't really have any other options.

20

Merlin and I both marched outside. He headed to the yard to do some work with his bird bath cauldron, and I climbed into my car and backed out of the driveway. It would take me about five minutes to reach the police station, which meant I had precious little time to sort through my latest thoughts.

According to Merlin, Officer Dash had lied to me about the poison that killed Harold. But why? The simple answer would be that the medical examiner couldn't trace the presence of magic and truly thought gas line antifreeze was to blame.

But something in my gut told me that wasn't quite right.

Had Officer Dash knowingly lied to me to see how I responded? But if she'd intentionally lied, did that mean she knew magic was to blame? Or had she yet to hear anything conclusive from the medical team?

Once again, I wound up lost in the churning sea of my thoughts.

So lost, in fact, that I forgot to pay attention to the road signs. I blew right through a stop sign at a quiet intersection that led out of my neighborhood, only realizing it once it was too late to brake.

Crud. I really needed to stop getting consumed by my thoughts and start paying better attention to traffic. I would be better after this quick trip to the police station. Maybe I'd start pulling to the side of the road when the urge to overthink became too great.

Yeah, that would make me less of a hazard to myself and others. And yet...

It seemed I'd made this vow too late, because a police cruiser pulled out after me and turned on its siren.

No, no, no!

Yes, I'd been caught and deserved to be punished for it. I'd find some way to pay the ticket. Right now, I was more worried about the delay in joining Merlin at the police station. Hopefully this routine traffic stop wouldn't add too much time to my trip. And, yeah, maybe Merlin would be mad about having to wait a few extra minutes, but it wasn't like running from the police was a viable option here, especially since I was heading straight toward their HQ, anyway.

I groaned and pulled over to the side of the road. The cruiser pulled over behind me, and I watched through my rearview mirror as a uniformed officer climbed out and slammed the car door shut.

Officer Dash, herself.

Double crud.

She motioned for me to roll down my window, and I instantly complied.

"Well, well, well," she said with a dry chuckle. "You just can't stay out of trouble. Can you, Springs?"

"I'm sorry," I murmured, hating this—hating it so very much.

"License, registration, and proof of insurance, please," she barked, all business.

I slowly reached into the glove department and grabbed the needed documents, then took my license from my purse and handed that over, too.

"I'll be right back," Officer Dash told me.

I stared straight ahead as I waited for her to run my information and issue my ticket. Time passed much more quickly than I would have imagined, because it seemed like only moments later, Officer Dash returned to the driver's side of my car.

"Out of the vehicle," she ordered with a cold, assessing gaze.

"What? Why?" I squeaked.

"Don't ask questions. Just do what I say!" she shouted.

Her sudden fit of rage frightened me so much that I stumbled out of my car as told. And though she frightened me, I hoped she'd be less frightening if I complied with orders.

"Hands against the vehicle," Officer Dash spat.

"What? No. I didn't do anything wrong!" I shouted.

Dash pushed me into the side of my car. Hard.

Pain shot through my shoulder, burning even worse as she grabbed my wrists and slapped a pair of handcuffs on them.

"I didn't do anything," I sobbed. "Please let me go."

"Stop whining and turn to face me!"

When I turned, a giant Cheshire smile filled the policewoman's face. She was loving every moment of this.

"I don't understand," I mumbled. "Did you find new evidence?"

Instead of answering, Officer Dash place a hand on my shoulder and forced me to meet her gaze. I watched in silent horror as her eyes changed color and shape, shifting from unassuming gray to a bright and robust green.

She blinked once... Twice...

21

I crashed into the earth, unable to catch myself, thanks to my wrists being cuffed behind my back. I kicked out with my legs and twisted my torso, struggling to bring myself into a sitting position. At last I rammed into a thick tree trunk and was able to wiggle myself upward.

Once I had a moment to take in my surroundings, I recognized the small garden cottage almost instantly. We'd come to Luna's, and I was pressed against the same Magnolia tree I'd clutched onto after my very first teleportation.

The front door of the quaint brick house flew open, and Virginia ran outside in bare feet. Her toenails were painted in a shiny lavender I wouldn't have expected from her.

"Oh, goody!" she cried, racing into the yard. "Is it time at last?"

"It is." Officer Dash spoke from behind me. I twisted in an effort to see her, but the thick magnolia tree blocked her from view.

"What do you want with me?" I shouted to whoever was willing to answer.

"I've got this one," Virginia announced, sauntering forward with a soft expression that belied the vitriol of her words. "You should've been in jail by now, but your bond to that stupid cat formed too fast, which means Plan B became necessary."

"I didn't kill Harold," I told her as I struggled to slip my wrists from the handcuffs. The task seemed impossible, but that didn't mean I'd stop trying. Especially since this seemed to be shaping into a try-or-die type of situation.

"Of course you didn't," Virginia said with an almost-pleasant smile. "I did."

"You?" I asked, my voice now shaking with fear. I hadn't even considered her. Luna, yes. But her powerless familiar? Never.

Virginia simpered at me. "Don't you remember asking me to leave the coffeehouse that day? I was sitting right there. I thought for sure you'd put it together when you showed up at my house yesterday, but no. Turns out you're not that smart, after all."

"You were the customer!" I shouted as the final pieces clicked into place. No wonder Virginia had seemed so familiar. She'd been sitting in plain sight that day. Amateur sleuth or not, how had I missed something so major in my investigation?

Virginia's smile widened. I had the sudden urge to slap it right off her face, in part for Harold and in part for me. "See, Dash. She does catch on eventually."

Officer Dash didn't respond, so I took the opportunity to ask a very important question. "Are you going to kill me, too?"

Finally, Virginia's tight smile disappeared. "Unfortunately, no. You've made things quite difficult for us, I'll have you know. You were supposed to take the fall for that old miser's death so the authorities could shut you up and throw away the key before your bond with Merlin had a chance to solidify. It was our best chance of getting rid of him, but you ruined that for us."

"What?" I snapped as I scowled up at her. "Do you want me to apologize?"

"Uh! No manners." Virginia let out a few slow breaths before continuing. "Any murders that happen within the magical community are instantly traced. If I would have killed you outright, then I'd find myself locked up. But since your former coffee boss knows nothing of the magical world, his death wouldn't have registered."

"Do we really need to do the whole villain monologue thing right now?" Dash growled from somewhere I still couldn't see. "We've caught her. Now we need to dispose of her."

"So you *are* going to kill me?" I shouted with triumph. I had been right, but I wish I hadn't.

"Worse," Virginia revealed with wide, bright eyes. She enjoyed this, the villain.

"What? What's worse than death?" I asked. I had to keep her talking, to give Merlin time to find and rescue me.

Virginia played straight into the wicked stereotype and threw her head back to cackle. "You'll see soon enough, my dearie."

"But I don't understand. Why did you want me out of the way? What did I ever do to you?"

"Absolutely nothing," Virginia admitted with a sniff. "But Dash wanted Merlin out of the picture, and I was all too happy to oblige, given the history between him and my boss."

So this was because my playboy cat had broken the wrong cat's heart. *Ugh!*

"People fall in love and break up all the time," I argued. "That doesn't mean you kill them."

"Oh, I don't care about that. Although all of Luna's incessant pining for that scruffy fleabag has certainly gotten on my last nerve."

"Then what do you want?"

"Magic is volatile. Did you know that? The more of it that exists within the same area, the more likely it is to cause an unwanted reaction. When Merlin took you on as his familiar, Luna's magic had to be dampened to protect the town. I certainly see no reason why either of us should be deprived of the level of power we've grown accustomed to, so when my companion here offered a plan to dispose of you both, I eagerly agreed to do my part."

"But how does getting rid of me keep Merlin from finding a new familiar?"

She hung her head and let out a deep laugh. "You really don't know much about how this community works. Do you? Once a familiar has been initiated, it's almost impossible for a witch to obtain a new one. Not after that whole mess with the two Merlins and Arthur way back when. And without his familiar close by, *our* Merlin can't legally practice magic. The powers that be would lock him up so quick, he wouldn't even have the chance to blink away."

"Enough!" Dash shouted from behind me. "She's just trying to buy herself time in case that kitty cat of hers shows up to rescue her. I'm done dawdling. Let's finish what we started."

22

As soon as she vowed to “finish what we started,” Officer Dash at last stepped into my line of sight. She looked the same as she always had, except the bright green eyes. Eyes like mine, like Virginia’s, like anyone who’d been touched by magic.

“You’re not a real cop,” I spat at her.

“Oh, really. What was your first clue?” The fake officer Dash laughed at me cruelly, then raised both hands and snapped her fingers above her head.

The air around her rippled and shimmered with a slightly green hue as she transformed from the sardonic police officer into a chunky black cat with a crooked tail.

I gasped, and so did Virginia.

“You’re a witch,” she cried, pointing an accusing finger at her accomplice. “This whole time you told me you were a familiar, too. That you were fed up with the status quo.”

The black cat smiled devilishly. “Dearest Virginia, one of those things is true. The other? Well, you played into my hand so easily, a fact which I most definitely appreciate. But now that your usefulness has expired, I no longer need you.”

The cat version of Dash clicked her tongue, and Virginia’s face grew into a mask of horror. Her mouth opened wide in a silent scream, and her feet shuffled hopelessly beneath her as she floated a foot from the ground.

“What did you do to her?” I demanded, struggling even harder against my bonds now. I couldn’t tear my eyes away from Virginia, terrified that I would share her fate. Why wasn’t she screaming? It would be easier to take if she screamed.

Dash unsheathed her claws and stared down at them, thinking. “Why do you care? She killed your boss and tried to send you to jail for it.”

“We both know you were the mastermind. Virginia was only a pawn in your scheme,” I shouted. We were on the edge of a large subdivision. Maybe if I screamed loud enough one of the neighbors would hear and come to my rescue.

“I bet you never even told her why you wanted Merlin out of the picture,” I muttered when Dash continued to stare down at her claws without even acknowledging my previous accusation.

“Virginia had her own silly reasons for what she did. She didn’t need to know mine.”

“Tell me,” I demanded, kicking my feet out before me to appear like more of a threat. “I deserve to know.”

“You deserve nothing!” Dash hissed. “And you will get nothing except what’s coming to you!”

With that, she leaped toward me. Rather than unleashing a storm of magic, she sliced a claw against my cheek. I instantly forgot the dull ache in my shoulders in favor of the sharp sting that took over. I screamed out in pain, but the movement in my facial muscles only made it hurt that much more. A drop of fresh blood rolled down my cheek and fell onto my shirt, leaving an ugly red stain.

Dash ignored my misery as she floated back to the ground and studied her blood-tipped claws, green eyes wide with wonder. “*Huh.* Well, that explains a few things.”

“What things? What’s going on? Why are you doing this to me?” I cowered against the tree, which seemed to please the evil black cat.

She paced back and forth for a moment before turning toward me once again. “My blabbermouth assistant already told you more than you need to know, but I’ll let you in on one last little piece of knowledge.”

Dash looked back over her shoulder at Virginia, who was still trapped in soundless torment. “Look at her. She’s currently living her worst nightmare.”

And I knew from the frozen mask of terror on Virginia’s face that Dash was being truthful with me now.

I shuddered, hating that the truth was scarier than a lie. Why else would Dash have revealed this to me? “What is it?” I sputtered, groping for words, willing to do anything to keep the conversation going. "Spiders? Clowns? Great White Sharks?"

Dash smiled. "That's the beauty of illusion magic. I don't need to know. The magic finds the fears, the desires, finds whatever I need and latches right onto it. Virginia was a fool, but it was even easier to convince her to fall in line when my magic probed her heart and found what I needed."

"You're an illusion witch?" I gasped. I didn't know exactly what that meant, but it certainly sounded scary.

Dash smiled at me again. "The very best that ever lived."

"I know why Virginia wanted to get rid of Merlin, but why you?" Strangely, I was beginning to wish that Dash would turn back into the ornery policewoman. This new feline version was much, much worse.

She shook her head. *"Ah, ah, ah!* I have no need to reveal my plot to the likes of you. I only told you about Virginia so you'd know what was about to happen to you and fear it all the more."

I met her eye, unwilling to cower in fear any longer. "You'll never get away with—"

But Dash cut me off by loudly clicking her tongue twice. As soon as she did, the whole world melted away, leaving me trapped in a sea of endless black.

Noooooooo!

23

"Hello?" I cried into the echoing void, but no one answered. Unnerved, I stumbled forward, unable to feel the ground over which my feet moved. I couldn't feel anything, not even the cool metal which had previously bound my wrists.

A pinprick of light appeared on the horizon, and I rushed toward it, desperate to get out of this dark place. I still couldn't bring my hands forward despite not being able to feel the cuffs on my skin, which resulted in my waddling more than jogging toward my destination.

As I moved closer, the tiny light pulsed and expanded, and out stepped Merlin in all his Maine Coon glory. Instead of normal shining green, his eyes were deep black, lifeless, soulless.

"I didn't choose you. I got stuck with you," he sneered, addressing my secret fear head-on.

"No, no. It's not true," I said, recalling our earlier conversation. I hadn't been his initial choice, but he was very happy that we'd ended up together.

"You're lying," I bit out.

And with that, the false Merlin burst into a puff of smoke and floated off into the darkness.

"You were an illusion," I told myself. "Just an illusion."

I'd called the imposter cat on his lie and he'd left me alone. I just had to remember to find the truth. Hopefully it would set me free from this awful place.

Another pale flicker of illumination appeared to the distant right, so I stepped toward it, bracing myself for what I might find there.

A tall man's silhouette appeared. I couldn't make out his features but recognized him as soon as he spoke. *Harold.*

"You may not have killed me, but it's your fault I'm dead," he told me with great anger.

What could I say to that? I couldn't deny the part I'd played. This accusation was perfectly true.

Harold kept going, feeding my guilt, making it grow bigger and bigger.

"I always knew you were a worthless employee, but I kept you on out of the kindness of my heart. And how did you repay me? Ha!"

"I'm sorry," I mumbled as tears began to form in the corners of my eyes, making my vision blurry. "I'm really, really sorry."

"A little too late for that," he scoffed. "And what happens if you get yourself out of this alive? Will you kill your next boss, too?"

"I—" My voice broke. "I didn't mean to. I'm so, so sorry."

"I have no one to mourn me, and it's your fault," he raged.

"No," I whispered, lifting my head high. "Your daughter Kelley misses you very much. All she ever wanted was the chance to know you. And she's still trying to find out who you were, even though you're gone, even though her mother doesn't want her to. And I'm trying to help. I shared stories with her. I helped her stand up to her mother..."

That's when it hit me.

"I never liked you very much," I continued, using this opportunity to get it all off my chest. "But I didn't want you to die. And it's not my fault you did. Yes, they were trying to frame me, but I didn't choose this magical world. It chose me. Even though I'm very sorry for what happened to you, Harold, it wasn't my fault."

Poof! His silhouette turned into a dark cloud of dust and blew away into the abyss.

"I'm done lying to myself!" I screamed into the encroaching darkness. "You may have trapped me in an illusion, but I know my own heart! I know my own mind!"

Officer Dash appeared as a semi-transparent hologram before me. Not the new cat form, but in her familiar cop garb. "You think you can outsmart my illusion?"

"I know I can," I shouted, wishing I could shake a fist at her.

She laughed softly at first, then more and more breathlessly. Soon Officer Dash was wheezing for breath. "You stupid girl. This isn't some family-friendly film where the princess just needs to believe in herself to defeat her much more qualified opponent. You're not a princess. You have no power, and you will not win."

"Yes, I will!" I shouted back at the hologram, but she only laughed harder.

"Fine. Do things the hard way. See if I care. Eventually you'll figure out it's hopeless." And with that, Officer Dash disappeared, leaving me in absolute darkness.

I staggered forward, unwilling to give up. I'd defeated the first two illusions. I could defeat more. I could escape this place.

And though I wandered for ages, no more lights appeared, and soon I grew tired searching for them...

Was this really how it ended?

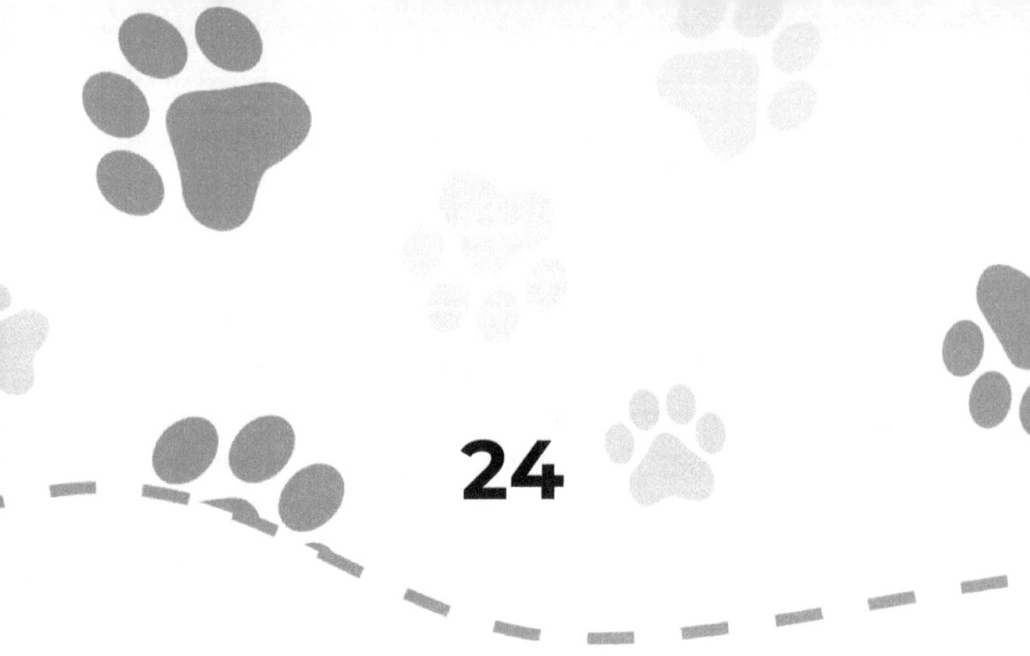

24

Even time was an illusion within that mental prison of mind. It ticked on and on leading nowhere. I would lose my mind here, if I hadn't already. I couldn't do any good for Merlin from in here, either, which meant soon he would find himself overtaken by the sinister Dash.

I didn't know why the dark witch had focused her attentions on us, but I knew now that we couldn't win. She was simply too powerful.

Battered but not yet fully defeated, I closed my eyes and tried to create my own series of mental pictures to break the monotony of the void. My mom's smile as we applied makeup side by side in that old mirror, Grandma Grace teaching me how to waltz in preparation for my first middle school dance, even Merlin speaking to me for the first time and opening my eyes to a beautiful and dangerous new world.

"Show me the truth," he said in my memory, then opened his

mouth and let out a shimmering huff of magic. The darkness folded in on itself, revealing green grass, blue sky, and bright sun.

No, this wasn't a memory. It was really happening now.

"I knew that truth serum was worth the extra few minutes it took to prepare," my cat told me as he brushed his soft fur against my wrists, freeing me from the cuffs.

"What's going on?" Virginia cried as she awoke from her illusion and staggered toward us.

"Not so fast!" Merlin commanded, then kicked his hind legs into the earth and sent a pair of small cyclones spinning toward Virginia. When they reached her, they braided around her torso, trapping her within the high-speed winds.

I'd never seen such a powerful display of magic from my cat before, and now that I had, I felt very glad he was on my side.

"How did you find me?" I asked, bringing my arms in front of me to ease the ache in my shoulders. Now that I'd escaped the illusion, everything hurt again.

"Easy," Merlin revealed, kicking up another pair of twisters and dispatching them toward Dash. "I followed our familiar bond. That thing is like a beacon."

I watched as the black cat deftly dodged the windstorm, darting wildly to the side.

"If you'll excuse me for a moment, please," my cat said, shifting onto his hind legs, then slamming back down and pounding the ground before him.

A flurry of sharp icicles shot down from the sky and formed a cage around Dash, much like the one made of flowers and thorns that Luna had crafted to contain Merlin.

"You'll never defeat me," Dash hissed as she rammed her body into the icy prison bars.

"Big words for somebody who's trapped in a cage," my cat quipped. "Why have you kidnapped my familiar? And what is this other one doing here?"

Dash's hackles rose. "I don't owe you—"

"Speak the truth," Merlin said, breathing out what was left the shimmering potion fog. Whoa, my cat was a witch and a magic-breathing dragon. I'd have to remember to reflect on just how cool that was later. You know, after we got out of this alive.

The black cat strained in an effort to remain quiet, but one by one the words came out. "The... Only... One... Who... Can... Stop... Me... From... Fulfilling... My... Destiny." She emphasized this with a long and angry hiss.

Merlin traipsed over to the cage and sat just out of Dash's reach. "Oh, so this is some funny prophecy business? Strange, I thought those were outlawed."

"Not prophecy. *Lineage.*"

As Dash choked and gasped for air, Merlin casually tilted his head to the side. "What does lineage have to do with anything?"

"My... Ancest—" Dash gasped and fell on her side, letting out a long pitchy yowl. "My secret dies with the two of you!" she shouted, no longer under his spell.

"Well, that's unfortunate," Merlin said as he stalked the perimeter of the ice cage. "Because we don't feel like dying today. Do we, Gracie?"

I shook my head and mumbled, "No."

Dash clicked from inside the cage and shifted into a tiny insect, flying easily between the bars. She transformed back into the black cat mid-flight and fell to the earth with an unsettling thud.

"Neat trick," Merlin said, raising his back and puffing out his tail like a cat on Halloween. "Wait until you see what I can do with a little bit of static electricity."

The sky darkened, and somewhere in the distance thunder boomed. I hoped the tree would shelter from me from the terrible storm that would soon be coming. Or that my cat at least had enough control to avoid hitting me with it.

"No! Merlin, stop!" a husky female voice shouted. A blur of white rushed onto the scene and thrust herself between the warring witches. *Luna!*

Virginia's missing witch had arrived, and I doubted she'd be on our side. Merlin had put up a good fight against Dash, but there was no way he'd be able to win against two more experienced witches.

I silently whispered a prayer for the both of us as I watched helplessly from the shadows of the large tree branches. I hoped I'd already stored enough magic for Merlin to be useful, because I had nothing else to offer in this fight.

25

"I told you to stay away from my property!" Luna shouted at both me and Merlin, sweeping her searing gaze over each of us. "Now release my familiar at once!"

Merlin stared straight ahead with wide eyes, instantly complying with the garden witch's command.

"No, Merlin. Don't!" I shouted, trying to snap him out of whatever spell he was under.

"But I have to listen to Luna," he told me with a blank expression.

Uh-oh, the spell she'd forced me to give to him the other day! It had now come into effect. I remembered how helpless I'd felt as I struggled against the directive to pour the potion into his water dish, as I attempted to warn him the next morning.

I hadn't been able to stop myself from doing as it commanded, and now it seemed that Merlin couldn't, either.

Ugh. We were so dead.

Luna ran to Virginia and did a quick check for injuries. "What's going on?" she demanded of her familiar.

"I don't know," the stylish old woman sobbed.

"Lies!" Dash screamed, appearing completely unhinged as her eyes bulged from her head. She glanced straight up into the sky, then did that clicking thing that signaled a coming spell. A mirage took shape before us.

In the shaky, shimmering image, Virginia sat speaking with Officer Dash as they made the plan to kill off Harold and place the blame on me.

"But what of your witch?" Dash had asked Virginia.

"She can die, too, for all I care," Virginia seethed in the mirage.

I couldn't see Luna through the mirage, but I could hear her ask, "You would betray me?"

"She already has," Dash announced, clicking her tongue to take the image away. Whether she'd shown us an illusion or a memory, I couldn't say. Either was equally probable—and equally devastating.

Luna swished her tail and let out a keening wail. The massive magnolia tree behind me rose up from the earth.

Virginia tried to run, but the tree used one of its limbs to lift her high into the air and hold her captive.

"Why?" Luna cried, visibly straining from the effort of commanding the gigantic tree.

"You left me no choice," Virginia bit out. "Magic used to mean something to you, but lately you've been such a lovesick fool that you've paid no attention to what's really important. With his new familiar imprisoned, Merlin wouldn't have been able to practice magic anymore, and you'd have to stop pining for him and shift your focus back to growing our power."

Luna lowered her eyes, and the tree threw Virginia high into the air, then caught her again with its branches just before she crashed into the ground.

The wretched woman screamed the entire time both up and down.

Luna's whole body shook and trembled, but she showed no signs of relenting. "There is no *our* power. It's mine. It's always been mine. You were but a servant."

"I think of you as much more than a servant," Merlin assured me as we both watched, dumbfounded.

"You don't deserve the magic you were blessed with," Virginia shouted down at her witch.

Luna cocked her head to the side, straining under the weight of her magic. "Is that so?" she asked, then nodded back toward the massive hole from which the tree had emerged.

We all watched as the tree walked on its roots and then climbed back into the earth and grew still. Once it had settled in, Luna shook off her fatigue and broke into a run.

Virginia scampered down, and the moment she touched ground, Luna jumped onto her shoulders, claws fully extended.

"Ouch!" Virginia cried, but none of us had any sympathy for her.

"You think me undeserving of my magic?" Luna asked, but didn't wait for an answer to her question. “Have it your way! I hereby renounce my power and sever the bond between us.”

The ground trembled, and Virginia collapsed to her knees.

Luna jumped clear just before impact.

“What’s happening?” Virginia cried as her image blinked and blurred and a cloud of shimmering green rose up from each of their bodies, creating a heavy fog that was difficult to see through.

“I am no longer a witch, and you are no longer my familiar. The magic is free!” Luna declared.

“Noooooooo!” Virginia cried, chasing after the departing fog and grasping greedily as if she could catch and hold onto the air. I couldn’t see her very clearly through the magical fog. Instead, I watched the air as it shifted and moved around her.

And if I couldn’t see, I doubted Virginia could, either.

Little by little, the fog condensed into itself, forming a thick, undulating wave.

Virginia remained fixated on the chase, swept away in the wave, so focused on her desperate grasp for power that she didn’t consider where the expelled magic was now heading.

I watched in shocked horror as she slammed into the well that had served as Luna’s cauldron and flipped over the edge, unable to catch herself before disappearing into the dark hole with the rest of the wave—returning to its source of power.

A moment later the magic had gone, and a loud crunch rose into the air.

“Well, she’s dead,” Merlin said beside me with not a trace of regret.

That was when I started to cry, useless non-magic entity that I was. Even though Virginia had tried to frame me for murder and send me to jail, she'd still been a living, breathing person.

Now she wasn't doing either of those things.

And with Luna and Dash still here and ready to fight, I could very well be next.

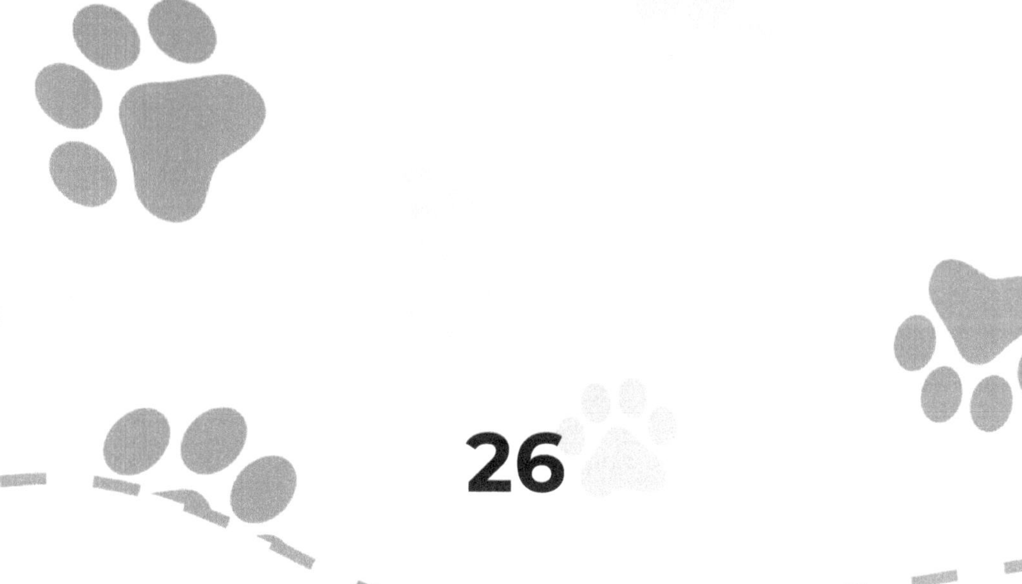

26

Luna let out a keening wail and ran to the well after her lost familiar.

"I didn't mean to kill her, only to stop her!" she cried. "Her brush with power had driven her mad. I should have been more careful before taking her on. This is all my fault."

"It's not your fault," I said, remembering my conversation with the fake Harold in Dash's illusion. Even though I'd played a part in his death, it hadn't been my fault.

The same was true for Luna now. Virginia had made her own choices. She'd betrayed her witch. She'd chased blindly after the fleeing magic, which resulted in her fatal tumble down the well.

Funny how I'd considered Luna an enemy when she was just as hurt by today's events as both me and Merlin. I actually ached for her now as I regarded the lanky white cat, whose formerly green eyes had already begun to fade to a pale almost sickly blue.

That reminded me—she'd given up her magic. She couldn't hurt us now. She couldn't hurt us ever again.

"Where's the other one?" Merlin shouted from beside me, already kicking up his back feet in case he had to summon a twister and resume the fight.

I glanced to Merlin and then to the larger garden. Luna sat sobbing at the well, but the far more deadly Dash was nowhere to be seen.

"No! She got away," I ground out. It seemed our true nemesis had used the distraction of the magical fog to slip away undetected. Which made me wonder, had that thick cover come from the severed bond or had Dash cast the illusion herself?

"A coward!" Merlin spit at the ground, then curled his lip in disgust.

"No, she was anything but." I shook my head, wishing my cat's assertion was true but knowing better than to hope. "Both plans A and B failed, so she retreated. She'll be back with a new plan and even harder for us to defeat the next time."

"Merlin, I'm so sorry," Luna mewed from her place on the lip of the old stone well.

When it became clear that she wouldn't leave her vigil there, Merlin and I stalked over to join her.

Luna fixed her gaze on Merlin, her eyes dull and sorrowful. "My familiar tried to destroy you. I thought I was helping when I cut our magical ties, but I just created an excuse for the other one to sneak away."

While I felt bad for Luna over Virginia's death, I still couldn't let her off the hook completely. She'd had a part in this, too.

"You mixed a potion," I accused, finally able to utter the words I'd failed to speak so many times.

Now that Luna's magic was gone, it seemed the spells she'd previously cast no longer worked, either. "You forced me to give it to Merlin and made it so that I couldn't warn him."

Luna's eyes grew wide as Merlin reared up and arched his back. "Luna! Is this true?" he demanded.

The white cat hung her head in silent shame.

"It's true!" I cried, wringing my hands. "She kidnapped me and used hair from both of us to mix the potion. I wanted to tell you, Merlin. I tried so hard."

"Gracie, it's okay. I understand why you couldn't resist the spell. You're still very new, but we'll work on building your defenses so that others have a harder time casting on you in the future. It will be okay." Merlin sounded almost fatherly in that moment. He may have been disappointed in how things had gone down, but it didn't make him love me any less.

The others were right. Our bond was strong. Not just magically, but emotionally, too.

Merlin's tender tone vanished when he turned to address the other cat. "Why, Luna? You said you had no part in the plot to imprison my familiar before our bond could fully actualize, and yet you did this?"

She let out a shuddering sigh.

"Speak!" Merlin barked, a strange sound coming from a cat, indeed.

Luna gasped and hopped down from the edge of the well and pressed her side against it. She looked to Merlin, then cast her gaze aside as if she'd been burned.

"Speak!" Merlin yelled even louder.

The lanky white cat turned her pale eyes to me. "I didn't want to hurt either of you. It was a..." She continued speaking, but her words became so soft and mumbled that I couldn't make them out.

"A what?" I prompted, leaning closer in an effort to better hear.

"A love spell. A potion to make Merlin fall back in love with me!" Luna's voice grew louder and stronger with each word.

I turned to look at Merlin, and he stood with eyes wide and unblinking, his mouth hanging slightly open.

"I love you, Merlin," she continued, stepping forward and coming to stand less than an inch from her flabbergasted ex. "I always have. I tried so hard to hate you once we took our familiars. I knew the laws of our society. And yet... Forgetting you was the one spell I couldn't cast."

She paused as they locked gazes, then took a small tentative step forward.

"Now I've given up my magic in the hope that we can be together. I will protect you all my days with or without magic to aid me. I will love you forever and always, no matter what. Will you love me, too?"

I held my breath as we both waited for Merlin's response... Honestly, I didn't know what to expect next.

27

The battle-worn Maine Coon took one step back, then another.

Luna had just poured her heart out to him, and yet he seemed to be in search of an escape route. I loved my cat, yet a part of me vowed I would kill him if he really was planning on breaking her heart a second time.

Yes, Luna had kidnapped me, but now that I knew why, it was actually kind of sweet. Add in the fact she had given up her magic on the slight chance he'd reciprocate her love, and these cats were the stuff of classic love stories. Provided Luna's affection wasn't unrequited.

C'mon, Merlin! Tell her you love her, you big fluffy jerk!

Merlin took another step back, then turned to face the opposite direction.

And he ran.

He ran faster than I'd ever seen him run before. He moved quick and low to the ground, then zig-zagged and sprinted in the other direction.

"REOWEOEOEOEOW!" he cried, a cat possessed. His tail had grown puffy. He panted heavily. But still he ran and mewed and ran some more.

"I'm sorry about him," I told Luna as we both watched the spectacle.

"What's to be sorry about? He loves me back! He loves me so much that he's got the zoomies!" Luna watched Merlin's celebration with the special wonder of a woman very much in love.

I broke out laughing, such was my relief and joy. "Is that what he's doing? The zoomies?"

Merlin slowed to a trot and made his way back to us. Ignoring me, he kept his eyes glued to Luna as he approached, then closed in tight and rubbed his face against hers.

Both cats purred loudly as they continued to lick and rub against each other. The whole scene made me a bit uncomfortable, to be honest. It also made me wonder if the three of us might have a litter of witchy kittens in our near future.

When at last they came up for air, Merlin moaned, "Oh, Luna. You didn't have to cast a spell on me. I never stopped loving you. Not for one moment."

I cleared my throat, knowing that if I didn't speak now, I'd quickly be subjected to another PDA session from these two. "Um, guys. I'm really happy for you and all, but we still have some problems that need to be addressed."

"All business, this one," Luna quipped. "It seems you chose your familiar much better than I did." She glanced briefly toward the well and sighed.

Merlin moved to Luna's side, pressing his body up against hers. Although she was a tall and lanky cat, Merlin's mass of brown striped fur made him appear much larger. In fact, half of Luna's body seemed to disappear into his magical fluffiness.

Both cats watched me with rapt attention, which I guess was my permission to speak freely.

So I let it out. "Harold was still murdered, and I'm still a suspect, I think."

"You think?" Merlin asked.

"Well, Officer Dash was the one inspecting things, and apparently she wasn't a real cop. That's the part I'm not sure about." I bit my lip as I waited to hear his theory on all of this.

"The illusion witch?" Luna asked, and I nodded. I guess I could take answers from whichever cat wanted to give them.

"She won't be sticking around here where she's so easy to find," Luna assured me. "Besides, your bond with Merlin is now unbreakable. He'll be able to find and rescue you from anywhere."

"So the investigation is dead in the water?"

"The investigation was never truly alive. Dash fabricated the whole thing from the start," Merlin concluded with a smug grin.

But I still felt uneasy. "How do you know?"

"Because I saw the body, remember? I could tell he'd been murdered by magic, but to the common human observer, it would seem as though Harold passed of a severe and sudden heart attack."

I shook my head, wanting to trust him on this but also needing to be sure. “I don’t understand. How did Dash expect me to take the fall for this, if everything looked normal?”

“We can’t know her exact motivations, but as an illusion witch, she had many options available to her,” Luna explained as Merlin purred at her side. “She could have posed as a jailer, fabricated reports, made you think you were being arrested by humans but then taken you to some kind of magical holding cell. The good news is she won’t try the same thing twice, so for now you can stop worrying about her.”

I sighed. “How can I stop worrying, knowing that she’ll almost certainly be back?”

“That’s a problem for another day,” Luna told me. “Right now, bask in the moment. Live your love.”

Oh, brother. I rolled my eyes hard, but neither of the two lovebirds seemed to notice or mind.

Still, I felt awful. “Fine, fine, so I’m off the hook for now, but an innocent man still died.”

“That is unfortunate, but it’s not like we can make it up to him,” Merlin told me.

“To him, no. But there is someone else. And I have an idea…”

28

After our big confrontation came to its official close, Merlin teleported the three of us home.

Eventually I'd need to find my way back to my car, providing it hadn't been towed in my absence. But for now, I just needed to pop a couple painkillers and take some time to veg out on my couch.

I changed into my favorite pair of pajamas and then lay across the sofa with my tablet, wholly prepared to binge that new Netflix show everyone had been gushing about. Unfortunately, the opening credits hadn't even finished rolling before Merlin jumped up onto my chest and blocked my view of the portable screen.

"I've asked Luna to move in with us, and she's agreed," he informed me with a rumbling purr.

Well, this kind of felt like a thing he should have asked me first, but even I understood that Luna had nowhere else to go. And even though I'd never known great love myself, I clearly recognized it in these two. I wanted them to be together and happy, even if that meant adding another roommate.

"Congratulations," I said with a sleepy smile.

Merlin nodded at me. "Okay. Just making sure you knew how things would be. As you were."

While I tucked into my show, Merlin gave Luna the grand tour of our house, which wasn't all that grand, given its small size and outdated furniture. Still, I occasionally heard her gushing and exclaiming over things like the shower curtain, coffee maker, and litter box. True, the coffee maker was impressive, but the other things? I guess she preferred my grandma's hodgepodge aesthetic to Virginia's all florals all the time.

Somewhere into my third episode, the pet door opened and closed with a swish. I assumed the two lovebirds had gone out for a walk through the neighborhood, but a moment later, Luna jumped onto the coffee table and waited for me to pause my show before speaking.

"I sent Merlin out for a while," she said, adjusting herself into a more comfortable position. "To give us two girls some time to talk."

I sat up and patted the couch beside me. "What's up?"

Luna hopped over and took a quick breath before launching into what seemed to be a prepared speech. "At first I wasn't sure you were worthy of my Merlin. That's why I gave you such a hard time. But today you proved yourself more than worthy. You were very brave, but moreover, you were there for him in a terrifying situation. And you did not run or abandon him. I was wrong about you, and I want to apologize for that."

I blinked slowly as I took in the weight of her words. "Of course I was there for him, he's my cat. And now that you'll be living with us, I'll be there for you, too."

Luna began to purr. "It will be nice to have a human who loves me for a change. Virginia only loved my power. I should have taken more care in choosing, but I was hurt and distracted, knowing that Merlin and I would have to end our relationship so we could each take our full places in the magical community." She paused for a moment. "I know we have only just met and that most of our encounters have been negative until now, but Merlin trusts you and that's good enough for me. I love you, as he loves you."

"Thank you, Luna," I whispered softly. "That means a lot."

She rubbed her nose against my face in affection, but I pulled back and let out a pained hiss.

"What's the matter?" Luna asked, concern reflecting in her cornflower eyes.

"Dash gave me a nasty cut," I said, raising my fingers to my face and wincing again.

"Oh, no," she wailed. "Merlin and I were so caught up in each other that we didn't tend to your wounds. The moment he is returned, he'll whip you up a nice salve."

"That would be nice," I admitted, unable to refuse the promise of help.

"Are you hurt anywhere else?" Luna wanted to know.

"My shoulders are sore from being handcuffed so long, but Dash didn't touch me at all. Except when she slashed me. It was really weird, actually. She looked at my blood and said it explained a few things. What do you think she meant by that?"

Luna shook her head. "I don't know. Normally illusion witches can't read biomatter, so if Dash did, she is exceptionally powerful."

I shuddered at this. "Well, that definitely doesn't make me any less afraid for our next battle."

"No." Luna stared off into the distance as if seeing something I couldn't. "But there is a way to learn what she knows."

"Oh?" Now she had my interest.

"Has Merlin told you about Nocturna?"

I shook my head, even though the movement caused the cut to sting all the more.

"It's only accessible at night, but many of our kind live in the open there," Luna explained in almost a whisper, as if the place itself were sacred. "We can take you, find a blood witch, have him tell us what he sees there."

"Can we go tonight?" I asked, hope creeping up anew.

"I don't see why not. It will be up to Merlin to decide, though. He's the only one of us with a magical passport now."

"Okay, I'll ask when he gets home, then," I said with a small smile of gratitude.

"Actually, sweetie. Leave that part to me. I know exactly how to get a yes from our Merlin." She winked, then hopped away.

I cringed but thankfully avoided summoning a mental picture of what Luna's persuasive methods might entail. I already had enough to worry about, thank you very much.

29

At this point I was just stalling. I knew I'd need to be up and active at night to visit the magical city Luna had called Nocturna, but before we could go, there was one more thing I needed to handle today.

After a quick conversation with Merlin to confirm I could actually do what I had planned, I shot Kelley a text asking her if we could meet up. She invited me to come out to the coffeehouse for another round of PSLs and frozen banana nut bread.

By the time I had fetched my car and driven over to Harold's, I found her working with the espresso machine. A big smile stretched across her face when she spotted me.

I raced over to hug her. "You look so much better today. Does this mean you got good news?"

Kelley's smile widened. "My dad's lawyer contacted me today about the will. He changed it up about four weeks ago and left it all to me. He may not have taken much opportunity to get to know me, Gracie, but my father did love me."

I hugged her again. "Oh, I always knew he did!" I cooed, even though I'd honestly had no idea. "He probably just wanted to be careful about how he approached your relationship, figuring he had more time."

We both became somber.

"I'm sure you're right," Kelley said.

"Officer Dash contacted me today," I revealed. This would be the only part of my confession that was actually true, but I knew Kelley would need to hear this in order to move on. "Your dad wasn't murdered, after all. He had a heart attack. The medical examiner who suggested he'd died by poison was fired for getting it so wrong."

"I'm glad he wasn't murdered," Kelley said, "But I'm still so sad that he's gone."

She finished preparing our lattes and we relocated to the big corner booth. Of course, I still hadn't revealed the biggest part of my plan but knew I couldn't put it off much longer or I'd risk losing the nerve.

"So what's next for you, Kelley? Will you be going back to Ohio with your mom?"

She shook her head. "No, definitely not. I mean, why would I do that when I now have my own business to run?"

"You mean...?"

"Yes! The coffee shop is mine. I'm going to be making some big changes to the menu and to the payroll... you should definitely be making more than you currently are... but I'm going to keep the name in honor of Dad."

"That's wonderful, Kelley. You'll be a great boss, and I can't wait to hear all your ideas!"

As it turned out, she couldn't wait to share them with me. "I can go over some of them now if you'd like. To start, PSL is no longer a seasonal item. We'll serve it all year round. And also—"

"I hate to interrupt, especially because I love that idea so much, but there's something I need to say," I said, my heart thumping hard in my chest.

Kelley looked at me with concern.

"Nothing's wrong," I promised.

"Then what's going on?" she pressed.

I reached into my purse and took out an empty water bottle. Merlin had helped me prepare the potion I requested, even though he warned me against it more than once. Still, I knew I was making the right decision with this.

I uncapped the water bottle and set it in the middle of the table. Nothing happened. At least that's how it looked to those who didn't know it held an invisible form of magic.

"What's with the empty bottle?" Kelley asked with one eyebrow raised.

"Don't worry about that," I said, waiting for her to shift her gaze back to me.

I didn't continue until her eyes met mine. "This is kind of a weird question, but I want you to tell me the first answer that pops into your head. Okay?"

Kelley shrugged, but said, “Okay.”

“If you could wish for anything, anything in the whole wide world, what would you ask for?”

She snorted. “Like a fairy godmother kind of thing?”

“Something like that,” I answered with a secretive smile. “You don’t have to blurt it out. You can take a moment if you need to, but not much longer. So, tell me, what’s your one big wish?”

A smile blossomed from cheek to cheek. “Well, I guess I—”

“Wait,” I cried, reaching over to the bottle and giving it a good squeeze. “Take a deep breath first,” I instructed, wanting to be sure she breathed it all in.

I watched as Kelley sucked in the invisible gaseous potion, waiting nervously to hear what she would say next.

But she knew exactly what she wanted. “I want to honor my dad’s legacy by making Harold’s House of Coffee the most successful coffee shop this town has ever seen,” she said with a firm-set jaw.

“You will,” I promised her.

After all, I’d just passed on my ask-for-anything familiar spell. Merlin had told me I shouldn’t, because he wouldn’t be able to make another one. And, yeah, now I could never get to be Lady Gaga, or King Arthur, or someone else crazy famous…

But Kelley needed this more than I did, and giving her this once-in-a-lifetime opportunity felt right, considering all she’d lost because of us.

I couldn’t bring Harold back, but I could make sure his daughter was well taken care of in his absence, and that’s exactly what I planned to do.

30

When I came home, I showed both cats the empty bottle I'd used to pass my wish on to Kelley.

"Yup, it's gone," Merlin whined, rolling onto his side dramatically. "I can't believe you gave that away."

"She's a good one," Luna told Merlin as she pressed her body against the side of my leg and shook her sleek white tail. "My familiar destroyed herself by craving power. Yours freely gave it away. You're a lucky witch."

"That, I am," Merlin admitted with a wink. "Even if she is a little bit crazy."

"What's done is done," I said with a shrug. Before I'd gone to see Kelley, Merlin had whipped up an anti-pain potion, taking the hurt out of both my shoulders and my cheek, which meant I could move freely now. "Let's focus on what we can still hope to change."

"Are you sure you're ready to enter Nocturna?" Merlin asked me tersely. "It's rather overwhelming for a first-timer, especially one so new to magic as you are."

"I'm sure," I said, pressing my lips into a tight line. "I'd rather have the knowledge than not."

"The sun is setting," Luna said, and we both stared at Merlin, waiting for him to speak.

"Then let's go," he acquiesced.

I followed Merlin as he slowly stalked toward the door.

He ran through, but Luna waited for me to open the big door. "Remember, you can do this," she assured me with a simple smile.

I took in a deep breath and stepped outside into the evening twilight.

Merlin had already seated himself upon the bird bath. "The moment the sun disappears over the horizon, we'll be able to use the cauldron as a doorway to Nocturna. Shouldn't be long now."

"How am I going to fit through that?" I squeaked, studying the small stone fountain.

"Magic, duh!" Luna answered with a laugh and then hopped up beside Merlin.

"Step forward," he said as he splashed in the water and placed a wet paw on Luna's forehead.

"Lean in close," he instructed. When I did, he dipped his paw again and touched it to my head. "Luna will go through first, and I'll go in last to make sure nothing goes awry."

"Goes awry? Wait. Does that mean this is dangerous?"

"Don't worry about it, sweetie," Luna cooed.

In the distance the sun finished its descent. The cauldron glowed a bright mint green, swallowing Luna whole.

"Whoa, I don't want to do this!" I whined and took a giant leap back.

"Too late," Merlin said, then summoned a gust of wind that sent me stumbling right into the fountain. I closed my eyes as I braced for impact, and I screamed and screamed and screamed, until I noticed that everything was absolutely fine.

When I opened my eyes again, I stood on a dark stone path. Both cats were at my side. The surrounding buildings had been built in a Bavarian style, white with dark crossbeams.

Luna nudged me forward. "What do you think?"

"It looks like something out of a fairytale," I said, instantly falling in love with the quaint magical city.

"This area was settled during peak popularity of the Brothers Grimm. Everyone wanted the German village look, and Nocturna was no different," she explained with obvious pride.

"Where is everybody?" I asked.

"Just waking up, no doubt. Remember, we cats tend to keep evening hours," Luna reminded me, and of course she was right.

"Follow me," Merlin commanded, and Luna and I both fell into step beside him. He led us to what appeared to be a covered wagon, although it had nothing hooked up to pull it.

"We need a reading," Merlin shouted from outside.

A moment later, a flame point Siamese popped its head out from the wagon. Its eyes grew wide as it caught sight of Merlin. "And what will you be offering in trade?"

"Anything but lightning," Merlin responded, standing tall as he waited.

"How about a rainstorm?" the Siamese asked greedily.

"Done," Merlin answered with a nod.

"Excellent. Now let's see what we have here."

Luna guided me toward the wagon. "Go on, sit down."

"But doesn't Merlin have to pay first?" I whispered to her.

"They have a spoken contract bound by magic," she explained. "Don't worry, everything will be taken care of."

"Is this going to hurt?" I asked the flame point who'd popped up beside me on the bench seat.

He scoffed. "I'm insulted. What kind of blood witch do you take me for?"

I fell silent, preferring not to discuss how badly Dash had hurt me when she took my blood. The Siamese blood witch moved to my lap, then held his paw to my neck. I felt nothing, but when he pulled away, blood tipped each of his claws, shimmering in the night sky.

He stared down at his paw with wide eyes. "Well, I'll be."

"What? What is it?" Merlin demanded, sounding even more nervous than I felt.

"This is your familiar?" the blood witch asked, glancing from his paw to me and then back again.

"Yes, she is. Is everything okay?"

"More than okay!" the Siamese crooned, as if hysterically happy. "Her blood is especially powerful. She's a descendant of the original dutiful familiar."

"Arthur?" Luna asked with a gasp.

"King Arthur, the Great Merlin's true companion," the Siamese verified.

"And you're descended from Merlin?" I asked him, recalling the story he'd told me when we first spoke.

My cat nodded but continued to stare blankly ahead.

"What does this mean?" I asked weakly, still unsure of how to take the news.

"It means that you have the most powerful bond of any witch and familiar living today," Luna supplied in a hushed whisper.

"No wonder we bonded so fast," Merlin murmured.

"We already knew about the bond," I pointed out.

"Yes," the Siamese said. "But keep it a carefully guarded secret, for there will be many who wish to separate you."

I nodded dumbly, terrified of what I'd just learned.

Dash already knew…

And she'd definitely be back.

MERLIN FIGHTS A GHOST

It was hard enough serving as my witchy cat's familiar when we only had to deal with threats we could see. Now he's gotten himself into a bitter feud with a newly dispatched ghost, leaving me to wonder... How in the heck are we supposed to defeat this thing?

I miss the simple days when all I had to worry about was finishing my thesis paper and not getting fired from my part-time job as a barista.

And, yeah, even though I didn't choose the magic life, it sure as heck chose me. Now all I have to do is to keep myself alive long enough to appreciate some of the perks.

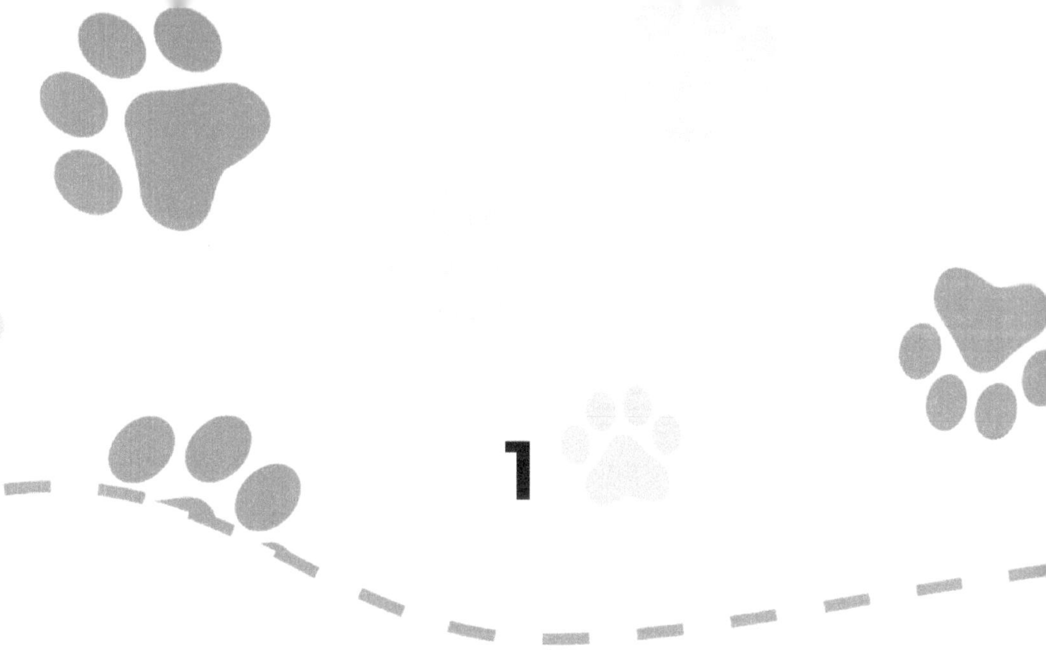

1

Hello, I'm Gracie Springs. I used to be a pretty normal girl, until about a week ago. You see, my boss got murdered by magic, then an evil witch and her accomplice tried to frame mc for it.

As it turns out, I'm descended from King Arthur. I've also been chosen to serve as my witchy cat's familiar. I used to call him Fluffy, but now I know he much prefers to go by Merlin. He has a famous lineage, too. He's descended from the original Merlin.

No, not the human imposter everyone thinks they know. The real wizard, who just so happened to be a cat.

Because of our intertwined ancestry, Merlin and I have an almost unbreakable bond. Almost.

The bad guy got away last time, but we both know she'll be back with a new plan to steal Merlin's magic from him for good.

While all this has been going on, I've also needed to keep up the appearances of a normal life by working my part-time barista job at Harold's House of Coffee. The shop is in the process of being remodeled, thanks to the very ambitious goals of Harold's successor, his long-lost daughter, Kelley.

Also, I'm very close to completing my master's degree in Sociology. I just have to finish my thesis, and then I can find work in my field rather than forever working as a part-time bean-slinger.

Lately, though, I'm plenty busy with getting the hang of my new role as a familiar. Both Merlin and his new girlfriend are more than happy to grill me at all hours of the day and night.

I need to be ready for when the next magical attack happens, and make no mistake, we all know it's coming soon.

I bet my grandma never would have guessed what was in store for me when she gifted me her small-town Georgia home and retired to the Florida Keys. She certainly didn't know that a certain magical Maine Coon had already been scoping her out to work as his familiar, or that he'd later choose me in her place.

Honestly, even though my life has taken a turn for the crazy, I wouldn't have it any other way. I love Merlin, and I love our adventures together, no matter how much they frighten the frijoles out of me.

I can't cast magic, but that doesn't mean I'm not important in our fight against the wicked illusion witch who has set her sights on us.

But this time when she finds us, I'll be ready to take her down.

An unholy shriek woke me from a dead sleep.

Meeeeeeeeeeeh!

I darted upright in bed and grabbed my cell phone to serve as a flashlight. “Who’s there?” I demanded.

But was only answered by Merlin thumping down the hardwood floor in the hallway.

Meeeeeeeeeh! the shriek sounded again, and this time I realized it was Luna crying her heart out.

And so it went. Shriek, scamper. Shriek, scamper. Until at last I made my way into the hall and found them both staring at the far corner of the ceiling with their ears pressed back against their little kitty heads.

“What’s going on?” I asked, knowing full well both of them were capable of more than just uncivilized meows.

“Gh-gh-gh-ghost,” Merlin said, then took another sprint down the short hallway.

I glanced up to the spot where Luna still had her large unblinking eyes fixed… and saw absolutely nothing.

Still, I asked her, “What do you see?” Generally, she was the more logical of the two—or at least the one more likely to open up to me.

“I can’t see anything,” she whispered without removing her gaze from the ceiling. “But there’s an energy that’s forming. It’s not wholly in our world yet. It will be soon, though.”

“So you see a pre-ghost?” I summarized.

“Something like that.”

“But how can you tell? You’re not magical anymore,” I reminded her.

Luna couldn’t stifle the hiss that escaped her. “I may not be a witch, but I am still a cat. Magical or not, we can all see into the supernatural realm."

"Like Nocturna?" I asked, referring to the magical nighttime city that was only accessible to magical creatures at the twilight hour.

Merlin growled and began to kick up his hind legs.

"Oh, no, you don't!" I cried, reaching down to pluck him into my arms. "No tornadoes inside the house."

He growled in dismay until I set him back down.

"We must get rid of it before it takes its full form," Luna told me as she worried her bottom lip with her top fangs.

"The fact that it's here so soon in its after-life journey is a very bad sign," Merlin revealed, and when I looked down at him he had arched his back and puffed up to maximum volume.

I grabbed him into my arms again. "Definitely no lightning inside the house!"

"Then what should we do?" Luna asked with a gasp.

"Let me make some coffee," I said, admitting defeat at last. It was clear that neither cat would let me go to bed until I found a way to bust this newborn ghost... or at least to send it off to haunt some place far, far away from here.

2

Coffee in hand, I settled myself at the kitchen table. The hard wood of the old chair did little to make me comfortable, but it did help keep me awake.

I took a slow sip from my mug, letting the steam warm my face, then glanced over at the two cats sitting across the table from me.

"So a ghost is coming," I said. "I can see how that would be a bad thing. Do either of you know how to make it go away?"

Luna shook her head sadly. "It's Virginia," she said, speaking of her late familiar. "I just know it is."

Merlin rubbed his head against his girlfriend's neck. "Her death wasn't your fault. It was her own greed."

"It feels like my fault," Luna mumbled. She'd been blaming herself ever since it happened. When she learned that Virginia had gone rogue in her thirst for magical power, Luna hadn't hesitated to sever the familiar bond, leaving them both powerless. And in her desperate grasp for the fleeing magic, Virginia toppled headfirst down a well and met her end.

Now apparently she was in the process of taking ghostly form and planning to haunt my house.

Was she after revenge?

Would she hurt me or one of the cats?

Whatever was going on, it definitely couldn't be good.

And just when I thought things were starting to settle down. *Ugh.*

My only hope now was that either the cats were wrong about the ghost or they had a different explanation for its presence.

I sucked in a deep breath, then let it out slowly. "I don't really know much about ghosts outside of what I've seen in old movies. Can one of you catch me up?"

Luna and Merlin exchanged a tense glance.

"What? What's wrong?" I asked with a heavy sigh. I almost didn't want to hear what they said next, but I needed to be prepared in case I found myself caught in the middle of another magical standoff.

Luna began to speak, but Merlin put the side of his paw against her chest to stop her.

"You're already distressed enough, my dear. Let me handle Gracie," he offered magnanimously.

"I don't like it when you talk about me as if I'm some kind of liability," I muttered as I wrapped both hands around my coffee mug to soak in its warmth.

"Look," said Merlin, approaching me slowly from across the table. "Luna and I are both young witches. Or, at least she was until... Anyway, the point is, I'm still a witch. A young one."

I groaned at his jumbled mix of explanatory stops and starts. I wish he could just tell it to me straight, no matter how bad. "Your point being?"

Merlin looked to Luna, who nodded for him to go on. He swallowed hard, then said, "Well, neither of us has had any experience with ghosts before now, either."

I didn't understand their worry. So they didn't have practical experience. Book smarts could do in a pinch, and these two witchy cats seemed to have a limitless supply of knowledge when it came to the hidden world of magic.

When neither said more, I put on a smile. "No big deal. You learned how to deal with ghosts in witch school, right?"

A growl rumbled in Merlin's throat, and he lowered his eyelids as if it pained him to look at me. "Oh, you humans. So myopic in your world views. Just because you need years of schooling to function in society doesn't mean other creatures do. In fact, we witches learn much of what is needed simply by observing our everyday surroundings."

I scowled right back at him. I didn't get out of bed in the middle of the night just to be insulted by my feline roommates. "Great. And what's that taught you about ghosts?"

He coughed and looked away. "Fair point," he admitted. "I guess we aren't really equipped to deal with some of the rarer magical conundrums."

I drew in another slow, deep breath. "So where does that leave us? Do we just wait for the ghost to finish materializing and then ask it to leave?"

"Oh, no." Merlin scoffed. "Surely not."

"Ghosts are incredibly uncommon." Luna's voice was hardly more than a whisper from her side of the table. "The deceased only return to our world when they have a burning purpose. Something they wanted so badly while they were living that the quest for it became embedded in their very soul."

I shivered despite myself. "Sounds serious."

Merlin nodded. "To want something that much. It's often not good."

"Virginia yearned for power," Luna said softly. "The same thing that killed her could have brought her back."

"Yeah, that's definitely not good," I agreed, taking another long slurp from my coffee.

Both cats stared blankly at me while I drank. Somehow they treated me as a sidekick but then expected me to have all the answers.

"Um, can we capture it in a positronic box?" I suggested with a shrug. I hadn't seen Ghostbusters in a long time, but it was really the only frame of reference I had here. And somehow I doubted Virginia would be returning to us as a chubby green pizza-loving cartoon character.

"We don't deal in science," Merlin said with an exaggerated shudder. "This is a magic household, and you'll do well to remember that."

"To Nocturna then?" I asked, referencing the magical city that we could only enter at nightfall and with Merlin's aid.

Both cats nodded. "Nocturna."

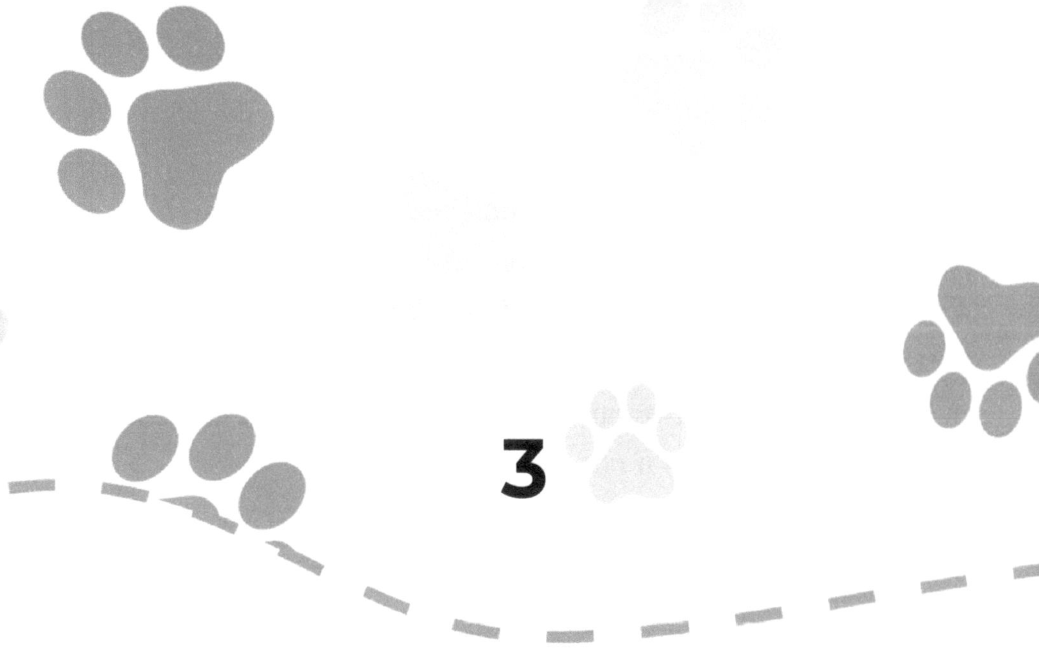

3

As much as I wish I could've gone back to sleep, the coffee had done its job—meaning I was now up for the day. I had several hours to kill before my shift at the coffee shop, and I would have liked to tell you that I spent them working on my thesis research.

But, yeah, that's not what happened.

Instead of being productive, I whiled away the hours by watching the two Ghostbusters movies from the '80s. I didn't have time to get to the more recent adaptation but promised myself I'd watch it after work, Nocturna, and whatever other surprises managed to set my day off-kilter.

Of course, I got so absorbed in my mini movie marathon that I lost track of time and had to do my makeup in the car. My dark circles would now be on display to anyone who bothered to look at me for more than a few quick seconds.

Stupid ghost disturbing my sleep and messing up my look.

Even though I hoped our visit from that ghost was a one-off thing, I knew better than to expect a sound night's sleep anytime soon. That was the thing about the magical world—nothing was ever as easy as you'd hope. Even the two-blink teleport thing was full of problems and could kill somebody if not done properly.

Nope, not for me.

I'd stick to going places in my car, which was probably equally dangerous but at least more familiar, thank you very much.

Given an absence of red lights on my journey, I only managed to add a bit of eyeliner and a sassy matte lipstick before pulling into the parking lot at Harold's, but it would have to be enough.

My new boss Kelley Carmine insisted on having her staff of baristas come into work, even though renovations kept the place closed to customers—and that felt odd to me.

Today, it seemed especially odd, seeing as our numbers had doubled. Before, only Drake, Kelley, and I had covered the majority of shifts, with the late Harold taking on whatever few we couldn't. When I arrived for work that day, though, three strangers stood huddled beside the brand-new espresso maker, watching as Kelley did the leg work for a round of pumpkin spice lattes.

That was her thing. While she'd kept the original name of the coffee shop to honor her late father, everything else about the business was undergoing a major transformation.

The most noticeable change was that every day was now pumpkin spice latte day. No longer could anyone order a simple latte, cappuccino, or Americano. Each now included at least some hint of pumpkin in the mix.

That was the hardest part of this transition for me, learning the new menu.

I fully supported Kelley's mission to offer PSL all year round, but that was before I realized the extent of her plans. We now had more than a dozen variants on the classic drink, including holiday versions that were also meant to be served year-round.

Want a cupid spice latte in August? No problem. We just need to add a shot of white chocolate and some red hot sprinkles to our classic PSL.

Blech. Just thinking of that monstrosity made my stomach churn.

"Welcome, Gracie!" my new boss cried with a giant grin on her eighteen-year-old face. "Now we just need Drake, and we can get started with the day you've all been waiting for!"

She paused as if she expected me to shout out some kind of answer. I didn't even know there'd been a question.

Kelley clucked her tongue. "C'mon, Gracie. You know better than anyone! It's one week until opening day, which means it's time to get everyone—including our lovely new hires—oriented to the new way of things. And..." She grabbed a pair of coffee stirrers and tapped them on the edge of the counter to imitate a drumroll. "That includes getting to taste everything on the menu! I hope you brought your appetites!"

How I managed not to throw up right then and there, I still don't know. Maybe Merlin's magic was starting to rub off on me, after all.

While I found Kelley's enthusiasm admirable, her commitment to the theme was just a bit too much for me. Still, I liked her and I wanted her to succeed. I also knew that no matter how far out into left field she went with this business, it was still destined to be a hit. I'd made sure of that when I secretly bestowed my one big wish upon her. Now I'd have to make my own destiny without any significant magical aid, and that was fine by me.

My life was exciting enough, thanks to my new adventures with Merlin and Luna... and our baby ghost. Plus I didn't trust myself not to waste the wish on something trivial—or something that would backfire on me spectacularly.

So Kelley got her PSL lovefest, and I got to keep my job. Let me tell you, the more things change, the more they just keep on staying the same.

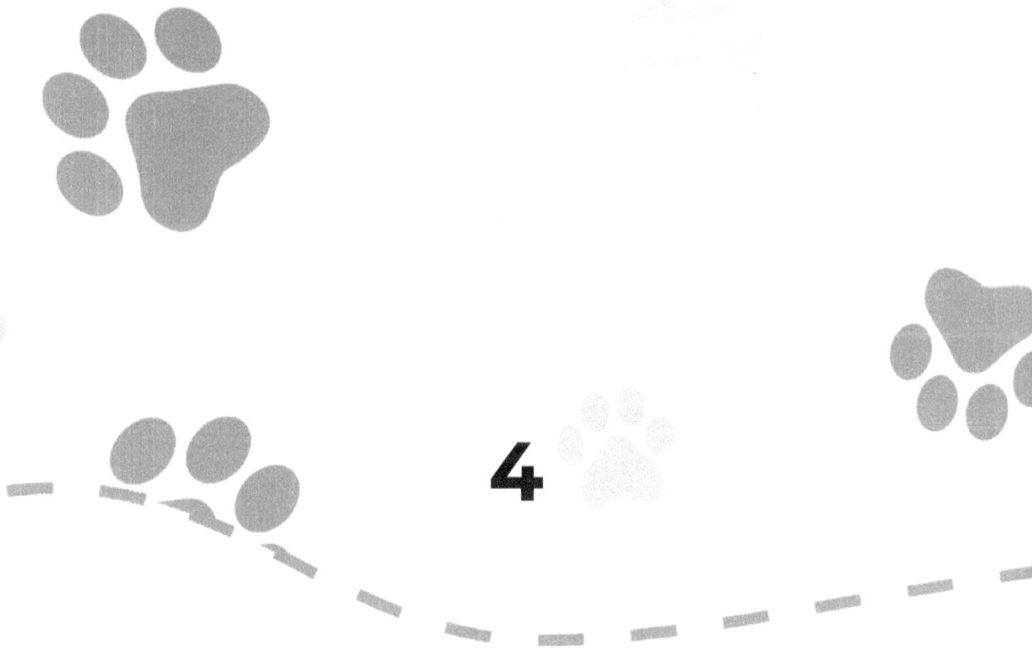

4

Drake dragged himself through the door about ten minutes later, which made him eight minutes late for his shift. Harold would have torn him a new one—and then made him work at least an hour without pay. Kelley simply put on her best smile, clapped her hands together, and announced that we'd be starting off with an icebreaker.

She even climbed onto a chair and cupped her hands over her mouth like a megaphone—an action that was definitely not needed, given that we were all huddled closely together in the tiny storefront.

"My name is Kelley, and my favorite pumpkin spice is ginger!" she shouted, then climbed down from the chair and motioned for me to climb up and take my turn.

I stumbled over, trying so hard not to be embarrassed as I rose up on that chair. "I'm Gracie, and I like cinnamon?" I said, having never really thought much about my favorite pumpkin spice before.

And so the day went, full of useless getting-to-know-you activities and overly sweet coffee confections. At one point, Kelley announced we'd be playing "Never have I ever" as her inventive, ice-breaking way of trying the new iced beverage line.

When it was my turn, I felt emboldened enough to say, "Never have I ever seen a ghost." It was kind of true. I knew there was a pre-ghost in my house, but only because my cats had told me.

What really surprised me was when Drake of all people kicked back his shot of pumpkin spice coconut dream.

Drake. Hmm. What did I know about Drake?

He had a bit of an attitude problem when it came to authority but had always been nice enough to me. The real question was whether he had taken a drink to be funny or if he'd actually seen a ghost. If he'd really come across one before, maybe he could help me with my problematic houseguest.

I had to find out, so I caught up with him in the parking lot as we were headed home from our mind-numbing afternoon of orientation activities.

"Hey, Drake," I called, jogging over to him. "Crazy day, huh?"

He shrugged casually with that same apathetic air he brought to everything. "It was pretty lame, but at least Kelley won't dock our pay like her old man did. That's something good, I guess."

I laughed, which made Drake raise one eyebrow and regard me with suspicion.

"Everything okay there, my PSL compadre?" he asked with a sly grin.

"Oh, yeah," I assured him, trying to ignore the heat that rose to my cheeks. "Just too much sugar today, I think."

He nodded and scooped his keys from his pocket. "Well, this is me." He motioned toward the shiny blue coupe we now stood beside. It was a much nicer car than I expected him to have. Seriously, how did he pay for this thing on his part-time barista salary?

"Okay, so bye, then," he said, when I remained silent for too long.

"Drake, wait!" I shouted before he could climb into the driver's seat and shut me out.

He settled on the seat but left the door wide open as he waited for me to tell him what I wanted.

I cleared my throat to buy a little time. This was an awkward question, especially if he'd been joking during our icebreaker. "I've been meaning to ask you—"

I didn't get to finish because he abruptly cut me off. "Yeah, sure I'll go out on a date with you," he answered, a debonair smile now on full display.

I blinked hard and took a step back. "Um, that's wasn't... Uh..." I had to make this right without alienating him so much that he'd refuse to share the details of his ghostly encounter. Unfortunately, this was a very new situation for me, and one I had a hard time putting into words. What were the rules of etiquette when it came to openly discussing the paranormal? And just how much could I share without risking my safety or freedom? Merlin had made it very clear that if I shared his witchy secret with non-magical folk, I would find myself locked away in a terrible supernatural prison for the rest of my life.

I was still debating how to frame my question when Drake spoke again.

"Your place at eight? Sounds awesome. I'll see you there."

And with that, he slammed the door shut and backed out of his spot, giving me one last mischievous look before he disappeared into traffic.

I jumped and waved my arms while shaking my head wildly, but I couldn't be sure that Drake caught sight of me in his rear-view mirror.

How had I messed this up so badly? I should have just blurted out my question. Trying to put things delicately had only made the whole situation worse.

Because now it seemed I had two problems on my hands.

And no idea how to solve either one.

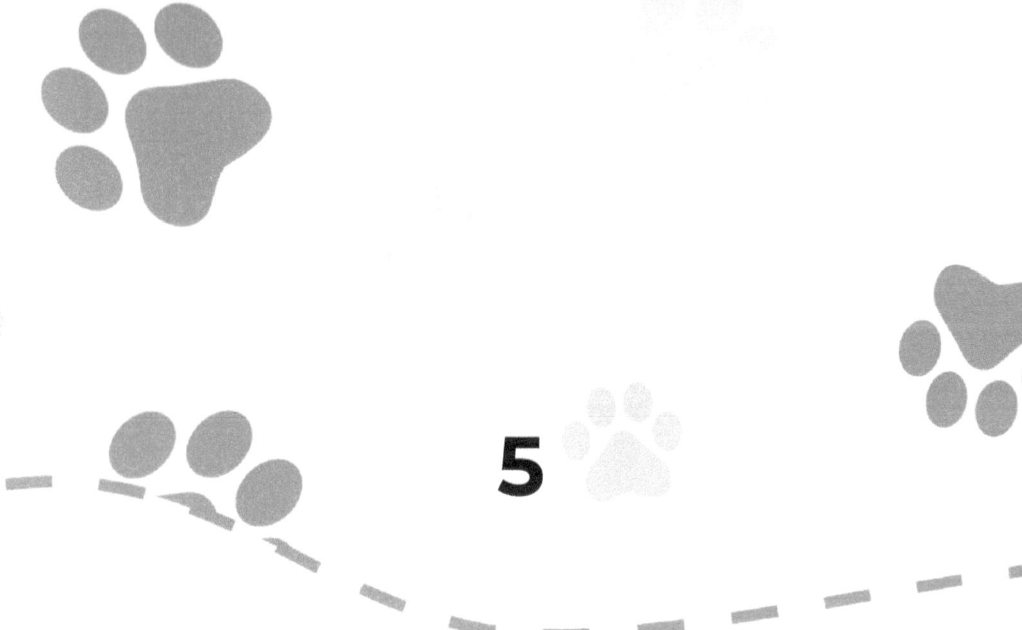

5

I returned home to both cats sprawled out and sunning themselves on my kitchen floor. As they slept, their tails twitched with dreams. I hated to disturb them, especially given how adorable they looked relaxing together . Perhaps one day I'd have a relationship as gratifying as that of my cats, but today would not be that day. And that relationship would not be with Drake.

"We've got a problem," I announced as I pulled out a chair and sat to remove my shoes.

"Bigger than the ghost?" Merlin asked with a yawn.

"Not bigger, but a problem nonetheless."

"Let's hear it," Luna commanded after she'd thoroughly stretched both her front and back legs and sauntered over to stand beside me.

"I kind of accidentally agreed, or maybe I invited... Um, I'm not sure how it happened, really, but I have a date with this guy from work." What was with me and words today? Why did I have such a hard time explaining even simple things? I must have done a poor job showing my displeasure, because both cats became very excited by my announcement.

"A date? That's fantastic." Luna's her blue eyes twinkled with glee. She sat taller and said, "Merlin and I have been worried about your love life lately."

"Seriously? It's only been like a week since you moved in here, Luna. How could you already be worried about my love life?" And was I really such a sad case that even my cats took pity on me? Cats famously didn't care what anyone thought about them, so why were they taking so much time thinking—and worrying—about me?

"Oh, a life without love is no life at all," Luna corrected me with a sigh. "Welcome to the living, Gracie."

"No, stop it." I hissed. Lately I'd been taking on more and more cat mannerisms, thanks to the influence of these two. The next thing I knew, I'd be licking the back of my hand and rubbing it across my forehead. God help me.

"This is not a real date," I continued, laying my displeasure on full display now. "It happened by accident, and he's coming over here tonight."

"But we're going to Nocturna tonight," Merlin reminded me, his whiskers twitching with newfound irritation.

"I know!" I shouted. Why was this so hard for them to understand?

"Then call and reschedule, dear," Luna suggested with a condescending air. I did not like this look on her. Or on me for that matter.

"I can't. I don't have his number."

Luna worked hard to maintain her smile, but even I could see it was faltering. "Then pay him a quick visit."

"I don't know where he lives."

"Then how does he know where you live, dear?" she asked with a sigh.

"That is a good question."

"You don't seem very excited for your date," she pointed out with a frown. "How did all this come about?"

I caught them up on all the ice-breaking activities and Drake's admission during "Never have I ever."

"That's a strange game. Why would humans want to brag about the things they haven't done? We cats like to share our accomplishments, not lack thereof," Merlin groused.

"The game is not the point," I snapped. "The point is that Drake has seen a ghost. And when I tried to ask him about that, it turned into this whole date thing."

"Well, a date is a perfect opportunity to ask him about his ghost, dear." Ah, Luna. Ever the optimist. It was starting to wear on me.

"Except we're supposed to be going to Nocturna tonight," I reminded them.

"You don't have to go everywhere we go," Merlin said rather grumpily. "If you want to abandon us in favor of your date, we'll live."

The beginnings of a tension headache crept up my neck and into my brain. Would it be wrong to turn a spray bottle on my cats to discipline them, knowing they could talk and that at least one of them could retaliate by conjuring lightning?

I tried very hard not to shout at the top of my lungs now. "That's not—"

Luna gently patted my hand with her paw. "It's fine, dear. Merlin and I will enjoy the alone time. We wouldn't want to be all up in your hair during your date, anyway."

"It's not—*UGH!*" This time I threw both hands in the air, then slammed them down on the table in frustration.

"So touchy," Merlin said with a sneer. "Don't worry, though, your highness. We'll do all the actual work that's needed to keep our home safe while you have fun entertaining your gentleman caller."

"You know what? Fine. Go to Nocturna. Have all the fun without me while I stay here and participate in a date I didn't ask for and don't want."

"Wonderful," Luna cooed. "So we're all in agreement then?"

I dropped my head into my hands and tried to focus on my breathing.

"Humans mature so much more slowly than cats," I heard Merlin whisper to Luna. "Perhaps I'd have been better off with the old lady."

"Is it too late to switch?" the femme feline wondered aloud.

"You know better than anyone that once the familiar bond is set, it can't be broken without—"

Luna drew in a sharp breath. "Yes, I know."

"So we're stuck with her," he added glumly.

"I can still hear you!" I shouted, then stalked off to my room and slammed the door.

Hmm. Maybe they were right about my maturity level, after all.

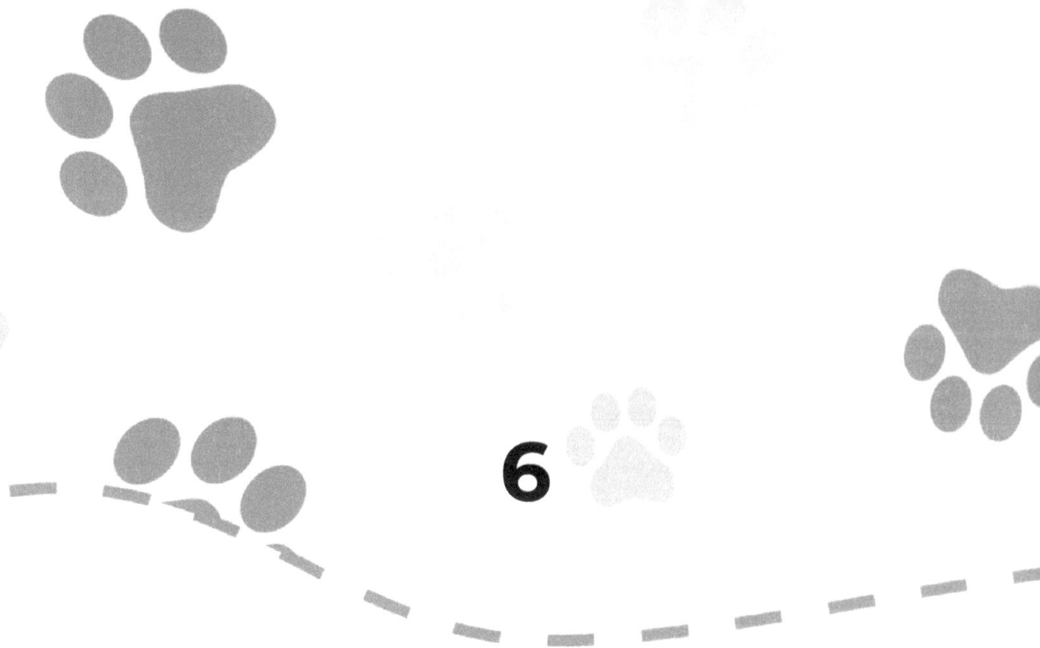

6

The sun was due to set about fifteen minutes before eight o'clock that night, which meant that if Drake arrived even a few minutes early, he'd see my cat's magic on full display right in the front yard.

"Maybe we should consider moving your cauldron around back," I suggested as Merlin and Luna were making the final preparations for their journey to Nocturna. What I wouldn't give to go with them instead of having to stay here and entertain Drake in what would surely be an awkward encounter.

"Are you serious?" Merlin hissed, his eyes turning sharp. "If we move the cauldron, we may damage it. If we damage it, our connection to the magical world could be lost for good."

"Okay, okay, sorry," I muttered, kicking at a patch of extra-long grass near the driveway. As much as I loved being a homeowner now,

I hadn't quite gotten the hang of the lawnmower yet. Every time I fired the thing up, the smell of freshly cut grass aggravated my allergies and sent me into a violent sneezing fit. But because the grass had to be cut one way or another, I end up running the mower back and forth over the yard as fast as I can, not bothering to make sure it gets cut evenly. Mostly cut was better than not cut at all, I figured, and since I didn't have the money to hire the job out, my neighbors would just have to deal with my uneven lawn.

"Next time, perhaps schedule your romantic tryst elsewhere," Luna purred. She began to rub against my leg, but I leapt out of reach. I was still not okay with the way she was treating me when it came to this accidental date—or to my love life at all.

"Not a romantic tryst. Not a romantic anything," I corrected between clenched teeth. "Remember, he invited himself over."

Merlin whispered something to Luna, just quietly enough that I couldn't make out the words. When he finished, they both turned toward me and began laughing.

"Just go to Nocturna already," I seethed, kicking another patch of mis-mown grass. "Stay there forever for all I care."

The cats continued to titter as they hopped into the birdbath, splashed around, and then disappeared in a glowing swirl of green. I doubted I'd ever get used to Merlin's strange modes of travel, either by turning his cauldron disguised as a bird bath into a portal or by blinking twice to magically teleport.

Every time my new life as a familiar began to make even a little bit of sense, something so bonkers came along I didn't think I'd ever be able to reconcile it with my previous understanding of the world.

I guess that was true of most things these days. Everything teetered somewhere between boring and safe or fascinating but stressful. I could pretty much guarantee that my life with Merlin would always fall into the latter category.

Now that he and Luna were gone, I had a little while to play with my makeup, provided Drake arrived exactly on time or even a little bit late. Given his work history, I was banking on him being late, which meant I had some time to work on my look.

I hadn't dared lift a cosmetic brush or poof to my face while the cats were here teasing me. Still, whether or not I had asked for this date, I wanted to look nice. And I'd take any excuse to trot out one of my bolder makeup looks, really.

I didn't have any real dates happening in the near future, so I might as well use this fake date to try out the mermaid eyeshadow palate I'd purchased from a popular online boutique.

I worked fast to apply the array of bright colors, but not fast enough apparently, because the doorbell rang about halfway through my application.

"Coming," I called, turning my head slightly from side to side. If only I had another five minutes. *Grrr.*

Exactly on time, I noted with a quick glance at the microwave clock as I passed through the kitchen. Definitely not what I'd expected from Drake.

I found him waiting patiently on my doorstep, wearing a black dress shirt, tie, and suit jacket with jeans and a pair of ordinary, scuffed-up sneakers.

"Hi, Drake," I said, my eyes landing on the single flower he held clutched within his hand. The bloom was a deep blood red with spiky looking petals, definitely not something I recognized.

"For you," he said with a small smile that I found almost charming.

"Thank you," I said, accepting the gift. "It's really pretty."

"That's a black narcissus, a cactus Dahlia," he explained in that smug way of his.

"I don't know much about flowers," I admitted with a slight frown. "Cactuses don't need water, right?"

"Cacti is the plural of cactus," he corrected with a chuckle, shoving both hands into his pockets now. "And the flower has already been cut. It will die, no matter what you do with it now. So go nuts."

"Oh," I said for lack of a better response to his unsettling instructions. "Well, thanks again. I guess you should come on in."

I hurried to the kitchen to find something to put my flower in. Surely, Grandma Grace had left a vase or two somewhere in here. In the end, I gave up searching and simply placed it in an empty pitcher that I'd used once or twice to make lemonade.

Drake definitely got points for bringing me a flower, I'd give him that. But since this wasn't an actual date, the points didn't matter a lick.

Come to think of it, I hadn't gone on a date since relocating to Elderberry Heights, nor had I wanted to go on one. At first, I'd been too busy settling into my new house and job while still pretending to make forward progress on my thesis. And now I was too busy solving murders, fighting mad mages, and corralling talking cats. At this rate, I'd be lucky to ever go on a real date again.

But Drake didn't need to know any of that.

I had one mission here and one mission alone—find out what he knew about ghosts and see if it could help with my little situation.

7

"So is this a Netflix and chill situation, or…?" Drake raised an eyebrow and smiled at me suggestively.

I couldn't suppress the shudder that wracked through me at that thought. "Eww, no. Just give me five minutes and then I'll be ready to go out."

"Go where?" he asked, following me toward the hall.

"I don't know. Wherever you want," I called over my shoulder before stepping inside the bathroom and closing the door.

"You're the one who asked me out," he shouted from the other side. "I assumed you had a plan."

I bit my lip to keep myself from giving it to him straight. If I ranted about how I'd never meant to invite him on this so-called date, he probably wouldn't be up to sharing what he knew about ghosts. So for now, I'd just have to play along.

"How about a moonlit walk?" I suggested once I emerged from

the bathroom, my look now complete. That at least put me in a better mood.

"Pretty eyes," Drake said with an approving nod. "I like that look on you."

"You know about makeup?" I squeaked.

"Not much, but I make it my business to know a little bit about a lot of things. Keeps life interesting. And, sure, I could go for a walk." He grinned and motioned for me to lead the way.

Suddenly I felt nervous.

Drake clearly paid a lot better attention to his surroundings than I previously gave him credit for. Did that mean I'd given off some kind of vibe suggesting I wanted to date him?

Outside, Drake offered me the crook of his arm, and I looped mine through, feeling extra fancy as we strolled through the neighborhood.

"So how'd you get into the bean business?" he asked as he kept his eyes fixed on the distant horizon.

"Putting myself through graduate school," I answered by rote. His was a question I'd answered often, especially when my professors and fellow students asked why I was distracting myself with this temporary job when I could simply finish my degree and find a much better gig. "How about you?"

"Just following orders." He flashed me an impish grin.

"What? Whose orders?"

He let out a fatigued sigh. "It's a condition of my trust fund. I have to keep a steady job to collect. So just to stick it to my old man, I keep the lowliest job possible, doing the exact opposite of what he'd intended for me."

"So you're a trust fund baby? That explains a few things," I said, thinking back to his shiny sports coupe.

"Darling, I'm a trust fund man, and don't you forget it." He smiled charmingly, and I couldn't help but laugh. This was something we had in common, at least. The people in our lives expected more of us—or rather different things. I knew I'd finish my degree eventually, but I still had no idea what I actually wanted for my life. In truth, I'd chosen Sociology as my field of study because it seemed to be one of the broadest majors available. I'd then signed on to grad school because that's what you were supposed to do when your bachelor's degree didn't offer a clear career path.

I still preferred that life be full of surprises, and settling into a 9-to-5 felt like the exact opposite of that.

"Don't you get bored, though?" I asked Drake now. "With only working part-time and having no aspirations outside of continuing to collect?" He didn't need to know that my own aspirations were as of yet undefined.

"Bored? No way. And who says I don't have aspirations. Like I said, I like to know a little bit about a lot of things. A modern renaissance man."

"Like gardening," I supplied with a slight grin. "And makeup."

He nodded. "And ghosts."

Oh, good. He'd given me the lead in I needed. I jumped for it. "Actually, I was wondering about that."

He hung his head and laughed. “Of course, you were. You don’t think I knew that in the parking lot?”

I stopped walking and stared after him. “But you—“

He also stopped a few paces ahead and then turned to study me. “I turned the situation to my advantage. I’ve been wanting to take you out for a long time. I figured this way you’d want it, too.”

“Sneaky.” Now my smile was so big it was busting at the seams.

He winked at me. “Or genius.”

“I’ll stick with sneaky,” I answered with a laugh, then began walking again and looped my arm through his once more. “So are you going to tell me about the ghosts?”

“Ghost,” he corrected. His smile had been replaced by a clenched jaw and furrowed brow. “I’ve only ever seen the one.”

“Tell me about it,” I practically begged as I gave his forearm a little squeeze.

His expression lightened again. “Well, I guess I got what I wanted out of tonight—that is, some extra time with you. I suppose it’s only fair to give you what you wanted. One ghost story coming right up.”

He cleared his throat to begin…

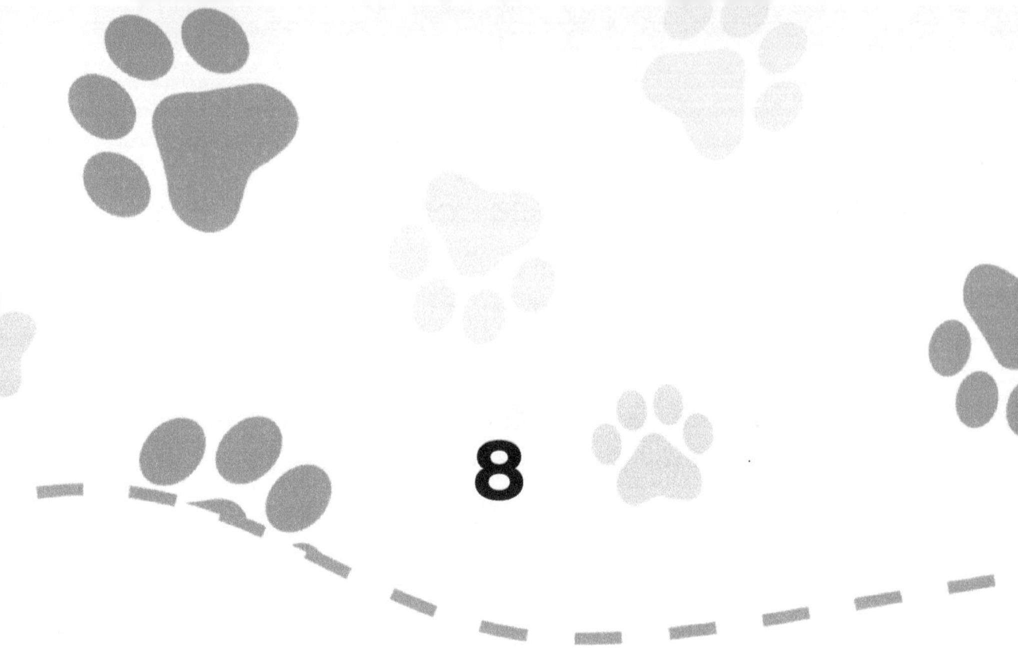

8

"Okay, so it was a dark and stormy night..."

I groaned and flung my head back dramatically. "Seriously?"

"If you want the story, then you've gotta let me set the scene," Drake said, his dark hair falling into his eyes as he smiled at me from just one side of his mouth.

I rolled my eyes and motioned for him to go ahead.

"Like I was saying, it was a dark and stormy night." He widened his eyes and glared at me, daring me to protest.

When I kept mum, he smiled with the other half of his mouth, too.

"I'd just turned twenty-one, which meant I'd finally come into my trust fund, and now I was in the process of driving all over the country in search of a new place to settle down. The only requirement? That it be as far away from my parents as possible. I was on my way to Miami when a giant storm whipped up, so I pulled over to the side of the road to wait it out. While I sat there, this lady in white appeared out of nowhere." His eyes became vacant as he journeyed deeper into the memory, and I had no doubt he was seeing the scene unfold anew in his mind's eye.

Drake took a deep, stuttering breath before continuing. "She wore this old-fashioned gown and no shoes. I could barely see her through the thick sheet of rain, but it was enough to tell that she was semi-transparent."

I gasped. "Wow, you really did see a ghost."

"Why would I lie about it?" he asked with one dark eyebrow raised in question.

The intensity of his gaze made me let go of his arm and take a small step to the side. "You're right. I'm sorry. Go ahead."

He shrugged. "There's not much else to tell. Another car showed up, almost drove straight into the thing, but then skidded off road at the very last minute. A soccer mom van stopped to help the person who'd crashed. Eventually the rain stopped, and I carried on toward Miami. Stayed there for a few months but got sick of all the sun. I came back up to Georgia, looking for the place I'd seen the ghost. Eventually I gave up my search. That was when I saw the help wanted sign at Harold's and decided to settle in Elderberry Heights."

"Wow," I whispered in awe, even though I had yet to process his story in its entirety. "So you definitely believe in ghosts?"

"Definitely," he declared unequivocally as if he'd been asked whether the sky was blue. "I've toured haunted houses and talked to psychic mediums in the time since, but everyone I've found has been a fraud."

I grabbed him by the shoulder and waited for him to bend down so I could whisper, "What if I told you I had a ghost materializing in my house right now?"

Drake's eyes lit up with intrigue. "Then I'd ask what we're doing out here. Can I see it? Can I talk to it?" He looked like a kid at Christmas.

"I'm not sure it can talk yet, but I know it's there. Weak, but seems to be getting stronger." I was proud of myself for not mentioning the cats in my explanation.

I worried that he'd ask questions I didn't know how to answer, but instead he whipped around and began walking quickly back toward my house, so eager he was to see this ghost for himself.

"That's my biggest regret, you know," he said as I struggled to match his pace. "That I just sat in my car the whole time rather than getting out and trying to communicate with it."

"But you said that a car ran it through," I reminded him, wrapping my arms around my torso as we walked. Even though it wasn't the slightest bit cold out, I still needed that added bit of comfort to counteract how this conversation had started making me feel.

He nodded. "Yes, another car scared it off, but there were several minutes of the spirit just floating there. It seemed like maybe she was waiting for someone or something."

This was getting creepy. I mean, it had already started pretty creepily, but the more Drake shared of his otherworldly experience, the more I began to worry about how my own might play out.

Could my house ghost even be scared off? And if I tried too hard to get rid of it, could the cats and I end up missing an important message from the other side?

If only I knew...

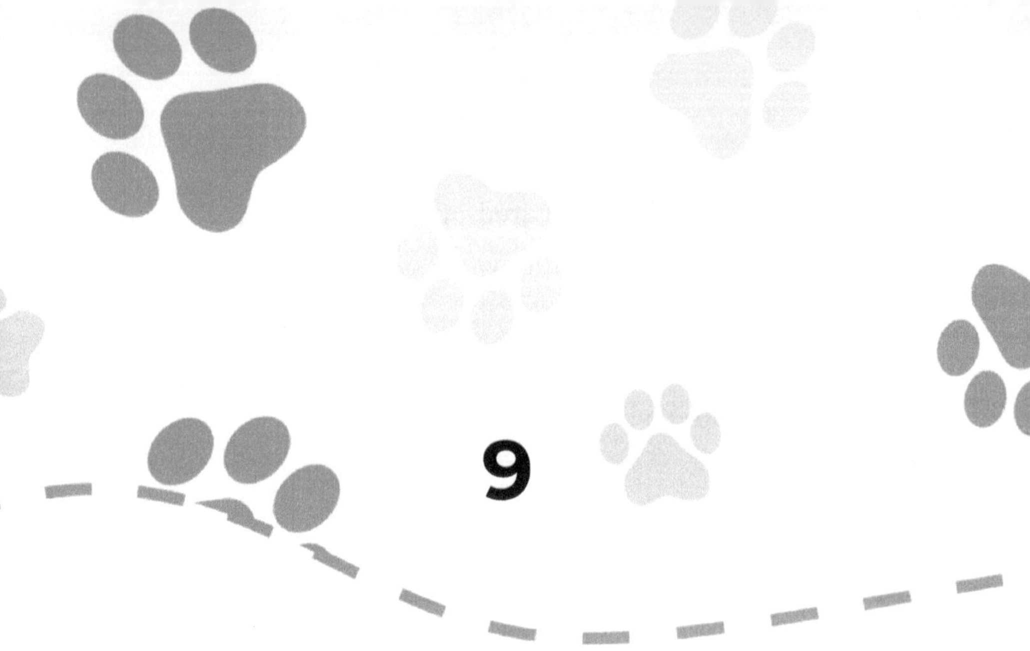

9

I led Drake back to my house and invited him inside to meet my baby ghost. I felt much better allowing him in this time. He now knew where we stood as far as this evening's non-date, and he'd already confided in me with his ghostly experience.

Granted, I still hoped he'd clear out before the cats returned from Nocturna. I didn't think I could endure another merciless round of their teasing.

"Well? Where is it?" he asked eagerly, glancing all around the house as if he'd be able to see it with his naked eyes.

"I'm not sure it's out yet. I think it's strongest at night, and the sun has only just gone down," I explained as I pointed to the top corner of the narrow hallway leading to my bedroom.

Drake marched right over to the spot I'd pointed out and reached up a hand with outstretched fingers.

"What are you doing?" I guffawed, resisting the urge to slap my palm into my forehead. "Trying to give the thing a high five?"

He turned back toward me and made a face, not embarrassed as I'd expect but more playful. "I'm checking to see if there's a temporal anomaly."

I chuffed at this. "And? Is there?"

"Well, I just realized that I have no idea what a temporal anomaly would feel like. Yeah, I've seen a ghost before, but that was more dumb luck than anything." He tilted his head to the side. "How did you know it was here?"

My heart thudded in my chest. I hated lying, but telling him the truth about Merlin would result in me being locked away in some dodgy magical prison for the rest of my life. That one simple fact made lying essential, but it didn't make me good at it.

"Oh, it's my, uh, intuition," I hedged. "Sometimes I can hear things other people can't." That was true, if only because the cats chose to talk to me instead of most other humans.

His eyes widened, and he seemed to look at me with a fresh perspective. "Whoa. So you actually heard it, then? Did it speak to you, like in words?"

I shook my head quickly. "No, no words. It's more like the sound of, uh, waves crashing softly on the beach."

"How does one crash softly?" he asked with a chuckle.

I couldn't tell whether that was a rhetorical question, so I chanced an answer. "It's hard to explain. Like *shhspspspspshh.*"

"Sounds like how some people call their cats," he pointed out with another soft laugh.

I smiled awkwardly. “Haha, yeah, it kind of does. Anyway, maybe I’m panicking over nothing. I mean, it all sounds pretty crazy, right?”

Drake walked back toward me at the other end of the hall. “Crazy is just what people like to call things they don’t quite understand. For what it’s worth, I believe you about your ghost, and I think it’s pretty freaking cool.”

“Thanks,” I said with a sigh of relief.

Drake raised his hand to touch my forearm. “You’re pretty freaking cool, Gracie. There’s something different about you. Especially lately. And, well, I really, really like it.”

I swallowed hard. “Th-thank you.”

His eyes softened around the edges as he ran his palm up my arm. “Look,” he murmured. “I know I backed you into this date, and that you were too nice to say no. But you can say no now. Okay?”

I nodded as his hand finally reached my shoulder.

He took another step forward. “May I kiss you?”

Oh, wow. That came out of nowhere. “No!” I said, perhaps a bit too emphatically.

Drake immediately dropped his hand and took a step back. He wore a smile, but it was definitely forced.

“I’m sorry,” I mumbled. “It’s just that I have a lot going on in my life right now, and—”

Drake held up a palm. “It’s okay. I get it. I didn’t think you were into me, but I had to find out for sure. I’ll leave you to your evening. If you need any more help with your ghost or just want to hang out, you know where to find me.”

He moved past me and made a beeline for the door.

"Drake, I'm sorry!" I called before rushing after him. "I do like you, and I've enjoyed hanging out with you tonight. But I just don't know you that well yet. And the part about having too much going on to make space for a relationship. That's one-hundred percent true."

He tilted his head slightly to the side. "You don't have to explain it to me. I'm definitely an acquired taste."

"Hey, then maybe I'll acquire it after we spend more time together," I blurted out stupidly. I didn't feel that way about Drake, and I wasn't sure I ever could.

He paused with his hand on the doorknob. "So you think you might get a craving for some vitamin D later?"

My mouth fell open. I tried to issue a response, but it came out as more of a disgusted groan.

Drake spun around to face me. "D for Drake! That's all I meant! D for Drake. Not… the other thing."

I nodded mutely, my eyes still wide from shock.

"Yeah, I'll just go jump off a bridge now," he said, pulling the door open and stepping outside.

For a moment, I debated going after him, but then—

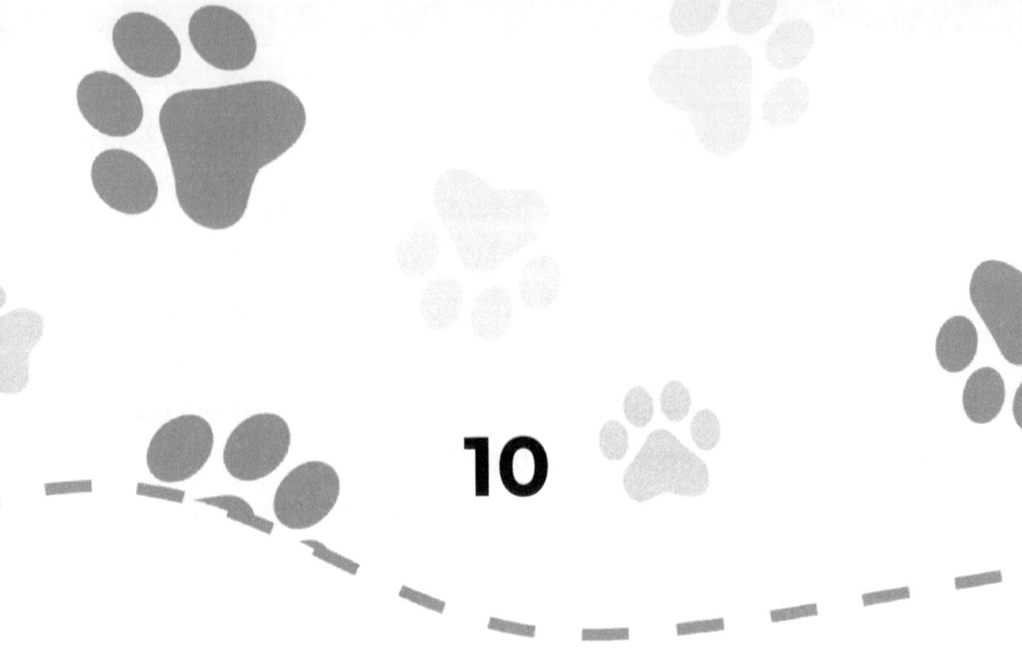

10

"Out of my way, out of my way!" Merlin yowled as he and Luna popped out from the birdbath in a cascade of green sparks.

"Hush, or someone will see you!" I whisper-yelled from my spot in the doorway. I glanced toward the road and was relieved to see that Drake had made his getaway before the magical display on my front lawn.

"That was a close one," Merlin muttered as he and Luna passed by me on their way inside the house.

I shut the door and locked it. Just in case.

"What happened?" I asked, almost afraid to hear their answer.

Luna stretched to lick Merlin's forehead, and he visibly let go of some of the tension he'd carried home with him.

"Thanks. I needed that," he purred to his lady love while continuing to ignore me.

Luna attached herself to Merlin's side. I wouldn't have been able to pry them apart if I tried. And I definitely knew better than to try.

"We ran into some cats from Merlin's past, and they weren't exactly happy to see him. Or to see us together," she explained in that lilting voice of hers.

"What did they do?" I asked. Merlin was hardly more than a kitten. Him taking me on as his familiar was the act that officially made him a full-fledged witch, and that had happened very recently. How could such a young cat already have such bitter enemies?

"They challenged him to a duel, which he—" She narrowed her eyes at Merlin. "—then foolishly accepted."

"Whoa, you could have died tonight?" I spat with equal parts surprise and anxiety. "What were you thinking?"

"He wasn't thinking," Luna answered with a sigh. "But you must also remember that we cats do things differently than humans."

"Duels with guns, right? Like in Hamilton?" I pictured Merlin wearing a period costume and circling another cat in colonial garb while they rapped about their grievances. Now there's a show I would pay good money to see.

"Certainly not," Luna said, her lip curled in disgust, almost as if she'd been able to picture the scene playing out in my head.

"Then?" I asked seriously.

Merlin spoke up at last, his fur twitching at the shoulders. "It wouldn't have been so bad. We cats fight with what's at our disposal."

He raised a paw and unsheathed his claws. "We use a combination of magic and good-old fashioned rough-housing."

Luna nudged him until he put his weapons away. "Cats strike with their paws. Magical cats strike with phantom claws."

I shook my head, not understanding the strange metaphor.

"We bat at each other's magic within," he explained, then pressed his ears back against his head, raised a paw, and hit at the air. "Like that, but we don't aim to injure faces or hurt pride. We attack each other's magic until one of us doesn't have enough left to continue the duel."

"You kill each other?" The thought seemed so barbaric. But I guess if humans could take each other's lives, then so, too, could other species. As much as I wished they wouldn't.

Merlin shuddered. "No, it's much worse. The loser lives on without magic. A fate worse than—"

"Ah-ah-ahem!" I cleared my throat loudly to stop him.

"What's your problem?" Merlin asked, then glanced to Luna at his side and dipped his head in regret. "Oh, right. Sorry."

"I know you didn't mean it," she said softly, still clearly hurt by his words. "Just as I know you wouldn't want to risk your magic when we have an imminent threat in our own home."

"Why did those other cats even want to fight you? Surely, nothing you've done could have been *that* bad." Sometimes he was sarcastic and off-putting, but overall, Merlin was a good cat. He didn't seem like the enemy type... Well, other than that thing with Luna. Actually, you know what? Never mind. He'd clearly made his fair share of enemies in his short life. Maybe that was just the way with magic. I was still new to this world and learning all its quirks.

Merlin growled. "Well, before Luna was my girl, she was Tom's."

"Tom," I repeated. "Tom Cat?"

"Yes, and when he saw her without magic, he blamed me. Tom became so angry, he challenged me as part of some misguided attempt to avenge her."

"That's actually kind of sweet," I said with a sappy smile.

Luna shook her head adamantly. "I do not need to be avenged by Merlin, Tom, or anyone else. I make my own choices, and I fight my own battles with or without magic. Of course, Merlin agreed to the duel before I had a chance to tell him any of this."

Merlin nodded somberly. "And when Luna made her displeasure known, the only thing we could do was run and hope we made it back through the portal before Tom and his cronies could catch us."

"Please tell me you got what we needed regarding the ghost before all this went down," I mumbled, upset.

"Of course we did," Luna answered with a wide grin, which quickly faltered. "Although it would probably be best if Merlin doesn't show his face in Nocturna for a while."

"But without Merlin, neither of us can go."

"I know," she said with a flick of her tail. "So consider Nocturna off our resource list for the moment."

Great. Our direct connection to the magical world had been temporarily severed while we struggled to deal with a very real, very immediate magical problem.

That would make things so much easier.

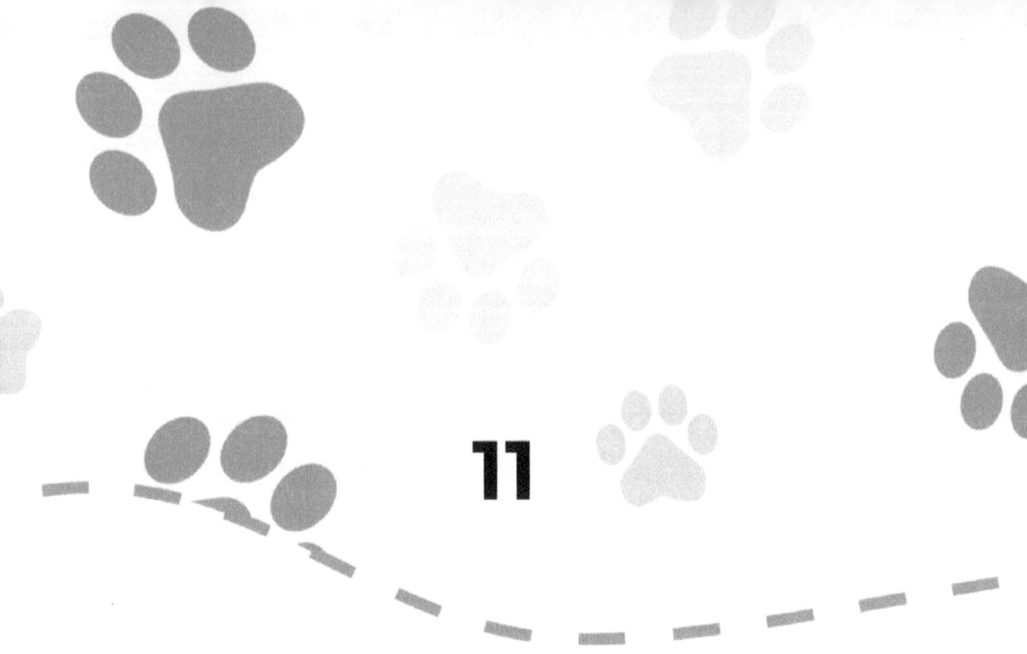

11

"But you said you got what we needed," I pointed out, hoping very much that this was true. Without the ability to access other magical creatures in Nocturna, we'd be truly alone in dealing with our unwanted house ghost.

"Relax, will you?" Merlin spat as he stared at me with large green eyes. "Don't you remember rule one?"

Yes, I remembered that I was supposed to trust everything he said without question. A terrible rule, but one he insisted on enforcing.

I pressed my lips into a firm line and waited for him to share more.

And once he was satisfied with my quiet compliance, he went ahead with his explanation. "We went to the library and found a spell we can use to trap the ghost."

My jaw dropped open. "Nocturna has a library?" I squealed with glee. Oh, how badly I now wanted to go.

"Yes. What's the big deal?" He wagged his tail wildly like one of those giant wavy men in front of an auto dealership.

"Nothing. I just love books, and—"

"Can we focus on what's important here?" Merlin snapped, clearly still out of sorts from his near duel with the rival Tom Cat.

Luna fixed me with a kindly gaze. "The library is lovely, but it is made for cats. I'm afraid you wouldn't fit through the door, dear."

Well, there was that dream dashed. I hadn't even been granted proper time to picture myself ensconced in stacks of magical old books. *Sigh.*

Merlin lay down in loaf form with his paws tucked beneath him, apparently now delegating the task of dealing with me to Luna.

She stood and stretched, keeping her tail high in the air. "We found the spell we need, and I should have all the ingredients for it in my garden. Since I am no longer magical, I won't be able to mix the potion myself, but I still have the knowledge. I can guide Merlin in its creation. Or even you."

Oh, that was right. As Merlin's familiar, I was also a vessel for his magic. Kind of like a portable battery charger. I couldn't cast any magic myself, but I always had a ready source for my feline overlord.

"One problem," I realized aloud. "Your garden is at Virginia's old place. We don't have access to it."

She grinned a devilish grin. "It's outside. All we have to do is walk up and take what we need."

I twisted my mouth in a grimace. "Isn't that stealing, though?"

Merlin laughed. "After all we've been through, you're worried about stealing? Besides, that garden is Luna's. She planted it, cared for it. How could it be anyone's but hers?"

"Don't think about it too hard. You'll just give yourself a headache," Luna suggested. She then pressed herself into Merlin's side. "Well, c'mon. We need to get those ingredients if we're to dispatch our ghost."

I sighed. She was right, of course. That didn't make me feel any better about sneaking around on a property that didn't belong to us. Just look at all the trouble it had gotten us into before!

Still, once the cats had made up their minds, there was no convincing them otherwise.

I placed a hand on the Maine Coon witch's back, resigned to what would happen next.

Merlin just had to blink twice, and the three of us were transported to the garden.

Well, actually, we ended up at the far edge of the yard near a thick tree that I knew all too well. I shivered, remembering the times I'd been here before. None of them had been pleasant. First Merlin and I had broken in, only to be threatened by our then-enemy, Luna. She also kidnapped me and used me to make a love spell, although I didn't know that at the time. The worst memory of all, though, was the showdown we had with Virginia and the wicked illusion witch who'd been pulling her strings. The same tree we found ourselves standing by now had been animated and fought right alongside us.

Creepy, creepy, creepy.

Was it any wonder I was so hesitant about returning now in the dead of night?

A flash of red caught my eye. I turned quickly, half expecting to see a crazed witch running right at me. But it was only the FOR SALE sign flapping in the gentle breeze.

Luna drew up to my side and said, "Virginia had no family. No next of kin. That's part of why I chose her. It's much easier to make a familiar of someone without attachments."

"Is that why you chose me?" I asked Merlin, wondering if I should be offended. Did the witchy cats choose people human society didn't want? Did this mean my cats thought I was a loser who wouldn't be missed?

"That's why I chose your grandmother," Merlin explained without looking my way. "I chose you by default when she left."

I chuffed. "Thanks for reminding me."

"Hey, I'm happy with my choice, however it was made."

That at least made me smile. "Okay, so we're here for ingredients, right? Let's get what we need and go. Whether or not anyone lives here now, I still don't feel right about snooping around."

"Your sense of morality is seriously questionable at times," Merlin said as he raised his head and sniffed the air. "But so be it."

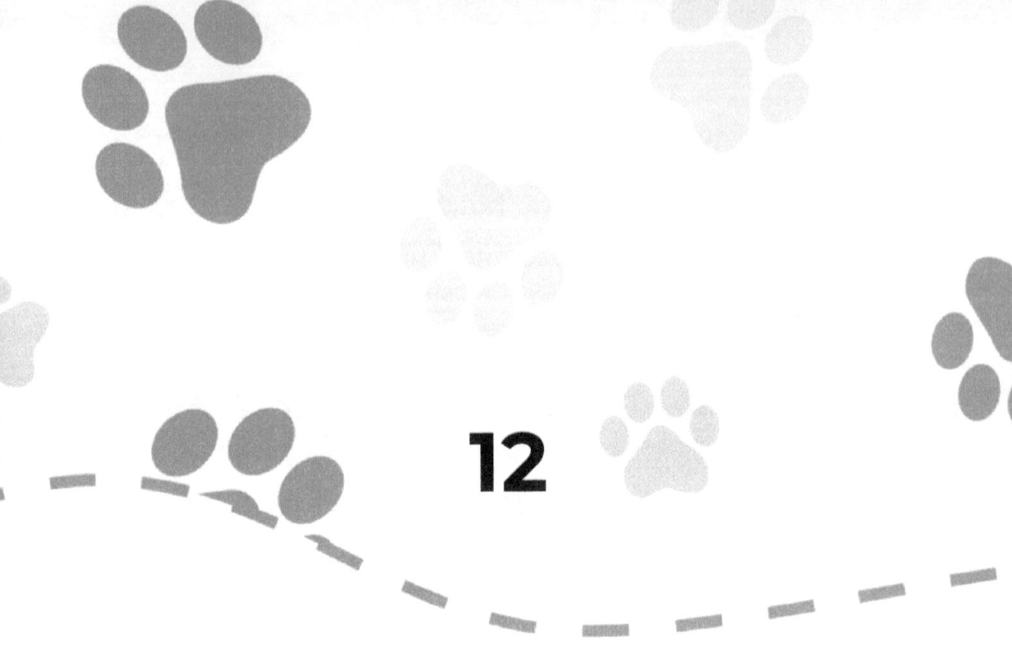

12

Luna led the way into the back garden. I had a hard time seeing much in the darkness of night, but neither cat hesitated as they plucked various herbs and flowers from the ground and laid them in a pile at my unmoving feet.

"Are you almost done?" I asked after several minutes of this.

That was when a flood light lit up the backyard, blinding me in its sudden brightness.

"Hello!" someone called from the side of the house as footsteps hurried our way. "Who's out here?"

I froze in place, hoping Merlin would transport us out of there before the other person made it back.

No such luck, though. Honestly, I don't think he even tried.

"Gracie?" the other person shouted with a gasp. "What are you doing back here?"

Finally my eyes began to adjust to the light. I squinted at the new arrival and watched as it slowly morphed into the familiar shape of my friend and boss, Kelley Carmine.

"Hi," I said with an awkward wave.

"What are you doing here?" she asked, stepping closer without hesitation now that we'd identified each other.

"Oh, you know..." I laughed to disguise my nerves. "Taking my cats for a nice moonlit stroll."

She tilted her head to the side. "In my back garden?"

I took a step back. "Your garden? I thought this place was for sale. I'm sorry, I didn't realize—"

"Oh, you're fine." Kelley waved her hand dismissively and made a funny face. "It's not officially mine yet. My offer was accepted just today, though, which means it will be soon."

"Kelley, congrats! That's amazing!" I broke into a relieved smile. I didn't like snooping around my friend's place uninvited, but it was much better than if it were a stranger's.

Her cheeks reddened slightly. "Yeah, now that I own a business here, I'm trying to put down some roots. It felt weird to live in my dad's old place, so I did some searching and found this cute little cottage. I just came by to take some measurements so I can start planning."

"Well, you picked a nice house. This garden is very pretty."

We both looked toward the rows of herbs and flowers that filled almost half of the back yard.

Kelley shook her head. "Do you think so? I don't even know what half these plants are. I was actually thinking of tearing everything out and replacing it with tulips. That's my favorite flower, and I hear they're much easier to take care of than some others."

Luna gasped and fell over onto the grass.

"Um, is your cat okay?"

"Oh, yes. Luna's fine. They're both fine. Sorry about appearing unexpectedly like this. The cats kind of lead the way, and I follow." This was the best misdirect I'd come up with yet, because it was totally true—just not in the current context.

"That's okay. Like I said, it's not mine yet. But when it is, you and your cats will be welcome anytime." Kelley then grabbed my hand and tugged me along after her. "Since you're here, you might as well come in and see it. Can you believe it, Gracie? I just bought an entire house! Or I guess I'm about to, but still! A house!"

I laughed as we made our way toward the front door together. While it was strange that Kelley had purchased this exact house, I wasn't the least bit surprised she was soon to be a homeowner. Her father would have been so proud.

I, however, couldn't let her know that I'd already been inside because then I'd have to come up with lies to explain myself.

Kelley fiddled with the Realtor's lockbox on the door and extracted a key. "You have to use your imagination a little, okay? The previous owner had terrible taste, but my agent assures me that everything will be cleared out of here well before I move in."

I smiled and nodded as she fitted the key into the lock above the doorknob.

"That's a lot of floral print," I exclaimed as soon as she flicked on the lights. Of course it was a lot of floral print—this place had been inhabited by a garden witch and her familiar.

"It's kind of sad, isn't it? I don't know how the previous owner died, but I know she had nobody to claim this house or any of her things. When I think of her, I picture this poor little old lady locked up in this time capsule of a house with only a cat or two to keep her company." She glanced over at me and worried her lip. "No offense."

Boy, had she gotten Virginia wrong.

"No offense about the cats?" I asked with a playful grin.

"About your house. I didn't mean to imply that retro can't be cool. It's just—" She motioned around the room. "There's so much floral in here."

Well now, apparently I'd become an old lady stereotype. *Fabulous.*

"My house belonged to my grandma," I explained as we both strode toward the kitchen. "I have lots of good memories that happened inside that house exactly as it is. I don't have the heart to change it."

Kelley's face immediately crumpled into a frown. "Oh, I'm so sorry. I didn't realize… My condolences."

I chuckled. "Grandma Grace isn't dead. She's just in Florida."

"Well, that's good, I suppose." She winked at me, then guided me into the small formal dining room. "Someday I'll have you and the others from work over for a real sit-down dinner party."

"Sounds great," I enthused.

"Oh, it will be," she promised, her eyes practically glazing over as if she were seeing that future scene before her.

I, however, couldn't see past Virginia and the horrible events that occurred here.

Well, at least I knew Virginia was haunting me and would probably leave Kelley alone. Because as hard as it might be to protect myself from an angry spirit, I imagined it would be even harder to help a friend without revealing the existence of magic.

13

After showing me the master suite, Kelley walked me back out into the hall and turned to me with worry reflecting in her pale eyes. “Gracie, do you think I’m taking on too much at once? With the coffee shop and now this house? I mean, I’ve hardly been in town for a month and, well, I’m kind of in a vulnerable spot, what with meeting my dad and then losing him, and—”

I placed a hand on her shoulder. “Kelley, it’s okay. It is a lot, but you’ve got this. You’ve already made such amazing progress with the coffeehouse, and you’ll do great things with this house, too.”

She blinked up at me with glistening eyes. “Do you mean it?”

“Of course I do. I believe in you, and I’ll be with you every step of the way.” It seemed I’d accidentally become Kelley’s mentor by helping her through her father’s death. That was okay, though. I really liked her and wanted her to be happy. I also hoped she never found out that I had initially suspected her of murdering her dad. I now knew she would never do such an awful thing. She just didn't have it in her.

Kelley sighed and offered me a tight hug. "I'm so lucky to have a friend like you. Seriously. It's like there's this vice around my chest. And as we move closer and closer to the grand re-opening, it tightens a little each day. It's already getting hard to breathe now. What will it be like when the big day is finally here? I worry that I won't have any oxygen left."

I patted the back of her head like one would do with an upset child. In truth, Kelley was little more than a child. She had an awful lot on her plate for an eighteen-year-old. Even though I was still pretty young myself, I had nowhere near as many responsibilities thrust upon me—that is, if you chose to ignore the whole magical cat with a seemingly unending supply of enemies.

"It's anxiety," I told her, recalling something my grandma had once told me. "It may seem like a bad thing, but it's good, too."

Kelley pulled back and looked at me like I was crazy. "A good thing? How?"

"It means you care. Life is so much better when you have things and people that matter to you. And the best part? You can harness that anxiety as motivation. Fuel. Use that nervous energy to propel you toward your goal, and you'll be there in no time."

"Seems like you speak from experience," she said with a tight smile.

I nodded. "Well, from my grandma's, at least."

"It's good advice. Did your grandma have anything to say about love?"

I widened my eyes at this. "Love!"

My friend turned bright red and looked toward the floor. "Well, it's a crush, and I know I have no extra time to think about things like this, but every time I see him come into the coffee shop, I— Oops, I've said too much."

"Kelley!" I gasped, grabbing her forearm and forcing her to look up at me. "Please tell me it's not Drake."

She shrugged coyly. "I know, I know. He's just so cool, like he doesn't care what anyone thinks of him. I wish I had that kind of confidence."

"It's important to you what others think, and that's okay. It's because you care about them. That's way better than Drake's cool confidence."

"Maybe, but he's just so smart, and he has all this random knowledge."

"He knows a little bit about a lot of things," I said, recalling his words from earlier that night.

"Exactly!" Kelley crooned. "Do you think I've got a shot with him?"

"Well, you're kind of his boss. I'm pretty sure there's laws against that kind of thing."

Her features pinched into a frown. "You're right. What was I thinking? I don't have time for a relationship right now anyway."

"Hey. There will be time for all that later. And you're going to make some guy very happy one day. Look at you with the business and the house!" I hated to discourage her, but I also knew that Drake was interested in someone else—me. What I would give for that not to be true, especially now that I knew Kelley would happily take my place as the object of his affection.

She smiled. "You're right about that, too. I should probably let you get back to your cats before they run away on you, huh?"

Right, the cats.

I gave her another quick hug. "Thanks for showing me around. It's a lovely house. Congrats again, Kelley, and see you at work!"

I let myself out and raced back around the house, using my phone light to guide me. I found both cats standing near the old well that had served as Luna's cauldron.

Luna had a lovesick expression on her face, and Merlin was the very picture of rage. Had I just walked in on my cats canoodling? *Really?*

"If you two have kittens, I am not raising them!" I growled into the night.

"That's enough out of you," Merlin growled right back. "It's not our fault you took forever in there. We had to do something to pass the time. Now are we ready to go, your highness?"

I nodded stupidly.

"Then lay your hand on me, and I'll teleport us back home," the cat commanded.

I hesitated. "Um, that's okay."

Luna stepped forward, her blue eyes taking on a red hue in my flashlight. "Gracie, dear. I know what you're thinking, and it's all right. We were only grooming each other."

Grooming, uh-huh.

Still, I didn't want to stay stuck in this awkward situation any longer than I had to. I placed a hand on Merlin's head.

He blinked twice, and we were home.

14

"Wait," I cried as my feet touched down on the linoleum kitchen floor. "We forgot the ingredients for the spell!"

"Already took care of that while we were waiting," Merlin said, jerking his head toward the table where an array of plant life had been spread across the surface.

"What's this for?" I asked, picking up the only non-organic object on the table—a ceramic garden decoration shaped like a frog with a giant, open mouth.

Luna smiled wistfully. "This was Virginia's. It used to sit on the edge of the porch. She used it to hide her spare house key."

"Yeah, her and everyone else in the state of Georgia," I quipped. Seriously, why have a spare key at all if you were going to make its hiding spot so obvious? "Why did you bring it back? Are you missing her, Luna?"

The normally docile cat snarled at me. "Heavens no! Why would you even think I'd miss that monster? We need something that belonged to the spirit in life. It will help us summon and trap her."

"As opposed to some other ghost?" I deadpanned. "Because we have so many ghosts knocking on our door."

Luna shook her head at my snippiness. "The potency of any spell is much stronger if you add an object that belongs or belonged to the intended recipient."

Oh, yes. I knew this. "Like when you took Merlin's hair for the love spell?" I pointed out with one eyebrow raised.

She let out a little cough. "Precisely."

"So is everything ready? Can we make the potion now?"

"Carry it outside for us, and we can get started," the she-cat told me, and I was quick to comply.

Once again, though, I questioned the wisdom of keeping the cauldron in our front yard, but it was at least late enough that we probably wouldn't need to worry about gawking neighbors.

The cats worked together in mixing the brew while I kept my eyes on the street, just in case I needed to sound the alarm.

Thankfully, it only took a few minutes for them to finish their witchy work.

"Gracie, come grab this," Luna called when they were done.

Inside the bird bath sat the little ceramic frog, its mouth filled with a dark green liquid. It looked like one of those disgusting concoctions my mother used to make in her juicer and then try to force me to drink in the mornings before school.

I didn't care that it had antioxidants, I refused to ingest something that looked like it had been scraped from the bottom of a pond—and smelled that way, too.

I could hardly suppress a gag as I lifted the frog full of potion and carried it into the house.

"Put it in the hallway near the back corner," Luna instructed. "The same place we sensed the ghost forming last night."

"Remind me what this will do," I said after following her instructions to the letter.

"It will help Virginia to materialize faster, and then it will trap her in place so we can deal with her."

"And how do we plan to deal with her?"

"Eh, we'll figure it out when the time comes," Merlin added with a long, lazy stretch.

"Wonderful," I muttered, pouring some crunches into the cats' bowl for them. "So glad to know we're doing everything we can to make sure we stay safe. Now if you don't need me any longer, I'm going to bed."

Both cats raced over to eat. Before lowering his head to the bowl, though, Merlin glanced over to the counter and frowned. "Luna, my love, did we forget one of the ingredients for our potion tonight?"

She stopped eating and raised her head. "No. Everything that should have been included was."

"Then what's that?" he asked, pointing his nose toward the counter where the black cactus dahlia Drake had given me still sat in a half-empty glass pitcher.

Both cats glanced toward the counter and then me.

"Gracie," Luna prattled in a sing-song voice. "That's not from my garden. Does it belong to you?"

No, no, no. I had hoped we'd all been busy enough that we could just skip past the part where the cats teased me about my non-date. They'd already laid into me pretty hard before Drake came over, and I just didn't have the energy to endure their teasing a second time.

"It was a gift. Don't worry about it," I said, crossing my arms over my chest.

"From your new boyfriend?" Luna cooed, her tail waving from side to side in delight.

"What was his name again?" Merlin asked, kicking up his back leg to scratch behind his ear.

"Drake," Luna answered promptly.

"Not my boyfriend. Not even close," I said through clenched teeth.

"But he gave you a flower," Luna pointed out. "Isn't that considered a romantic gesture among humans?"

"Yeah, he wants me. I don't want him. In fact, my other friend does. Ugh, never mind. Can we just move past this whole elementary school thing, please?"

"What's elementary school?" they both asked, completely transfixed on me now.

"It's a place human kids go when they're like six."

"I'm only one year old," Merlin said with a shrug.

"Me, too," Luna chimed.

"So I guess it's not past us then," Merlin said with a sinister smile. "Now tell us, did Drakey Wakey kiss you nighty wighty?"

"I'm going to bed!" I shouted, then stomped off and slammed my bedroom door for the second time that day.

15

I woke up the next morning to bright rays of sunlight shooting through my blinds. Ugh. I really needed to invest in some blackout curtains if I ever wanted to sleep past sunrise again.

After a quick pit stop to the bathroom, I trudged into the kitchen and straight to my favorite appliance, then popped in a dark roast pod and waited for it to brew.

My morning coffee was becoming increasingly important to me now that everything at Harold's was pumpkin spice flavored. I used to love getting those special lattes during the fall, but now that I'd been subjected to a PSL overdose at Kelley's hands, I firmly believed seasonal drinks were seasonal for a reason.

"What are you doing?" Merlin asked, hopping onto the counter and rubbing his face against the coffeemaker.

I pushed him to the side. "Don't do that. I hate it when you get your fur in my morning cuppa."

"But it's so warm and buzzy," he groaned.

"Speaking of warm and buzzy, I didn't like what I saw in the garden last night. I think it might be time to consider getting you and Luna fixed." My brain hadn't had the chance to wake up fully yet, but I still couldn't get that picture of them out of my head. It's like the disgusting scene was seared in my memory.

Merlin crept back up to the Keurig and rubbed his cheek against it again. This time he let out a contented purr as he asked, "Fixed? Why? We aren't broken. Well, I mean Luna's lost her magic, but other than that she's perfectly fine."

"It would be irresponsible to bring more kittens into the world, what with all the poor cats waiting in shelters." Also somehow I felt that my familiar duties would extend to playing nanny too, and my life was already complicated enough without having to be responsible for other living things—especially small and delicate living things.

"Wait. Are you saying—?" Merlin arched his back up and let out a terrible hiss. He even went so far as to take a swipe at me.

"You want to alter my privates? I thought such tales of human barbarism were but mere myths, made up to scare young witches at bedtime. But you... My own familiar? Please tell me you were joking!" He swooned and fell over onto his side, pumping his legs as if running in a dream. Apparently this is what a panic attack looked like on him.

Oops. I kept forgetting just how differently humans and cats viewed the world when it came to certain matters. Honestly, I should've known better on this one.

The coffee finished brewing, and I had to use a spoon to fish out the long, striped cat hair that had landed in my brew. I never should have initiated this conversation without a full cup of caffeine already buzzing through my system.

Unfortunately, since I'd started on this topic, I now needed to finish it. "It's a minimally invasive surgery, especially for male cats."

Merlin popped back onto his feet, but his hackles were still raised. "If it's such an easy surgery, then why don't you have it?"

"It's not exactly the same for humans. Besides, I may want kids one day."

Merlin became Halloween cat again. Yup, I definitely wasn't winning any points with him this morning. "And you don't think Luna and I would like to pass our love down to the next generation? Besides, if you'll recall, I'm the last living descendant of the original Merlin. I can't let such an important magical bloodline die with me."

"But what about the shelter cats?" I whimpered pathetically.

"Look, heart to heart here. Luna has already lost her magic. Don't take motherhood away from her, too."

I raised an eyebrow, then took a careful sip from my mug. And still wound up with cat hair in my mouth. *Gross!*

The cat sighed. "Again your sense of morality confounds me. Still, if the shelter cats are so important to you, we'll find a way to help them. There's plenty of room in Nocturna. You get them here, and I can get them there."

"You promise?" I took another swig of my morning java.

"If that's what it takes to maintain peace in my home while also keeping my privates intact, then I agree." He came to the edge of the counter with his tail raised amicably, and I patted him softly on the head.

"Thank you. While we're talking openly about this, I do think you and Luna should wait to start your family."

"Why? We're already a bonded pair. Cats don't need a piece of paper telling us what we know to be true in our hearts."

"Be that as it may, we're kind of dealing with a lot right now. With the ghost. And we both know Dash will be back before too long. It just doesn't seem like the right time to bring a child—or, um, litter—into the world."

"Fair point. Now are you done with this strange heart to heart? Because I am very, very done."

I flushed. "Yes, sorry."

"I mean, you didn't even ask about the ghost. After all the work we put in. You went straight to talking about my privates."

"You're right. I'm sorry. Now can we please stop talking about your privates?"

He shrugged. "If you don't want to talk about something, then don't start the conversation."

"Sorry, sorry, sorry. Now tell me about the ghost," I practically begged.

Merlin arched his back again, but this time in a stretch. He then jumped over to the table and waited for me to join him. "Well..." he began.

16

I hated when Merlin drew things out like this. "Well, what? Did we catch our ghost?" I demanded, and then realized something else strange about that morning. "Hey, where's Luna by the way?"

I almost never saw the cats apart from one another. Each morning when I woke up, they were together and basking in the glow of their new love.

Merlin sniffed at the air before responding to my questions. "Luna is out on a morning stroll. She said she needed some time to herself. From the smell of it, she's about two blocks out and making her return to us now."

Time to herself? Hmm. Did this mean trouble in paradise? The cats had already gone from lovers to bitter rivals and back to lovers again. I was beginning to think I had the Ross and Rachel of felines on my hands. They better not plan on taking a break any time soon, because I was so not prepared to deal with that!

I kept this all to myself, of course. Merlin and I had just been discussing family planning, and that hadn't gone over well. At all. I needed to resist the urge to play the role of therapist here. Those two were far more experienced in matters of the heart than I was, anyway.

When I didn't say anything in response to his news of Luna, Merlin continued on. This time telling me about the ghost. "It didn't come," he said with a bored yawn. "Luna and I waited all night, and that rotten ghost didn't even have the courtesy to drop in for a hello."

I gripped both hands around my coffee mug and sighed.

"That's a good thing, right? I mean, we don't actually want the ghost to be here."

"If it came here once, you can bet it will come again. By not returning last night, it's just drawing things out for everyone, and that irritates me." He flicked his tail to punctuate this remark.

"Maybe she knows we set a trap for her?" That would keep me away. Maybe it was stopping Virginia from returning as well.

"Maybe," he answered pensively. "I don't really know much about it. But I would assume she wouldn't know about the potion until she began to materialize, and by then, it would be too late." He had a point. There was so much we didn't know when it came to our baby ghost, and that made this whole thing so much harder.

The cat door flapped open noisily, and Luna came trotting inside.

"How was your walk, my love?" Merlin asked, then hopped down from the table to rub his face against hers. It was the scene with the coffeemaker all over again. Well, at least Luna was already covered in cat hair.

"It was nice to get some fresh air while I thought about why Virginia failed to visit us again last night," the white cat answered promptly.

Ah, so I'd been totally wrong about the whole trouble in paradise thing. I was glad I hadn't pushed the issue. I really needed to butt out of my cats' relationship and let them handle things for themselves. Lesson learned.

"You need to stop blaming yourself," Merlin said softly.

They both jumped up on the table to reengage me in the discussion.

"Tell him, Gracie," Luna begged, her blue eyes fraught with remorse. "Virginia was my familiar. I chose her. I failed to see that she had been corrupted. It's all my fault."

I reached out to stroke her back. "Merlin's right. You really can't blame yourself. Bad things happen to good people—um, cats—sometimes. That's just the way of life."

"Well, then life sucks," she said with a sniff.

"Sometimes," I agreed. "But you have a lot to be grateful for. Why, just this morning Merlin—" I stopped short. I was doing it again, interfering in their relationship. "Told me how lucky he is to have you."

The Maine Coon winked at me, and Luna appeared to relax somewhat.

"What conclusions did you reach on your walk? Why didn't Virginia visit us?" I prompted when I grew tired of the extended silence. That was the thing about talking with cats. They were huge fans of the dramatic pause. They also had no sense of urgency, meaning simple conversations could draw out for hours if I didn't help to push them along.

"Maybe the ghost wasn't Virginia," Luna said. "Maybe it wasn't even here for us at all, but rather for the house."

"That's an interesting theory," I said slowly, even though I 100% disagreed with her assessment.

"If it's Virginia, we're prepared with our potion. If it's not, then we have nothing to fear," Merlin summarized.

"Yes, I suppose that's right," I said, taking another sip of my coffee. It was now dangerously close to room temperature, so I chugged it down fast and then rose to make a fresh cup.

"Anything else we should do about this now?" I asked while I sifted through my bucket of multi-flavored K-cups and selected a nice French roast.

"Now we wait," Merlin said in a bored drone. "Either the ghost will return and we can deal with it then, or it won't return at all, and we'll be in the clear."

Luna and I both nodded our agreement, but somehow I doubted it would be as simple as Merlin claimed.

And I think he knew that, too.

17

Several days passed with no more signs of our spectral visitor. As much as I'd doubted Luna's theory, I now had to admit it was fully possible that some ghost other than Virginia had dropped by. Just in case, though, I called my Grandma Grace to make sure she was alive and well. She didn't have much time to talk since life in her retirement community was full of exciting social events that were not to be missed, but she assured me she'd never felt better and would drive up to visit soon.

And so as the days ticked past, I focused on work and even managed to get some thesis research in. Drake and I chatted more at work than we had in the past, but I made every effort to keep all of our interactions platonic so that Kelley wouldn't be jealous and he wouldn't get the wrong idea about me.

He was an okay guy, but I had no time for close human relationships while I was settling into my role as familiar. And when eventually I did re-enter the dating pool, I needed someone with more direction and ambition than Drake. I could just picture the two of us drifting through life on handouts from my grandma and his parents while we both continued to work at the coffee shop until the day we died. That was not the life I wanted—nor the one I deserved.

Kelley at least had enough chutzpah for the both of them. They'd be a great couple, if Drake ever decided to return her feelings. Whatever the outcome, it would be interesting to watch their story unfold.

I, for one, was glad I had time to consider such matters. With each new day that passed, I worried less about the ghost. Each night I slept better. Each day I was able to focus on the people and cats in my life, try new makeup techniques, and just generally relax and enjoy myself.

It was divine.

I was right in the middle of a fantastic dream in which I won a lifetime supply of cosmetics from my favorite cruelty-free company, when—

Meeeeeeeeh!

REOW! HISSS!

Meeeeeeeh!

I bolted upright in bed as both cats continued to caterwaul in the hallway. This could only mean one thing. Our ghost had returned. And just when I was starting to believe our first visit had been a fluke.

I pulled on the robe that hung from the back of my door and

stepped out into the hallway. Sure enough, both cats were going ballistic.

And I do mean ballistic.

Merlin had even begun kicking back his feet in that familiar chicken scratch maneuver, which meant—

"No! Stop! No lightning in the house!" I screamed, but my warning came too late.

A zipping bolt came crashing straight through the roof, illuminating the wayward spirit in the process. Suddenly a bright swatch of blue appeared right where my cats had been staring. Now I saw it, too.

Oh, Merlin. He'd meant to destroy the thing, but he'd only given it more power.

The house let out a giant whomp, and everything went silent—and even darker than before.

"Merlin, you fried the electricity," I shouted, unable to tear my eyes away from the transparent blue blob floating just a few feet away from me in the hallway.

And then it started to rain inside the house.

"Merlin!" I screamed.

"It wasn't me," he shouted back.

I raised my eyes and saw that—yes—the rain was coming through a newly made hole in the roof. That would not be cheap to repair. "You better be able to fix that with magic," I mumbled.

"You're worried about that when we now have this?" Luna cried, motioning toward the ghost frantically.

The sudden motion startled the spirit, and it took off down the hall and moved on to rattling about the kitchen.

"Why wasn't it captured by your spell?" I demanded of the cats.

Meeeeeeeeh!

REOW! HISSS!

Meeeeeeeh!

Not the answer I was looking for. Clearly they weren't much help in this situation, given their desire to scream about the ghost rather than to capture it.

Come to think of it, I'd been shouting a lot, too. Ugh.

Never mind my initial reaction. Someone had to deal with this thing, and I guessed that someone might as well be me.

I marched into the kitchen and stumbled right into the table. Ouch!

The only light came from the ghost itself, thanks to Merlin's lightning-induced blackout. The pulsing blue blob didn't appear human, but what else could it be?

"Hey, Virginia," I called out, working hard to hide the quiver in my voice. "Why are you here? What do you want?"

The ghost floated closer to me, and it took everything I had not to run out of the house screaming. I guess I couldn't hold the cats' reaction against them when I wished I could do the exact same thing.

The spirit continued to inch forward, slow as molasses. I could have run, but I stood transfixed, unable to pull my eyes away from the spectral sight.

Moments later, it completed its journey, stopping less than a foot in front of me.

And then it spoke in a terrible rasping echo that sent a shiver straight down my spine. "Who's Virginia?"

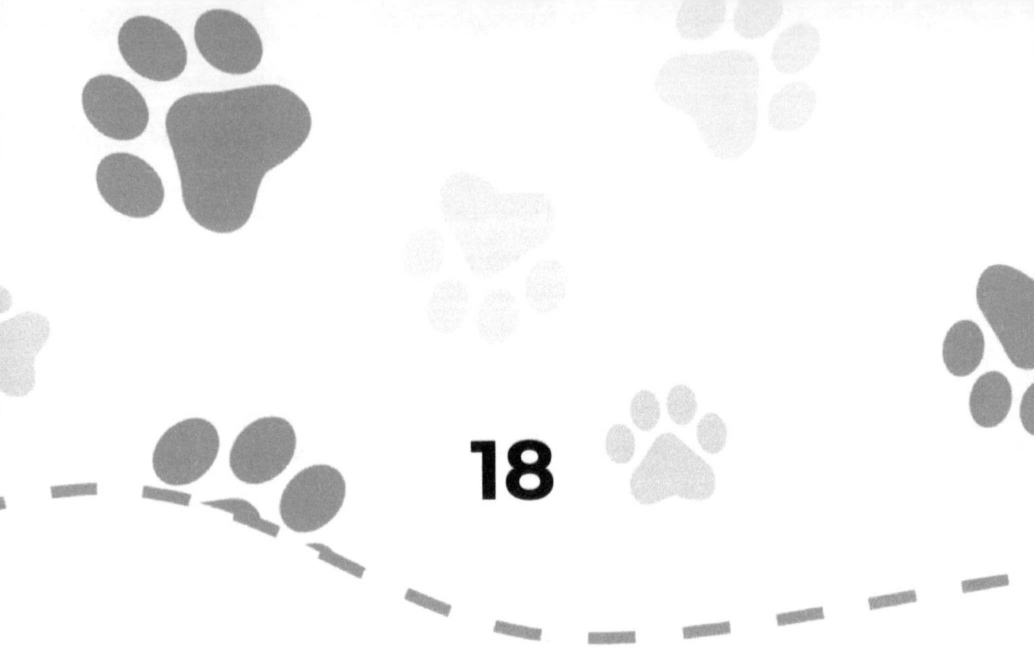

18

It was hard to tell given the strange echoing quality of its voice, but I was pretty sure our ghost was a boy.

"Who are you?" I murmured. I couldn't believe I was talking to a ghost. This topped all the strange things that had happened so far these past weeks. I'd reached a new peak of weirdness here and wasn't sure I liked it. Well, at least the spirit seemed gentle. That's definitely better than I'd have gotten were it actually Virginia.

"Gracie?" the ghost asked, moving so close to me that the glowing blue blob was but a hair's breadth from my face.

"Uh, ghost?" I responded stupidly.

"I never wanted to be a ghost," the strange creature moaned as its blue light undulated. "I don't know why I'm here, and I don't know why I came to you."

That was when I finally recognized something familiar in that eerie voice. This wasn't Virginia, but it was someone I'd known—someone I'd watched die not too long ago.

"Harold?" I asked in serious disbelief. "Is that you?"

"It's me," the spirit confirmed. Wow, I couldn't believe my former boss had returned from the spectral plane to pay me a visit. He'd hated me, and even more than that, he hated *paying me* anything—especially not what I was owed for all the hours I put in at his coffeeshop.

"No wonder the spell didn't work," I murmured to myself, thinking of the useless ceramic frog in the hallway. "It was made for Virginia. And you clearly aren't her."

"Who's Virginia?" Harold echoed.

"Don't worry about it," I shot back quickly. I really preferred not to tell him that Virginia was the one who had killed him in the first place. Instead, I swallowed hard and asked, "Why are you here? Why did you come to see me, Harold?"

"I don't know," he answered as his blue light pulsed yet again. I wondered if the color he'd taken on was a coincidence or if it was something more of a mood ring. Would evil ghosts glow red? Magical ones green? Interesting to think about, but not what was important at the moment.

"Do you have unfinished business of some kind?" I asked after licking my dry lips.

"It's hard to remember much in this form," he said in that jarring echo of his. "But give me a moment, and I'll try."

While I waited for Harold to collect his thoughts, the two cats slowly moved out of the hallway and came to stand beside me in the kitchen.

"What does it want?" Merlin asked, swishing his tail so hard it thwapped me in the leg.

"A talking cat!" Harold exclaimed in fright and zipped back toward the sink.

"Yes, he's a talking cat, and you're a ghost. Which seems scarier to you?" I asked, tilting my head to the side in disbelief. "Besides, you just saw him talking in the hallway. You also watched him summon lightning, remember?"

"Oh, I think I do." The blobby blue Harold bobbed back over to us, coming dangerously close to crashing into Luna this time. "And this one threatened me!" the ghost cried when he recognized the white cat.

"I have a name. It's Luna," she hissed, arching her back at him.

"Eek! A talking cat!" Harold screamed and raced about the house.

Oh, boy. This was going to take a while.

I needed to take charge here, or we'd be at this all night. "Harold, you came for a reason. I know you're having a hard time remembering, so I'll ask some questions to see if that helps. Okay?"

He bobbed up and down, which I took to mean he agreed.

"Is this about how you died?" I ventured carefully.

"I was poisoned."

"Yes, that's good, Harold! Yes, you were poisoned." Oops, my voice sounded all high and babyish like it did when I talked to Merlin —before he started talking back, that is. When I'd still assumed he was just a regular fuzzy wuzzy. Even though Harold seemed harmless, there was nothing fuzzy or wuzzy about the ghost before me.

"Well, you don't have to sound so happy about it," he booed.

"Oh, trust me. I'm not happy about it."

Sigh. I might as well tell him the truth and get it off my chest. He'd forget it in a few seconds any way. "I'm sorry, too. You were murdered because someone wanted to hurt me."

"But she avenged you," Merlin added, hopping up onto the table to get closer to the talking blue orb. "She risked her own life to punish those who hurt you."

"So my killer is now dead?" Harold wanted to know.

I shrugged for lack of a better response. "Um, yes and no. The mastermind is still on the loose, but the one who pulled the trigger is definitely dead."

"No, I wasn't shot. I was poisoned," he insisted in another wailing echo.

"Right." No tangents, no metaphors. Straight simple language. "Does your visit have anything to do with your daughter? Kelley?"

"My daughter," the ghost mumbled and then flashed bright cerulean and shouted, "Kelley! Yes, I wanted to thank you for helping her."

I smiled. Harold would have been a good dad if he'd been given more of a chance. "Of course I helped her, she's my friend."

"But you gave her your one wish. You didn't have to do that."

My jaw would have hit the floor if it could reach. "You couldn't remember that cats can talk, but somehow you both knew and remembered that my cat brewed a potion which I then gave to Kelley so her biggest dream could come true?"

The blue blob tilted to the side. "Memory is strange as a ghost. It comes and goes."

"Well, you're welcome for helping Kelley. She wants to do your legacy proud. You have a very good daughter there. It's too bad you didn't get much of a chance to know her."

Harold's hue turned dark like midnight. "It is too bad."

"Tomorrow is the grand re-opening of the coffeehouse. She kept the name," I informed him. "To honor you."

He brightened once more. "Would you please tell her I'm proud of her?"

Well, this was sweet and all, but I really needed to get some sleep since I was scheduled to work a double shift tomorrow. "I'll see what I can do. Thank you for the visit, Harold. Was that all?"

"Wait!" The ghost raced around the kitchen before returning to face me. "I have a warning to deliver from the other side."

"That might have been a good thing to start with," Merlin said snippily.

I shushed him, then softened my voice to speak to Harold. "What is the message?"

His voice grew deep and clear, changed. "Seeds that have been sown will soon bear dangerous fruit."

I gasped. "Harold? What does that mean?"

He spun slowly as if surveying the room. "What does what mean?"

“The message you just gave me,” I pressed. Please remember, please rememb—

“I don’t remember,” he said and then flashed out of view.

19

The next morning I woke up with a killer headache. Not only had the whole fiasco in the kitchen taken an unpredictably long time, but when it was over I lay awake for close to an hour pondering the meaning of Harold's ghostly warning.

Seeds that have been sown will soon bear dangerous fruit.

What did that mean?

For all I knew, Harold heard it in some movie before he died and now summoned it back up, confusing it for a real memory. It certainly sounded like some weird prophecy that had come straight out of an epic fantasy film.

The more I thought about it, the more confused I became. I guessed I'd just have to wait and see what happened next, as much as I hated not being able to prepare.

It would be a busy day.

The coffeehouse's grand re-opening had arrived. I had to give her credit, Kelley had made especially fast progress in retooling the menu and retraining the staff. Now the moment of her public debut as owner of Harold's House of Coffee had arrived.

She'd need all hands on deck because today was going to be non-stop busy. The magic I'd secretly given to her guaranteed it would be so.

At my urging, Kelley had scheduled the full staff to work a double shift for the day, including me.

When I arrived at Harold's, I found her wearing a white '50s inspired party dress with little pumpkins and horns of plenty patterned all over it. She ran over to me with a huge grin on her face. "Gracie, hello! Are you ready for our big day?"

"Your big day," I reminded her with a grin. "And yes, I'm definitely ready." No need to let her know I'd lost several good hours of sleep last night, thanks to the paranormal soap opera my life had become.

She nodded, and a pair of jack-o-lantern earrings bobbed along with her. "Good news, the new uniform shirts arrived last night. Grab one from the office and get changed."

Oh, no. Harold had allowed us to wear whatever we wanted because he was too cheap to invest in uniforms, but Kelley had gone all out by commissioning a series of custom T-shirt designs that would change each month.

I sifted through the box until I found a large, then pulled it on over my other shirt. On the front, my new uniform said "#PSLIS-

BAE," which was the new hashtag Kelley was trying to get started on social media. The back read, "Ask me about my favorite pumpkin spice!"

Lord help us all.

When I came back out of the office, I found Kelley standing near the creamer station and staring up at the wall. As I drew closer, I discovered she was studying a framed picture that hadn't been there when last I worked two days ago.

The photo was the same one that had been on display by the casket for Harold's funeral. It was a close-up of his face, complete with chubby cheeks, narrow eyes, and receding hairline. Kelley should thank her lucky stars that she'd inherited her good looks from her mother.

"Do you think he'd be proud of me?" she whispered when I reached her side.

"I know he would be," I said giving her shoulder a supportive squeeze.

Kelley turned toward me but didn't meet my eye. "Really?" she mumbled. "You don't think I'm overdoing it with the pumpkin spice?"

"People are going to love it. Just you wait."

Now she looked at me. Her eyes held all her dreams and secret fears. This was so much more than a grand opening to her. It was an opportunity to bond with the father she'd only just begun to know. "What makes you so sure?" she asked.

"I just know," I assured her, and then, "Hey, should we take a couple quick shots of pumpkin roast espresso to help get us pumped?"

"That's a great idea," she gushed, stepping past me and rushing toward the industrial sized espresso maker. "Everyone gather around!" she called as she worked the machine.

The three new hires had already arrived. I'd been so focused on my many magical problems this past week that I hadn't really made any efforts to get to know them outside of Kelley's team-building activities. Now that I knew our ghostly visitor had been Harold of all people, maybe I could start to relax even more. To let other people in.

Drake flew through the door just as Kelley was pouring the last shot into a little paper cup. "Sorry I'm late!"

"Actually you're five minutes early," Kelley said as she handed him a shot.

Drake jerked his head toward the door. "Should I go back out and come in a little later?"

"Oh, stop." Kelley hit his chest playfully, and I watched as stand-offish, sarcastic Drake blushed. He actually blushed! Perhaps there was hope for these two, after all.

"A toast!" I said, raising my own paper cup in the air.

"To Harold's. Long may his legacy live!" Kelley cheered.

"To Kelley. Long may she overlook my tardiness!" Drake countered.

"To all things pumpkin spice," I added.

The newbies shouted a combination of "Cheers!" and "Hear, hear!"

And then we all took down our shots of espresso.

“Ah, hot, hot, hot!” I cried.

“That went straight up my sinuses,” Drake whined.

The others just laughed and laughed.

Yup, we were ready to slay.

20

I dragged myself home at the end of my double shift, reeking of cinnamon, nutmeg, and ginger. As much as my feet ached and my back twinged, I couldn't be happier. Kelley had truly risen to the occasion, and I loved seeing the way her face lit up as she basked in the success of a job well done.

I was happy, but now very ready to unwind.

Thank goodness the power outage last night had been the result of a sudden electrical overload and not permanent wire damage. A quick trip to my house's fuse box had restored power. The hole in the roof, on the other hand, would be much more difficult to fix.

I tried not to worry about it as I popped a TV dinner in the microwave, then settled on the couch and scrolled through Netflix. After my hard day of work, I deserved to indulge in the sleaziest, most over-the-top reality series I could find. I settled on one of their original series that asked people to get engaged before ever meeting face-to-face. This would be trashy television gold.

And, yeah, it was interesting right away. I could hardly tear my eyes from the screen when the microwave dinged, alerting me that my slimmed down version of mac and cheese was ready for consumption.

So transfixed I was by the ridiculousness playing out on screen that I accidentally stumbled over one of the cats on my way to the kitchen.

Luna mewled and ran to my bedroom for cover.

"How dare you!" Merlin boomed, marching straight up to me from wherever he'd been.

"I'm sorry, Luna! It was an accident!" I called after the retreating feline.

Then I turned toward Merlin. "Don't lecture me when you put a hole in our roof just last night! I called a fix-it company for a rough quote while I was on break, and they want more than I make in a month! So I hope you've learned your lesson about summoning the elements inside our house."

"Don't start a family. Don't summon lighting. You have so many rules!" the giant fluff of a cat spat.

I scoffed at him. "They're very reasonable rules."

"I think you're forgetting who's in charge here. I'm the witch."

"And I'm the homeowner," I exploded. I seriously didn't have one drop of energy left to deal with his nonsense today. "I'm also the one who pays all the bills. And I've just had a very long, tiring day at work, so don't push me!"

"You're lucky you're not a cat, or I'd challenge you to a duel right here and right now." He stamped his little kitty foot in rage, but it didn't scare me either.

"Merlin! Gracie!" Luna cried. "Enough!"

We both looked to her and grimaced.

"It was an accident, and I'm fine." As she approached I noticed something different about the way she moved. Oh, I really hoped I hadn't hurt her too badly with my careless mistake. "But you two have both been way too tense lately. Remember, we are all on the same side."

Merlin moaned. "But she—"

"But nothing. We're all dealing with a lot right now, and the last thing we need is to start turning on each other. You're both stressed, and I understand. I think you need a bit of space to cool off from each other."

"I'm sorry, Luna. You're right. I'm just really stressed about the ghost and the warning I can't make heads or tails of, and the hole in the roof, and—"

"I know you are, dear. I would fix the hole for you if I could, and I would have been able to, if I still had my magic. Never matter, Merlin will travel to Nocturna at the first available moment and find a garden witch who can assist with the repairs."

"But Tom Cat!" Merlin argued. "If he sees me, he'll challenge me again. I could die, Luna. Die!"

"Then you'll just have to make sure he doesn't see you," she coaxed. "Now I want the two of you to make up this instant."

"I'm sorry, Merlin," I said, casting my eyes to the floor. Luna was good at the whole disappointed parent thing. She'd make a great mother one day when she and Merlin were officially ready to start their family.

Luna walked over to Merlin and nudged him with her paw. "Now you."

"Sorry, Gracie," he muttered while also rolling his eyes.

Luna nodded, missing that last gesture. "Now, Gracie, why don't you get back to your show? Merlin, let's go on a date. It may be our last chance before the children are born."

"What?" I exploded.

"Run, my love, run!" Merlin cried as they both launched themselves at the cat door.

Well, that was one more huge thing to worry about. Perhaps I should stop assuming that life would settle down and get back to normal. Chaos was the new normal. And soon kittens!

For today, however, I let the melodramatic reality show soothe my anxieties somewhat as I chowed down on my soggy cheese noodles.

And I didn't even make it to the end of the first episode before I drifted off on the couch.

21

I awoke sometime later, confused at first as to where I was. Then I spotted the message from Netflix on my TV screen: *Are you still watching?*

I switched off the television with its remote, then sat up and stretched my arms overhead. I needed to move myself into bed, but I was still so, so sleepy.

Just as I was about to force myself to stand, I heard a series of clicks and scratches coming from across the living room. *What the heck?*

I tiptoed over to take a look and saw the silhouette of a cat in the window. My cat.

"Merlin, what are you doing out there?" I cried, racing to open the window.

But before I could make it across the room, a bright green light burst forth from the wall and blocked my path.

"Harold?" I squeaked, even though there was no mistaking the figure before me.

"So we meet again," a ghostly Virginia drawled. Unlike Harold, she was much more than an amorphous glowing orb. Her face was fully formed in a perfect replica of how she had looked in life—except now she was green and semi-transparent. She was also missing most of her body. In fact, her figure ended slightly below the armpits, giving her a bust-like appearance.

Virginia charged at me and gnashed her teeth.

I dodged out of the way just in time. "Get out of here, and leave us alone," I shouted, running for the hallway.

Virginia followed, cackling as if she were a witch and not a ghost. Maybe she was a witch now, too. She was certainly glowing green with magic, which put me at a double disadvantage. I couldn't wield any power of my own, and I had zero idea how to kill a ghost. *Wonderful.*

I groped about in the corner of the hallway until I found the ceramic frog with the potion pooled within its open maw. As soon as I got a firm grip on it, I spun and thrust it toward my assailant.

"Take that!" I shouted, proud of my quick thinking despite the fog of fatigue that enveloped me.

"What are you doing with my frog?" Virginia asked with a dry laugh. "And why are you waving it at me like a weapon?"

I braced myself with feet shoulder width apart. "I hereby bind you, ghost!"

"Silence." Virginia's bellow echoed, reverberating through the entire house.

I pushed the frog at her again, but it flew from my hands and crashed into the wall. When I tried to speak, I found my mouth was sealed shut.

"That's better," Virginia said with an approving nod. "Now enough with the theatrics. I'm here to kill you. Nothing more, nothing less. You'll pay for what you and your witch did. I have more magic in death than I ever had in life, and now I will use it to avenge my untimely death. So, any last words?"

She rotated her head on her stump of a torso and released her magical hold on me.

I gasped, then shouted at her the second I was able to move my mouth. "Where are my cats?"

Her green dulled with apparent disappointment. "Well, that's a waste of words. If you must know, I've magically sealed this house. They can't get in, and you can't get out. You're entirely at my mercy. First I'll take care of you, and then I'll finish them off as well. It's almost too easy."

"You don't have magic. H-h-how is this possible?" I sputtered. If I could keep her talking, I could keep me breathing.

Virginia had such a large ego she not only wanted to murder me, but she also wanted me to bask in her brilliance before she did it. The quintessential villain divulging her master plan instead of actually implementing it.

"Oh, anything is possible if you have the right friends. Luna was an amateur, a fool! But my new master appreciates what I am, what I can do." She was so textbook bad guy, I almost felt sorry for her. Unfortunately, I felt much sorrier for me in this moment, though.

Virginia had no morals that I had seen, and she wouldn't hesitate to deliver on her promise of my demise.

Even though I was still shaking in my boots, I forced myself to roll my eyes. "Dash, you mean? You're still working for that witch after the last time literally got you killed?"

"I know what you're doing, and I'm not stupid enough to fall for it," a glowing, green Virginia hissed.

"Funny choice of words. Fall for it? Isn't that how you died the first time? Maybe it's how you'll die this time, too?" I would have crossed my arms over my chest, but I needed to have them ready in case Virginia flew at me again.

"I am immortal in my new form!" she boomed triumphantly. "The only one dying tonight will be you. And your little kitty friends." She hurled herself at me with her ghostly mouth wide open and clamped down on my shoulder.

Ouch, ouch, ouch. It hurt so bad! Much more than any bite should have stung. Somehow I knew she had infected me with magic.

But what kind?

And what would it do?

I swooned on my feet. No, I couldn't let her win.

Especially not so easily.

But then I swooned again.

"What did you do to me?" I croaked.

22

"I created a drain. Soon the magic within you will begin flowing to me," Virginia revealed, circling me with glee. "And once I have enough of it, I will use it to end you. How's that for poetic justice?"

Virginia sure was full of herself. But even I had to admit that her plan was a good one. Killing me with my own well of magic.

Just wow.

I hadn't even made it a full month as a familiar, and already my ties to the magical world had led to my imminent death.

Sorry, but no.

I was not going down without a fight.

My cats couldn't get inside to help me, but I could still hear them at the window. I could still talk to them, let them guide me in this battle. I hurled myself down the hall, passing straight through the enemy ghost, and raced to the living room window.

Merlin sat waiting as I unlatched the window and pried it open. "Gracie, behind you!" he shouted.

I dodged to the side to avoid another painful bite from my spectral opponent.

Virginia passed through the window, screamed in rage, and then hurled herself back the other way.

"She used most of her magic to create her barrier spell," Luna called from out of sight. "It's why half her body's missing. Even with the drain she placed on you, she is regenerating very slowly."

Yes, Luna was right! By silencing me, she'd lost her stumpy little arms. Her figure now ended at the collarbone. If she cast another big spell, she might blink herself out of existence.

The ghost drove at me again, and I leapt out of the way. Were all these physical attacks meant to distract me while she recharged her magic? And what was the worst she could do to me without magic? Bite me again? That would hurt, but I already knew I could survive it.

Well, two could play at her little game of wait and see.

I ran to the closet and grabbed my broom.

Virginia laughed at me, mocking my choice of weapon. But then I slammed it into her face, grody bristles first, and sent her flying backward.

"You'll pay for that!" she promised, her green transforming into a blazing emerald as she spat curses at me. "Freeze!"

My feet fused to the floor. I could still move my upper body, but the lower part was now stuck like a fly in honey.

As soon as she muttered this magical command, the rest of her ghostly shoulders disappeared from view. Now she was just a bobbing head and a neck.

"You can't kill me without killing yourself," I said as if this were fact and not just my current theory. She'd told me she was now immortal as a ghost, but that didn't mean she could stay on our earthly plane for long.

"I'm already dead, thanks to you!" she bandied back. As her frustration grew, her words came out faster, more slurred together.

"Gracie!" Merlin shouted from the window. I glanced through Virginia and saw both he and Luna sitting on the sill now.

"We can bind her, but I'll need ingredients from my garden," the she-cat yelled.

"No, the frog didn't work." If it had, this whole thing would have stopped almost as soon as it started. If only.

Luna didn't give up, however. "It was too old and lost its potency, but a new batch will work."

"I can't leave."

"Try the door," Merlin shouted. Thank you, captain obvious.

"I can't. I'm stuck." I motioned toward my legs and let out a groan.

This whole time Virginia was shouting insults at us but not actually casting any more spells. It seemed I was right about her not having the requisite power to finish the deed she'd come to commit. She probably hadn't realized how much the barrier spell would take out of her. It's not like she was a real witch, anyway. She'd never had magic in life and was inexperienced with it in death.

I scanned the room, all the while searching for some kind of solution that would unstick me from the floor. I spotted my phone lying on the coffee table a good six feet away. I couldn't reach out and grab it, but I did have a broom in my hands. If I could distract Virginia long enough to get ahold of it, I could send an SOS text to Drake.

Luckily he'd insisted on programming my number into his phone after our failed date. He'd also offered to help with my ghost, should I need it. And I definitely needed it right now.

"Hey, loser!" I shouted loud enough for Virginia to hear me over her deranged ranting. "Think fast!"

23

I pretended to cast a spell. Yes, I couldn't use the magic within me, and, yes, Virginia knew that. But thankfully my ruse still worked.

I raised the hand that wasn't holding my broom and made an elaborate twisty gesture. "Merlin, lightning!" I cried.

Sure enough, Virginia spun around just in time to see Merlin summon a bolt of lightning right outside the window. His magic couldn't cross the barrier she'd erected, but the ghostess couldn't help but watch transfixed as Merlin's attempt to come to my aid "failed."

Quick as a shot, I swept my broom to the side, then pulled it back to me like an oar. This sent my phone skittering across the floor and straight toward me. Thank goodness I'd invested in a good phone case, or this plan would not have worked.

I stooped down still rooted to the spot and grasped the phone in my hands. With a quick swipe to unlock it, I opened my contacts and typed a quick message, both of my thumbs flying impossibly fast over the screen.

Drake, SOS!

Come help me!

I sent each text separately, not knowing when Virginia would manage to wrest the phone from my hands and silence my cries for help.

Ghost is— Virginia reeled back around and tore the phone from my hands with her magic before I could finish. It flew and smashed against the wall, much the same as the frog had. So much for that heavy-duty case.

RIP, my iPhone.

Drake would come. I knew he would. What he'd be able to do to help, now there was a question I hadn't quite thought out.

I studied Virginia to see if any more of her had faded from view, thanks to her most recent use of magic, but it seemed she had lost no ground. Which meant the drain she'd placed on me was beginning to work.

No, no, no. What else could I do to stall her?

"Merlin, I'm scared!" I shouted, making Virginia positively glow with *schadenfreude.*

"I won't leave you," he promised from his spot at the window. "Even through the barrier spell, my presence is keeping you strong. And yours is also protecting me."

"But the drain…" My words fell away as if my energy was also being sucked from me along with the magic.

Merlin stood and pressed his paws against the barrier, giving me a full view of his furry tummy. "It's my magic you carry. A small part of it is going to Virginia, but most of it is able to escape to the barrier and come back to me. I can't leave or the magic will have no place else to go."

"Stop helping her!" Virginia raged, but she was also unable to cast through the barrier. To land an attack on Merlin, she'd need to go outside. And we all knew he was a much more powerful magic user than she was, especially with my additional energy flowing into him now.

"You're stuck until you've generated enough magic to enact whatever death spell you have planned." Merlin addressed the ghost directly, his voice cold and haughty.

To me, he said, "Ignore her. She can't hurt you yet."

"Oh, yes, I can!" Virginia screamed and then lunged and bit me again. She came at me so fast, I hadn't been ready with my broom. Darn it!

This new wound throbbed with pain, but I could survive it. She couldn't bite me to death, and right now my primary objective was to not die. Honestly, it was kind of my only objective.

"Memorize this list of ingredients," Luna called to me from beside Merlin. "When your boyfriend gets here, send him straight to my garden. If he brings back what we need, Merlin and I can make a new binding potion."

"But he'll see you practicing magic and hear you talking!" I objected. Merlin had drilled it into my head from the start that I could not reveal magic to non-magical people. What was the point of surviving my ghostly encounter only to wind up in a dingy prison for the rest of my life?

Luna's voice came to me strong and confident. "We have not revealed ourselves to him, so he will only hear meows. And his eyes will invent other scenarios to explain away our actions. Everything will be fine. Just be careful. Now memorize this list. Hawthorn, celandine..."

Luna shouted out at least ten ingredients, and we went over them again and again until she was sure I had them all right.

Virginia continued to spit and howl, but at worst she only made us repeat ourselves a few times to be heard over the din.

Why did it feel like my epic magical encounters always dragged out? Life-or-death confrontations in movies always happened so fast. There was no waiting for a ghost's magic to recharge or biding time until the correct potion could be brewed.

Real magic was both more exciting and much more boring than the magic in the movies. At least the movies couldn't kill me.

Virginia, on the other hand...

She swept toward me again, and I hit her away with the broom. I was getting kind of good at this. She rounded back to attack again, but a pair of bright white lights burst through the window, interrupting her efforts.

Drake had arrived.

24

Everything seemed to stop as Virginia and I waited mid-battle for Drake to turn off his engine, exit the car, and come inside.

He pounded on the front door. "Gracie! Is everything okay? Let me in!"

The barrier spell! Would he even be able to enter? And if he did, would he be able to get out again?

"Drake," I cried out, my voice hoarse from all the screaming I'd been doing that night. "Don't come in!"

"What's going on?" he demanded, rattling the doorknob, but it remained shut tight.

"Don't come in!" I begged, hoping he wouldn't waste time arguing. I needed him to act and act fast. "Please, I need your help. I need you to go to a garden and get me a list of ingredients."

Drake pounded on the door with all he had. "What? Gracie, why? What's going on? Is the ghost back? Are you okay?"

"It's here, and it's very angry. I need to bind it before—"

"I'm not an it! Show some respect, you weak mortal!" Virginia hissed and swooped around the room.

"Whoa," Drake cried, and his pounding stopped. "Was that the ghost? You're right, it does sound angry!"

"It, it, it! I am not an it! And you, foolish boy, have just been added to my hit list," Virginia was in fine form, glowing the brightest I'd seen yet. Pride was an important sticking point for her. Hmm, maybe if Drake came in he could talk her to death by getting her to use her magic so much she dematerialized, but I couldn't risk his safety. And I also much preferred ridding myself of her permanently. It was Luna's potion or bust. I just needed to convince Drake to leave and get what she needed.

"Drake, it's okay. Don't listen to her," I called, hoping that Virginia's threats hadn't caused him to lose courage. "Just go to the garden. Bring back what we need. It's the only way. Do you have your phone? Take down this list."

A brief moment of silence, and then, "I'm ready."

I recited the ingredients to Luna's nodding approval and also gave Drake the address. "Now hurry please! I'm counting on you!"

I listened as Drake's feet slapped the pavement in retreat, then his engine roared to life and he sped away.

"What now?" I asked the cats who were both still watching from the windowsill.

"We wait and hope that he brings us the correct ingredients. And swiftly," Luna answered.

"Drake knows a little bit about a lot of things," I said, recalling the conversation I'd had first with him and then with Kelley. "Gardening is one of them. Besides, he can always look up the ingredients on his phone and make sure he's picking the right ones. He won't mess this up."

For some reason, I believed this with every fiber of my being. Drake would not let me down. In fact, he would save me. Everything would be okay.

I just had to be patient.

"I'm growing stronger by the minute," Virginia reminded me in a serpentine whisper. And she was right. She'd regained the form she had when I first saw her—a full bust that filled out to just a little below her armpits. "I will kill you, Gracie, and I will make your boyfriend watch. Then I'll rebuild my power and kill him, too. Next will be Luna. I'm saving my former master for last. Before the night is through, you will all be dead."

"No one is dying today, you old goose," Merlin heckled her through the barrier. "Especially not my familiar and not my unborn children!"

Virginia gasped and spun toward the window. "What did you say?"

"We have the power of love on our side. Your hate will never win," I yelled, because that seemed like the type of thing a good guy would say in a showdown like this.

"It seems I left you at the right time, Luna," Virginia said coldly.

"At least as a witch, you had some power. But you gave that all up, didn't you? And for what? To play house with some walking hairball and to bear his brats?"

"I owe you nothing, Virginia," Luna ground out, a growl underlying the words. "And you can never understand that power comes in many forms. My children will grow to be strong and kind and to help rid the world of monsters like you."

"They will die or live cursed lives. That I can guarantee." As the ghost shared this eerie promise, I knew better than to doubt her words.

As much as I'd thought this wasn't the right time for my cats to start a family, I would fight with everything I had to protect Luna's litter. Virginia had meant to scare us, but she'd only given me more motivation.

I would defeat her once and for all.

Those kittens would never know how close they'd come to ending before they'd ever had a chance to begin.

Auntie Gracie was on the case.

And she would not let them down.

25

By the time Drake returned, Virginia's ghostly body had materialized down to her navel.

And those twenty-odd minutes of waiting, trapped in place, while she ranted and raved and told us all how awful we were, proved to be among the most excruciating of my life. A few times she charged at me, but I was able to deftly knock her away with my broomstick.

Honestly, I think we were both relieved when Drake's car pulled into my driveway for the second time that night. This time, however, two sets of footsteps approached my door instead of just one.

"Drake?" I called out warily. *Please let it be him. Please let it be him.*

"It's me," he called through the door.

"And me," a second voice chimed.

"Kelley?" I croaked. Why on earth would he have knowingly

brought her into a dangerous situation? Now that my friends were at risk, too, I felt the pressure mount. Me, Luna, Merlin, the kittens, Drake, Kelley—I had to save us all and fast. Virginia was reforming more and more quickly. Soon she'd be able to cast whatever she had planned for me, and then she'd take us all out one by one.

"I ran into her at that house," Drake shouted to explain Kelley's presence. "How come you didn't tell me it was hers? Anyway, she wanted to help, so I brought her back with me. Now will you please let us in?"

"No, don't come in!" I shouted, but it was too late.

Virginia used a small bit of her accumulated magic to throw the door open and pull both Kelley and Drake inside.

"Gracie, what's going on?" Kelley trembled as she caught sight of Virginia's imposing presence.

"Whoa," Drake said on the wings of an exhale. "Why is she green?"

"She has magic. She trapped me inside, and now I fear she's trapped you as w-well," I sputtered. I was determined to win, but also terrified I wouldn't be able to. We needed to mix the potion in the cauldron and either lure Virginia outside or bring the mix inside to bind her. But how, if no one could move through the barrier without her consent?

Virginia must have realized this as well, because she chose that exact moment to let out a textbook perfect evil laugh. "And now you've brought me one more. I shall kill her, too."

Kelley choked out a sob, which only made Virginia laugh harder. Oh, she would pay for that!

Drake took Kelley in his arms and made soft shushing noises. "I'll protect you," he promised, then glanced up toward me. "Both of you."

"She's erected a barrier around the house. Nobody can go out or come in unless she allows it. And I can't move from this spot," I explained, gesturing toward my useless legs.

"Yeah, no. I'm not letting some ninja turtle looking banshee tell me what I can and can't do," Drake declared. He guided Kelley into my waiting arms and then marched back toward the front door.

No, no, no. For all I knew the barrier was electrified. Sure, it hadn't hurt Merlin when he touched it, but Drake wasn't magical. Could he withstand the sudden shock of making contact?

"Drake, stop!" I yelled. "She—"

But then he stepped outside. Turning to me, he pushed his hair back with a flip and flashed us all a debonair grin. "You were saying?"

"How is this possible?" Virginia screamed and spun around the house.

At the same time, Kelley launched herself from my arms and went flying toward the door. When she reached the threshold, though, she slammed into it with a *thwack* and fell backward with a heavy thud. "I don't understand," she sobbed. "Why can he leave, but I can't?"

Drake reached through the doorway and offered her his hand, but hard as he tried, he couldn't pull her through. When he let her go, Kelley pushed herself against the wall and curled into a whimpering ball.

“How did you do that?” I demanded of him. And would I be able to do it, too, once I was able to move from this exact spot on the floor?

Drake shrugged. “I don’t know. Sometimes I can just do stuff others can’t. Or sometimes I just know things, like how I knew where you lived without you telling me.”

“You followed me,” I said, preferring the explanation that made more sense. Even if it was creepy and stalkerish.

He shook his head. “Nope, I just pulled it from of my memory. Weird thing is I don’t remember making the memory in the first place, but there it was, ready to be of service.”

“Enough of this,” Virginia seethed. “Let me recharge in peace.”

“Why would we do anything for you?” I snapped. “You’re just going to kill us.”

“And, oh, how I am looking forward to that.” She flashed bright as her ghostly hips now started to materialize. We were running out of time.

“Drake, take the ingredients you got from the garden to the birdbath in the front yard, mix everything together, and then put it in some kind of container and bring it back inside.”

“How much of each thing? I mean, if I’m making a recipe, surely there are certain measurements required to get it right?”

He had a point. But how could he be so nonchalant about this all? I’d already known all about magic, and yet I was terrified. Kelley lay curled in the fetal position, but Drake was fine with talking casually about everything?

“I… I don’t know,” I mumbled.

But then Luna appeared outside the open door and promptly

introduced herself to Drake. "Hi, I'm a cat. I used to be a witch, but I'm not anymore. Still, I can help you save Gracie if you'll let me guide you in making this potion."

Drake stared at her with wide eyes.

Kelley's sobbing intensified.

I waited, afraid to look away. Afraid of what would happen next.

Drake let out a long, stuttering sigh. "Yeah, okay, cat lady. Let's go do the thing."

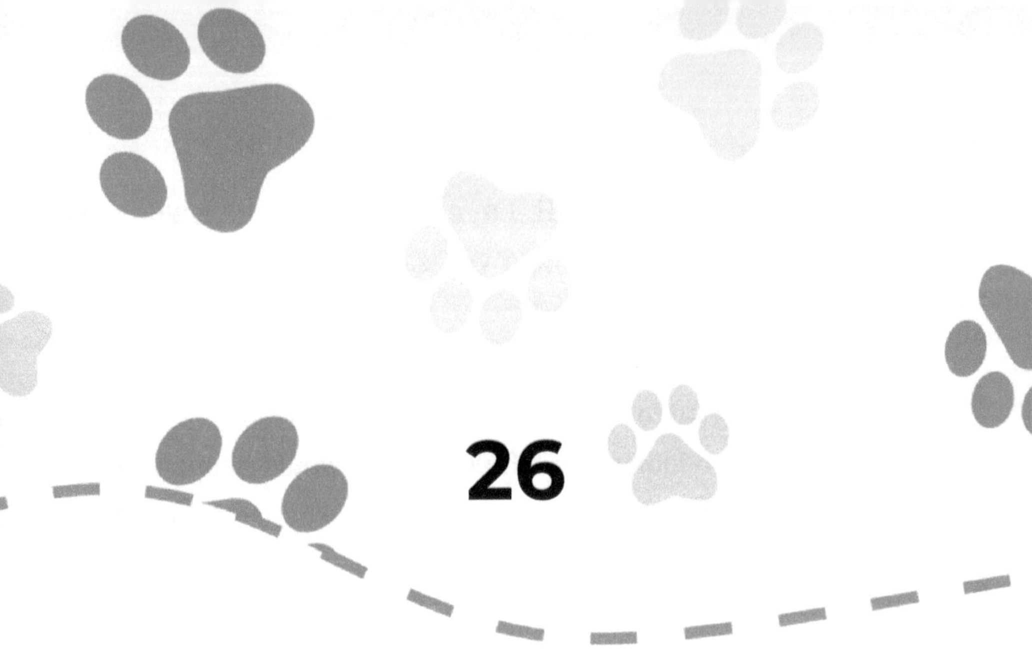

26

It was agony not being able to watch Luna and Drake prepare the potion. Merlin did move to the open doorway to offer an update, but Virginia quickly slammed the door in his face. He then moved back to the window so that the magic flowing out of me would have an easier time reaching him.

"Gracie, do you have a pitcher or something?" Drake called, charging back through the front door so easily Virginia shook and flashed with rage.

"Never mind. Found one," he called out a moment later. As he passed by me, I realized he'd taken the same pitcher I'd used as a vase for the flower he gifted me. I wondered if he noticed.

He stopped before reaching the door, then turned to address me again. "Oh, the cat lady said I need a piece of some frog to finish the potion. Know where I can get that?"

That's right. We still needed something that had belonged to Virginia. Even though her little garden creature had shattered, those shards could still be of use. That was a relief.

"Hallway," I directed Drake, jerking my head to the side, and he took off to retrieve the needed ingredient.

He held up a shiny piece of ceramic as he took his return trip through the living room. "Got it."

Virginia shrieked and threw herself at him.

I tried to push her away with my broom, but she and Drake were both beyond my reach. "Look out!" I cried helplessly.

Drake glanced up just as Virginia crashed into him... Or rather, through him.

"What are you?" she cried in a quavering voice.

"What are you?" he shot back, then seeing that he was unaffected by her advance, carried on toward the door.

He disappeared outside and returned a couple moments later carrying the pitcher now filled with murky green potion. "The cat lady said to give this to you," he said, placing the vessel in my hands.

"But what do I do with it?" I offered Drake my broom in exchange.

He didn't have time to answer before Virginia came flying at us.

He tried to bat her away, but the broom in his hands passed straight through her.

The angry spirit tackled me, and I would have fallen flat on my butt if not for the fact she'd frozen me in place earlier during this encounter.

I remained standing tall, the pitcher clutched firmly within my hands.

Virginia, on the other hand…

"What is happening?" she cried as all the color drained from her form and swirled into the pitcher.

I watched in awe as my vessel filled with pure light, magic.

When I looked back up at Virginia, she was drab and gray. She'd also regained her full body all the way to the tips of her ghostly toes.

"You stole my magic. Give it back!" she hissed and grabbed for the pitcher, but her hand passed straight through. She tried again, only to receive the same result.

"Where'd she go?" Drake asked, still holding the useless broom like a baseball bat.

I pointed straight ahead. "She's right here. Can't you see her?"

"No, Gracie. She's definitely gone." He let out a dry laugh as if he thought I was trying to trick him.

Merlin's voice floated to me through the open window. "We couldn't dispatch her fully because her unfinished business is killing you, Gracie. Until that's fulfilled, she will be trapped in our realm."

"Then how do we get rid of her?" I asked, craning my neck to search for him, but he was gone from the window.

"I will kill you!" Virginia growled and dove at me, but remained invisible to the others.

"The potion we brewed relieved her of her magic and bound her to this house," Luna announced after she and Merlin ran inside through the cat flap. It seemed that Virginia's barrier spell had fallen when she lost her magic.

"So she's stuck here? With us?" I screeched. Our house was full enough as it was, especially with kittens on the way. The last thing we needed was another roommate, especially one whose greatest desire was to kill us all.

"Yes, but she can't harm us. Or anyone else." Luna nodded slowly. I guessed she didn't like this arrangement any better than I did.

"Die, brat, die!" Virginia swooped at me once more, but the harder she worked to get my attention, the more her voice and image faded.

"Also you're not stuck. You can move again," Merlin informed me, nudging my foot with his paw. "So stop standing there, and move."

I jerked my foot upward, expecting the simple movement to be extraordinarily difficult. But this only resulted in my losing my balance and stumbling into Drake.

He caught me and helped me stand up tall. "Careful there, compadre."

"That's the second time you've called me that," I told him with a curious glance. "Why?"

"It's just a colorful way of reminding myself I live in the friend zone," he said with a wink. "And it's especially important now that I know you're this awesome witch who fights evil spirits on the regular."

Ugh. That was right. Drake pretty much knew all my secrets now. Sure, he didn't know about my Arthurian ancestry or the fact I was a familiar rather than a witch, but he still knew way too much.

I hoped the cats had a plan for dealing with that, and also that I wouldn't be heading to a wretched magical prison for sharing too much with a mortal.

I may have had a hard time with the ghost, but I'd still beaten her. I doubted I would have such an easy experience with hardened magical criminals while trapped inside an inescapable box.

27

"Hello? Is it safe to come out now?" a haunting voice echoed through the walls.

"Let me go!" Virginia cried, but her words were hardly more than a whisper now. At least that would make it easier to ignore her, if we would truly be living together for—what?—the rest of my life now, I guessed. Besides, Drake and Kelley clearly couldn't see or hear her anymore. Not even a little bit. That, at least, was a relief.

"Is that you, Harold?" I called out.

A blue hand reached through the living room wall and offered me a thumbs up. Nice to see he was coming into his full form now.

Kelley glanced toward me with glistening eyes. "M-my d-dad?" she sputtered. "Is he really here?"

"C'mon out, Harold!" I called with a smile. And it felt so good to feel my cheeks rise in happiness that I actually laughed aloud.

Harold phased into the living room. He was still mostly a blob, but he did have hands and a face, which was something.

Kelley slowly pushed herself to her feet but hung back from our new arrival.

"It's okay," I assured her with another smile. "He's not like the other one. C'mon."

When I motioned to her, she came over to stand beside me. "Dad?" she asked, unsure that a ghost could be trusted, even if it was one she'd known in life.

"Kelley," Harold responded in that melodic echo of his.

She kept her wide eyes directed at Harold, but spoke to me. "What's wrong with him?"

"He's still a new ghost, so he hasn't formed all the way yet. Go ahead and talk to him. He won't hurt you."

Harold's chubby cheeks bounced as he hovered in the air before us. "All I wanted was to see you one last time," he confessed. "To tell you I love you, and I'm sorry I wasn't around."

Kelley let out a little laugh and swiped at her freely flowing tears. "You didn't know about me. Not until the end."

I turned and saw Drake watching the scene unfold in awe. He and Kelley could both clearly see Harold, but no longer could they see Virginia. All this ghost business was terribly confusing. I doubted if I'd ever learn the exact rules that governed how they interacted with the world of the living.

"I should have spent more time with you once I did know, but I was scared I'd disappoint you. I thought we'd have more time."

Kelley choked on another sob but was all smiles now. “Me, too. But maybe now that you’re back, we can—?”

Harold’s light dimmed, and she stopped short. “No. I can’t stay. I will watch out for you, but it will be from the other side.”

“Why won’t you stay here with me?” If Kelley had possessed a ghostly light, I expect it would have faded then, too.

“Because my business is completed.” Harold spoke matter-of-factly, but I could see how much it pained him to deny his daughter’s wishes. He had changed so much since just last night. Not only was he speaking full sentences, but he was remembering. Emoting. “You now know how much I love you and wish things could have been different. I’ve seen you again, and I’ve given Gracie my warning.”

“Um, speaking of that,” I interjected, raising one index finger to draw everyone’s attention. “Virginia’s bound now. She can’t hurt us. Thank you for the warning. It helped, I think.”

Harold raised his disconnected hands and steepled them in front of his face. His brow furrowed as he drifted toward the ceiling and looked down on both Kelley and me. “No, my message was not about her, but another. One who still lives,” he said at last, using the same strange voice as he had when first delivering this warning. “The seeds that were sown will soon bear dangerous fruits.”

Kelley gasped, but little could surprise me at the moment.

“Yeah, can you give me more specific details? Like who, what, when, why? Any of that would help.”

Harold dropped his hands and returned to my eye level. His blue had become pale and much more transparent than before. “I’ve already said more than I should. The dead aren't supposed to interfere with the living. And also I don't remember enough to say."

He shifted his gaze back toward Kelley. "Stay well, my dear. I'll see you on the other side one day. Not too soon, though, okay?"

Kelley stretched her fingers out and touched her father's ghostly hand.

He bobbed for a moment before fading from view.

"That was so cool," Drake said from his spot on the couch.

Kelley stumbled over to join him. "I can't believe that was my dad."

"He seems like a pretty decent guy," Drake enthused. "I take back every bad thing I ever said about him."

While those two kept each other company, I snuck into my bedroom and motioned for the cats to join me. Once we were all inside, I gently closed the door behind us.

"What do we do now?" I whispered to them in a sudden burst of desperation. "They both know about magic. Does that mean I'm going to prison?"

Merlin chuckled in delight. "The thing about that is..."

"We found a loophole," Luna exclaimed with a rumbling purr.

I looked from one cat to the other. Both seemed pleased as punch. "What are you guys talking about? What loophole?"

"Well, technically Virginia is the one who revealed magic to them both. Not you," Merlin shared with pride.

"And I only spoke to Drake after she'd shown the true nature of her powers," Luna added. "Which means you won't be punished."

I was so relieved, I could almost feel the heavy emotional burden as it lifted from my shoulders.

"Neither of us will," Luna said with a Cheshire grin.

I let out a slow, long exhale. Ah, it felt so good. "Awesome. Well done. But what do we do now?"

"Gracie, we have a plan," Merlin promised, then motioned for me to lean closer so he could share all the details.

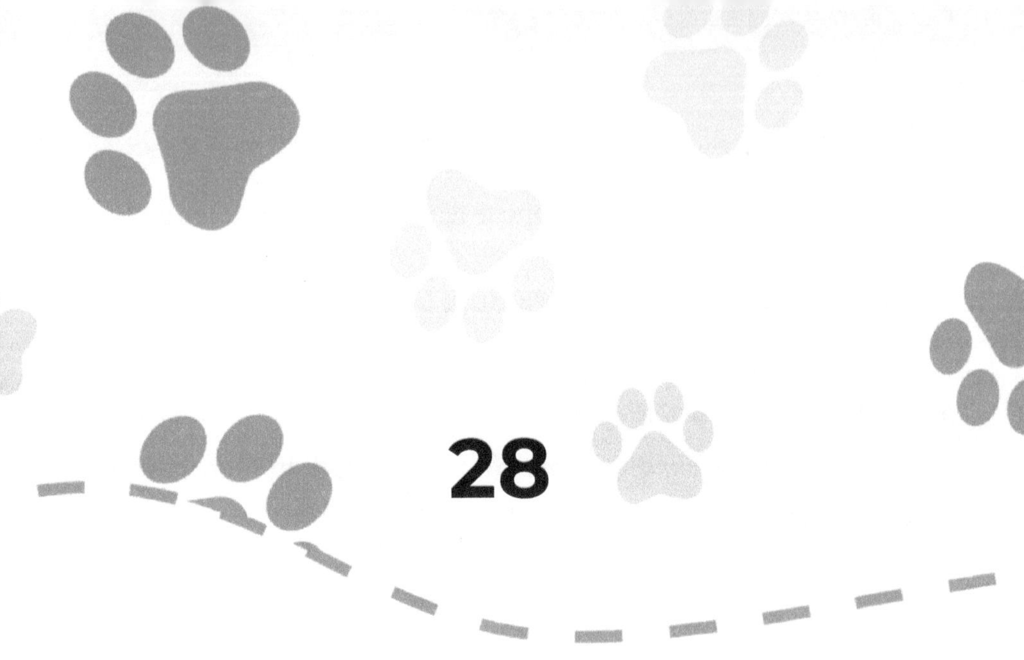

28

As it turned out, the cats really had thought of everything. While neither of them had ever possessed the magic to alter memories—that was an illusion witch specialty—Luna was able to successfully guide Merlin in brewing a powerful sleep potion.

They prepared it in gas form so it would be far easier to administer to our subjects. And once Drake and Kelley were out cold, Merlin teleported the lot of us back to Kelley's new house.

Virginia's old furniture hadn't been cleared out yet, so we moved both of our sleeping beauties to the floral-print couch. I took extra care to position them snuggled together with Drake's head in Kelley's lap. Just in case that helped to get him thinking about her as a potential girlfriend.

Our primary hope, though, was that they'd wake up in the morning and believe everything that had occurred was nothing more than a crazy dream, one they'd somehow managed to create and move through concurrently.

I, of course, would deny any involvement in their ghostly adventures. While I hated gaslighting my friends, it really was for their protection—and sanity.

It would have been nice to have human friends with whom I could share my magical comings and goings, but it would be selfish of me to expose them to any long-term risks that came with knowing. Without any witches to claim and protect them, they would be on their own and, thus, in grave peril. At least that's what the cats told me.

Anyway, Kelley and Drake both had enough to keep them busy with how popular the newly improved Harold's House of Coffee had already proven to be.

The day after our great nocturnal adventures, Kelley was scheduled for another double shift with the new hires set to help during the morning rush and me and Drake to join her later in the morning. Yeah, she'd definitely have to expand the staff again soon, but I trusted her intuition when it came to knowing when to act.

And when I arrived to start work, I found Drake had already beaten me to it—something that had literally never happened before. I also found that he was holding hands with Kelley while she rang up a customer and one of the new staff members worked the espresso machine.

"Good morning!" I cried joyfully once they'd finished tending to the customer. "I got a great night's sleep and am ready for whatever today throws at us."

Okay, so maybe I was selling the ruse a little too hard, but they didn't know that. I'd taken great care with my eye makeup that morning to ensure not even the faintest of dark circles graced my visage. And now I would be chipper and upbeat for the entirety of my shift, no matter how much I wanted to crawl back into bed and sleep it off.

Drake yawned openly, refusing to let go of Kelley's hand. "What's so good about it?"

I nodded toward Kelley. "It seems like something's good. Or at least something's different."

They both blushed, and frankly, it was adorable.

Kelley motioned for me to come closer.

"We spent the night together last night. I don't remember him coming over, but when I woke up, there he was." She smiled as Drake pressed a kiss to her cheek. They'd really gone from zero to sixty in hardly any time at all.

"I don't remember, either," he said, "but that's not so unusual. I forget stuff I should know all the time and know stuff I shouldn't."

Kelley dropped her voice to a husky whisper. "The weirdest part, though, is that we both had the craziest dream. The same dream!"

"Really?" I squeaked, doing my best to imitate surprise.

"You were there, too," Drake pointed out as if he expected me to remember. "Did you by chance dream about ghosts and magic talking cats last night?"

I shook my head emphatically. "Nope. I slept like a log."

"Isn't it so funny how the little bits and pieces of daily life can fuse together to create this whole big adventure in the dream world?"

Kelley asked, shaking her head. "Like my dad was there as a ghost! And there was this other ghost trying to hurt us, but Drake saved everyone. That's when my dad came and told me how much he loved me. I swear, you just mentioned ghosts one time as part of our icebreaking games, and it turns into this!"

"Yeah, and the wildest part is how we both dreamed the same thing," Drake said, narrowing his eyes at me. "The exact same thing."

"That is pretty wild." I nodded toward their joined hands. "It seems to have brought you together, though."

"Kelley's a pretty cool chick. Or should I say, pretty and cool," Drake responded before giving her little butterfly kisses with his eyelashes.

I was happy for them but also felt like if the pumpkin spice didn't make me puke today, their sickeningly sweet antics might.

"I've gotta go do the shift-end debrief with the new guys," Kelley announced with a sigh. "Be back soon."

Drake accepted a quick peck on the cheek and wiggled his fingers goodbye, watching her the whole way as she sauntered back toward the office.

"So you and Kelley?" I asked, not even trying to hide how happy I was about this turn of events.

"I know it wasn't a dream," Drake told me in a raspy whisper. "And I know you know it, too."

"I have no idea what you're talking about," I said with a shrug, then flipped my hair and went to wipe down the tables.

All the while I was panicking on the inside. How could he remember? And what would that mean for everyone going forward?

29

I returned home to two very happy cats and one very unhappy ghost. Merlin and Luna sat waiting for me on the kitchen table with huge matching grins spread between their whiskers while Virginia's nearly invisible form swooped around the house muttering muted curses.

"How's the new roommate settling in?" I asked the cats as Virginia swept toward me and then phased through me. Physically, I felt nothing, but it still felt like a violation.

I shuddered and yelled at her not to do that again.

"Or what?" the ghost asked so silently I had to strain to hear.

"Well, you are already grounded," I said with a laugh. "Give me time, though, I'll think of something."

Both cats laughed with me as Virginia disappeared into another part of the house.

"She hates it, and we love it," Merlin answered with bright eyes.

Luna seemed less amused despite her earlier laughter. "I still feel somewhat responsible for this all."

"You can't control the evil within someone else," I said, running my fingers over her smooth white fur. "And besides, now your children will know much more about ghosts than you ever did. That's a good thing, right?"

"I suppose," she said with a sigh and leaned into my touch.

"Never mind about that." Merlin stood and arched his back in a deep stretch. "We have a surprise for you."

I raised one eyebrow. "Oh?"

"Right this way, if you'll please."

Both cats hopped off the table and trotted down the hall to my bedroom. They stopped before entering, though.

"Look up," Merlin said with wide, eager eyes.

I looked up and saw nothing—or at least nothing that wasn't supposed to be there. And the sight of that plain, boring white ceiling made my heart leap with joy.

"You fixed it!" I cried, stooping down to pet both cats in thanks. "How? I thought you needed to go to Nocturna to find someone?"

"As much as I'd like to take credit, it was all Luna," Merlin announced with pride. "Tell her, Luna."

The she-cat looked embarrassed by her good deed. "Well, you know how we've been going to my garden so much lately?"

"I do."

"I figured if there were other garden witches nearby, they would have similarly well-stocked gardens." She paused, and Merlin picked up where his partner left off.

"We spent all day teleporting to various neighborhoods around the state until at last we found what we were looking for two towns over. A place called Beech Grove. There we met a magical human of all things! The garden was his, but he introduced us to a cat he knew named Mr. Fluffikins."

"And Mr. Fluffikins came with us and fixed the roof with just a swish of his tail. Can you believe it?" Luna cried. If I didn't know any better, I'd say this Fluffikins had left quite the impression on her.

Merlin didn't seem the least bit jealous, though, and I admired how secure their relationship had become after its rough start.

"I can't believe you went through all that for me. Thank you."

"Well, it was Merlin's fault, but now he knows better than to summon lightning indoors. Right, dear?" Luna glared at him.

Merlin's head drooped toward his chest. "Yes, dear."

"I appreciate you making it up to me, thank you." I gave them each another pat on the head before rising back to my feet.

"Oh, that's not him making it up to you," Luna said in a stern voice, directed more at Merlin than at me. "That's just setting things right. Merlin has another surprise for you as part of his apology, though."

Merlin took a deep breath. "I thought a lot about our talk the other day, and how important it is to you that Luna and I embrace human customs while living in the human world..." His words drifted off, leaving me confused. What was he getting at?

Luna nudged him with the side of her paw. "Well, go ahead. No need to dilly-dally."

The Maine Coon raised his head and regarded me with glowing

green eyes. “And as such, Luna and I have decided to get married. Officially. Before the kittens come.”

I clapped my hands together in excitement. “You guys, that’s great! I’m so happy for—”

“And you will plan it for us,” Luna gushed. “Isn’t that wonderful?”

My smile faltered for a moment. “Uh, you guys don’t have to do all this on my account.” Especially if you expect me to do all the work, I added silently. I’d never planned a human wedding before, let alone a cat wedding. Where did one even begin?

“Think nothing of it, dear. We want to do this for you,” Luna assured me. She really had no idea.

“Thanks,” I said, trying so hard to keep some form of a smile plastered on my face. “When is the happy day?”

“This weekend!” they both cried in unison.

Oh, boy.

30

And so one adventure came to a close while many others loomed large on the horizon. I had a cat wedding to plan post-haste, a litter of kittens on the way in less than two months, a ghostly roommate I now needed to work hard at avoiding for the rest of my mortal existence, and the big bad was still out there.

I had no doubt we'd see Dash again, especially given Harold's eerie warning about sown seeds and dangerous fruit. Still, we had no idea how to find her, which meant we'd have to wait for her to come to us.

In the meanwhile, Merlin and I would just have to work to become as strong as possible so that we'd be ready when she returned. Thanks to Virginia's drain, I'd lost a good portion of the magic I'd accumulated since becoming Merlin's familiar. Luckily, my witchy cat was able to patch me up just fine. I had also started taking on magic faster the more and more time we spent together.

Everything would be fine. I had to believe that, or I would most assuredly go crazy.

The one thing that bothered me most about everything we'd just gone through, however, wasn't the near-death experience at the hands of an enemy I thought had been killed once and for all. It was the fact that my current coworker and former admirer Drake now knew about me and my cats—and who knows what else?

He had special abilities that none of us did, and he took them all in stride. The ghost hadn't weirded him out or broken his cool. He'd treated it like everything else in his life, somewhat interesting but mostly just... normal.

I longed to ask him what he was, but I figured he'd have no problem telling me if he actually knew himself.

He definitely knew what I was, though. And he often tried to talk to me about that night's events when we found ourselves alone at work.

Let me tell you, the tabletops at Harold's had never looked shinier, thanks to all the good polishes I gave them whenever I needed an excuse to avoid him.

For now, Drake was taking care to speak to me only when we were guaranteed privacy, but what if he started blabbing to others? Would I be held responsible by magical law enforcement and forced to pay for this exposure?

Merlin and Luna had said I was in the clear since Virginia was the one who exposed herself to him, but I still felt sick about him knowing.

I trusted him with my safety, but my secrets?

Not a chance.

I had a feeling I'd need to make some very difficult choices soon in order to protect him, my magical family, and myself.

And with a sweet, innocent litter of nieces and nephews on the way, I couldn't afford to make any mistakes…

MERLIN KILLS A ZOMBIE

When my cat brought me a dead bird as a present, I cringed.

When that dead bird suddenly flitted back to life, I screamed.

At first, I shrugged it off as one of the random things that happens when your roommate is a magical cat, but then it kept happening.

Turns out a familiar foe is creating an army of undead creatures with the goal of forcing us to surrender. But Merlin and I refuse to let dark magic prevail—not when the entire existence of magic is now at stake.

And if magic dies, so too will all who wield it.

Oh no, my cat will NOT become a casualty in this unholy war. I'm ready to fight my way through a million zombies and then take out the big bad, too. Nothing can come between this witchy cat and his familiar—and I'm ready to prove it.

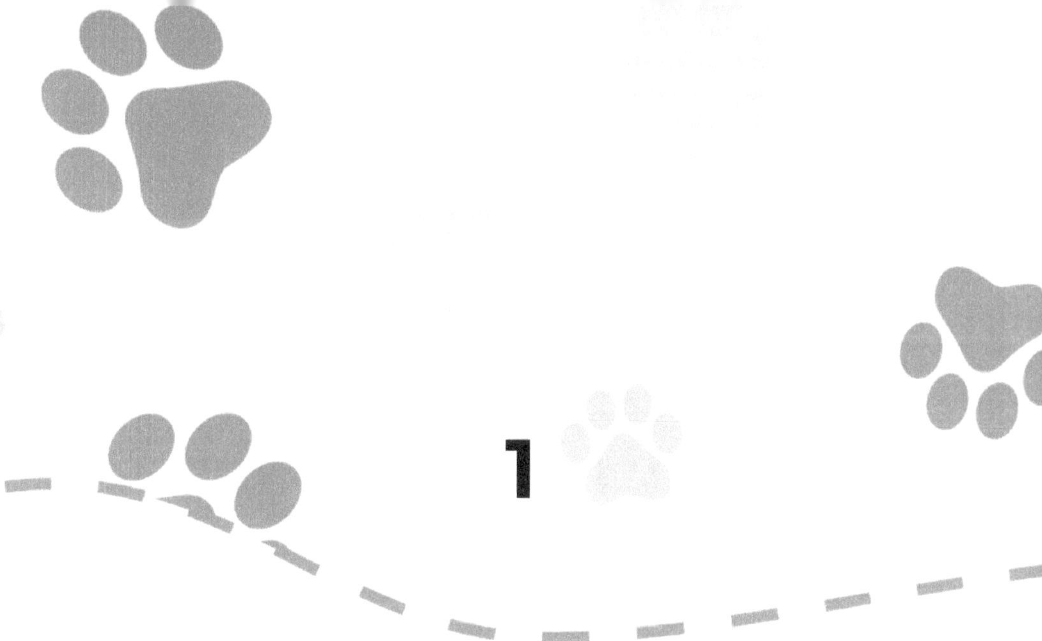

1

Hey there, I'm Gracie Springs. I'm a twenty-something barista working my way through grad school. Okay, I should have gotten my degree several months ago, but I haven't found the time to finish my thesis yet.

You can't really blame me, all things considered. Seriously, you try working as the human familiar for a magical cat with at least two dangerous enemies and tell me how well you keep up with the everyday things.

Ever since my Maine Coon Merlin revealed his powers to me, it's been one attempt on my life after another.

When I first moved to the tiny Georgia town of Elderberry Heights, it was just me and my normal kitty cat living in the house my grandmother gifted me when she retired to the Florida Keys. But now Merlin's pregnant wife Luna has joined us, and so has Luna's former familiar, a somewhat disgruntled and super evil ghost named Virginia.

Yeah, it's getting a little cramped, and the kittens haven't even been born yet!

Another fun twist?

I'm descended from King Arthur, and my witchy cat has a famous lineage, too. He's descended from the original Merlin.

No, not the human imposter everyone thinks they know. The real wizard, who just so happened to be a cat.

Because of our intertwined ancestry, Merlin and I have a nearly unbreakable bond. It's also put a gigantic target on both of our backs.

Our original enemy, Dash, hasn't turned up for a while, but we have no doubt she's regrouping and will make a play for us again soon.

What she wants with us, I honestly have no idea. And I'm almost too afraid to find out.

Because honestly? The more I learn about the magical world, the less I seem to understand it. I can't cast magic, but I can hold it inside of me. That's my main role as Merlin's familiar, in fact: to be a walking vessel for his magical overflow. If he were a normal witch, becoming tied to him wouldn't have upset my life all that much.

However, since my cat is anything but normal, it's one life-or-death encounter after the next.

It may seem like I'm complaining, but actually I'm happy to help. Someone has to take on the bad guys, after all.

So why not me?

Famous last words, I know...

. . .

"Eek! Why me?" I shrieked when Merlin dropped a dead bird at my feet just as I was trying to fix my morning coffee.

"It's a gift," the fluffy Maine Coon announced with pride. He didn't even seem the least bit offended by my reaction to his grotesque gesture.

I cringed as I studied the limp avian form at my feet. "What could possibly make you think I'd want this?"

"Why wouldn't you want this?" he countered. The tip of his tail flicked, revealing the beginnings of his irritation with me. "And how can you know you don't like it until you try it?"

Proof that even though we could talk to each other, we didn't necessarily stand one another.

"Um, thank you," I said, bending down to examine the "gift" more closely. I'd have to find some way to dispose of it when he wasn't looking. The problem was, Merlin always seemed to be looking.

"See, now that wasn't so hard," my cat said, a smug smile spreading across his whiskered face.

I was trying to work out what to say next—it took quite a bit longer when I hadn't yet had my coffee for the day—when the bird flitted to life.

I screamed and fell backward, landing hard on my butt.

"Don't worry, Gracie!" Merlin cried as he pounced into action. "I'll save you from this feathered fiend!"

I watched in stunned silence as he leapt into the air, sunk his fangs into the bird, then landed back on the linoleum floor, all in one fluid motion.

"Coulda... sworn—he's... dead," he mumbled through a mouthful of bird. Then much to my horror, he crunched down hard.

Oh, that poor little red-breasted robin.

Merlin dropped the now thoroughly murdered bird at my feet again, then began to groom himself with long, sweeping licks across his side.

I didn't know what to say. I certainly couldn't force out another thank you, but I also couldn't really punish my cat for doing exactly what cats do.

As I stared at the bird in bewilderment, it began to twitch back to life. First it was just the tips of one wing, but then one black beady eye shot open.

I crab-walked backward until I bumped into the fridge.

"Oh no, you don't!" Merlin cried and pounced again before his victim could take flight.

He crunched down on it once more, this time breaking its neck so that it hung at an unnatural angle.

I breathed in and out deeply, praying that such a scene would never ever unfold in my kitchen again. Coffee or not, I was now fully awake—and also undoubtedly scarred for life.

"Is it really dead now?" I whispered after a brief pause, afraid that if I wasn't quiet enough, my words would rouse the songbird from its sleep of death. Provided it was actually dead this time.

Merlin and I both stared down at the disfigured mound of feathers and watched as it once more twitched to life.

This was most assuredly not how I'd planned to start the morning!

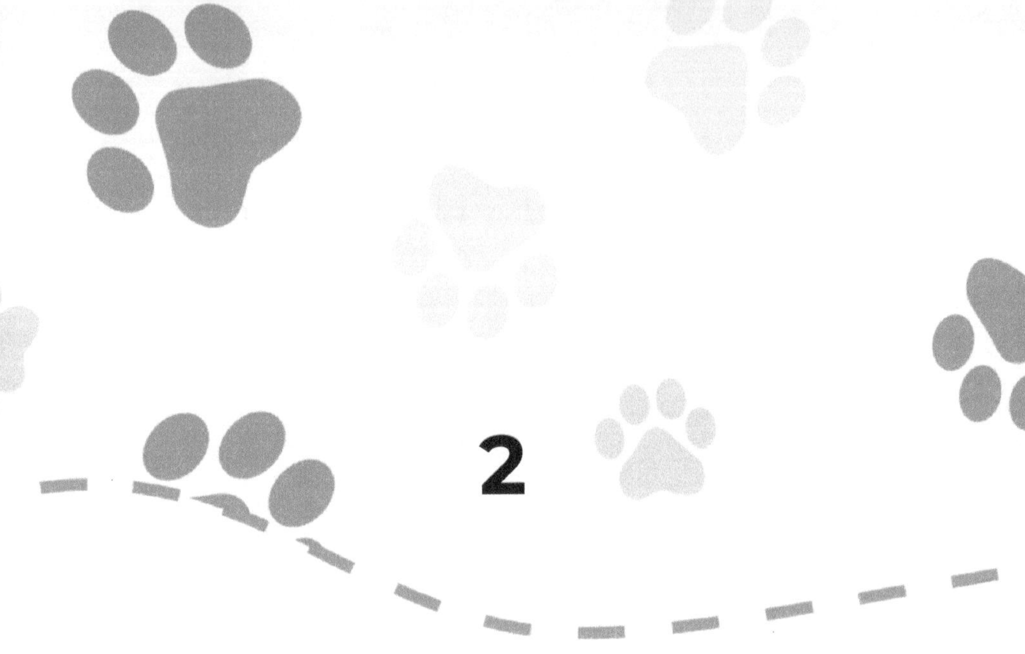

2

"Why won't it die?" I cried, scrabbling for purchase as I attempted to push myself into a standing position.

"Dark magic is afoot," Merlin declared before pouncing on the dead-or-dying-or-undead bird. "Go to Luna. I'll take care of this fiend!"

Well, he didn't have to tell me twice. I ran out of the kitchen and straight through the front door without even taking the time to slip on a pair of shoes. The morning dew clung to my socks, but I didn't care. I could easily put on fresh footwear, but I couldn't stand to watch as Merlin had his way with the sharp-beaked monster in the kitchen.

I rounded the house in a flash and found Luna sprawled out on the grass and soaking up the sun. Ever since becoming pregnant, she'd taken to spending much of her day in the back garden. I'd even helped her plant some flowers and herbs to help with the homesickness she sometimes felt.

Seeing me, she gently rolled onto her feet, still the perfect picture of grace and elegance even toward the end of her pregnancy.

Yes, we were getting quite close to kitten time. The cats had given me one week to plan their wedding after they'd found out they were expecting. They reasoned that since holy matrimony was important to humans and not so much to cats, I should be the one to put in all the work. That had been a few weeks ago now. The happy newlyweds had spent a couple of nights away from home to celebrate their honeymoon, and then life had gotten back to normal—well, as normal as it could be when you had two talking cats and a ghost as your roommates.

I'd almost started to believe that the magical baddies of the world were done with us, but now we had a very messed-up robin to prove otherwise.

"Oh, dear," Luna said after noting my worn expression. "I told Merlin you wouldn't appreciate that gift, but he insisted. He said you hadn't been yourself since Virginia moved in, and he wanted to do something to show you that you're appreciated."

"That's actually kind of sweet," I said with a half smile as I rubbed at my sore backside. "But, yeah, you were right, the bird was a terrible idea. Especially considering it won't stay dead."

Luna's ears shot back, and her blue eyes grew wide. "What do you mean it won't stay dead?" she asked in a low whisper.

"Exactly that. That thing would seem dead, but then pop back up a few moments later. I'm pretty sure I watched Merlin break its neck, but even that didn't stop it." I shuddered at the memory—that one would, no doubt, reappear in my nightmares many times over. "Also I think maybe I'm a vegetarian now."

Luna hissed. "Don't even joke about such terrible things."

"Which of those things do you think was a joke?" I sputtered in disbelief.

Luna studied me for a moment. "Oh my, you are serious. Aren't you?"

"Dead serious," I said through gritted series. "Or, I guess, undead serious."

"Yes, that seems to be the situation we have on our hands now," Luna agreed with a solemn nod.

"Do you mean...?" I couldn't even finish the sentence. The very word seemed so improbable.

"Zombies," Luna confirmed my suspicion.

"But how?" I exploded, cursing our bad luck. Although something told me a lack of luck had nothing to do with this.

"The how is quite simple," Luna explained patiently. "It's the why I'm more worried about."

"Well, now you have me curious."

The she-cat stared at the house without saying anything.

"How are zombies made, Luna?" I prompted.

She blinked up into the sun, then turned to me slowly. "Well, you know how cats have nine lives?"

"Sure," I said to hurry us along. I'd always assumed that was just an expression, but obviously not. I'd have to remember to ask about that later, when we weren't facing down a zombie in the kitchen.

"It's not all cats. Just witches. We're not immortal, but we are granted extra lives."

"Okay," I said, nodding. "I guess that makes sense."

"We can bestow our lives upon others. It's a complex but relatively well-known spell. Normally it's a benevolent spell used to help mates match each other's lifespans."

"But I'm guessing that's not the case with the bird Merlin brought me," I ventured.

"No," she said, searching the distance. "There's a corrupted version of the life-share spell. It can be used to reanimate the dead."

"But that bird only just died. I saw it," I reminded her.

Luna's face took on a drawn expression, which did not provide me with very much comfort. "Yes, that means our dark witch is close."

"Do you think he'll make more zombies?"

"I'm guessing the first one wasn't an accident, so more will likely be on the way."

"But why would someone surrender all their lives just to spook us a little?" That was the part I didn't understand. Even if we couldn't kill the bird, we were still much bigger and stronger and could find another way to overpower it.

"That's what worries most," Luna whispered. "The truly evil among us—the kind who would use a spell like this—can also control the minds and wills of others. It's possible the culprit has an army of helpless witches at his disposal and that each of them have a cadre of zombies at theirs."

I sighed and dragged a hand through my hair. "So things are about to get bad, huh?"

"Really bad," Luna bit out, as if speaking the words would also make them true.

Luna was the bravest among us. If this new zombie situation spooked her, then we were in for some tough times ahead.

This day just kept on getting worse and worse...

3

"Now that you know what we're dealing with here, I'm sure you understand that we can't leave Merlin alone with that thing any longer." Luna ran around the side of the house, back to the front.

I loped after her somewhat hesitantly. One undead songbird couldn't do that much on its own, but what about a whole flock of them? There's a reason Hitchcock's aptly titled masterpiece was one of the most enduring horror films of all time.

When I entered the house, I found Luna pacing tight, worried circles around Merlin, inspecting him closely. "Are you sure it didn't get a scratch or two in?"

Merlin puffed up his fur and then shook out his coat. "Even if it did, I'm fine. The life-share spell can't be conducted through a third party. If someone wants to turn me into a zombie, they'll have to do it face-to-face."

Luna let out a sad mewl. "That's what I'm worried about, dear."

Merlin rubbed his face against his wife's. "Don't worry about me, my love. Just keep growing our children in your belly, and I'll handle the rest."

Luna narrowed her eyes and flicked her tail. She loved Merlin, but she definitely didn't like being ousted from our adventures. When she'd still had her magic, she'd been the more powerful of the two cat-witches, and every now and then she seemed to question the sacrifice she'd made—whether that was fighting ghosts or inspecting strange noises at night.

"Luna caught me up on the magical side of things," I said with a nod her way. "I think I understand all that, but what happened to the bird?" I glanced around but didn't see the cursed thing.

Merlin strode across the kitchen and sat at my feet. "I defeated the vile fiend in the best, most enjoyable way possible." He paused, lifting his nose with obvious pride.

"You a—"

"I ate it!" Merlin finished with wide eyes. "I'm not usually a fan of dark magic meat, but a meal is a meal. And I had to get rid of it somehow. At least this way we know he won't be coming back."

I shuddered at the thought of the mangled carcass stirring in my cat's stomach. *Yuck, yuck, yuck.*

"But who would send a zombie after us, and why?" Luna asked, concern reflecting in her wide blue eyes.

"Surely you've noticed we collect enemies like they're going out of fashion," Merlin teased. "Granted, things have been suspiciously quiet for the last few weeks."

"Hang on. There's someone else we should be asking these questions," I murmured, then marched up and down the hallway, banging on the walls. "I know you're in there!" I shouted. "Come out. We need to talk to you!"

It didn't take long for one very angry ghost to phase through the wall and regard me with an icy glare.

If looks could kill... Actually I think our resident ghost was hoping her sour expression *would* render me dead, but she was completely powerless and also bound to our house.

Virginia spent most of her time inside the walls, the only real place she could get any privacy. At first she'd enjoyed popping in and out of rooms and trying to spook us, but the less we reacted to her jump-scares, the more she'd voluntarily begun to fade into the background.

Still, the former evil henchwoman might know something about our new zombie master foe. And anyway, it never hurt to check.

"Why did a zombie attack us today?" I demanded as she bobbed before me, nearly translucent from her lack of magical energy.

"Is that what all the fuss was about?" she asked drolly. "And no one thought to wake me? I love seeing you three get your derrieres handed to you." Virginia was too classy to talk about butts in English, clearly.

I rolled my eyes at her. Half the time our elderly ghost reminded me of a sassy teenager—and that was when she wasn't trying to kill us somehow, someway. I had to hand it to her. She didn't give up easily.

"Had I known a zombie was coming, I'd have done what I could to help," she added with a *humph*.

"Funny, I'm pretty sure you don't speak bird." Luna growled and crouched low as she faced Virginia.

"Nor do you, *dear*," the ghost said, mocking her former master's affectation.

"You've been spying on us," I countered. It wasn't a question.

Virginia shrugged. "Remember, you're the one who made it so that I can't leave this wretched place. Of course I'm spying. Problem is I've got nobody to tell."

I bit my lower lip and nodded. Virginia was right, of course. She couldn't talk to anyone who wasn't inside the four walls of this house. Meanwhile the cats and I knew better than to let unvetted strangers into our abode.

One thing was immediately clear: our zombie maker wasn't working with our ghost. On the one hand, that was good news. Nobody had unfettered access to us the way Virginia did.

But on the other hand?

I had no idea where to look next.

And something told me it would be much harder to defeat zombies if we didn't know when or where they'd be coming. Well, at least we'd had the last few weeks to rest up. A fight was definitely brewing, and judging from this morning's showdown, it wouldn't be one that we could easily win.

4

"Should we go do some research in Nocturna?" I asked the cats, referring to the hidden fantasy city that was only accessible via an active witch's cauldron—or in our case, via the birdbath in the front yard where Merlin also brewed his potions as needed.

"We can't always run straight to Nocturna. There are other ways of solving things," my cat groused. One of his sharp teeth protruded over his bottom lip, giving him an irritated yet comical appearance.

"So says the guy who has a certain Tom cat looking to take him down," Luna teased. One thing I'd learned quickly while hanging around these two was that cats' love lives were even more complicated than humans'. First they'd broken up to pursue their magic, then they'd become sworn enemies, had a big showdown, got back together suddenly, and now kittens were on the way. Merlin had also upset a few of Luna's other suitors who believed she'd made the wrong choice. One had even challenged Merlin to a magical duel, which the Maine Coon had foolishly accepted.

Returning to Nocturna meant risking Merlin's magic, because if he fought and lost, he'd have to spend forever without it. Unfortunately, Luna and I couldn't enter Nocturna without Merlin since he was the only active witch. And if he lost his magic, not only would we be permanently locked out of the city, but we'd also be sitting ducks on this side of the cauldron. Whatever supernatural entity was after us now might not stop pursuing us if we lost our only source of magic, even though we'd be completely helpless without it.

And that's what made this whole thing so frustrating. Our zombie master was literally manipulating life and death. I preferred to remain among the living, thank you very much.

I wrung my hands as I glanced from one cat to the other. "If not Nocturna, then where do we start? Do we try to capture one of the zombies and ask it what it knows?"

Virginia drifted closer to me, and I flapped my hand as if she were a foul smell I could send floating in the other direction.

She simply laughed and moved in even closer. "You only bested me out of stupid luck. Don't expect to get so lucky again. There's no way someone as ill-equipped as you—all three of you—could possibly take out a master of the undead. Soon I won't be the only ghost around here, mark my words."

Luna raised her hackles and swiped at the air. "Go away, you nuisance! The only weak one here is you. You signed your own death warrant when you decided to betray me in your quest for power. And you have no one to blame but yourself, and possibly that awful illusion witch."

Merlin nodded thoughtfully, but I could tell something had distracted him. "We can capture a zombie, yes, but there's no point in keeping it alive—erm, animated. They aren't intelligent enough to do anything more than go after their mark. They're disposable. The perfect henchmen, because they won't get distracted and they won't betray their maker."

"You really think you stand a chance, don't you?" Virginia laughed even louder.

Merlin spun to face her, anger glowing in his green eyes. "Quiet, or I'll eat you, too!"

Virginia opened her mouth to say something, but Merlin continued to glare at her with all the hostility he could muster, which just so happened to be quite a lot.

She sighed and floated toward the edge of the room. She stayed near enough to keep spying, but at least she'd removed herself from the active conversation.

"Do we think this could be Dash?" I asked the two cats. "It seemed like a pretty sure thing she'd be coming back to challenge us again. Is that what's happening here?"

"It's as good a guess as any, dear," Luna agreed before licking her paw and rubbing it over her forehead.

"She could be anywhere, though," I pointed out. "She could look like anyone or anything. How will we know when we've found her?" Dash's ability to manipulate others' perception is what had allowed her to get so close to us the first time around.

"We won't know," Merlin said stonily. "At least not at first. But I'm pretty sure she wants us alive. At least long enough for her to carry out whatever plans she has for us. I say we let her capture us, and then take it from there."

"Darling," Luna gasped, stomping her front paw down on the ground and drawing a startled expression from both of us. "That's incredibly dangerous! Think of the kittens!"

"I am thinking of the kittens, which is why I need you to stay here." Merlin licked Luna's forehead and then marched over to the door and waited, all the while wagging his tail impatiently.

"C'mon, Gracie," he called in a voice that brooked no argument. "The sooner we get this started, the sooner we can finish it, once and for all."

I didn't want to put myself into the middle of their argument, but we didn't have a better plan for sussing out our zombie wrangler and I couldn't bear to stand by and do nothing while we waited for him or her to strike again.

I sighed and offered Luna an apologetic glance as I slipped my feet into a pair of shoes, grabbed my keys, and followed Merlin outside.

"Let's go catch ourselves a bad guy," I said once I'd securely closed the door behind us.

"Actually," Merlin said with a smug grin. "We're going to let a bad guy catch us, instead."

I nodded and followed my cat down the street with no idea whether our slapdash plan would work at all.

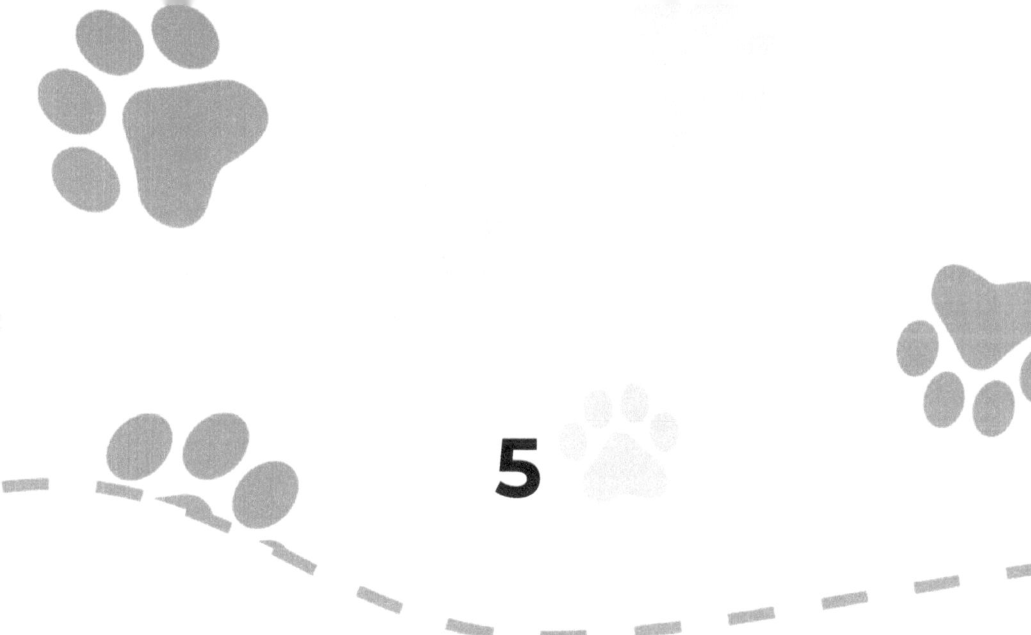

5

I strolled down the street, trying to appear casual despite the giant housecat walking determinedly at my side.

"What should I be doing?" I mumbled to Merlin when I was sure nobody was looking our way.

"Act... natural," he said through a closed mouth.

We turned the corner and found old Mrs. Harkness watering her begonias with a pleasant smile on her face.

"Good morning, Grace!" she chimed. "And good morning to your furry little companion there, too."

I waggled my fingers in a wave and put on my best smile. "Yes, it's a great morning!" I called back.

"I said *act natural,"* Merlin hissed from below.

"What's that, sugar?" Mrs. Harkness responded with a furrowed brow as she shut off the hose and blinked into the sun.

"Oh, j-j-just admiring the natural beauty of the day!" I said, quickening my pace before she could figure out who'd really spoken.

I waited until we were an entire block away before speaking again. "That was too close." I kneeled down to stroke Merlin's head and kept my voice low. Hopefully any passers-by would just think I was cooing over my pet. "You shouldn't talk while we're outside. Anyone could be listening."

Merlin winked at me, and I straightened back to a standing position, ready to continue on our way.

But then Merlin let out a terrible yowl and kicked up his back feet in distress.

I reached down to pet him, but he swatted at my hand. "LU! NA!" he half shouted, half meowed.

I glanced down the block, and sure enough, I spotted a tiny white blur on the horizon. I don't think I'd ever seen Luna move so fast, but I also had no doubts it was her, especially given Merlin's unhappy reaction.

When she caught up with us, she plopped her butt on the ground right in front of Merlin.

"I told you to stay home!" he seethed.

"And I told you I'm not sitting this one out," she shot back in a raspy whisper.

"And I told you we need to avoid talking while we're outside where anyone could hear."

"You didn't tell me that, dear," Luna pouted. "See, I'm already missing things. I refuse to be written out of our adventures just because I'm about to become a mom. We work best as a team. You need me."

"Okay, but seriously, stop talking while we're in public!" I hissed as a beat-up minivan rolled past us. The driver gawked at me like I was some kind of crazy person, and he was absolutely right.

Once he passed, Luna let out a high-pitched meow and rubbed her face against my hand—to signal her agreement, I supposed. Well, at least one of them saw things my way. And Luna was right, too. She'd been an integral part of our adventures so far, and we wouldn't have escaped either alive without her help.

Merlin stared at us both with wide green eyes, flicking his tail back and forth unhappily. He didn't speak again, though, so I guess that meant he agreed to keep mum for a bit.

"I have no idea where I'm going," I admitted in a whisper, crouching low again. "Can one of you take the lead?"

Luna meowed and trotted ahead, turning back only for a second to make sure we followed.

Merlin emitted a low rumble, but otherwise fell in line. He hated when he wasn't the one in charge, not that such a thing happened very often.

Luna set a pace much faster than my normal gait, and after a few more blocks I found myself breathing heavy as sweat beaded at my hairline.

"This isn't working," I complained. "Nobody is paying any attention to us."

Merlin opened his mouth, ready to come at me with either an "I told you so," or "serves you right for trying to silence my voice."

"Oh, I wouldn't say nobody," a smooth voice responded from a nearby azalea shrub before Merlin could speak. All the words ran together with no breaths in between, creating a creepy, snake-like sound. Still, even though I couldn't immediately place it, I knew I'd heard this voice before. I mean, how could I forget something so eerily distinct?

Luna charged straight into the bush while Merlin hung back on the sidewalk with me. Soft feline voices whispered back and forth, and a few moments later Luna peeped her little white face out and motioned for Merlin and me to come closer.

Oh, I really hoped the owner of this azalea didn't make an appearance anytime soon, because I had no idea how I'd explain my way out of this one. Merlin entered the bush easily, but I had to drop to my hands and knees and bring my face close to the earth to see through the tangle of leaves and branches.

Three glowing pairs of eyes met mine—blue, green, and yellow. When it came to the new arrival, I couldn't see anything more than those bright, sun-like eyes, but that was enough for me to place him.

Mr. Fluffikins had arrived.

Which meant we definitely had trouble on our hands.

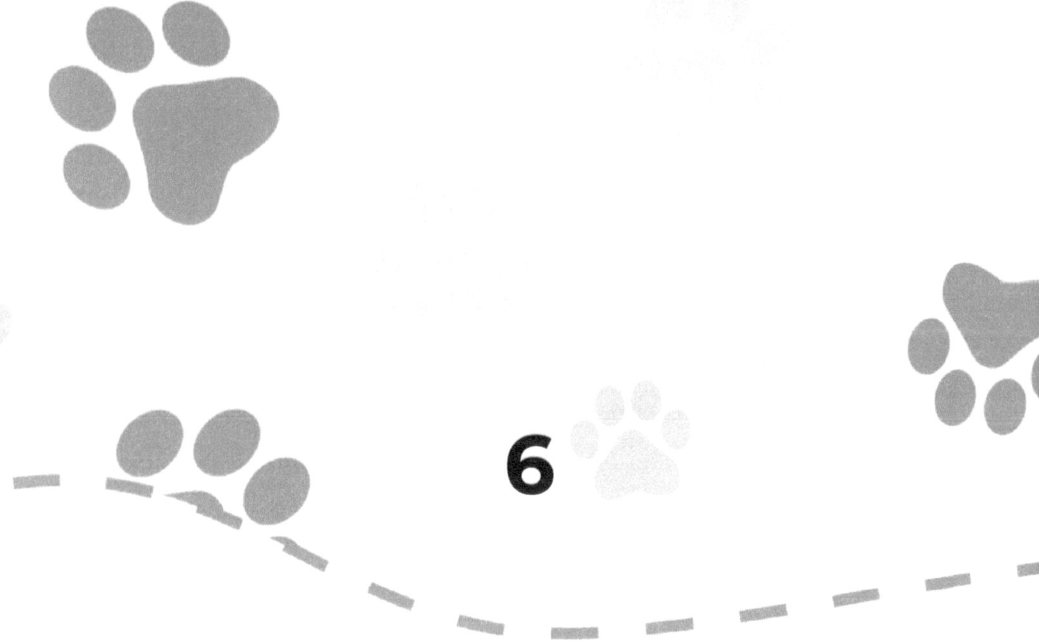

6

"I was called to investigate a disturbance in the area," the black cat explained.

We first met Fluffikins after Merlin had summoned lightning in the house and blasted a hole straight through the roof. I didn't have the money to fix it, and Merlin didn't have the correct type of magic, so he and Luna phased in and out of various neighborhoods around Southern Georgia until they found Mr. Fluffikins.

His magic was different than what Merlin's was or what Luna's had been. Instead of being tied to a particular element in nature, Fluffikins wielded a special kind of magic generated from the earth's core, and with it, he could do almost anything.

He used his elite skills to manage a team of mixed paranormals in the nearby town of Beech Grove. While small, Beech Grove served as the magical hub for this region of the state, which made the little black cat crouched before us the single most powerful magical being for miles. If he'd been called in to investigate a disturbance himself, then that definitely meant it was something big.

I bit my lower lip, trying to keep all the questions I wanted to ask from tumbling out one after the other.

As I'd learned at Merlin and Luna's wedding, Fluffikins was all about ceremony and precedent. He wanted things done a certain way —nay, *demanded* they be done a certain way. And when it came to magical hierarchy, my cat outranked me mightily.

Sure enough, Merlin took the lead for our side of the conversation, holding his nose high to show that the other cat didn't intimidate him, even though that may not have been true. "Might that disturbance be related to zombies?"

Fluffikins tilted his head to the side; his eyes appeared to float in the darkness. "Zombies, no. Nothing so terrible as that."

"Well..." Merlin shifted his weight from paw to paw before continued. "I'll have you know that we got attacked by a zombie robin this morning and have reason to believe more will be on the way."

"More? Are you sure it wasn't just a one-off? A new magic user practicing the life-share spell that accidentally transferred it to the wrong entity?"

"We're sure," Luna answered with a grave expression.

"Well, since I'm already here, do you need my help?" Fluffikins offered. "It's the least I can do while I search for my mark."

"Who's your mark?" I asked, unable to hold back my curiosity.

Fluffikins let out a weary sigh. "It's an unfortunate thing. A young vampire is running rampant in your town. He risks exposing all of magical kind to the humans due to his recklessness."

"I haven't noticed anything unusual," I said with a shrug. "Maybe it's not as bad as you think."

"We've been lucky so far, but if he isn't reined in soon, we'll have quite the situation on our hands." He paused and turned away from me, redirecting his attention on the highest-ranking individual here. "Merlin, do you need my help handling your zombies?"

My cat sniffed the air and shook his head. "Thanks, but no. We are fully capable of dealing with this on our—"

"CHEE TEE TEEE YAAAAAH!" A loud cry rent the air unlike anything I'd ever heard before. Shortly after, a small projectile shot through the bush and landed before us.

It rose on two legs, expertly shaking off the force of the impact, then turned toward Merlin with murder in its dark, glistening eyes.

"CHYAHHHHHH!" It belted out again, throwing itself at the Maine Coon's face.

Merlin staggered backward, but his tiny attacker grabbed onto his whiskers and clung tight, refusing to be shaken away.

Luna and Fluffikins both jumped into action. Luna hurled herself at the invader, slashing out with sharp claws in an urgent desire to defend her mate.

Mr. Fluffikins summoned a swirling pink tendril of magic and used it to lasso the creature and pry it away from Merlin. Once captured, he held it up for a closer inspection.

The little thing hissed and snarled, trying desperately to break free. When Fluffikins didn't let it go, the creature began to gnaw at his shoulder.

That's when I recognized the creature for what it was—a squirrel. No sooner had I figured that out than the attack squirrel broke his arm clear off and slipped from a surprised Fluffikins's magical grasp.

He bounded out of the bush and screamed again. *"TCHI-TCHI-TCHIIIIIYA!"*

Mr. Fluffikins spun in a circle, then sent a burst of magic straight into the air. It exploded around us, and I threw my hands over my head defensively.

"No one in a one-block radius will see or hear us, but we must dispose of this vile creature quickly!" he shouted. And just like that, all three cats bounded from the bush, ready for one heck of a fight.

7

Squirrels rained down from above, a veritable army descending from the sky—or at least from a nearby tree branch. Being that I was stuck on my hands and knees with my head pushed into a bush, I found myself completely at their mercy.

Tiny, clawed hands scraped at my back, and—oh—how it hurt! I backed out of that azalea as quickly as I could and scrabbled to my feet, but the tiny fiends hung on tight.

Merlin, Luna, and Mr. Fluffikins charged forth and fell upon the squirrels who'd attached themselves to me.

But more kept coming in a steady wave. Black, gray, brown, even red squirrels, all with crazed looks in their eyes, all determined to tear us to shreds.

And honestly I didn't know how to fight them. Nor did I want to.

I'd always loved watching the playful squirrels who came to snack at the bird feeder in our backyard.

While just as agile, these squirrels were decidedly different. Unhinged. And given the spectacle the first one had treated us to, I was willing to bet they were also undead. It seemed our zombie master had found us, which meant the plan had worked. In hindsight, it was a horrible plan.

Another worry zoomed to mind. Could undead squirrels still spread rabies? I'd have to add visiting the hospital for a screening to my long list of things to do later that day, providing we even survived this heckin' crazy battle.

One of the little bucktoothed monsters sunk his teeth into my neck, and I roared in pain. Served me right for getting so lost in my thoughts when I should have been present in the moment.

I'd only just shook off the last squirrel when another assaulted me and a turbo-charged acorn thwapped into the side of my head.

What the...? I turned sharply to the side as a half dozen more nuts and assorted other projectiles slammed into my face.

Oh, that did it!

Gone were my inhibitions about hurting the cute little animals. They were already dead-ish anyway, and if I didn't fight back, then one of the cats or I could follow in that unfortunate wake.

Ms. Gracie Springs was no pushover, no sirree!

I began to stomp around, trying to crush the little monsters beneath my feet. However, not even that could keep them down. The flattened beasts rose again, slithering on their bellies as they sought out their revenge.

"There's too many!" Merlin shouted. "I can't eat them all!"

Luna's gorgeous white fur was streaked with blood as she continued to bite and claw and pounce. Even Fluffikins looked worse for wear as he wielded his magic like a whip to keep the undead hoard at a distance.

A roaring engine sounded somewhere out of sight. I jerked my head toward the sound, and one of the combatants used that opportunity to scamper up my side and plant itself on top of my head.

I screamed and threw my hands up, desperately trying to roust the thing before he could chomp down and possibly give me a permanent scar for all to see.

The noisy engine grew louder and louder as the vehicle approached. Whoever it was would see us embroiled in battle: woman and cats versus angry, deformed squirrels. How was I supposed to explain this one away?

Wait, no. Mr. Fluffikins had cast a shield. Our secret was safe, but were we? There were only four of us, and the zombie master seemed to have an endless army of squirrels at his command. Were we sure it was Dash? That whoever this was wanted us alive?

Vroom, vroom. The noisy engine drew closer and closer before turning a sharp corner and revealing a motorcycle and helmeted rider.

A second squirrel climbed onto my head and yanked at my ponytail. I glanced toward Merlin, but he was now pinned like Gulliver waking up on the island of the Lilliputians. It took two dozen of the smaller creatures to hold him down, but they'd managed to overpower him by working together.

The bike revved and picked up speed.

I whipped my head toward the sound, watching in horror as it lifted up onto the sidewalk, coming straight for us with no signs of slowing down.

We may be protected from prying eyes and ears by Fluffikins's shield, but that wouldn't stop the motorcycle from crashing into us. The rider didn't even know he was in danger.

This was it. If the speeding bike didn't kill me, the zombie squirrels would.

Oh, of all the ways to die!

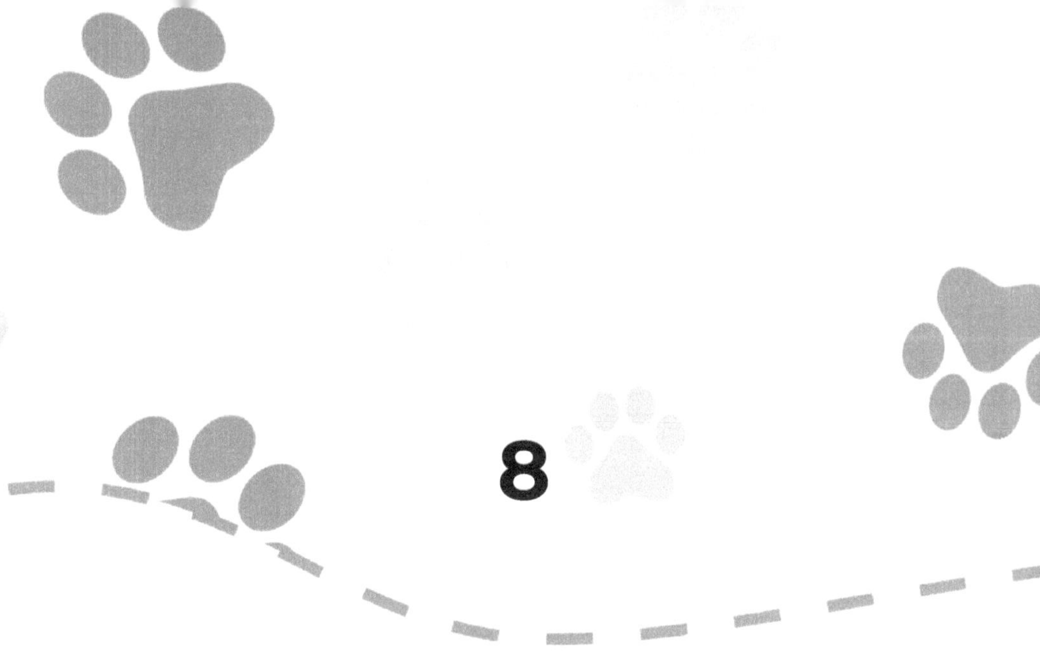

8

The motorcycle jerked to the side, only narrowly missing me as it took out several of the squirrel fighters, its thick rubber tires driving their little bodies into the cement. Still, the furry zombies twitched and attempted to pry themselves from the ground.

The bike reversed, then came to a stop a few feet away from me. The rider lifted his visor to reveal the sharp features of my fellow barista and kind of friend, Drake.

"Grab the cats and hop on," he shouted before dropping the visor once more.

Well, he didn't have to tell me twice, and I didn't have to tell the cats at all. We piled on, even as the remaining squirrels jumped at us and pelted us with acorns.

I briefly wondered how he'd managed to spot us despite the protective barrier, but I was both too shocked and too grateful to question this lucky circumstance. Besides, magic was weird when it came to Drake. This wasn't the first time he'd been able to do what others couldn't.

"Hang on tight!" Drake revved the engine and the bike jolted to life.

The remaining squirrels cried and chirruped, moving impossibly fast in their pursuit.

We were definitely out of the warded bubble now, which meant magical and non-magical alike would be able to see our panicked departure and the angry animal mob giving chase.

Drake kicked things up, moving at least double the legal speed limit now—or at least that's what it felt like to my unpracticed mind.

Merlin and Luna both dug their nails into me as we took a sharp turn.

Mr. Fluffikins produced some kind of swirly pink magic that, while just hardly visible, firmly glued him to the bike. I wished he would have taken the time to also help my cats, but no.

My poor thighs!

We zoomed past my house, and I moved one of my hands from Drake's waist to squeeze at his shoulder. "Aren't we going to stop?"

"No way!" he yelled back, his voice just barely audible over the roaring engine and rushing wind. "Those little suckers looked like they meant business. I'm getting you as far away from here as possible." Or at least I think that's what he said.

We drove with only the sounds of the engine and speeding wind to keep us company. After about twenty minutes, we at last came to a stop outside of a stylish bungalow at the edge of town.

"Welcome to *mi casa,*" Drake announced, parking the bike in the driveway next to a Segway of all things.

"Thanks," I muttered breathlessly. The world felt like it was still rushing past me even though I stood on solid pavement once more.

Drake lifted his helmet to reveal a swash of hair styled to within an inch of its life with hard, spiky gel. "I'm glad I didn't miss that fight. Zombie squirrels? Who knew such a thing even existed? I mean, I'd hoped but..."

"Wait, how did you know they were zombies?" I asked, my mouth gaping open in shock.

He bent down to check his hair in one of the bike's mirrors and winked at himself. "Oh, you know. I like to know a little bit about a lot of bit. Zombies included. And that vacant expression in their eyes was a dead giveaway."

"Undead," I murmured, unable to help the small smile that played at my lips. Leave it to Drake to bring his signature levity to any situation.

"Why were they attacking you, anyway?" he asked with an inquisitive gaze, turning his full attention to me now that he knew his hair still looked the way he wanted.

"Um..." I started, then immediately stopped.

Because seriously, how could I even begin to explain? Earlier, he'd seen Virginia's ghost and found out that my cats were magical and could talk, but we'd given him a special potion to wipe his memory and cover our tracks. Despite our best efforts, though, he refused to attribute all the strange things that had happened that night to a wild dream as we had planned. He knew something was up, which meant I had to tread lightly here.

But how could I possibly explain away a homicidal squirrel hoard?

Mr. Fluffikins saved me from having to explain myself when he hopped away from the bike and rounded on Drake. "Why, if it isn't just the man I was looking for," he said with an unhappy smile splashed across his face.

"What's up, little cat dude?" Drake asked with a laugh, leading us all through his garage and into his home.

Fluffikins kept his tail low and curled at the end. "I'm here to get you registered with your local supernatural board. It seems you've been creating quite a few issues during your nocturnal wanderings."

Drake stopped inside the doorway and stared at the bossy black cat through squinted eyes. "Come again now?"

Fluffikins entered behind him and then hopped up onto the counter, refusing to break eye contact with Drake. "Have you registered? If not, I'm taking you in right now."

Luna, Merlin, and I stood just outside the door, watching the scene unfold with wide eyes. I think we realized what was happening before Drake did.

"Why would I need to register?" he asked with a nervous chuckle. "You said this was for a supernatural board? That's great and everything, like, fine I'll register, but I'm not supernatural."

Mr. Fluffikins sighed. "Please don't tell me you don't even know what you are."

Drake dipped his hands into his pockets and rocked on his heels.

"I'm just an average-ish guy living off his trust fund and keeping busy."

The boss cat let out a dry laugh. "Average guy? Not even close."

All eyes were on Mr. Fluffikins. Nobody spoke. We were all waiting to see whether Drake would figure this out on his own.

What a revelation. I'd always known something was off about Drake, but this?

My friend shook his head and crossed his arms over his chest. "Sorry, I don't follow."

Fluffikins shook his head and sighed. When he looked up again, he spoke slowly, as if to an imbecile.

If Drake was offended, he didn't show it.

"You are a supernatural creature and need to register with the board."

"Oh yeah?"

We all nodded.

"And what kind of supernatural creature am I, Mr. Pussy Cat?"

"A vampire," Fluffikins said around a growl. "And don't you dare ever call me Mr. Pussy Cat again."

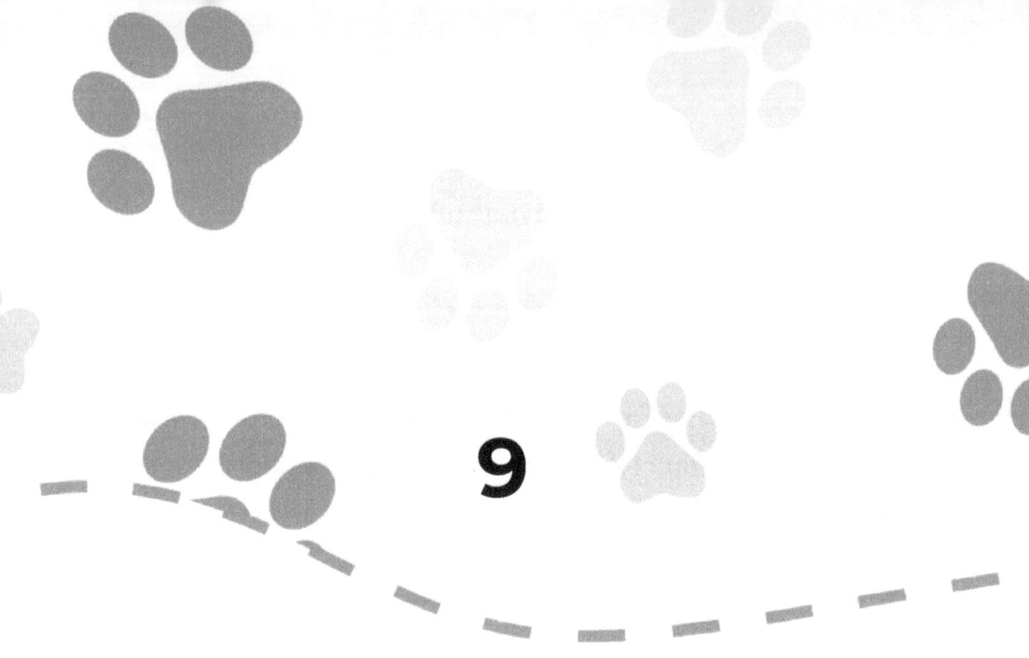

9

Drake took a step back and leaned into the wall. “No,” he said, shaking his head. “That’s not possible. I mean, I think I would know if I were a vampire.”

I glanced toward Merlin who was rolling his eyes.

Luna at least showed some compassion but didn’t speak a word.

“It’s okay, Drake. Really. You’re still you,” I offered with a small smile.

Drake groaned and shook his head. “No. I’m not. I can’t be.”

Mr. Fluffikins lifted a paw and extended one claw. “Looks like I need to convince you, so here we go. Let’s start with the easy stuff. Do you ever just know something that you shouldn’t? Like memories of things that haven’t actually happened?”

Drake nodded mutely, and Fluffikins extended a second claw.

“And do you ever wake up somewhere with no recollection of how you got there?” he pushed further.

Drake nodded again.

Fluffikins added a third claw to his furry fist. "Do you have an insatiable craving for wealth and knowledge?"

Drake said nothing.

"You know a little bit about a lot of bit," I said, quoting him back to himself. "And you do live off a trust fund."

Drake's entire face had drained of color by now, giving him a much more vampirish appearance than before. Honestly, I'd never seen him look so unsettled, not even when Virginia's ghost was actively trying to murder us. I watched now as his hands groped at the wall, unable to gain purchase.

When he spoke again, his voice came out broken and pitchy. "B-b-but I don't drink blood. I would never ever do such a thing!"

Fluffikins's claws retreated back into his paw, and he set his foot on the tile floor. "Did I say anything about drinking blood?" he asked with a low growl. He then turned to me with a peeved-off look. "You humans and your stupid lore. You've set vampires back hundreds of years, thanks to your so-called entertainment. Hundreds of years, that's when they actually did drink blood. It's been ages!"

"I'm s-s-sorry," I muttered, more a question than a declaration. Why was he blaming me for this when I was the only one here who was actually trying to help him!

"Normally new vampires aren't left on their own. Something must have gone wrong with your turning." The black cat blinked slowly while watching the newly revealed vampire for his reaction.

"So I wasn't born a vampire?" Drake's voice still squeaked like a preteen as he pushed out words in a hurry. "My mom and dad aren't—"

"Heavens no, nobody is born a vampire. How ridiculous!" Now it was Mr. Fluffikins who was rolling his eyes. Cats were not the most patient creatures, something I'd learned early on in my employ as a familiar.

But Drake didn't know any better. Even if he'd been okay with my magical stuff, this was different. He'd just found out that he was a monster, and one who had been unintentionally causing havoc at that.

He sank to the floor, cradling his head in his hands. "I'm dead," he murmured. "I'm legit dead."

"Well, technically you're undead," Fluffikins clarified with a sniff.

"Just like those squirrels," Merlin added with a laugh.

Luna shot him an irritated glance. "Go gentle on him, dear. Can't you see how upset he is already?"

Fluffikins had started laughing, too, but managed to pull himself together quickly. "If you're friends with this guy, how did you not figure out what he was?" he asked me.

"That's a good question," I said, turning my eyes back to Merlin.

He puffed up defensively. "What? I can't know everything about everything, okay? I knew something was up with the guy, but most vampires are loud and proud. How was I supposed to know what he was when even he didn't?"

Well, he had a point there.

"Settle down, you." Luna brushed up against Merlin's side and purred, nuzzling him until he at last deflated.

"You three will be able to see yourselves home from here, right?" the boss cat asked Merlin, then walked up to a gently sobbing Drake. "You need to come with me."

He continued to cry, not acknowledging Fluffikins or any of the rest of us. As for me, I didn't know exactly what Mr. Fluffikins did on a day to day, but I knew he wasn't used to taking no for an answer. And I also knew he would be unlikely to back down now.

Sure enough, the black cat extended his claws and tapped at Drake's arm. "Did you hear me, vampire? I need you to—"

"Perhaps we could be a little more delicate with him?" I suggested. "And maybe since you're here, you can help us with our zombie problem? I mean you did offer earlier. Let's take a break from vampires and talk zombies. Sound good?"

He shook his head from side to side. "That was before I'd found my charge. As you can see, I got what I came for and now I need to get back to Beech Grove. Many pressing matters await the vampire and me there."

"Are you kidding me right now?" Luna piped up. It wasn't like her to go on the offensive like this, but apparently she'd been pushed too far. "You're the diplomat for this entire region, and you're not at all worried about a zombie invasion?"

"It was very clear they were coming for you and you alone, so it's not an issue that takes precedence. This guy on the other hand…" He jerked his head toward Drake. "He's been causing trouble all across Peach Plains. We need to rein him in, and ASAP, or risk the exposure of our kind."

"So what? You're just going to let us die at the hands of this rogue zombie master?" I exploded, glaring at the cat with all the hostility I could muster.

"Tell you what," Fluffikins said with a sigh. "Submit your request in writing, and the board will get back to you in 5-10 business days."

I nodded dumbly. It was the only way to keep from screaming at the helpless jerk.

Fluffikins tapped Drake with his claws again and cleared his throat. "Now are you coming with me or what?"

Drake sobbed and moaned but didn't offer any words in response.

"Fine, then. We'll do it the hard way," Mr. Fluffikins bit out, and then both he and Drake disappeared in a swirl of sparkling pink magic.

10

The three of us that weren't swept up by Mr. Fluffikins's flash magic marched out of the house and into Drake's backyard. Once there, Merlin blinked twice to take us home. It was always easier for him to navigate outdoors rather than from inside an unfamiliar place.

"Well, a fat load of good that did us," the Maine Coon grumbled before padding over to his water dish for a quick drink.

"It was a good plan, dear. Really," Luna coaxed. "But Drake rescued us before our zombie master could capture us."

"I'm very angry with you," Merlin said to his wife after licking a few errant drops of water from his lips.

Her tail shot straight up, then arched forward at a sharp angle. "Don't be. I'm fine."

Merlin's tail immediately rearranged itself into the same position. "I said it would be dangerous and that you should stay back, but you refused to listen. Look what happened! You could have been hurt. One of the kittens could have been hurt!"

"I'm not a delicate flower, and I'm not a child," Luna hissed as she stood ramrod straight, refusing to budge.

"Oh, you think—"

"Enough!" I cut in. "We're all on the same side here. If we fight among ourselves, we don't stand a chance. As it is, we have no idea what we're doing. Let's not make this even harder than it already is."

Luna relaxed her stance and dipped her head apologetically. "You're right, dear. Of course, you're right."

Even though Merlin was technically my boss, I decided to take charge of the situation. It was the only way we'd make any progress at all. "Merlin, I know you just want to keep your family safe, but you have to let Luna decide for herself what that entails. You know she wouldn't knowingly put herself or the kittens in danger. She's smart and strong, and we need her help if she's willing to give it."

Neither cat said anything, but at least they didn't argue with my hasty decree.

After a few moments of tense silence, I went on. "Okay, our first plan wasn't exactly a success, so I think it's time to make a new one. I know you're *catsona non grata* in Nocturna, Merlin, but I really think that's where we ought to go next. I mean, we think our zombie master may be Dash, and we know Dash is interested in our bloodlines."

"We already met with the blood witch. We know exactly what we are and how we're connected." Merlin still stood in an awkward stance, though he had lowered his tail to a less hostile position.

When I shook my head to disagree, his tail shot back up into that mean forward hook.

I sighed. Why did everything have to be a battle for dominance? I just wanted to figure out this zombie thing before we were attacked again. If we could avoid that, I'd be one happy lady.

Still, I proceeded carefully. "Clearly there's something more that we're missing. I think we should go back and see if we can find out what that is."

Luna stretched out her back legs as she moved toward me. "And before you say anything, I'm coming, too."

"Neither of you can go if I refuse to take you there," Merlin pointed out with a half-hearted snarl. He'd already begun to deflate again.

"Then it's a good thing you're not refusing," I said with a cheeky grin.

"What about Tom and his cronies?" Merlin asked. "They're probably still looking for me so we can finish our duel."

More than a month had passed since that run-in, but I knew very well that cats could hold grudges for longer that. "Can't you use magic to change your appearance?" I suggested with a shrug.

"I'm a sky witch, and you know that. Illusions are out of my wheelhouse." He yawned and fell over onto his side dramatically.

"I can give you a makeover if you want?"

"Hard pass." Merlin jumped up and stalked down the hall.

"Where are you going?" I called after him.

"The portal to Nocturna doesn't open until sundown. I'm taking a nap," came his mumbled reply.

Luna yawned. “That sounds like a good idea,” she said before heading through the cat flap and to her favorite spot in the rear garden.

That just left me, alone in the kitchen.

Maybe I could pound out some work on my master’s thesis, make something of this day yet.

“I see you’re still alive and well. How awful for me,” a ghostly Virginia droned as she phased through the wall and came to hover before me.

Yeah, no. I was not dealing with her if I could avoid it.

I grabbed my keys and left the house in a hurry.

I had no idea where I was going, but hopefully I could at least get a few hours of peace and quiet before diving even deeper into this zombie adventure of ours.

11

My life was in a sad state, considering the only place I could think to go was my place of work, Harold's House of Coffee. No, I was not scheduled that day. Yes, my social life had probably hit rock bottom.

In truth, I hadn't taken the time to get to know many people since relocating to Elderberry Heights. All my family was back home in Michigan, other than Grandma Grace who'd moved to the Florida Keys. I'd left my friends back in my old college town, and all my new neighbors had a good forty years on me.

My boss Kelley had become a good friend over the last couple months, though. I'd supported her through her father's death and the resulting murder investigation and stayed by her side as she rebranded Harold's House of Coffee to serve all pumpkin spice lattes all the time.

She was also dating Drake, which made her the perfect person to mine for some info about him and the nighttime troubles Mr. Fluffikins had spoken of.

As far as I knew, Kelley was one-hundred percent certified human. But I'd assumed that Drake had been, too.

Who even knew anymore?

"Hey, girl. What can I get you?" Kelley sang out the moment I walked into the cafe.

"Just a hot tea. Thanks." I'd never been much of a tea drinker, but I'd recently become very anti-PSL. Too much of a good thing and all that. It was easier to pretend I didn't want coffee than to hurt Kelley's feelings. Because if I refused to accept her offer of a free drink, she'd just go ahead and serve me up whatever new concoction she was testing for the masses. Ergo, my request for hot tea despite the hot weather.

"How's today been?" I asked when she slid a mug of nearly boiling water to me over the counter. I casually plucked a bag of hibiscus tea from the display and dunked it into my cup.

"Busy as usual," she answered with a bright smile.

"Hey, have you heard anything from Drake?" *Real smooth, Gracie!* It was no small wonder I'd managed to survive all my recent scrapes, given how poor my people skills could be at times. Then again, I was mostly dealing with cats and other supernatural types lately.

Kelley shook her head. "Not since this morning when we texted hello. Why? Is something up?"

"Oh, yeah. I mean, no. Everything's fine!" I hurried to reassure her as I poured a couple packets of sugar into my mug and grabbed a stir stick. I kept my mouth pressed in a firm line as I finished preparing my drink. Why hadn't I at least attempted to come up with a plan on my way over here?

After mentally scolding myself once more for good measure, I raised my eyes to meet Kelley's and asked, "He's just been acting a little weird lately. Don't you think?"

"Weird how?" she said distractedly as she got to work making an iced drink for a customer.

"It's hard to describe," I ventured, not wanting to give away any of Drake's or my secrets. "Just, you know, weird."

Kelley tilted her head to the side as she thought, all while effortlessly engaging the blender. "Well, Drake's always been different. That's why I like him so much."

"You're right," I said, disparaged at how quickly I'd reached a dead end. "We shouldn't be surprised by anything he does."

"Yeah, like how he bought that Segway for no rhyme or reason," she said with a giggle.

"And the motorcycle," I added with a laugh.

Kelley shot me a silly look. "Yeah, guess which one of those two I like better." She shuddered, then poured the blended drink into a tall glass. "Segways really aren't meant for two people, but that didn't stop him from picking me up for our date using that thing last week."

I joined her in laughter, and it felt great to occupy my mind with something so frivolous for a change. We chatted about other things for a few minutes, but I knew I shouldn't stay too long and disrupt her work, especially given the fact that Harold's was always busy and needed all hands on deck.

"Well, I should probably--"

"Hold that thought!" Kelley interrupted, fishing her phone out of her apron. I hadn't heard it chime, but that wasn't exactly surprising since she tended to keep it on silent mode.

"Oh, hey, it's Drake!" she announced with a giddy grin, but as she read on her face rearranged itself into a frown. "He says he's going to be out of town for a few days and wanted to know if I could find someone to cover his shifts."

Kelley lowered the phone but continued to stare blankly where it had been. "We're supposed to go on a date tonight, but apparently he's already left. He didn't even say why."

"Maybe he's planning a surprise for you," I said, forcing a fresh wave of enthusiasm. Of course, I knew the truth about Drake's sudden disappearance. If I saw him before she did, I'd have to tell him to do something special for Kelley or to risk losing her as his girlfriend. Then again, if he was truly a vampire, maybe she was better off without him.

"Or he's cheating," Kelley said with a groan.

"No! He would never!" I reached over the counter and squeezed my friend's arm reassuringly.

"You did say he was acting weird lately. Do you know something I don't?" She raised an eyebrow my way.

"No, no, no. No way! I didn't mean that at all. Drake is crazy about you. Don't doubt that for a second. Anyway, I got to go."

And I rushed out of there as fast as I could without actually breaking into a run. Definitely not my finest moment.

12

After leaving the coffee shop, I drove around town for about an hour trying to gather my thoughts. During the relatively peaceful past few weeks, I'd begun to fantasize about getting back to a normal life. I'd actually thought that danger *wouldn't* be waiting around every corner, that I *wouldn't* have to strain so hard to keep my cat's magical world a secret.

Oh, how very wrong I'd been.

The more I thought, the more I despaired the current state of my life. I mean, what was the point in even finishing my master's degree at this point? It's not like I'd ever be able to get a normal job, not so long as I had my responsibilities as a familiar.

I'd once flirted with the idea of going even deeper into my education to land a doctorate. I loved school and would have enjoyed being a professor. But how could I ever truly make myself available to my students and colleagues if the enormity of my cat's secret always came first?

At least now I had an understanding boss at the coffee shop. I still couldn't summon the time or the passion needed to finish off my half-done thesis. What made me think I could take things to the next level with a doctoral dissertation? Or add classes on top of my current off-balance load?

Then there was the glaringly painful fact that I'd obviously never be able to fall in love, get married, have kids—all the things I didn't want now but knew I'd desire one day.

My cat and his magical needs always had to come first. Which meant I always had to come last.

I loved Merlin and Luna and knew I'd be crazy for their kittens, but what would happen if I ever wanted more?

Yeah, I probably shouldn't have been so fixated on the future, seeing as I didn't know whether we'd survive our current predicament—or the next one, or the one after that.

I was definitely getting ahead of myself, but I also couldn't help it.

It wasn't just me, though. I worried about Drake, too. A part of me had broken seeing him crumble to the floor like that.

I'd always viewed him as the ultimate chill guy, but even he had his limits. What would life be like for him now that he knew what he was?

I guess I should have been grateful that my problem was so small compared to his. Not only had Drake become a creature of the night, but he was all on his own. My magical servitude came with a whole family who loved me dearly, who had my back, no matter what.

It was with this one final thought in my head that I returned home, only to find one very angry kitty waiting at the kitchen table. "Oh, look who finally decided to show herself!" Merlin yowled. "Our water bowl has been empty for hours!"

"I was only gone an hour and a half," I said, shaking my head and forcing myself to take slow, deep breaths so I wouldn't lose my cool.

"Likely story!" Merlin shouted back at me.

I bit my lip as I reached down to grab the cat's stainless steel water dish. I also reminded myself of the resolve I'd had in the car—this was my life, and these cats were my family. I loved them, even when they were working my last nerve. Still, I'd given up the chance to become a respected academic to work as the servant to one very spoiled kitty, regardless of the fact that he was also magical.

I finished filling the dish and set it on the table beside Merlin.

He took one hesitant drink, then sneezed and whispered, "It's not the right temperature. What are you doing to me here, Gracie?" proving that no matter how magical our world became, at the end of the day, Merlin was still an average, everyday cat, too.

"My apologies, your highness," I said with a mocking curtsy.

Merlin flicked his tail and narrowed his eyes at me for a moment before finally relenting with a sigh. "Fine, I'm sorry I'm being so rough on you. I'm having a hard time today, but I shouldn't be taking it out on you."

Wow, an actual apology. This would go down in history as one of my favorite days ever, despite the multiple attempts on my life via various undead creatures.

"Because of the zombies, you mean?" I asked tenderly as I picked up his bowl and carried it over to the sink. If he could apologize, then I could try a little harder to meet his needs, too.

"What?" Merlin stared across the room at a sunbeam he probably wished he was lying in rather than sitting here talking to me. "The zombies? Oh, no. I mean, sure they're a problem, but what really worries me is my Luna."

I set the bowl back down, and he came over to investigate. When Merlin decided the water was at the right temperature for consumption, he leaned forward and lapped it up heartily.

"I know you're only looking out for Luna," I said gently. Yes, I'd already made my opinion known on this matter, but it still weighed heavily on my cat's mind. I also felt like I needed to stick up for Luna here. Girl power and all that.

"Please don't tell me I need to apologize," Merlin mumbled, lifting his head momentarily.

"Well, that wouldn't be the worst idea."

"I already tried, but she wouldn't accept it."

Well, that was a shocker. "Are you sure?"

"Of course, I'm sure," Merlin snapped, then had the good sense to look ashamed for losing his temper. "Sorry, sorry. I know it's not your fault, but I'm not making any of this up. When I tried to apologize, Luna said she was too tired to argue anymore and asked if we could discuss it later."

"Oh," I said, not knowing what else I could offer. "Well, I'm sure everything will be fine. She probably just wants to deal with one thing at a time, and the zombies should definitely take precedence."

"Mmm-hmm," Merlin said, turning back to his water.

Yikes. I really hoped these two made up before the kittens arrived.

13

When at last night fell, the two cats and I marched out to the yard and straight over to Merlin's cauldron, aka the unassuming stone bird bath that served as his tie to all things magical, including the city of Nocturna.

We had to wait for a couple odd cars to drive past, but as soon as the coast was clear, we hightailed it to the cauldron. Merlin jumped up and splashed at the water, then motioned for me to jump on through.

This was only the second time I'd traveled via cauldron. My heart beat wildly as I plunged into the tiny opening to the next realm, but at least I managed to land on my feet. The cats joined me a few seconds later, and together we surveyed the bustling cobblestone streets of the old city. The buildings mimicked the Bavarian style and were made to accommodate cats rather than people. This gave everything an adorable fairy-tale quality, and I found it quite enchanting.

"Well, this is your plan, so what next?" Merlin asked, beaming up at me. It seemed our little talk in the kitchen had softened his demeanor some, thank goodness.

"We should see the blood witch," Luna said. It wasn't like her to interrupt, but I understood that tensions were high between her and Merlin. She probably just wanted to get this little trip finished as quickly as possible.

I nodded. "Yes, that's what I was going to say, too."

"Then let's go." Luna trotted down the cobblestone walkway, leaving us to follow.

Merlin and I exchanged curious glances before following after her. The sooner we got this over with, the sooner we could find a way to exterminate our zombie problem once and for all.

As we strolled through the darkened streets of Nocturna, a few friendly cats called out to us. But nothing could stop Luna on her quest to reach our destination without delay.

As we rounded a corner, my toe caught a crack in the stone path, causing me to stumble and fall to my hands and knees.

"Are you all right?" Merlin asked, racing over to examine my skinned palms.

I let out a slow, shaky breath. It stung, but not bad enough for me to request magical aid. "I'm fine. It's just a bit hard to see without any lights," I offered as I slowly rose back to my feet.

"We have the moon to guide us," Luna said, tilting her head to the sky.

"Yes, but I don't have night vision like the two of you," I reminded her. The feline residents of Nocturna didn't need artificial light to see, which resulted in some paths being better lit than others. The one we had just turned onto had nary a lantern or lamppost to be seen.

"Right." Luna sat and waited for me to get my bearings before continuing on.

Our little party had almost made it to the old covered wagon where the flame-point Siamese had his blood witch consultancy when a shadowy figure exploded from the alleyway and pounced on Merlin.

"Ah-ha! I knew you couldn't hide forever," a fat orange tabby snarled.

As a young Maine Coon, Merlin hadn't quite reached his full size. However, it was rare to find any other cats who were larger than him. Somehow, though, this chunky assailant seemed to outweigh him two to one.

"Get off him," I shouted and stomped my foot while Luna watched the scene unfold from several paces away.

"This scaredy cat owes me a duel," the orange chonker decreed, clueing me in to his exact identity.

"You're Tom," I said, pointing at him with an angry, shaking finger.

He flashed us a wide smile, showing off his pointed fangs. "Gee, what gave me away?"

"We have nothing to fight about," Merlin ground out, still trapped beneath the larger cat's bulk. "Luna made her choice, and it wasn't you."

"That's right! You tell him!" Luna called out but kept her distance. "Now, please leave us. We have somewhere we need to be."

Tom scoffed at her request. "More important than this? I think not. I've been waiting weeks to put this guy in his place. Where you been, Merlin?"

"I have a life outside of Nocturna. And if memory serves, that's the whole problem in the first place." Merlin growled, then jerked his head to the side in a fast fake-out maneuver.

Tom toppled off him, giving Merlin the chance to escape his hold. Now both cats stood with their hackles raised, facing each other as they hissed wildly.

"You're jealous," Merlin bit out.

"Nah, I just don't like to see good things happen to bad cats," Tom countered. "Now, are we going to do this right here in the middle of the street, or what?"

"No, no." Merlin glanced toward Luna, and she nodded reassuringly. "I don't want anyone to get hurt. Let's take this to the fields."

Tom took a step back, then lowered himself to a sitting position. "I'm counting on you to be there," he said without taking his eyes from Merlin. "Five minutes, or you forfeit."

"You have my word," Merlin replied with a slight bow of his head.

And with that, Tom flashed a sinister smile, blinked twice, and disappeared into the night.

14

Luna tiptoed over to Merlin and me. "Come. We have to be quick. There's still time to visit the blood witch before that thug returns."

Merlin mewed morosely and hung his head in shame. "I know you want to keep me from fighting, darling, but you know what happens if I forfeit."

"What happens?" I asked, feeling so out of the loop when it came to Nocturna's unique methods of conflict resolution.

"An All Paws Bulletin will go out to every single witch in the area. By refusing to fight, I'll have effectively surrendered my magic, and it is their right to take it from me." Merlin spoke passionlessly, as if he'd already accepted the worst possible outcome. It wasn't like him at all.

I shook my head emphatically. I'd believe in my cat enough for both of us, if that's what was needed. "We can't take a risk like that.

Jeez. I'm so sorry, Merlin. I shouldn't have forced you to come back here. You tried to warn me."

The Maine Coon lifted a paw to silence me. "No. This is my fault entirely. I shouldn't have egged Tom on. I knew he was jealous, and still I took great pleasure rubbing my happiness in his face."

"But the blood witch..." Luna mewled pathetically.

"We can visit him once this is finished," I told her. I got that she didn't want Merlin to fight, but she could at least admit the hypocrisy rather than trying to act like she had other reasons for wanting to hold him back.

"What if you lose?" I asked Merlin somberly. As much as I didn't like it, we had to consider all possible outcomes. If Merlin lost the magical duel, he wouldn't die, but he would be left forever without his magic... And where would that leave me?

Merlin sighed. "Then I'm willing to bet the zombie master will be far less interested in what I do going forward."

"Well, that's one way to solve the problem, I guess." I forced a smile because I knew Merlin needed someone in his corner and Luna was oddly detached at the moment.

"In truth, I'm lucky that Tom didn't put out the APB the first time I disappeared. My guess is he'd find it far more satisfying to land a few good strikes of his own than to simply rob me of my magic due to a technicality."

I nodded slowly and glanced to Luna. Her blue eyes were wide as she took everything in, but still she remained silent—letting Merlin decide this one for himself, no doubt. Luna wanted Merlin to let her make her own decisions about what was safe versus what held more risk than acceptable, and now she was returning the favor.

"Is there anything we can do to help you get ready?" I asked after a brief moment of silence passed.

"Yes." He rose to all four feet and stretched. "I need you to remain as close to me as possible once I'm on the field while also keeping a safe distance from harm."

"How will I know what that is?" Too close and I'd put myself at risk. Too far away and I'd put Merlin at risk. This was not going to be easy, but it was the least I could do.

Merlin rubbed his head against my shin. "I don't know, but I'm trusting you to figure it out. Your presence will give me an advantage over Tom. He doesn't have a familiar, which means only I will have access to extra reserves if needed."

Oh, that was right!

Maybe we could win this thing after all. It could all come down to me. I could save Merlin's magic, and then once he defeated Tom fair and square, we wouldn't have to be afraid to return to Nocturna.

Finally my status as his familiar meant something; it gave me a bit of power—power which I fully intended to use for the greater good.

With any luck, Merlin would clinch a quick and painless victory, and we would still have the time we needed to visit the blood witch before the morning sun came out and put the city into a slumber.

If not, I'd need to be ready to bunk down in a town that wasn't made with humans in mind. And if Merlin lost his magic...

"I have a question," I blurted out. I didn't want to add to his anxiety over the pending duel, but I also needed to know.

Merlin plopped onto his rear and stared straight up at me. "Yes?"

"If you lose your magic, what happens to me?" I whispered meekly.

"Well, you remember what happened to Virginia when Luna cut hers off. It severed the tie. Just don't go chasing after the fleeing magic and try to avoid any wells, and you should be fine." He smiled half-heartedly, and I reached down to stroke his head.

"Oh, and there's one more thing you should probably know," he added sheepishly. "If I lose, then Luna and I will be able to leave with another cat's aid, but Gracie... You'll be stuck in Nocturna forever."

15

Stuck in Nocturna? But what would I do here? How could I make a life in a world to which I simply didn't belong?

"Can't another cat help me out, too?" I squeaked.

Merlin met my eye briefly, then looked away. "It's my blood to which you're tied. Our connection is what enables you to transport here. Without my magic, that connection is severed."

I gulped down the tangled knot of emotion that had formed in my throat. Merlin needed a strong second right now, not a liability. I had to push past my fears of what could be and do what he'd asked of me without any added doubts or hesitations on my part.

Merlin was a powerful witch. He'd proven that many times over.

He could win this.

In fact, he would.

Yeah, I just had to keep believing.

After all, he'd given me no reason to doubt his abilities before.

I clapped my hands together with more pep than I felt. "Then we'll just have to make sure you win this thing. Let's go!"

Merlin nodded slowly, then blinked twice, transporting the three of us to an open clearing far past town. An outcropping of buildings was just barely visible on the horizon, thanks to a ceiling of roaring fire that hung above us, illuminating the sky in all directions.

"Um, Merlin, what kind of witch is Tom?" I whispered, unable to tear my eyes away from the flames that threatened to come crashing down on us at any second.

"Volcano," he said with a tightly clenched jaw as he scanned the field for his rival.

I followed his line of sight but saw no one. Least of all Tom.

"Huh. Maybe he realized he bit off more than he could chew and decided to forfeit?" I suggested hopefully, but Merlin appeared unconvinced.

Above us, the sheet of fire undulated like a gentle wave, and I jerked my face up to watch the spectacle. As I watched, the waves began to crash angrily against an invisible barrier, then sloshed over its edges in massive plumes of lava.

Cracks appeared in the ground beneath my feet, and I jumped to the side to avoid being swallowed up by the sudden quake.

That tiny crack grew into a chasm as it raced off in the distance and exploded upward, creating a throne of dirt and rock.

The flames above reformed into a solid sheet and chased after the snaking fissure in a deadly dance. Both elements converged in a cyclone of grandeur born of destruction, and Tom leapt down from the throne, passing straight through the wall of fire.

"It's about time you showed up," the orange tabby said with a sinister smile. "And isn't it just like you to show up at the last possible minute?"

"Isn't it just like you to show up in a literal blaze of glory?" Merlin bit back with open contempt. "It'll take more than a few silly party tricks to impress me, though."

"Enough with the chit-chat. Your tail is mine, cat!" Tom chuckled cruelly as he raced toward Merlin on fast and steady paws.

I also moved swiftly toward the Maine Coon, knowing that the closer I clung to him, the easier it would be for him to put this guy in his place.

As Tom ran toward us, flames shot up behind him, propelling his thick mass even faster.

Merlin stood rooted to the spot as if entranced by the spectacle before him. And just when I was certain Tom would crash into him headfirst, Merlin spun around in a tight circle, kicking up a storm of his own.

A howling cyclone formed above him and launched toward Tom. By now the tabby had built up so much momentum that he couldn't stop himself in time. He crashed right into the maelstrom and was sucked inside, flames and all.

Merlin shouted something into the wind, but I couldn't hear it over the roaring gusts.

The twister spun faster and faster, lifted Merlin's opponent higher and higher. But Merlin wasn't done yet. He kicked his feet back behind him in a familiar maneuver. This was the power of his I most dreaded—after all, it had shot a hole straight through my roof.

He kicked faster and harder, again and again. His feet were a blur, and dust flew up, obscuring my view of the field.

And then from the sky…

CRACK!

A mighty bolt of lightning struck the cyclone, and I swear I saw Tom's skeleton flash before me, just like in the old-timey cartoons I'd watched on Saturday mornings as a child.

Merlin stumbled and fell forward. He'd just used his two most powerful spells back to back, and it had clearly taken a toll.

The tornado dissipated, and Tom thumped down onto the ground.

Neither cat moved, other than to take in giant racking breaths. Tom's magic sparked and flickered around his body.

Merlin did nothing.

"Merlin!" I called out to him. "You have to summon the rain. That's an easy one. You can do it!"

My witchy cat raised one paw to the sky but couldn't hold it up long enough to cast his magic.

I ran toward him. Maybe my touch could give him the strength he needed to finish this battle. I'd almost reached his side when a column of tightly packed mud shot straight from the earth, blocking me from moving any farther.

I darted to the side, but another pillar rose up to obscure that path, too.

"Merlin!" I screamed and pounded my fists against the earthen cage that had now ensnared me on all sides.

No, no, no!

If I didn't get to him—and fast—this could be the end for both of us...

16

I couldn't see anything except for occasional flashes of fire lighting the sky overhead. I screamed and pounded on the walls of mud that stretched high above me but couldn't break free.

"Surrender," Tom roared above it all.

I stopped screaming and fell quiet, waiting for Merlin's response.

"Ne… ver," he managed between pants.

"Your magic is mine," Tom rasped, proving that he, too, had taken quite the beating. "All I have to do is reach out and take it."

A terrifying silence stretched for what felt like ages.

What was happening? Was Merlin getting back up to fight? Had Tom already relieved him of his magic? And what would happen to the magic once it was gone? Would it spill back into nature as Luna's had done, or could Tom truly wield both his and Merlin's at the same time?

"This is your last chance," Tom said with heated passion. "Get up and fight me like a cat, or give up now."

Something fell on my cheek, startling me. I jerked back just as another something hit my shoulder.

Rain!

Merlin had done it. He'd managed to bring the rain. It came hard and thick, beating down on me with increasing strength.

He was still in this!

The cats growled and hissed, continuing to fling magic at one another. Meanwhile, the rain began to pool at my feet, rising quickly from my knees to my shoulders, higher, higher.

I treaded water, waiting for the chance to pull myself out of my temporary prison and do whatever I could to help Merlin seize victory.

When at last I was able to peek above the enormous earthen wall, I caught a quick glimpse of Merlin with his claws poised at Tom's throat, ready to strike. I couldn't hold myself for long and fell back into the pool beneath me.

I pulled myself up a second time and clambered onto the narrow strip of land with shaky feet. I stood at least fifteen feet off the ground with no idea how to get safely down.

Both cats whipped their heads up and turned toward me.

A wicked smile flashed across Tom's striped face as he dodged to the right in a similar fake-out to the one Merlin had pulled on him in the alleyway. He wriggled free and summoned a massive ball of fire. A second later, he catapulted the thing straight toward me. I jumped to the ground, no longer concerned with how I would take the fall.

The important thing was to not die.

Just before I smacked into the earth, a gentle stream of wind caught me and lowered me gently. Merlin had saved my behind, literally.

Unfortunately, Tom had counted on Merlin shifting his attention to rescue me, and now their positions had reversed.

The enormous orange tabby straddled my Maine Coon, swinging his paws wildly as he batted at Merlin's face, chest, anywhere he could reach—attacking the very source of his magic.

"Oh, Merlin, did you think you could win?" he jeered as he struck out at Merlin and sent him flying.

This was all my fault. If I'd just stayed put...

I choked on a sob but refused to make a noise. I'd cost Merlin too much already. At least he could escape with his life. He still had his family. Luna, the kittens...

Luna's bright white fur caught my attention as she stalked across the field, closing in on the dueling cats. She didn't have any magic, so what was it she planned to do?

I got my answer in short order when she crept up behind Tom and sank her claws and teeth right into his neck.

Tom flailed against her, but she held tight, impossibly strong. She wasn't only taking his magic, I realized as Tom's slack body fell to the field. All the life had been drained right out of him. Luna had done that.

She'd ended this duel by breaking every rule in the book.

"Luna," I cried, racing toward the cats. "What did you just do?"

"He was losing," she said simply with a shrug.

"But you killed him!" I argued as tears splashed down on my cheeks. So much had happened in such a short span of time, and I was having a hard time processing it all. "Why did you kill him?" I barked out.

"Merlin needs his magic," Luna said coldly, then turned on me with claws extended. She leapt toward me, her eyes red with rage.

I took a step back, but it wasn't enough to escape the oncoming attack.

Luna fell upon me, and everything went black.

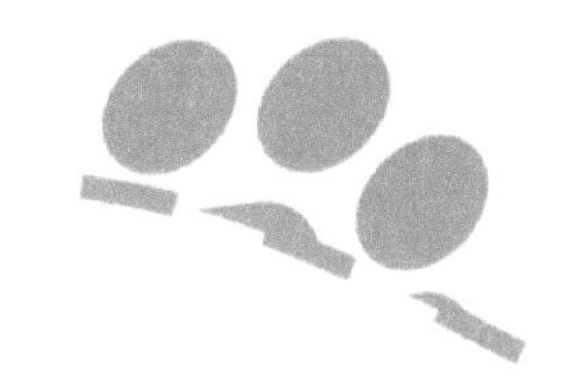

17

The next thing I knew I was struggling back to consciousness in a very unfamiliar place.

Standing.

Chained to a boulder.

On top of a mountain.

Oh, boy...

I yanked against my chains, but they had zero give.

Merlin. What had happened to Merlin?

My eyes strained as they scanned the darkness, at last landing upon a small metal cage, not unlike the kind a human would use to trap a skunk or raccoon that had gotten too close to the house.

Merlin lay unconscious inside.

"Merlin! Wake up!" I whisper-yelled. Even though I didn't see anyone else up here with us, our captor could still be nearby. We needed to find a way to escape before it was too late.

"How did we get here?" I asked him, but still he didn't stir. That's when I remembered.

Luna.

She'd killed Tom and then turned on me. But why?

Merlin moaned in his sleep but didn't acknowledge my pleas for help. At least I knew he was alive, even though he wouldn't be helping me make an escape plan any time soon.

I struggled against the chains again, grunting and pulling until I ran out of breath.

"Give it up," a deep and eerie voice commanded from somewhere nearby. "You can't win."

I scanned the summit but couldn't see anyone.

"Who are you? And why have you brought us here?" I shouted into the darkness.

"Pretty demanding for someone who has no options left," the voice said with a cruel chuckle. Well, at least he found this entertaining. I, however, was not amused. I also couldn't place the voice. It was familiar and strange at the same time.

My eyes narrowed in on the sound and finally spotted a black cat perched at the edge of the mountaintop.

Beside the cat, a cauldron flared to life, glowing a hideous swampy green.

"Mr. Fluffikins?" I asked cautiously. But hadn't he departed for his own town with Drake in tow? And wasn't he supposed to be one of the good guys?

The cat spun to face me, backlit by the brewing magic. "Recognize me now?"

The cat's chest was pure black, its eyes a bright glowing green. Mr. Fluffikins had a tiny patch of white on his chest and golden orb eyes. This wasn't him.

But what other black cats did we—? *Oh.*

"Dash," I said through gritted teeth.

"Took you long enough." The dangerous illusion witch simpered at me as if this were all a game. "But then again, I believe you know me better like this."

A poof of magic obscured my view. When it cleared, a no-nonsense police officer scowled back at me. This was the original form in which I'd met Dash, as the cop investigating my old boss Harold's death. Of course, it had all been a trap. As an illusion witch, Dash could take on any form she pleased.

At least I'd always thought of Dash as female since I'd first met the illusion witch under the guise of a police woman. Now, however, I was almost certain the black cat was male. Wait, why was I wasting time trying to figure out pronouns for a cat who almost certainly wanted to kill me?

Think, Gracie. Think!

"Where's Luna?" I demanded as I broke out into a cold sweat.

Another cloud of magic filled my vision, and out stepped a pure white cat with glistening blue eyes.

"I'm right here, dear," Dash said in Luna's voice.

I should have known. Luna would never betray us. It had been Dash the whole time—or at least since we'd entered Nocturna.

I tried to lunge forward, but the chains held me securely in place. "What did you do with her?"

Dash shifted back into her natural form. A plain and unassuming black cat. "I don't see why it matters. You'll never see each other again."

"Tell me where she is!" I yelled, fighting against my chains with renewed fervor.

"Relax. Enjoy your last few hours of life. If it helps settle you down, I can assure you that the white cat is just fine. You on the other hand? You're going to die." Dash let out a dry chuckle. I'd never wanted to smack an animal so badly, not even the zombie squirrels who had tried their best to kill me earlier that day.

Dash looked up and silently studied the night sky full of stars for a moment, then said, "You all could have lived, you know? My plan was simple. Get you to Nocturna to see the blood witch. Take said blood, and none of you would ever be the wiser. I could have carried out this plan with zero casualties. But now because of you, many will die."

I swallowed hard, unsure of how I would get out of this one, especially without Merlin's aid.

Right now, I needed a miracle.

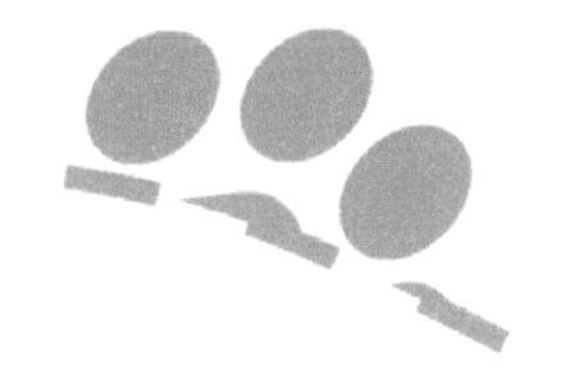

18

"Let me go," I demanded, refusing to die silently—or at all, if I could help it. "Nobody has to get hurt. We can end this all now."

"And why would I do that?" Dash asked, returning to the glowing cauldron and studying the brew.

"Because deep down you're good," I chanced.

Dash laughed bitterly. "Someone has been watching too many fairy tale movies, I think. Because I can assure you I'm bad to the bone."

The notes of that famous old song played in my mind, and I cursed the black cat for adding a catchy ear worm to my current list of problems. I shook my head to regain clarity, focus. Only one thing mattered right now, and that was escaping.

"Why are you doing this?" I asked. "What's in it for you?"

Dash turned a pair of stark green eyes on me. "Oh, that's really quite simple. When I realized what you and Merlin were, the connection you shared, I knew I'd finally found what I'd been waiting centuries for."

"Centuries? Nobody's that old."

"Once again, you are wrong. I am nearly one thousand years old."

I gasped. Hadn't expected that one. "But how?"

Dash smiled, baring sharp white fangs. "You are but an ancestor, the last scion. I, however, am the original."

"You're the imposter Merlin," I said, knowing innately that it was true. It was the only thing that made sense, given how interested she —or, I guess, he—was in Merlin's and my lineage. "But I thought you died."

A puff of magic replaced the little black cat with a very old man whose white beard stretched to his ankles. "Everyone thought I did. Lucky for me, my illusions kept me hidden until I could find what I needed."

"You were the first familiar. You pledged your loyalty to the real Merlin!" I spat at him, disgusted.

Dash appeared unfazed. "Yes, well, why be the servant when one can be the master?"

This was awful. The only other familiars I'd met had both turned evil in their lust for power. If I survived this, would the same happen to me?

I thought back to the last time we'd faced Dash in a confrontation. If I could keep him talking, it would buy us time. We could still get out of this, Merlin and me.

"Why did you send those zombies after us?" That part still didn't make sense to me.

"Oh, that's easy. Have you really not figured it out yet? I needed to get you to Nocturna. Luckily, you're nothing if not predictable. You came here just as soon as you could get your master to agree, didn't you?"

"Merlin and I are really more of a partnership," I corrected, glancing to my fallen ally in his cage. *Please, please wake up.*

"Does it matter when you'll both die at daybreak?"

"Why do you want to kill us?"

"Why not? By the way, I know what you're doing. You're trying to keep me talking to delay my evil plan. But it doesn't matter. This all has to go down at a very specific time, and I already told you when that is."

"Daybreak," I said through dry lips. "And even you call your own plan *evil.* Shouldn't that tell you something?"

"Good, evil," Dash droned. "They're more alike than you think. The perception of both changes with time. You may consider me evil, but future generations will see me as a god."

"You're a monster," I spat, which took some effort since my mouth was well on its way to going dry.

"And your opinion doesn't matter. You are nothing more than a footnote in the legend of my glory. With your blood connection and the stars in perfect alignment, I will reforge the mighty Excalibur and use it to gain ultimate power over both the magical and the mundane worlds alike."

"You sound like a crazy person," I said.

"You try waiting almost one thousand years for your revenge, and see how you like it."

"Revenge? Against who?"

"Merlin granted me one ultimate wish as his thanks for my taking on the role of his familiar. And when he didn't like it, he tried to trick me out of what was due to me."

"You asked to be as powerful as him," I shouted. I knew Dash's logic made sense in his own mind, but it certainly didn't ring true in mine. "Familiars are only supposed to be vessels."

"Now!" Dash-Merlin-whoever exploded. "Why do you think those rules are in place? Hmm?"

"He cursed you. How did you survive?"

"No, he forced me into hiding. Once the magic was granted, he couldn't take it back. Not without this." He reached two hands into the cauldron and extracted a glittering sword.

"Is that—?" My breath hitched.

"Excalibur. Yes. At least it will be. Nearly one thousand years ago to this day, your ancestor Arthur pulled it from a stone, declaring it the ultimate weapon. But that's not why Excalibur was made, nor what it was meant to do."

I blinked hard. None of what this guy was telling me lined up with what I knew of the original legends. "Come again now?"

"Merlin made it for me. Not because—"

"I'm sorry. This is getting really confusing. We're up to three Merlins now, and it's making it hard for me to follow."

The dark wizard groaned. "Very well. The original cat sorcerer created this weapon, not to take one's life but to take one's magic."

"It was meant for you."

"Yes, but I'd already managed to escape. He became so frustrated that he jammed it into that stone. And by doing that, he couldn't extract it himself."

"Or he would lose his magic," I concluded.

Dash smiled wide. "Precisely."

"So Arthur…?"

"Was a means to an end. Because he pulled the sword from the stone, he would never be able to wield his own magic, even if he wanted to. And that made him the perfect subservient familiar… Oh, look who's finally decided to join us."

My eyes zoomed toward the cage where at last Merlin—my Merlin—was beginning to stir.

19

Merlin roused and attempted a standing position, but his back thumped the top of the cage, forcing him back down in a crouch. He shook his head before glancing around the summit.

"Gracie!" he shouted when his eyes landed upon me.

"Merlin, it's okay," I called back, relief flooding my chest. With Merlin's help, we still had a chance. "We're going to get out of this."

"Haven't you been listening to anything I said?" Dash demanded, stomping over to me in a fit.

"Yeah, I heard you. But you lost before, and I'm willing to bet you'll lose again."

"Oh, a bet? What are the stakes? Oh, I know. How about your life." The old wizard chuckled, clearly amused with his own banter.

"Who's this guy?" Merlin asked, his words coming out slurred.

The lack of magic still weakened him. We were at a definite disadvantage.

I sighed. "It's a long story, but that's Dash who also happens to be the original imposter Merlin. He's going to kill us so he can reforge Excalibur or something like that."

Dash rounded on me, his gaze filled with venom. "Hey, show a little respect. I worked hard on that plan. And you're leaving all the best parts out."

I shrugged, enjoying the fact that I was getting to him. Right now that was the only way I had to fight back. "It's kind of a convoluted plan, if you ask me. Is that the best you could come up with when you practically had a millennium to do so?"

"It's flawless," he shouted, sending a spray of spittle my way. "Granted, that ridiculous duel set things slightly off course, but the end result will be the same. Many years ago, our ancestors formed an eternal bond when Arthur pulled Excalibur from the stone. The sword was forged by the cat wizard to rob me of my magic, but instead Arthur was the first person to succumb to its curse, meaning the three of us and our bloodlines were thusly tied for eternity."

I cracked a smile. "Thusly, huh?"

"Enough!" Dash's shout echoed across the distance, proving just how isolated we were on top of this mountain.

"Yes, I think I've heard enough," Merlin ground out, still trapped in an awkward crouch position, thanks to the relatively small size of the cage. "You're the imposter wizard, but I'm the real deal. The last in the most powerful magical line to ever grace this planet. Which means I can beat you, you big fake."

True, he didn't have much room to maneuver in the cage, but that didn't stop Merlin from lightly kicking back his feet in his classic lightning summoner maneuver.

Nothing happened outside the cage.

But inside, Merlin let out a stuttering gasp and fell flat on his stomach.

Dash laughed evilly. "You think I wouldn't lightning-proof that thing? It's a magical cage. Anything you try to cast will only feed the cage and make it stronger. There's no way out."

Merlin panted as he rose and threw himself at the side of the cage.

Nothing, much to Dash's amusement.

But I refused to accept defeat. Magic couldn't free us, but I'd never had any of my own in the first place. We needed a non-magical solution, and I would find it.

Dash returned Excalibur to the cauldron and continued to work on his potion, doing what I had no idea. My eyes grew heavy as I watched him.

No! If I fell asleep, it would all be over.

"You never told us what you plan to do once you reforge that thing. Other than kill us, I mean."

Dash ignored me.

"Yoo-hoo!" I called. "Earth to Dash, or Merlin, or whoever you are!"

The bearded wizard spun to face me. "I am many people in one. I am everyone, thus no one."

"Uh-huh. So what about the rest of your plan? Don't you want to share it with me?"

"Why? You'll be dead anyway." A small smile played at his lips. I'm glad the thought of my demise could bring his dark little heart a bit of joy because I would definitely not be the one dying today. Still, I had to play to his vanity to get him to keep talking.

"True, but I'm still curious," I managed.

"Well, it's still a bit early, but I see no reason why we can't get things ready." Dash returned to the cauldron and extracted the sword once more. He carried it over to me, stopping a few feet out of reach. Then returned to his cat form.

This was my chance to fight.

I kicked out but missed by a mile.

He ignored me as he raised a paw and extended his claws, then dragged them across his chest with a gasp of pain. Blood dripped to the ground, splashing onto the sword.

"With our three bloodlines combined, I will reforge Excalibur and use it to seal the portal between Nocturna and the human world, so none can ever rise against me again. And then I will rule as a god, the most powerful—the only—magical being left in the mundane universe. Happy?"

Dash leapt on top of the boulder to which I was chained and jumped down to my chest, staring me in the eye.

"And now it's your turn to contribute. I'll just be taking some of your blood now."

"Like heck you will!" I raged and writhed but still couldn't free myself.

Dash struck out with a paw and slashed me across the face. I squeezed my eyes shut tight as he made impact, and when I opened them again I found myself someplace entirely different.

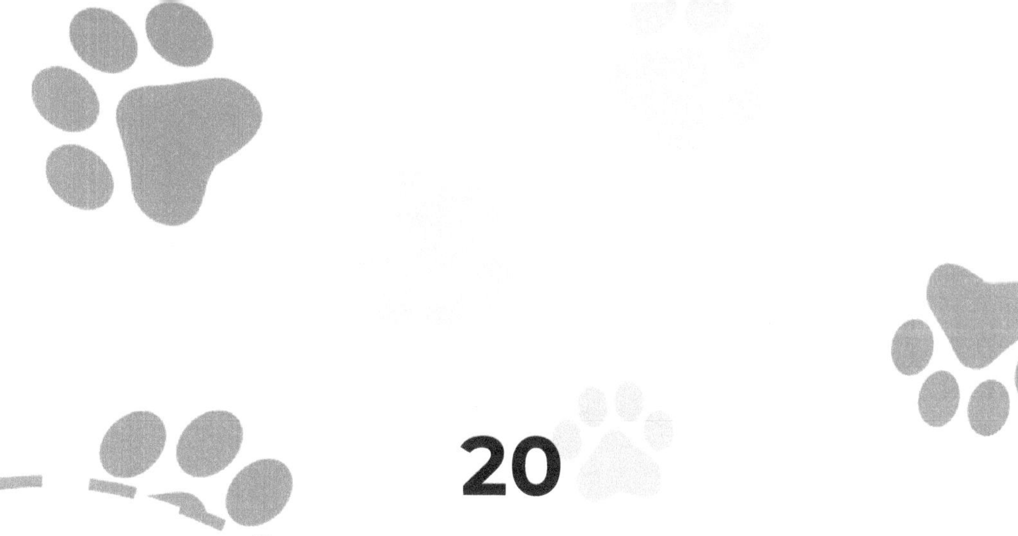

20

I stared down at the cash register. It blinked the numbers *$4.15* at me—the price of our thirty-ounce classic pumpkin spice latte, plus tax. In my hand, I clenched a crisp five-dollar bill.

Glancing up, I saw a customer waiting with one hand extended as he used the other to scroll through something on his cell phone.

Right. I must have really spaced out there for a second.

I made the correct change and handed it over. "Your drink will be ready soon," I said with my best customer-facing smile, then walked over to Kelley who had already fired up the espresso machine and gotten to work on the order.

A thick fog crowded the edges of my mind. I hadn't felt like this since I foolishly attempted to down twenty-one shots on my twenty-first birthday. I'd only made it to seven before I barfed all over my date for that night and forever gave up recreational drinking.

I didn't remember drinking last night. In fact, I didn't remember anything about last night at all… Or this morning, either. I just woke up, and I was here at work.

Huh. It seemed I really could do this job while sleeping. Next I'd have to try one hand tied behind my back.

"How has your day been so far?" the next customer asked me with a grin.

I returned her smile and turned back to the cash register. I loved our friendly customers. Increasingly, people treated me like a nuisance, an inconvenient distraction from whatever they were doing on their phones—even though they themselves were the ones who'd chosen to come to the coffee shop.

"It's a good day. Beautiful," I answered, even though I couldn't remember much of it so far. But no customer—no matter how friendly—wanted to hear the ravings of a mad barista.

Because I was going crazy, right?

Or losing it?

It being my memories.

I took the customer's order and cashed her out. As soon as she left, another came to take her place.

Then another.

And another.

I had no downtime between orders. Granted, Harold's always tended to be busy, but this was ridiculous. I didn't even recognize a single person who came in, and normally we had a steady flow of regulars.

"Kelley?" I asked, walking away from the register and the new customer who stood waiting.

"Hmmm?" she asked as she continued to work the espresso machine.

"Does anything seem off to you today?" I ventured, shifting my weight to one side.

She continued her work without even taking a second to glance up at me, but at least she answered. "Off how?"

I shrugged, wishing I could explain it.

Kelley chuckled. "Looks like someone had a few too many cold ones last night."

I grabbed her arm, but still she didn't look at me. "I don't drink, Kelley. You know that."

"Must have slipped my mind," she said coolly. "Now get back to the register. You have a line."

I followed my boss's orders, even though I now felt more out of sorts than ever. Kelley always made time for small talk, no matter how busy we got. It was important to her to keep up staff morale. And I was one of her best friends. If I came to her because something was wrong, she'd stop everything to help me through it.

"Welcome to Harold's. I'll be right back," I told the customer at the front of the line, then zipped back toward Kelley to test a theory I'd just developed.

"Do you think Drake could be cheating on you?" I asked her. Admittedly, this was a risk. Last time we'd spoken, she'd been intensely worried that Drake's sudden trip away meant he had another woman on the side.

I didn't want to rekindle that worry in my friend, but I also needed to get a stronger response out of Kelley. That would at least ease my own worry, that nagging feeling that something just wasn't right here.

"He wouldn't cheat on me," she said with a dreamy smile. "We're way too happy for him to go and mess things up like that."

Okay, that did it!

Where was I and who was this standing before me? Because it definitely wasn't the Kelley Carmine I knew and loved.

"Sorry, but I've gotta go," I told her, tearing off my apron and dropping it onto the floor.

"You can't just walk away mid-shift!" she shouted.

"Watch me," I called back as I raced around the counter and toward the exit.

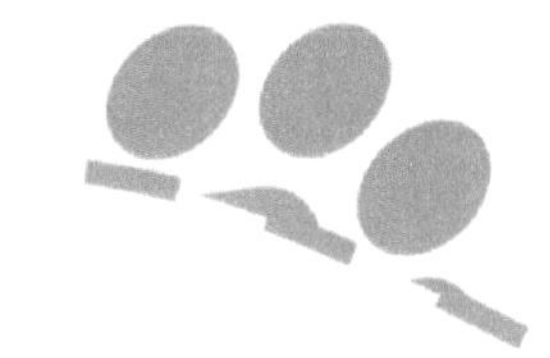

21

Before I could make it to the door, a strong hand reached out and grasped my arm.

Drake.

"Hey. Where are you off to in such a hurry?" he asked with his usual chill demeanor, a stark contrast to the sobbing heap he'd become when last we met.

"Something's not right here," I informed him, my voice low to keep the milling herd of customers from overhearing. "I have to go."

"It's weird, right?" came his reply. "One second I was hanging out with Fluffikins and the gang in Beech Grove, and the next I'm here at work."

I took a second to process this. "So you were somewhere else, and then suddenly you ended up here? I think maybe that's what happened to me, too." I racked my brain trying to remember but still came up infuriatingly short.

Drake rocked on his heels. "Yeah, probably, considering this is an illusion."

"A what?" That word sounded familiar, but why?

"An illusion," Drake repeated slowly. "You know, as in, fake. Not real."

"Illusion," I mumbled aloud, tasting the word, meditating on it.

And at last everything came into focus.

Dash!

He'd done this. Illusions were his specialty, and he'd had almost a thousand years to practice this particular skill. He'd captured me and Merlin, taken us to the top of that mountain. He was going to use our blood to do something terrible. He already had some of mine, but I didn't know if he'd gotten to Merlin yet.

I had to get back, just in case there was still time.

"Merlin's in trouble," I told Drake as fear squeezed at my heart. "I have to get to him."

"Okay," he said with a shrug. "See you later, then."

He let go of my arm, and I pushed through the door into the blinding sunlight.

No, it was all white. When the light faded, I realized I was back at the cash register staring at the numbers *$4.15.* By trying to leave, I'd reset the illusion.

I ran to Drake, who seemed to be the only sane person in this place.

"That was trippy," he confided.

"How come you're you when nobody else is?" I demanded, staying close and keeping my voice to a whisper.

"That's a weird thing to ask," he said with wide eyes as if I was blowing his mind right now.

"I'm serious. Kelley isn't herself. She's acting weird, but you're the same as always. Why?"

Drake tilted his head as he thought about this. "Now that I think about it, I'm not really me."

I pursed my lips, not knowing how to respond to that.

Luckily, he continued on. "Like my mind is here, but my body isn't."

"Drake, I'm looking at you right now. You. Your body."

He shook his head. "No, I don't think so. Watch."

I stared at him, but nothing happened except that he fell silent for a few moments.

"See," he exclaimed after about a minute.

"See what?" To my eye, not a thing had happened, but Drake appeared giddy.

"I left," he enthused as if I were supposed to not only take this all in stride but also be duly impressed. "I went back to Beech Grove and said *what up* to Mr. Fluffikins."

"Drake, you didn't go anywhere. You were here the whole time," I argued as the beginnings of a headache pressed at my temples.

He touched his chest and frowned. "Not me. This isn't the real me. Well, this body isn't. The inside me is here with you, but the outside me is back with Fluffikins."

"Drake, listen to me," I said pulling him toward the wall so we had a bit of privacy. "Right now I'm battling a really strong illusion witch. He sent me here as a distraction because I was asking too many questions or something. But I have to get back."

Drake nodded along. He was *laissez faire* about everything, but at least he wasn't stupid. I clung to that now.

"How did you leave just now?"

He twisted his hands in front of him. "I don't know. I just did it."

I groaned. So not helpful. "But how? I need to leave now. Can you teach me?"

He thought about this for a second before speaking again. "I just opened my eyes, my real eyes, and then I was in Beech Grove. When I closed them again, I was here. I don't really know how else to explain it."

"Okay," I said, licking my lips. "I'm going to try that."

I closed my eyes and tried to picture the summit I'd left behind. When I opened them again, I found Drake watching me in anticipation.

"Did it work?" he asked with a curious expression.

"No. Let me try again." And I did. I tried at least half a dozen times with increasing frustration, but I couldn't get it to work.

"Drake, I'm stuck," I whined in frustration.

He thrust one hand into his pocket and brought the other up to grope at his opposite arm. "Sorry."

"I'm stuck..." I said again, realizing something. "But you're not. You can help me!"

"Sure. What do you need?"

"Okay, listen up, because this is very important. I need you to go back to Mr. Fluffikins and tell him that an evil wizard has captured me and Merlin and taken us to the top of a very tall mountain in Nocturna. I'm trapped in an illusion, and Merlin is in a magical cage. We have no way out, and the wizard is going to use our blood to cast a very bad, super evil spell. I need you guys to come and save us."

His eyebrows rose one after the other. Finally I had piqued his curiosity "Nocturna? I've never heard of that place before."

"Yeah, but I'm hoping Mr. Fluffikins has. Can you do this, Drake? Can you save the world?"

"Sure, I don't see why not." And then he was gone, leaving behind the lifeless shell of his illusion.

All I could do now was wait and hope that I had put my trust in the right man—er, vampire—for the job.

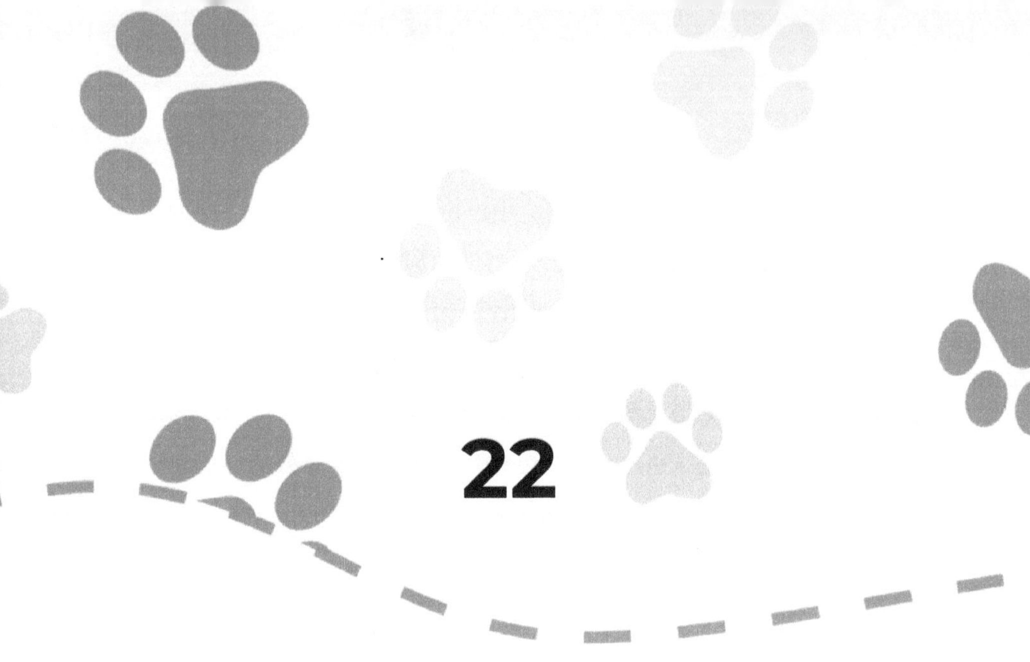

22

I blinked my eyes open with a start. The brightly lit coffee shop had transformed into a dark and barren nightscape. I couldn't see anything, save for the glowing light of the stars and moon that hung heavy in the sky above.

One more thing glowed, too—a cauldron filled with rolling bright green liquid.

I was back at the summit!

But how?

A swirl of pink caught my eye, then another surge of green.

Two black cats tumbled in a tangle of magic, Fluffikins versus Dash, good versus evil.

"Drake?" I shouted into the darkness.

"I'm here," he said, level-headed as he stood dangerously close to the edge of the mountaintop.

"You found us!" I was so happy I could cry.

"Took a few tries, but we got here. There are a lot of mountains in this place."

Now I really was crying. Perhaps I wouldn't die today, after all.

"Do you know you're chained to a rock?" Drake asked as the cats continued to fight tooth and nail.

"Yep. Can you free me?" I asked hopefully, struggling against my bonds to show him I was incapable of releasing them myself.

Drake started toward me with a steady stride, focused but not hurried, as if he had all the time in the world.

I tried not to groan, sigh, or roll my eyes. I knew he was capable of emotion. I'd seen it when Mr. Fluffikins had revealed that Drake was secretly a vampire. Did our current situation really not even warrant a bit of pep in his step?

Drake had cleared more than half of the distance between us when all of a sudden his eyes grew wide, and he slumped forward onto the ground.

Dash stood behind him, assessing the damage with obvious pride.

"Drake!" I screamed. "Get up!"

"That should keep him out for the count," the evil wizard said just before Fluffikins hurled into him like a blazing comet, and the cat fight resumed.

I watched them for a while, but it was impossible to tell who was who in this nighttime battle of magical black cats. The only saving grace was that their magic sparked in different colors. I wondered why Merlin's matched Dash's green and not Fluffikins's pink.

"Merlin?" I cried out, remembering my cat was still here somewhere, too. "Merlin, are you okay?"

"I'm okay," he said, sounding groggy. "But I still can't escape."

"Did Dash take any of your blood yet?"

"N-no, I don't think so."

"Then we're not too late." We could still do this. And now that the infantry had arrived, we would do this.

"The sun will rise soon. We don't have much time," Merlin warned.

"As long as we can keep Dash from getting your blood, we'll be okay," I promised, hoping that it was one I'd be able to keep.

The two black cats hissed and growled as they rolled about the mountaintop, locked in their magical battle. Dash was much stronger than either me or Merlin, but Mr. Fluffikins could easily hold his own.

My eyes darted from them to Merlin to Drake, waiting for the perfect opportunity to present itself. Somehow or another, we would win. We had to.

The cats tumbled into Dash's glowing cauldron, knocking it over. The swampy liquid sloshed out and seeped into the ground.

"You're too late," Dash boomed in that strange deep voice of his. "The sun is upon us. I just need one last ingredient and Excalibur shall be reborn."

Sure enough, the sun now peeked over the horizon. I'd never been so unhappy to see the dawn of a new day, but now, if we survived this, I would always view the sunrise differently. As a possible end rather than a promising beginning.

Fluffikins glanced up toward the sun. Only for an instant, but it was enough.

As soon as his opponent was distracted, Dash charged for Merlin's cage, ready to steal his blood and bring the cursed artifact back to life.

"No!" I screamed.

But Dash was already at the cage, fiddling with the lock. Although he kept his black cat form, he bespelled one of his claws into a key that fit the lock in question perfectly, no doubt.

Merlin pressed himself against the back wall, trying to put as much distance between himself and the dark wizard as possible.

From the corner of my eyes, a blinding shot of pink streaked across the summit and slammed into Dash like a speeding freight train. It didn't stop with impact, but kept pushing, charging straight off the mountaintop and out into the pre-dawn sky.

The ball of pink magic curved, reversing course and whipping back toward us. It stopped at Drake's side, and the magic faded to nothingness.

"What happened?" I asked Mr. Fluffikins.

"He wasn't paying attention, so I pushed him off the mountain," the big boss cat said, his chest puffed with pride.

"And you are so going to regret that," the dark wizard's voice boomed as he crested over the mountain. But he wasn't a cat anymore, nor was he a hoary-bearded human.

An enormous dragon now treaded air before us.

And he did not look happy.

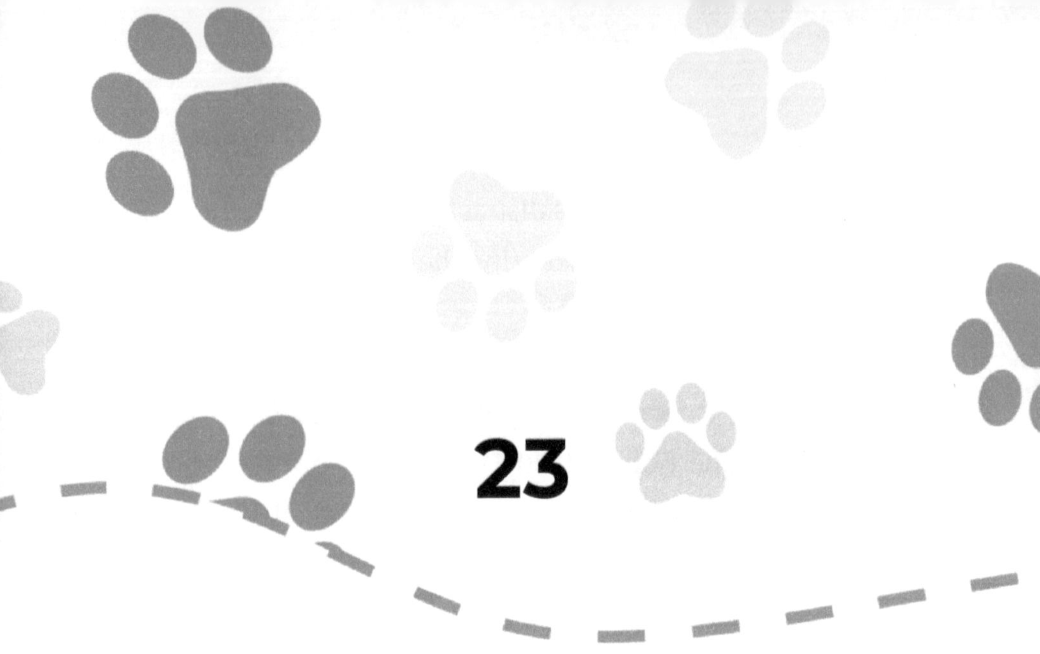

23

I stared at the monstrous green dragon with my mouth hanging wide open. I'd witnessed a lot of magic in the past few months, but none of it had shaken me quite like the sight of the awful behemoth flapping its wings before me now.

Dragon Dash roared and unleashed a torrent of flames that charred the grass at my feet.

"What's happening?" Drake shouted, finally waking up and scrambling to his feet. "Whoa, cool special effects."

The dragon puked flames and sent them weaving toward Drake.

"No!" I screamed just as the inferno enveloped my poor friend.

The dragon laughed and moved on to his next victim: Mr. Fluffikins.

I stared at the pillar of fire, still burning bright several paces away. Sweat beaded at my brow and above my lip. There's no way Drake could have survived that.

And it was my fault. I'd brought him into this.

In the distance, the cats resumed their battle. Although Dash's new form greatly outweighed the little black cat, Fluffikins did not back down from the battle. He launched himself straight at the menace and picked up the fight exactly where they had left off.

I left the cats to it and hung my head in remembrance as the fire burned itself out.

"Ouch, that was hot," Drake murmured, and when I glanced up I saw him stepping away from a scorched mound of earth. He didn't have a single burn on him. Not even a smudge of soot.

"Drake," I whisper-yelled, when I was sure the two witchy cats were fixated on each other and not paying attention to us.

When he looked my way, I nudged my chin to the side to motion for him to come closer.

"Aren't my new vampire powers awesome?" he asked with an enormous smile. "I literally just walked through fire."

"Yeah, super great." Of course, I had a billion questions to ask about that, but something told me Drake didn't have any of the answers, either. Besides, we had more important things to focus on right now.

"Listen," I continued. "I need you to get Merlin out of that cage. Dash unlocked it before Fluffikins pushed him off the edge of the mountain, so you should just have to unlatch it. Okay?"

"Okay."

"And move slowly and quietly. Dash doesn't think you're a threat, and the last thing we want to do is change his mind about that."

Drake gave me the thumbs up, then crept across the summit to Merlin's cage several yards away. Sure enough, he was able to simply unlatch Merlin's cage, no fancy lock fiddling required.

I expected Merlin to jump out of the cage with magic blazing, but instead he crept out with a faltering gait. The poor guy had been through a lot in the last twenty-four hours, and I wasn't sure how much more he could take.

I wanted to shout encouragements at him, but that would risk revealing his new freedom to Dash. For now, I just had to trust that my cat knew what he was doing.

And he was definitely doing something.

Merlin moved slowly but decisively toward me. Was he coming to break my chains? Would I finally be able to join this fight rather than just cheerleading from the sidelines?

No. The Maine Coon stopped a few feet shy of me and my boulder, and I realized in horror what he planned to do.

"Merlin, you can't," I rasped, barely above a whisper. I still couldn't risk alerting Dash to his freedom.

Merlin glanced up and met my eyes for a brief moment before returning his attention to the discarded sword. "We have no other options left," he said stoically.

And before I could stop him, he raised one clawed fist into the air and brought it down hard, swiping against his chest, exactly the same as Dash had done before.

His blood spread across his long fur, then at last dripped down onto the sword.

My cat had just reforged Excalibur, the weapon meant to destroy us.

24

Now infused with the blood of the final member of our cursed trio, the ancient sword glowed a hot and angry white.

Merlin took a deep breath and pulled himself up onto his hindquarters, then pounced down on the sword with both of his front paws.

The sword hissed and sizzled, extending its glow to Merlin's body as well. Together, they shone like a beacon, drawing the dragon's attention straight to them.

"No!" Dash pulled away from Fluffikins and sped toward the light.

"Drake," I yelled, motioning for him to join me again.

"I have a plan," I said as the dragon frantically tried to separate Merlin from the sword, but it seemed as if the two had now fused into one.

I whispered my plan to Drake, but he met me with a grimace of uncertainty. "I don't know. That seems pretty crazy."

"Just trust me on this one. It's our best shot."

He nodded and sauntered away.

"What have you done?" Dash bellowed, though he didn't seem to be asking anyone in particular.

Finally the sword released its hold on Merlin, and my cat fell to his side, completely spent.

The dragon grappled for the sword and easily gained hold. No one was left to fight him for it. With renewed confidence, Dash lunged at Fluffikins, slicing with enormous strength.

"Look out!" Drake and I both screamed.

Mr. Fluffikins produced a pink whip of magic and grabbed onto the sword, easily breaking it free of the dragon's grasp. He then used his magical whip to point the sword at the dragon's heart.

And as his magic held onto Excalibur, it became abundantly clear that the sword hadn't fulfilled its intended purpose. Mr. Fluffikins's magic still burned strong and sparkled bright.

"You idiots have ruined my beautiful plan," the dragon cried when he, too, realized the artifact had failed to rob the other cat of his magic. "For this, you will die!"

Dash and Fluffikins continued their battle, both still equipped with their full abilities. Excalibur fell to the ground, little more than a useless relic now.

Merlin cracked an eye open as he lay panting on the earth.

Drake crouched in the distance, waiting for the perfect moment to act on our plan.

I remained chained to that danged boulder.

"What did you do, you silly cat?" I asked Merlin. Once again tears streamed down my cheeks. I was really turning into quite the crybaby.

"My blood," he said with a shudder. "It's no longer magic. The spell is broken."

"You reforged the artifact and then nullified it so no one else could use it," I realized aloud.

"Yes," he said before passing out again.

"Merlin!" I screamed, but nothing I said or did could wake him.

Please don't be dead; please don't be dead.

It couldn't end like this. We couldn't win this battle only to lose the war. Merlin couldn't die. And he hadn't. I refused to accept it.

Fluffikins and Dash continued to fight for what felt like ages. It must have felt like a long time to Drake, too, because he decided to depart from the original plan.

"Yo, dragon breath!" he shouted, jumping up and waving his hands in the air.

"You! I thought I already disposed of you!" Dash roared and pulled away from Fluffikins, making a beeline for Drake.

Oh, that stupid jerk. Now he was going to die, too. Why couldn't he have just waited like I told him?

I was still weighing this question in my mind when Drake disappeared right before my eyes and reappeared on the dragon's back, driving him on toward the magical cage that had imprisoned Merlin earlier.

At the last possible second, Drake disappeared again. No, that wasn't it. He moved so fast, he became invisible to my human eye.

He leapt from the dragon's back right before the massive monster crashed into that tiny cage.

Being a magic cage, the second the dragon made impact, his power was absorbed into its bars, returning Dash to his natural form.

The old man with the long beard.

First Merlin's magic and now Dash's had made the cage even more powerful, and it easily quadrupled in size to accommodate its new humanoid cargo.

"Lock it!" I screamed, but Drake was already on it.

Fluffikins flew over and landed on the ground with a heavy thump. "It seems your first lesson with Connie went well."

"Yeah, turns out being a vampire isn't so bad," Drake admitted, jamming his hands into the pockets of his jeans.

"All right, you're coming with me," Mr. Fluffikins said to the pitiful creature in the cage before summoning a thick pink mist and flashing them both out of existence.

That just left me, Drake, and Merlin.

"Let me help you with those," Drake said. He zipped over to my side with impossible speed, then grabbed hold of my chains and pulled them apart like they were nothing more than the finest of threads.

I balked. "Could you have done that the whole time?"

"Probably," he admitted. "But I'm still getting the hang of things."

I gave him a high five, then fell to the ground at my cat's side. I scooped Merlin into my arms, and he nestled into my chest. He was still alive but would be mighty embarrassed about this later.

"We have to get back to town and find Luna," I told Drake.

"Let's get going, then," he returned.

"Wait," I said, staring into Merlin's little kitty face. His tongue stuck out slightly between his lips. He looked so innocent in that moment.

"I can't go with you," I said with a sad smile. "I can't leave Nocturna. Not anymore."

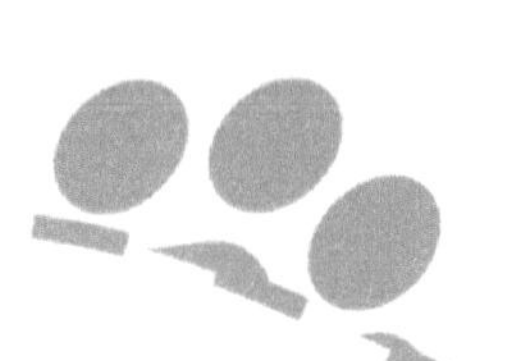

25

"If you're not leaving, then I'm not leaving," Drake insisted, totally catching me by surprise.

"I'll be fine," I said, flapping my hand. "Go, if you can."

He kicked at the burnt earth. "Okay, but how?"

"Well, how did you and Mr. Fluffikins get here in the first place?" Honestly, I'd been wondering about that for a while now.

"That pink magic stuff of his," Drake answered without missing a beat.

"I'm sure he'll come back for you once he's done making sure Dash is nice and cozy in that prison he mentioned."

Drake nodded as if it didn't matter. "But what about you?"

I sighed and stared down at the unconscious cat in my arms. "Only Merlin could take me in and out of Nocturna. I'm bound to him as his familiar."

"But he doesn't have magic anymore, right?"

"Right."

Drake's face wore a mix of emotions, so different than his usual tranquility. "So how are you going to get out of here?"

I shivered and hugged Merlin tighter to my chest, suddenly realizing how cold it had become now that the adrenaline had worn off. "I'm not."

He scrunched his nose as if in disgust, then shook his head. "Well, you can't stay on this mountaintop. Let me take you somewhere."

"No, Drake. Really, that's o—"

But before I could finish my argument, he snatched me into his arms and took off down the mountain at a blinding speed. I clung to Merlin as best I could, terrified of dropping him to his death.

"This a good place," Drake said, setting me to my feet a short while later.

I kept my eyes squeezed tight, afraid to look. At least it seemed like the world had stopped spinning around me.

After drawing in a deep, calming breath, I cracked one eye open and stumbled.

Drake reached out a steadying hand, holding me as I held Merlin, who was still out cold.

"You brought me back to the village," I said, surveying the miniaturized Bavarian town that rose up around me.

Drake shrugged. "Seemed as good a place as any."

We both glanced around the quaint village. An old Himalayan couple strolled past us on the other side of the street, but otherwise the place was deserted.

"Excuse me," I called out. "Might I ask a favor?"

They paused and stared at me with huge, unblinking eyes.

"Could you help my friends get back to the other side?"

"Yes, we can help," the lady cat answered with a cute, squeaky voice. "Our house is just down the road. Meet us back here about ten minutes before dusk, and we'll ready our portal."

"Thank you," I said, dipping my head in a bow. Unfortunately, I'd just realized my mistake.

The Himalayan couple returned my bow and carried on their way.

"They'll get you out of here, but not until later. The portals only open at night," I confided in Drake. Well, at least I'd have company as I figured out this new life of mine.

We both glared up at the sun, which had reached the top of the sky.

Drake offered me a cautious smile. "Well, I can think of worse ways to spend the day, especially since I'm going to have so many of them in my long, immortal life."

"Are you really immortal?" I asked as we navigated the empty walkways of Nocturna. Its feline residents had ambled off to bed by now, it seemed.

"There are still ways I can die. But not many. Most vampires stick around a very long time." He pushed both hands in his pockets and let out a deep, stuttering breath.

"How do you feel about it? Being a vampire, I mean?"

He shrugged. "At first it was a shock, but I'm used to it now."

"Already? I mean, you only found out yesterday."

"Yeah, but I guess I've been one for a couple years now.

Remember how I told you about that time I saw the white ghost in the rainstorm?"

I nodded, engrossed in his story.

"I think it happened that night. Fluffikins and his team are trying to help me retrieve that memory. They think it's the key to finding out why I'm different." He frowned for a moment, then rearranged his features into his signature mask of apathy.

"You've always been different, Drake," I pointed out with a laugh.

He chuckled, too, but I could tell his heart wasn't in it. "Yeah, but they mean something else. I can do things vampires aren't supposed to do."

"Like walk through fire?" I suggested.

"That, and other things." He shrugged again. "I dunno. There's a lot for me to figure out."

I wanted to help my friend, but I didn't know how. All I could do was listen while he was in Nocturna and hope for the best after he left it. It would take some getting used to—the idea that all my friends and family would have to carry on their lives without me. They wouldn't even know what had happened...

My phone buzzed in my pocket with an incoming call.

"Really? I have cell service in another dimension?" I fished it out of my pocket and saw that Kelley was the one calling.

"I've gotta take this," I said to Drake before pushing the button to accept her call. "Hello?"

26

"Gracie!" Kelley shouted into my ear via the cell phone. "You'll never guess what!"

I put her on speaker so Drake could hear, too, but lifted a finger to my mouth so he would keep quiet. The last thing Kelley needed was to find out that Drake and I were together in the wee hours of the morning. It was all innocent enough, but there was zero percent of the truth I could readily share with her, and I was far too exhausted to create a compelling lie.

"What?" I asked, adding as much cheer to my voice as I could muster.

"Well, I had a hard time sleeping last night because I was worried about me and Drake," she began.

When she paused to take a breath, I rushed to Drake's defense. "Kelley, I already told you. You two are—"

"No, listen. That's not important. I mean, it is, but that's not why

I'm calling." She took a hurried breath and jumped right back in. "I couldn't get to sleep, so I went outside for a little fresh air. And I think I found your cat."

I glanced down at Merlin, still cradled in the crook of one arm as I held onto the cell phone with my other. "Really, because he's right here with me."

"Yeah, but you have two cats, right? The big fluffy brown one and the smaller white one."

I gasped. "Did you find Luna?"

"I'm pretty sure I did. Hang on, I'll text you a picture."

My phone chimed, and I swiped up to open the text message. Sure enough, Luna's bright blue eyes beamed back at me.

"It's not a good one, but it's the best I can do," she said as I studied the image.

"Is Luna okay?" I pleaded. "Is she with you now?"

Kelley yawned as if to prove her story about missing out on sleep last night. Well, she wasn't the only one.

"I've been trying to call all night," she said, fatigue still evident in her voice, "but I only just now could get through. Where have you been?"

On top of a mountain fighting a dragon, among other things.

"Um, that's not important," I said. "Is Luna okay?"

"Yeah, I mean, I think so. She's stuck at the bottom of my well, so I'm not one-hundred percent sure, but she's been meowing up a storm. That's how I found her in the first place."

I could just picture Kelley standing over the well and glancing down at Luna as we spoke. Thank goodness, she had found her. Merlin would be so relieved when he woke up.

"Oh my gosh, Kelley, you have to get her out of there," I shouted, drawing a strange look from a wiry calico as she trotted by.

"I already called the fire station," my friend assured me. "They help cats out of trees, so why not wells? They said they'll stop by when they have a free moment to help. So I'm just hanging around waiting. Luckily, I planned to take the day off anyway. Hey, so when are you coming over?"

I lowered the phone and gulped back a fresh wave of nausea. What could I say? I couldn't come to her house now or ever again. I was stuck in Nocturna forever but had no way of explaining that to her.

"I'll be there as soon as I can," I managed to choke out before ending the call.

"Luuuunaaaa," Merlin moaned and turned over in my arms.

"She's safe. Kelley found her," I told him with a huge smile. I was so happy that the little cat family would be okay, even if I wouldn't be part of it anymore.

"We have to get back," Merlin insisted, tapping me with a paw. "Put me down. I have to go to Luna."

"But it's already morning, and we're stuck in Nocturna until at least tonight," I informed him, but set him on his feet, anyway. I was glad he'd regained his full consciousness. That was one less thing to worry about in this very worrisome day.

"Hey, that thing works, right?" Drake pointed to my phone. He used his other hand to extract his phone from his pocket and glance at the screen.

"No bars," he informed me, waving it before me. "Remind me to switch to your carrier when we're out of here." He held out his hand, open-palmed. "May I?"

"Uh, sure." I placed the cell phone in his waiting hand and watched as he copied a number from his phone into mine.

"Shh, it's ringing!"

Someone picked up on the other end of the line. I could just barely hear a muffled hello.

Drake's face lit up like a bonfire. "Tawny, hey. Put Fluffikins on."

27

"Um, could you put somebody else on evil-wizard babysitting duty and come get us, please," Drake said once Fluffikins had answered and he'd switched the call over to speaker phone.

"Where are you?" the black cat demanded in that creepy snake-like voice of his.

Drake blinked up at the sky and then looked around, presumably searching for landmarks. "That city. Nocturna. Right near the town square. There's a fountain."

"But Drake," I started to argue. "The portal only opens at—"

I stopped talking when Mr. Fluffikins appeared standing a few feet before us in his famous pink burst of magic.

Drake ended the call and handed my phone back to me.

Meanwhile, my jaw practically fell to my chest. "I don't understand. How?"

"Your cats' magic and mine are different," Fluffikins explained like the answer should have been obvious. "The same rules don't apply."

"Is that why their magic is green and yours is pink?" I asked, still dumbfounded.

"Something like that." The black cat plopped his rear onto the cobblestone walkway and flicked his tail thoughtfully. "I'll admit, I haven't quite figured out how so many magical systems can exist in the same space without following the same rules. But I assure you I won't rest until I figure it out."

"Are there more out there? Besides yours and what I had?" Merlin asked, settling himself at my feet.

"Yes. Yours originated in England some thousand years ago. Mine is much older than that, as old as the Earth itself, if not more." A smile stretched from one whiskered cheek to the next. Mr. Fluffikins clearly took pride in the seniority of his magic system.

"What else is out there?" I asked, crouching down to run my fingers through Merlin's thick fur.

"I don't know, but I intend to find out. Once I've finished training my replacement—"

"Tawny," Drake provided with an enormous sappy grin. Someone definitely had a crush. Not good news for Kelley, but then again, she and Drake probably wouldn't last much longer, given his new creature of the night status.

"Yes. Once Tawny takes over my post as diplomat for the Peach Plains region, I intend to travel the world and learn all I can about the various magic systems out there and how they fit together."

"Does that mean you can get Gracie out of here?" Merlin asked. It was only now that I realized his previously green eyes had settled into a honey brown. The magic inside him had died, and by his own paw.

"I can try," Fluffikins responded with a nod. "Everyone stand close and place a hand on me."

We scrambled over to him and did as instructed.

A pink mist swirled around us, then dissipated, leaving me all by myself on that cobblestone street.

A few seconds later, Mr. Fluffikins returned.

"I'm sorry, Gracie," he said. "It seems you are tied to the Nocturna system of magic and thus bound to its rules."

Tears threatened to fall, but I forced them back. "I understand."

"They can still visit you here," he offered, blinking up at me.

I nodded sadly. "I know."

"And I will search for an answer in my research, a way to bring you back to the mundane world."

"Thank you," I murmured.

Mr. Fluffikins shot me one last doleful look, then vanished for good this time.

Alone again, the full weight of my exhaustion settled over me. I hadn't slept at all last night. Instead, I'd been embroiled in one deadly battle after the next.

I was so, so tired.

And so I lay down, right there on the street, and closed my eyes. It didn't take long for me to drift off into a world all my own.

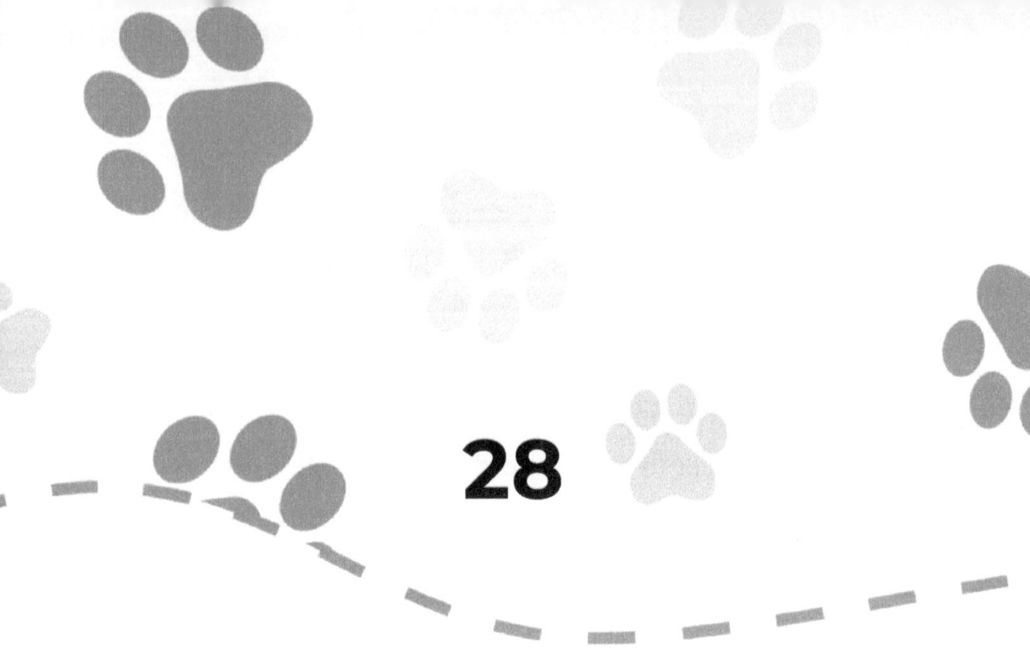

28

I woke up to a soft pair of paws kneading into my side.

"Merlin?" I mumbled. "Luna?"

But when I opened my eyes, I saw the elderly Himalayan female sitting at my side wearing a concerned expression.

"Do you still want to use our portal?" she asked as she continued to paw at me.

"I'm fine, thank you." I sat up and rubbed the sleep from my eyes.

"Are you all right, dear? You look pretty run-down."

Dear. That was Luna's pet name for me. If I closed my eyes again, I could almost imagine that she and Merlin were right here with me. But no, I was all on my own.

Forever.

I broke into a giant racking sob and let loose a pained wail.

"Let's find you something to warm your belly. Come with me," the kind stranger said, and I let her guide me toward her home.

"I don't think you'll fit comfortably inside, but please wait here and I will bring you a bit of milk," she said before running into her small, thatched cottage.

I waited, my tummy rumbling at the thought of obtaining nourishment. I'd been too scared, sad, tired, what-have-you to notice my hunger until now.

I tried to focus on my surroundings rather than the deep hunger in my belly.

Nearby, the village began to rouse. Nightfall was fast approaching, which meant it was time for them to start their day. And I watched as cats of all colors and stripes exited their homes and set out on journeys to places unknown.

A litter of black and white patched kittens followed after their mother in a little line, moving their paws quickly in an effort to keep up.

I smiled to myself. My world had ended, but all around me life went on. There were still happy endings and new beginnings. And I could make them happen for myself as long as I didn't give up.

I spied a brown fluffy cat racing up and down the pavement with an all-white kitten clutched in its mouth. As the pair drew closer, I realized that the baby couldn't have been more than a few days old. Its eyes hadn't even opened yet.

Oh, gosh. I hoped everything was okay.

I stood and moved toward the Himalayan couple's front door, knocking gently. "Excuse me, ma'am. I think there might be some trouble."

She hissed in fright, then peered at me through the window. "What trouble did you bring to my door?" she asked with wide eyes.

"I didn't mean to. I mean, I don't think, I—"

"Cat got your tongue," Merlin said from behind me. His voice came out muffled, but I would recognize it anywhere.

I spun to face him, and there he stood. He was the brown fluff ball racing through the streets with that white kitten in his mouth.

"Is that…?" My voice cracked, and I began to cry.

Yes, again.

"Here. Take him," Merlin said through a mouthful of fur.

I stretched my palms forward and allowed him to lay the tiny kitten onto my hands, then stood, lifting him to my face.

"So tiny!" I squealed.

"What's his name?" I asked with the biggest smile ever lighting my face.

Merlin raised his head high and sniffed at the night sky. "He doesn't have one yet. Luna and I had something more pressing to take care of first."

"Luna! Is she okay?"

"Yes, she's no worse for the wear. Came through the birth like a champ to deliver four healthy babes. Three girls and this boy."

"Oh!" I cried again between peppering light kisses to the tiny fluffer-nutter in my hands. "Thank you for bringing him to see me."

"I didn't bring him to see you," Merlin corrected, his face lightening into a smile. "I brought him to take you home."

I straightened with a start. "What?"

"My genius wifey pointed something out to me after I returned."

"Yeah, and what was that?"

"You're tied to my blood."

"Yes, and you're no longer magical, which is why I'm stuck here."

"I'm not, but I'm no longer the only one with my blood."

I stared down at the baby in my hands. "You don't mean."

"He got me here," Merlin pointed out. "Now let's see if he can get you back home. We need you there, Gracie. You're one of us."

Cue a whole lake of tears from Ms. Gracie Springs. At the end of the day, it seemed my last name fit me like a glove.

"Thank you for helping me, but I'm going now," I called to the peeping seal-point Himalayan before crouching back down to meet Merlin head-on.

"Let's go home," I said, holding the kitten in one hand while petting him with the other.

"Finally. I thought you'd never ask."

29

Everything back home was exactly as I'd left it the night before. Everything except the addition of four squirming newborn kittens.

"I just love them. Every single one of them," I gushed to Luna as she introduced me to each of the three girls. They all looked just like their father, while the sole boy took after his mother.

"You'll have to help us figure out what to call them. Merlin and I can't agree on a single name," she said, helping the smallest of the three girls latch on for feeding time.

"I'd be happy to."

Virginia chose that precise moment to pop out of the wall and shout, "Boo!"

The kittens shrieked and burrowed into Luna for safety.

"You did not just scare my cat nieces and nephews!" I bit out, seething with a rage like I'd never felt before.

Virginia cackled. “I’m going to like having the bitty brats around, I think.”

“It was you!” I snapped, carefully pushing myself to my feet and charging at the ghost.

“I have no idea what you’re talking about,” she said, already growing bored with me apparently, as she floated back toward the wall.

But I refused to let her off that easily. “You were spying on us for weeks. You told Dash when he could get a clear shot at Luna to make the switch. I’m guessing you also told him where he could hide her. Or was it just a coincidence that she ended up at the bottom of Kelley’s well?”

“My well. My house!” Virginia corrected. “And what does it matter? Somehow you fools still managed to win in the end, so who cares about what part I had in things?”

“I care,” I said, jabbing my thumb toward my chest. “Especially since you’re spooking the babies.”

“Oh, boo hoo.” Virginia laughed uproariously at her own joke.

I reached into my pocket and took out my cell phone.

“What are you doing?” Virginia asked, fright creeping into her voice.

“Calling the exterminator,” I said with a deliciously wicked grin.

Drake answered after the second ring. “Yellow.”

“Hi, Drake. Are you with Mr. Fluffikins?” I asked breathlessly.

“Yup.”

“I need a favor.” I quickly explained our problem.

“Yeah, we can help with that,” Drake said before hanging up.

About five minutes later, Drake, Mr. Fluffikins, and an old man with a long white beard popped into my living room.

I screamed and stretched out my arms to form a protective barricade for Luna and the kittens. "Dash is right behind you!" I yelled in warning.

Drake stared at me, his brow scrunched with confusion. "What? Oh, that's not Dash. This is—"

Virginia let out a terrible wail, drowning out Drake's words.

I glanced over just in time to see the Dash doppelgänger swish a massive scythe and suck Virginia's disembodied spirit into the blade.

"What just happened?" I asked, equal parts thrilled and terrified.

Drake waggled his eyebrows. "You had a soul to reap, so I brought my reaper friend."

The old guy in the suit bowed, then went to check out the contents of my fridge.

"Thank you," I called after him.

He simply lifted a hand in acknowledgment and returned to foraging about my refrigerator.

"He doesn't talk much," Drake said with a shrug.

"C'mon, you two. I want you to meet the kittens," I said, grabbing Drake's hand and pulling him after me.

Mr. Fluffikins followed us to the far corner of my bedroom where Luna had arranged a pile of blankets and old clothes to create a nest for her and the kittens.

Merlin joined us, too, having returned from whatever he was doing outside. He didn't say, and I didn't ask.

"They're so tiny," Drake crooned as he settled himself cross-legged on the floor.

"You should have seen them a few hours ago," I said, every bit the proud aunt. "I swear, they've at least doubled in size since then."

We all sat and waited for the kittens to finish their meal.

The little boy was the first to pull away from Luna. He wiggled his paws against the floor and scooted away from his mother's belly. Being that the kittens were still incredibly young—still less than a day old at this point—they never strayed far from Luna.

Right now, however, the little tike was moving determinedly across the room. I'd never seen any of the babies venture so far from their mother. But, I'll be darned, that white kitten kept going until he bumped into Drake's foot, then he stopped and mewled.

Drake laughed and scooped the baby into his hands.

"Whoa," he said, after lifting the baby to his face. "How come it has red eyes?"

I chuckled. "Don't be silly, Drake. They won't open their eyes for another week at least."

He slowly turned the little boy around so I could see his face. Sure enough, his eyes had popped open and were now glowing a bright and angry red.

"Well, this isn't good," Fluffikins said.

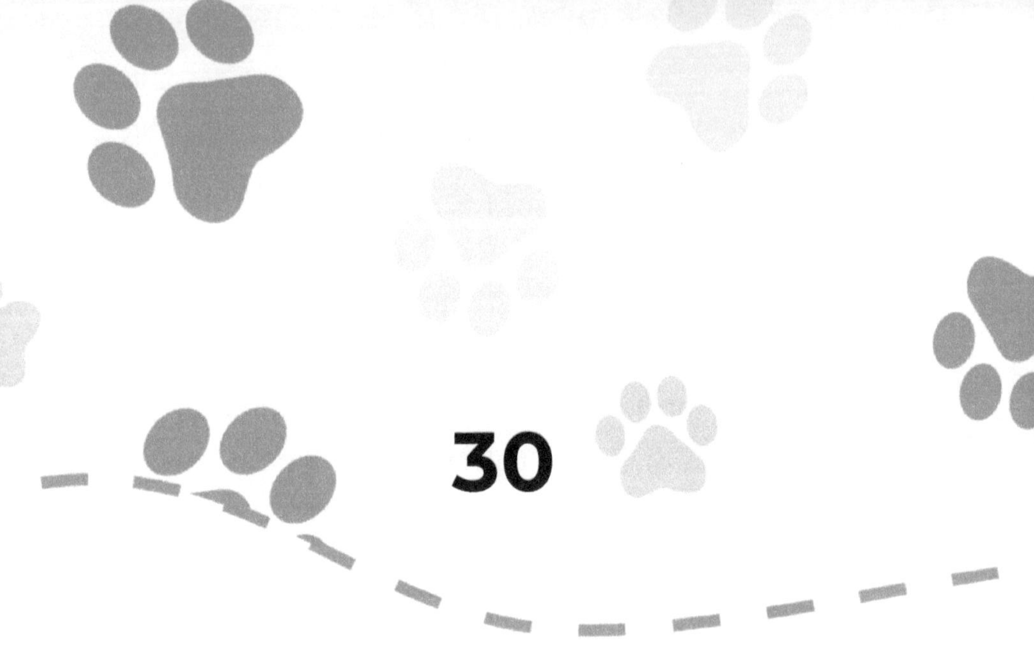

30

For the next week, Drake and Mr. Fluffikins visited every day. They said they just wanted to see how we were getting on after the big showdown with Dash, but it was quite obvious that they were actually observing the little white kitty with red eyes.

None of his sisters had opened their eyes yet, and they still mostly scooted and paddled to move from place to place. Our boy, however, was now able to run, scamper, and pounce. His favorite activity was playing with the laser pointers I'd picked up at the local pet store. Strangely, he was able to catch the dot each and every time we played, frying the battery on the laser pointer and effectively running our game.

Then there was that one time he sneezed and summoned a tiny tornado right in the house!

When he started biting Luna during nursing time so that her milk mixed with blood, Merlin and I knew we had to do something fast.

That day when the Beech Grove crew showed up for their visit, we left Drake with Luna and the babies while Merlin and I pulled Mr. Fluffikins outside for an important discussion.

"What's wrong with my son?" Merlin asked.

"He's a vampire," Fluffikins stated plainly.

"He's a witch," Merlin countered, kicking up his back feet in anger. He could no longer summon lightning—or anything else for that matter—but he still retained some of his magical mannerisms.

"Actually, I think he's both," I offered in quick order. Both cats turned to me. "I think something happened with Drake the first day they met. They bonded."

"And now Drake is his familiar?" Merlin asked, aghast.

"I'm not sure which is witch," I said, chuckling at my pun.

The cats, however, didn't even crack half a smile between them.

"That day when you came to take Drake," Merlin said, dancing on his front paws. "You said that vampires don't drink blood anymore. That it's an outdated practice. Then why is my boy doing it?"

Mr. Fluffikins cleared his throat before saying, "Human vampires don't."

"What about cat vampires?"

Mr. Fluffikins shook his head and sighed. "I don't know. There's never been one before."

We all drew quiet at this revelation.

"Will he be okay?" I asked at last.

The black cat nodded. “He’s very strong and developing at an accelerated rate. Surely, you have noticed that.”

Merlin and I both nodded, too.

“As hard as this is to hear, you need to let him go. Let him leave with Drake. They need to be together.”

Merlin’s eyes searched the horizon. “But how will I know he’s okay?” he squeaked.

Fluffikins reached forward and set a paw on top of Merlin’s “You have my word. I’ll treat them both as if they are my own.”

My cat turned to me. “Luna won’t like this.”

“I know,” I said with a sad smile. “I don’t like it either. But I understand.”

“Me, too. But let me talk to her alone,” he said, and then without waiting ran back through the cat flap.

A few moments later, Drake came out to join us in the front yard.

“I heard you broke up with Kelley,” I said conversationally, because it felt like a lighter topic than the whole vampire thing. She’d called me a few days back and cried her eyes out as we both dug into cartons of ice cream and streamed a sappy chick flick together on Netflix.

“It was the right thing to do,” he said. “Please promise me you’ll find a good guy for her, someone who deserves her.”

“Of course, I will!” I practically shouted. So much had changed in the last week, but Kelley was still one of my best friends. That would never change.

“I’m moving,” Drake added softly. “Not Beech Grove, but somewhere new.”

"There was an opening for town vampire," Mr. Fluffikins explained. "I vouched for him."

"Well, congratulations. I'm sure you and your kitten will love it there." I was too consumed with sadness over the departing kitten to offer him a smile now.

Drake looked to Fluffikins, confusion evident in his expression.

"You two share an unbreakable bond. Much like Gracie and Merlin," the cat boss reasoned.

It was true. Even after Merlin sacrificed his magic, I still remained tied to him and his family. Now anyone who saw Drake and the kitten together knew they belonged together.

"Well, at least I know I'll have a friend where I'm going."

"What will you name him?" I asked, hating that the kittens were more than a week old and still didn't have names.

"Hmmm." Drake thought for a moment, then broke out into a comical smile. "Since he's a vampire like me, I think I'll name him after that dude from Twilight."

I laughed, which only goaded Drake on.

"Yup, Jacob, it is," he declared.

I didn't have the heart to tell him that Jacob was the werewolf. He seemed so proud of his namesake.

Merlin reappeared and gave us a solemn nod. "Luna understands. She just wants a promise that we'll be able to visit him sometimes."

"Dude!" Drake shouted. "Of course, you can. Come whenever you want. Any time. Seriously, any time."

"Then we should make haste before mama cat has the chance to change her mind," Fluffikins said.

Merlin and I returned to the cat family's nest to say goodbye.

"Bye, Jacob!" I called right before Fluffikins, Drake, and that precious little vampire kitty disappeared in a swirl of mist.

Luna blinked up at me. "Jacob? Since when is that his name?"

"Drake decided just now," I said, almost like an apology.

She sighed. "Then we should name the others, darling."

Merlin nodded. "Before we do, I have a request for Gracie."

"Sure. You can ask me anything. You know that." I settled onto the floor to bring us closer to eye level.

Merlin curled up on my lap, glancing up at me with huge honey brown eyes. "When I surrendered my magic, I freed you of the familiar contract. It was the only way to save you. But make no mistake, you were the best familiar a witch could ever ask for. I love you, and I'm so grateful that we found each other."

"I love you, too, Merlin," I said, admittedly tearing up now.

"Gracie, would you please help me find equally wonderful familiars to serve my children? I know it won't be easy, but I want them to have the best, just as I have had the b—"

"Merlin," I interrupted. "Choose me. I love your kittens as if they are my own. And I will serve them as I have served you. We'll all stay together as a family. That is, if it's okay with you."

Merlin and Luna exchanged glowing looks of love.

"We do not deserve you, dear," she cried. "But I am so happy we have you in our lives, anyway."

"Yes, Daisy, Rosie, and Honeysuckle are absolutely the luckiest kittens alive," Merlin said, bending down to lick his wife on the forehead.

Luna beamed up at him. “You mean…?”

“I know it was hard seeing our boy set off so young. We should give the girls the names you picked for them. Besides, they’ve grown on me.”

The cats licked each other again, and I slowly backed out of the room to give the furry family its privacy.

I was part of that family, too, and I would devote myself to those three young ladies as long as I lived.

Sure, it wasn’t the life I had planned for myself, but it’s the one I’d made along the way.

And I was going to love every second of it.

My name is Gracie Springs, and I’m not a witch. But my life is pretty darned magical all the same.

WHAT TO READ NEXT

Mr. Fluffikins is the small black cat responsible for overseeing the most powerful supernatural beings in the small Southern town of Beech Grove. He's also charged with keeping the world of magic hidden from those without it.

Enter Tawny Bigford. She's a snarky part-time novelist who's both new in town and about to stumble headfirst into a magical murder investigation.

What's a bureaucratic cat to do? Well, he might as well hire her as a temp to keep her close until all this funny murder business is solved.

And they're going to need all the help they can get, especially considering the cat's various arch-nemeses looming large. Throw in a sexy cop, matronly angel, sarcastic vampire, down-to-earth shifter, and a mysterious old guy wearing a suit, and now Mr. Fluffikins and Tawny are ready to get to work.

If you love quirky humor and madcap magical adventures, then you do not want to miss this hot new series from a USA Today bestselling author. Here it is! This is your chance to binge read the first three books— Witch for Hire, Psychic for Hire, and Vampire for Hire—in this special boxed collection... Enjoy!

The *Paranormal Temp Agency: Books 1-3 Special Collection* is now available.

Get your copy so that you can start reading this zany mystery series today!

SNEAK PEEK

WITCH FOR HIRE

"Aaaaaaaaaah!" A scream tore from my chest as I leaped away from the frigid stream gushing out of the old showerhead.

Normally I loved starting my mornings with a slow and steamy rinse while I let all of my thoughts boing around my brain and eventually meld themselves into some kind of plan for the day. Ever since moving to Beech Grove a couple weeks back, however, I was lucky to get a good five minutes of warmth before the water heater suddenly gave up the ghost and a punishing spray of liquid ice ruined my good mood.

"That's it!" I shouted as I twisted the faucet off. My landlady would be hearing from me today, whether she liked it or not.

For her part, old Mrs. Haberdash had given me very careful instructions when I signed up to rent the small guest home at the back edge of her hilltop property. Even though she lived in the main house, just a short walk away, I was never ever supposed to visit her there. Anything I needed could be explained via a phone call or better yet—*at least according to her*—an old-fashioned letter.

Yeah, no.

I tried to do it her way, but so far my attempts at getting help with the plumbing had gone unanswered, and unfortunately, a useless shower made for a useless me. I'd tried playing by her rules and still had nothing to show for it. Now it was a time to play by mine.

Still dripping, I bunched my soapy hair into a bun to get it off my shoulders, threw on a shift dress and flip-flops, and headed out to finally confront my apathetic landlady.

I guess now would be a good time to introduce myself.

The name's Tawny, Tawny Bigford. Tawny is short for *Tanya,* a name I've hated ever since Tanya Mills stuck a chewed-up wad of bubble gum in my hair during our second grade spelling test. So now I'm Tawny.

I'm 35, love my showers—as you already know—and am wonderfully, happily, unapologetically single.

Sure, I had a husband once. George was his name. But several years into our marriage, he decided he made a much better pair with some PTA mom named Patricia.

A PTA mom!

As the story goes, they'd bumped into each other outside of the local middle school one afternoon, and it was love at first sight. Why George was there in the first place, I'll never understand. It's not like we had kids of our own or any other reason for him to find himself at exactly the wrong place and wrong time.

But it happened and changed all of our lives in the process.

Honestly, I'd have rather he slipped off with his younger, prettier secretary. At least then I could bemoan the cliche.

But he and Patricia, who is two years his senior, are disgustingly happy together. Most days I just pretend that neither of them exists.

Okay, so I may sound *a little* bitter. And I may live by myself in a rented guest house, but—disappointing showers not withstanding—I absolutely love my life. Basically I write two books per year, ship them off to my publisher for a paycheck, and then do whatever I want with the rest of my time.

Yes, I could write more to make more, but why? I'm perfectly happy to live frugally because that means living freely. And as such, I have more hobbies than any one person should probably ever have.

But I digress...

This wasn't the time to discuss my hobbies, it was the time to confront Mrs. Haberdash and to demand a steady supply of hot water that lasted more than five minutes per day. It was, after all, a simple and basic necessity.

On her doorstep now, I sucked in a deep breath to calm my rage, raised my hand, and knocked gently.

Just kidding, I pounded on that door with every bit of ire I had in me.

When no one answered, I started to shout. "I know you're in there! And I need to talk!"

Still nothing, so I tried the doorknob and was surprised to find it unlocked, given how much I knew the woman valued her privacy.

I pushed it open and charged in, ready to give old Mrs. Haberdash a piece of my mind.

Unfortunately, while all this righteous storming was going on, I hadn't kept an eye on my feet. I hadn't thought I needed to, but something big and heavy was lying on the ground just beyond the threshold and I slammed right into it, lost my balance, and thudded to the ground in an awkward tangle of limbs.

Not just my own, but Mrs. Haberdash's, too. *Uh-oh.* My stomach churned with an aching certainty.

"M-M-Mrs. Haberdash?" I asked, my voice quavering with fright as I turned my face toward the old woman sprawled across the entryway floor.

Her mouth remained firmly closed, her eyes glued open, her body even colder than the shower I'd just escaped.

Yup, she was dead, and—thanks to my unfortunate stumble—I'd just gotten my DNA all over her corpse.

No, no, no! I attempted a scream but came up short.

And here I thought a cold shower was the absolute worst way to start the day. Oh, when would I ever learn to leave well enough alone?

Witch for Hire* is available as part of the *Paranormal Temp Agency: Books 1-3 Special Collection.

Get your copy so that you can start reading this zany mystery series today!

ABOUT MOLLY FITZ

While *USA Today bestselling* author Molly Fitz can't technically talk to animals, she and her three feline writing assistants have deep and very animated conversations as they navigate their days.

She lives with her child and their own private zoo somewhere in the wilds of Alaska. Molly will occasionally venture out for good food, great coffee, or to meet new animal friends.

Learn more about Molly and her books, and be sure to sign up for her newsletter at **www.MollyMysteries.com**.

ALSO BY MOLLY FITZ

Learn more about Molly's collected works, so that you can decide which book you'd like to read next...

PET WHISPERER P.I.

Angie Russo just partnered up with Blueberry Bay's first ever talking cat detective. Along with his ragtag gang of human and animal helpers, Octo-Cat is determined to save the day... so long as it doesn't interfere with his schedule.

Start with book 1, ***Kitty Confidential***.

MERLIN'S MAGICAL MYSTERIES

Gracie Springs is not a witch... but her cat is. Now she must help to keep his secret or risk spending the rest of her life in some magical prison. Too bad trouble seems to find them at every turn!

Start with book 1, ***Merlin Takes a Familiar***.

PARANORMAL TEMP AGENCY

Tawny Bigford's simple life takes a turn for the magical when she stumbles upon her landlady's murder and is recruited by a talking black cat named Fluffikins to take over the deceased's role as the official Town Witch for Beech Grove, Georgia.

Start with book 1, ***Witch for Hire***.

THE MYSTERIES OF MOONLIGHT MANOR (WITH TRIXIE SILVERTALE)

Sydney Coleman has it all—until she doesn't. No sooner does she launch her bed and breakfast, than a trio of ghosts turn up oppose her at every turn. They insist she solve the murder of their mistress, but Sydney is desperate for cash. If she can't book some guests fast, her haunted mansion is utterly doomed.

Start with book 1, ***Moonlight & Mischief***.

CONNECT WITH MOLLY

Sign up for my newsletter and get a special digital prize pack for joining, including an exclusive story, *Meowy Christmas Mayhem*, fun quiz, and lots of cat pictures!

Sign up: **MollyMysteries.com/subscribe**

Now, if you ever wished you could converse with cats, here's your opportunity! This is me officially inviting you into my whacky inner world as part of my Cozy Kitty Book Club.

For those who just can't get enough of my zany cat characters and their hapless humans, this book club will provide new content to devour and the chance to get to know my best author friends.

From exclusive stories, behind-the-scenes trivia to never-before-released bonus content, and monthly giveaways, there's a lot to love about the Cozy Kitty Book Club. Join today to find out what we're reading next!

Join: **MollyMysteries.com/club**

www.ingramcontent.com/pod-product-compliance
Lightning Source LLC
Chambersburg PA
CBHW030629310726
48979CB00003B/930

* 9 7 8 1 6 4 4 5 1 5 8 2 2 *